SHADOW'S PAST

NATALIE JOHANSON

Tea & Dagger
Publishing

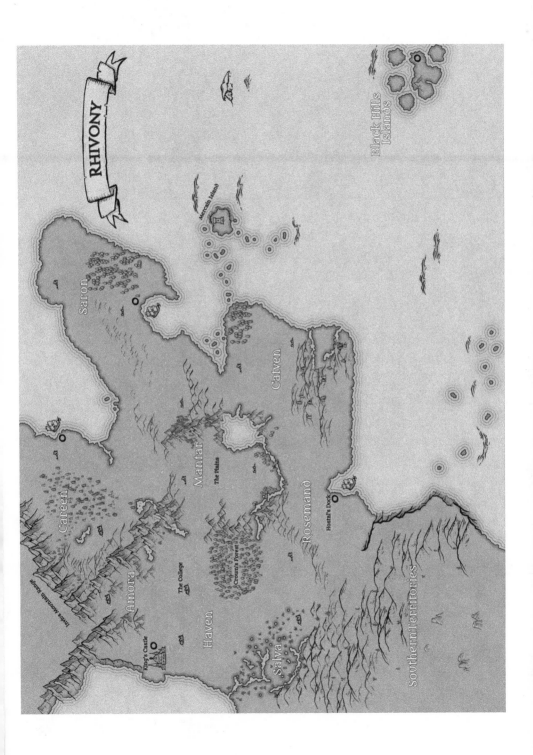

CHAPTER 1

*R*ose opened her eyes to stare at the ceiling in the dim morning light. Blinking lazily, she rolled her head and checked the small window of her room. The winter wind rattled the shutters and even with the rags stuffed in the gaps, the freezing wind forced its way through the cracks. She sighed and rolled out of bed, having chased sleep unsuccessfully all night. Even if the howling wind hadn't kept her up, the nightmares did. Her sleep was fitful, and disturbing. Her dreams were haunted by gray wastelands and whispering ghosts. Recently, her dreams had taken a turn for the worse. The attempted coup on the castle over the summer had left different marks on Rose. That fighting, that type of pain was different than anything she was used to. It had left new scars, hidden and visible, on Rose.

Swinging her legs over the edge of the narrow bed, she absently rubbed the smooth burns that circled her wrists. Despite the thick wool socks, her feet quickly grew cold from the floor, and she glared at the faintly glowing stove. The orange coals did little to heat the small room.

She pushed off the bed and shoved her legs into plain trousers and a simple tunic hanging off the back of the long chair in her room. It was a small box of a room, large enough for a narrow bed, a desk and a chair. The stove was shoved in the corner between the bed and desk. Unfortunately, the only coat she had was the deep blue uniform coat of the Light Horse: the messenger service of the king. Her belongings were sparse, and her actions over the summer required her to play the part of a Light Horse Officer. And, as her items were few and far between, she'd kept the uniform items. Shoving her arms into the coat, ignoring the feeling of being an imposter as she did so, she walked into the hallways in search of the kitchens.

They'd be warmer than her room, and maybe there was still a snack or two left lying about she could steal before attempting this feat called sleep.

Her life felt stalled. She'd come to the castle, after carrying the message for a dying Light Horse Officer, with the intent to leave again and continue her journey. But then she'd found another person with her magic. Something Rose thought was a mistake of nature or a curse of the gods, and then there was D'ray, the B'Leakon who'd attempted to overthrow King Micah. He appeared and upheaved her whole world.

And so she'd stayed, despite her fear of staying in one place, with the hope of learning more about her magic, of finding answers to questions she'd had all her life. Now, months later and winter fully set in, she had discovered nothing.

The stagnant feeling of her days added to her irritability and inability to sleep.

As she walked, she entered the older parts of the castle. Here the tapestries were older the further away from the public halls. Time had faded the once bright colors to dull, washed out fabrics, but you could still see the epic tales of warriors and kings sewed into their weave. One of the previous kings must've had a fondness for the sea, because along the hall to the kitchens, the tapestries were tales of sailors, great sea monsters, and the beginnings of the royal navy.

The suits of armor along these walls, tucked into the alcoves weren't the shiny, polished displays for the public. These were tarnished, grimy, and damaged from time. She glanced at them as she passed and wondered where these went when they were replaced. Did the castle just throw them out? Or was there a giant room in some dusty old wing stuffed to the brim with old armor parts?

Outside, the raging blizzard beat against the castle and the hallways were frigid as a result. The wind rattled the shuttered windows and howled. The once thick carpets along the floors had long since been worn down by the hundreds of servants' feet over the years. The stone floor poked through in many places. The halls were dark, the few lanterns burned low, and the flames made dark shadows flicker along the stone walls and the suits of armor.

She tucked her fists into her pockets and trudged around the corner.

"Everything alright, ma'am?" A guard paused in his stride down the hall. His black and amethyst uniform made him blend into the dark.

"Yup," Rose said and kept walking.

He dipped his head in a marginal nod and turned back down the hall. She continued on her journey to the kitchens, further into the belly of the castle.

Finally, at the door, feeling the residual heat of the hearths from inside the kitchens, Rose took a deep breath. Her bones were tired. A weight had settled in her limbs since the summer. She wanted to sleep. To sleep for days, but she worried the weariness that she carried wouldn't be cured by sleep.

"Ma'am?"

Rose jerked at Aaron's voice and found him sitting at the large kitchen table in the center of the room. The candlelight lit up little of his face, but with the shadows, Rose could see his high cheekbones and dusty blond hair. His face was full of sharp angles and lines. She was sure some would call him handsome.

"Everything alright?" he asked, his voice soft but attentive. She'd never seen him lose his attention or his patience.

Rose sniffed, annoyed she'd jumped, and settled across from him at the counter. "Yes. Can't sleep. What's your excuse?"

Aaron, one of King Micah's personal guards, glanced at her before returning to the block of cheese he was cutting into. "I'm getting off shift and needed a snack before heading to bed."

Aaron was a tall mountain of a man that managed to sneak around and move with barely a sound in a way Rose was jealous of. She guessed he was a few years older than her, maybe somewhere in the later half of his third decade. He carried himself like a warrior, and she'd seen him fight to know there was no lie in the lithe, lethal way he moved. It made her wary, but she'd never once seen him raise his voice.

"Oh. Well, tell me, Aaron of the guard." She nicked the cheese he'd sliced off the block and he frowned at her. "Do you enjoy it?"

Aaron frowned at her but sliced off another piece before pulling the teapot off the fire and settling at the table. He poured them both a cup before speaking. "Shield. Those who guard the royal family are Black Shields. And yes, it is a very fulfilling position."

Rose raised her eyebrows and sipped the tea. "You enjoy following a man around all day, every day? And what royal family? It's just him here."

"There's more to it, and you know that," Aaron said with a sardonic look. "And yes, right now, only the king. But when his cousins or his aunt visit the castle, their protection falls to us. And eventually, the queen and heirs."

"I see." Rose ducked her head, shame burning her cheeks. She did know that. She'd seen the work and risk Aaron and the other Shields had taken to protect the king last summer. She shouldn't have insulted him so. "I apologize. I'm in a mood, it seems." She stared into her tea. "Sleep disagrees with me."

She pushed strands of her hair out of her eyes and tried to tuck it behind her ear.

Aaron nodded and pushed his plate toward her. "After the battle this summer, I'm sure many find sleep hard to come by. It will pass in time."

She would bury these nightmares just like she has with all the others. These will just take her more time. More time and more rum. She started to rub the smooth scar on her wrist and had to tell herself to stop.

"Are you still training with Archie?"

Rose chuckled. "Everyone really does call him Archie when he's not looking, don't they?"

Archie, or Archibald as he preferred it, was one of the Swordmasters in the castle that trained new and upcoming recruits. His younger sister, Mariah Sayla, was captain of the Light Horse. She was currently trying to convince Rose to become a Light Horse Officer herself. Rose still had her doubts about that being a good idea. Assassins didn't belong in castles.

Aaron laughed, a deep, baritone laugh. "Yes, and I'll denounce you as a liar if you tell him."

Rose laughed too and it felt good to laugh, like something had loosened in her chest with the sound. She hadn't laughed since the summer attack on the throne room, when her magic had gone to shit, and she'd been trapped there after exhausting her magic, after letting the shadows in too far. Her hand went to the scars on her wrist again. D'ray had burned her wrists when he'd forced her memories out with his magic in an effort to assassinate the king. "Your secret is safe with me."

He nodded his thanks, a smile still on his lips. "How's your training going? It's hard work, and not many stick with it. Archie must see something in you to keep you on, without being paid," he eyed her with a raised eyebrow, "or a member of a corps."

She crooked a smile and ignored the jibe. "It's a challenge, and I like challenges." It also lets me clear my mind and not... think or feel or... "It's just me and the sword and trying not to get smacked." She paused and chewed her cheek. "Although, I don't like the broadsword. Archie started me with a long knife, but... I'm much better with my little daggers."

Aaron scrunched his brows together as he thought, and Rose took the opportunity to steal more cheese. "I have watched you fight in the practice rings. All of the Shields are Swordmasters, but we are also trained in... a variety of weapons aside from the broadsword. You should train with us sometime. Maybe I can train you in some weapons more to your style."

Rose nodded noncommittally. She wasn't sure if she wanted to commit to more training with more people. The more ties she made here, the harder it would be to leave. Some part of her didn't want to disappoint so many people if she disappeared, and fewer ties meant less disappointment. Although, she wasn't sure when she started caring about what others felt. The thought made her frown. She was already becoming too attached here, and she wasn't even sure she was going to stay.

The bells started their chimes, and even down in the depths of the kitchens, they heard their faint echo. "I really must be retiring. I suggest you try to do the same."

Rose nodded and watched him leave. She stood and checked in the back of the cheese larder and found the bottle of brandy was still there.

"Mine," she whispered as she grabbed it, stuffed it in her pocket, and finally turned back to her room.

LATER THAT AFTERNOON, while nursing a rather impressive headache, Rose sat curled in the stiff, overstuffed armchair in the common room for the Light Horse. The room was filled with a scattering of tables, and benches. The hearth had a large bookshelf built into the stone around it. Random knick knacks from the years were scattered on the plain wood shelving. A carved horse. A mismatched collection of books. Some trophy from a race she didn't know. The room was old and shabby, but it was lived in and loved. She felt like an intruder sitting here.

The fire roared in the hearth, making the large room warm and cozy. The sound of wood popping and crackling in the flames filled the room. The storm continued to blow outside; the window on the far end of the room was crusted with ice.

In the back of her mind, the shadows were restless, no doubt adding to her brandy headache. Something was stirring them, the denizens of the Shadow Land. She could feel them prowling in the shadows, could feel their irritation. She'd never felt them behave like this before. Normally the shadowy beasts existed on their own and, up until this summer, kept to themselves. She didn't know what it meant, but whatever it was… they were angry about it.

"What is causing such a frown?"

Rose blinked, focusing her eyes again, and turned to Sam Fiben. He sat across from her on the equally battered and old couch. He watched her with his expressive, eager eyes. Sam was also a member of the Light Horse and, like so many of the officers, had a magical ability. While it wasn't a requirement, as far as Rose was aware, the corps seemed to attract lost souls with odd magics. Sam controlled fire. Poorly, but he was learning. The stoic captain also had magic and could read minds. A skill that had set Rose on her nerves when she'd first arrived.

"Was I frowning?"

He nodded, a small grin on his lips. His piercing blue eyes seemed to twinkle at her. "You looked quite bothered."

"Hmm," she hummed and set her eyes back to the fire. "Something's changed."

"What has?"

"I don't know," she murmured and rolled her shoulders. But she needed to find out.

She stood with a sigh, head pounding behind her eyes, and turned from the room. She could feel Sam's eyes on her, but she ignored the stare on her back. The people in the Light Horse were so open, so used to sharing their cares and troubles with each other, but she'd survived by keeping her secrets close to her. She didn't know how to share. Didn't know if she wanted to.

Instead, she retreated to her drafty room, her boots clicking on the stone floor with her hasty steps. Closing the door behind her, Rose's hands shook. The last time she'd used her magic, it had taken control. It had harmed people, the king. She'd nearly lost her mind to the shadows. But the hells be damned, she wasn't going to let them control her.

She closed her shutter, blocking out the little light from the afternoon. In her dark room, Rose dropped into the shadows, into the Undertunnels. Like stepping into a room, she entered the world that existed between worlds. It lived in the shadows, the darkness, the between spaces of the world. Here, the world was awash with blues and grays and a heavy mist settled around her knees. The dark world is broken up by little 'windows' looking into the world at places where light meets darkness.

She could feel the wolves pacing in the darkness, could sense their agitation. Perspiration broke out on her forehead at their nearness, but they made no move to break into her mind. A wind stirred the mist in a flurry, and dew gathered on her face.

"What's happening?" she asked, her voice wispy. She ground her teeth in annoyance.

Red eyes appeared in the darkness and soon, the darkness condensed into a snout, a head, the body of a wolf. Standing nearly to her chest, the red-eyed beast stared at her, hackles raised and dew-drops dotting its fur.

"What is happening?" Rose asked again. This time her voice was firmer.

The wolf lifted its lips in a silent snarl, white fangs gleaming in the darkness.

"He's awakened." The voice echoed in her mind.

She fought back a grimace and told herself, again, that she was in charge of these beasts. Not the other way around. "Who?"

"He ruins the Balance. He should not be!"

More wolves appeared in the darkness.

"Who!" Rose shouted at them.

They froze, all blazing eyes turned to her. A stillness settled in her bones, and even the swirling mist seemed to hang suspended.

"The Earthmover."

CHAPTER 2

*R*ose blinked, sweat dripping into her eye. "The what?"

The wolves dissolved into the darkness with a huff, the fog swirling up and around in a torrent. She took a step back instinctively even though she was surrounded by shadow.

"Earthmover," they growled, dozens of voices over top of each other.

"What is an Earthmover?" she asked, raising her voice over their clamor.

Their growls were the only answer they gave. She sighed in frustration. Just once, she wanted a simple answer out of them. Just once.

"You must stop him. You must right the Balance."

The pressure behind her eyes started to build, her headache growing. She'd gone too long without using her magic, and now the drain was worse. An ache started in her shoulders, the tension held there, turning into a knot.

"How?" Rose asked, not expecting an answer.

The wolves, the shadows, they played by their own rules. They claimed impartiality in the world yet seemed to interfere in hers whenever they wanted. She huffed when they remained silent and stepped out of the Undertunnels.

She shivered in the cool darkness of her room. The dew that had clung to her skin and dampened her sleeves added to the cold. She closed her eyes and sighed. Just more questions. That was all she had. It frustrated her to her soul, and that weight in her bones seemed extra heavy. There were always more questions. Never answers.

With gentle movements, her head pounding and eyes aching, Rose stoked the fire in the little stove and set a pot to boil. She had very little in the way of items. A pot she'd nicked from the kitchens for tea. A small chest at the foot of her bed with even fewer items in it. Most, not hers. A vase with a wilted rose that sat on the rickety nightstand was all she claimed as her imprint on the room. She dragged the chair out from the desk and wedged it as close to the stove as she dared before flopping onto it.

Looking around her room, she wondered again why she was still here. She could leave in the middle of the night, and there would be nothing left in her room to mark she'd been here. A huff of a sigh escaped her as she poured steaming water into her mug of dried Subpulent berries. She knew why she was still here. She'd promised the king she wouldn't disappear in the night. Why she'd even made such a promise escaped her now, but even an assassin has to keep their promises.

She curled her hands around the too-hot mug and sipped the bitter berry tea. The Subpulent berries were the only thing known to help counteract the toll of using magic. Though, it tasted like shit. She grimaced and pulled her lips back from her teeth at the bitter taste.

Was this Earthmover connected to Gerik? His mind had been trapped in a book guarded by the shadows for hundreds of years, only to be set free by D'ray during the coup last summer. Now, this mage from a different time was alive and plotting only the gods knew what. After the failed coup he'd disappeared. His magic was, in part, the same as Rose's. Although he had other magics as well. She'd never seen anyone with more than one magic ability before. She sipped more tea and let her head fall back against her chair. She needed answers and was starting to think she wasn't going to find them here.

NIGHTMARES OF BEING TRAPPED in the desolate wasteland of the Shadow World, forgotten by everyone and chased by whispering ghosts, woke her not long later. Her heart pounded in her throat, and her breath came in sharp bursts. The voices of the castle inhabitants whispered to her through the shadows.

"Shit," she breathed and ran a shaky hand over her throat as she focused on pushing the shadows away. Rose could see and hear anything touched by darkness. As a child, she'd learned early on to block out the constant sound of people. It was almost second nature for her. It had been years since she'd let her control slip so much.

Her tea had gone tepid, and she set it aside with a curled lip. It was disgusting when it was hot. It was unpalatable when it was cold. Rose rotated her neck, stiff from how she'd been sitting. She wished she could go outside and sit in the silence of the Rose Garden, but with winter raging outside, that wasn't an option anymore. The gardens always seemed to calm her, settle her anxious soul. Her eyes were drawn to the wilted and dead rose on the nightstand. The company of the gardens helped too, she was loath to admit.

Rose pushed to her feet, bones aching more than they should be in her second decade, and turned to the hallways. She wandered the hallways, mostly empty this late in the afternoon. The winter storms meant there were no visiting nobility, no entourages of lords and ladies. Wishing to find a place to substitute her gardens, she wandered further and further, sleep making her careless in her path. She wandered far past anywhere she'd been before. Past anywhere the common public would've had access. She went further still into the new wing. Here the tapestries were elegant and bright. Beautiful scenes of horses and the lush forests of Rhivony decorated the walls. The rugs along the stone floor were fine and bright violet.

She stared at the carpets, her steps growing hesitant until she stood still. She turned her eyes again to the detailed tapestries, the shining armors along the wall. All decorated with shields adorned with the Ellsworth family crest.

Oops. She shoved her hands into her pockets and debated whether or not she cared that she'd wandered into the royal wing.

"Nope." She decided and continued walking, albeit with softer steps than before. Just the king was here. What were the chances she'd actually run into anyone? She just wanted to find a quiet, warm space to nap. Someplace to let her nerves settle.

She turned down another, smaller hallway and paused at the guards along the walls. None moved to stop her, and none acknowledged her. She continued her search slowly, half-daring them to stop her. When they didn't, she moved to a closed door at the end of the hallway.

Glancing out the nearest window, Rose saw the castle wall bend out in an arch past the door, implying a large room inside. Another guard stood next to the door. She raised an eyebrow at him and slowly put her hand on the handle. He made no move to stop her as she opened it and slipped inside.

What she found inside shocked her to stillness. Green. She saw green plants, large potted trees, and flowering bushes. Rows upon rows of green. Large windows adorned the east and west walls that would fill the room with sunlight during the day. She wandered slowly through the plants, noting the clusters of seating areas scattered throughout the room. There were the giant leafed plants from the southern swamps, some rimmed in bright purple. She curved her lips in a smile and let her fingers skim across the soft leaf. She'd only ever read about them. The leaf was larger than even her head. Further down were the bright flowers of the sta'aka plant. Three petals of shimmering gold and purple berries clustered under the leaves.

Rose glanced around the room before plucking a couple of the berries off and plopping them in her mouth. She groaned at the sweet juice that popped. The growers would dry these, grind them into a powder, and sell it for outrageous prices to be mixed into with milk or baked into some bread. Rose moaned. Fresh was best. Not that she'd had many opportunities to try them.

She continued on, resisting the urge to steal more berries, and passed small figurines for the gods scattered among the pots. She found Taspa, his hands opened and out like he was offering up something. The priests said he was offering hope. A few vases of lilies over, and she saw Hath, god of war and protection. His shield was held aloft, his sword tip planted in the ground at his feet. Protection, then. When his sword was up and at the ready he was going to war.

A few others she didn't remember from their figures. She wasn't a particularly religious woman, having seen too much evil to believe there were any gods paying attention to the prayers of the frightened, but there were a few that she still muttered a prayer to every now and then. Better safe than sorry.

A soft scratching sound drew her attention toward the eastern wall.

Shit. She followed the sound through a cluster of large leafy plants into an opening with plush seating set against the windows. Small tables with lanterns and a rug completed the area.

She walked closer but stumbled to a stop when she recognized the other person as they looked up.

"Sire?" She retreated a step. "I apologize. I didn't mean to interrupt."

The king set his small book aside, a charcoal stick in his other hand. He looked up at her, his hazel eyes widening slightly. His hair was disheveled as if he'd been running his hand through its length. Normally tied at the nape of his neck, it hung loosely around his shoulders.

"Miss Trewin. You're not interrupting. Sit."

Rose glanced around the small sitting area, half expecting a guard to jump out at her, before hesitantly sitting in the lounge seat across from the king. She was still surprised by the king's young age, not that much older than Rose's years. Though the stress from the past months shown in the pull of his shoulders and the tilt of his lips. He appeared to have aged far too much.

"Is it alright that I'm in here? No one stopped me when I came in." She was kicking herself for testing her luck by wandering down here.

"Of course." King Micah wrapped the stick of charcoal in a strip of cloth and tucked it in his pocket. "How did you find this place? It's pretty far off from the main section of the castle."

"I was looking for somewhere quiet," Rose said as she shrugged. "You have an indoor garden?" Of course, he does. He's the king.

"This room is quite the retreat in winter months. It was originally called the Queen's Room. Or maybe it was the Queen's Solarium. I don't remember. Whatever the name, this was the room given to the queen to do with as she wishes. My grandmother turned it into the garden it is now. I haven't bothered to change it. I rather like it."

Rose gazed around the room. "Are you sure it's alright if I sit here, then, if it's supposed to be the Queen's?"

"Oh, yes," he said with a soft smile, his eyes lighting up with the smile. "Besides, I do not have a queen."

She had to look away from that smile. There was so much left-over tension from the night in the throne room; when he'd called her back to him, said she was his. She wasn't sure what to make about him yet. The king, someone who had more power and social standing than anyone in the country, was also the only person who could pull her out when her magic tried to take over. He knew more about her magic and secrets than anyone else... and that made her nervous. They seemed bound together because of her magic, and Rose didn't want to be bound to anyone.

But at the same time, she glanced at him. She didn't dislike their quiet talks. There was an ease around him, and if she let herself admit it, she never would, he wasn't bad to look at either. Strong jaw and defined cheeks. His brown hair, loose as it was, made him look more common and less regal. She cleared her throat and looked away. She needed to remember he was regal.

"Are you sleeping alright?" he asked, his voice light and casual.

Rose narrowed her eyes at him. "Why do you ask?"

He shrugged, but it was too quick, too jerky, and she knew his next words would be a lie. "Just making polite conversation."

She narrowed her eyes at him again and looked away.

He opened his sketchbook and pulled out the charcoal when it was clear she wasn't going to answer.

Rose watched him warily for a moment before settling back in the chair. In the warmth of the room, her eyes were already feeling heavy.

In the silence of the room, the soft scratching of the charcoal across the paper, her words were pulled from her. He always seemed to pull words from her.

"I can't sleep. The shadows are restless about something. Won't let me sleep," she finally said and dropped her head back against the head-rest and sighed. "Just wanna sleep."

He watched her, no doubt waiting for her to elaborate more, before nodding. "Well, if this place offers you any peace, come here all you wish. It is sorely underused."

Like the Rose Garden, she thought with a soft sigh. She was the only one allowed in there as well. Despite feeling like he was giving her these privileges for a reason, she couldn't bring herself to walk away from the peace that was in this room. The quiet it offered. She also missed the peaceful moments of the Rose Garden where they would silently sit in each other's company.

"Do you mind if I sit just here?"

"As long as you don't mind if I sketch."

Rose raised her eyebrow at his well-worn book but nodded. She wondered what it was he drew, if it was more horses or something different.

Maybe one day I'll ask, she thought as she curled her legs under herself. Soon, the soft scratching of the pencil soon put her to sleep.

CHAPTER 3

*G*oron slowly sipped the dark, almost black, liquid the locals called pa'tva. It was bitter, thick, and disgusting, but he liked it. His body was still sore, tired from the centuries he'd slept under Gerik's spell. He had an odd floating sensation Gerik had ensured him would wear off soon, but it made him queasy.

The An'thila people moved around him, chatting in their rolling, clipped language. This land, he'd been informed, was called the Southern Territories, and it was a hot, arid place. The land was dead and dusty. How these people managed to work crops and a living out of it was a trick to see. He could feel the potential in the dirt, deep down, but no one in these dusty lands had the Earthmover Blood in them. They knew how to work it thanks to generations, knowledge, and maybe a little luck.

He sipped more pa'tva. The communal dining hall was loud and boisterous. It reminded him of the longhouses his people built. Looking around now, they'd grown much in his years sleeping, waiting for Gerik to wake him. When he'd last been to these lands hundreds of years ago, it had been a smattering of people scattered around the desert. Now, they were a thriving people. Huge towns had grown where there were just tents and a few horse corrals before.

"What're you grinning at?" Gerik asked as he lowered himself into the bench across from him at the long table.

Gerik. His longest friend and general. It was still strange seeing the man in this new body. Goron had never met a B'leakon before in his years. They were a tall race, tall even to him, and their wide, changing eyes set his teeth on edge. He hadn't learned, yet, what all the colors meant, but it was easy enough to guess at most of them.

"Nothing," he rumbled and sipped more of the drink. "Thinking of old times."

"Old times," Gerik murmured and eyed the pot of pa'tva with clear disdain, his lips pressed thin in a grimace. "Our old times are nothing more than a failed memory."

Gerik made another face as Goron watched silently. He'd been told how the war was lost after he'd slumbered. How Gerik's mind had been trapped, and because of that, he'd slumbered for hundreds of years. Slept while his friends and family, and their families, grew old and died.

Goron finished off his drink and finally asked, "what will you have me do?"

Gerik winced, and his hand went to his chest where the still healing wound lay. It was a red, inflamed thing, ugly and festering. The girl, the young Shadowstalker, had given him the injury.

"Until this heals, I'm weak." His eyes swirled red. "I cannot travel, cannot use my magic. I was barely able to wake you. I cannot risk another engagement with her until I am ready. I need eyes in Rhivony. Soon, our plan will be in motion, and I need to make sure the Rhivony king is hampered in his response. Head north and keep me apprised of the doings."

Goron nodded. Many of the An'thila were already at the north border, making raids across it into Rhivony. The next step, as Goron understood it, would be much more than simple raids.

"Most importantly," Gerik continued.

Goron pulled his eyes back to Gerik's rolling red eyes. They swirled red and molten.

"I need it. My Orthalen. I need it back. Without it, I can't work the other magics. The Elemental forces. I can barely work my shadow magic with this wound. I need that back. Find it," Gerik growled, his eyes growing darker, "and find this girl's Anchor and kill them."

He grinned. Any chance at causing long-lasting pain and misery to the Shadowstalker was something he was more than willing to do. The last Stalker, the one from his time all those long years ago, had taken much from him. It was time for some blood.

"But do not," Gerik said, low and deadly. His eyes burned dark blue, and the color was so cold, so deadly it made his blood run cold. "Do not kill the girl. The Shadowstalker. Her blood is mine."

Goron nodded once, his eyes locked on Gerik's strange and deadly ones. "I swear. Her kill is yours."

Gerik grinned, his teeth stark white against his sun-tanned skin, and it was lethal.

CHAPTER 4

*B*linking against the bright light, Rose opened her eyes to a rather bemused Aaron staring down at her. She squinted up at him, the room far too bright for her tired eyes, and tried to blink the sleep from them.

"What're you doin' in my room?" she slurred, tongue stuck to the roof of her mouth.

Aaron's smile grew, and Rose distinctly felt like she was the butt of a joke. He cocked his head and glanced around the bright room. "Where," he asked once his dancing eyes looked back down on her, "do you think you are?"

She blinked while waiting for her brain to catch up. When it did, she sat up so fast the room spun, and she had to hold her head. "Shit," she breathed and looked around the room. The Queen's Solarium. Not her room. "I fell asleep… "

"You sure did." He straightened, hand on his hip, as he stared down at her.

"Stop looking like an upset schoolmarm. Why didn't anyone wake me up earlier?"

Aaron chuckled low in his throat. "The king told us to leave you be. But, now that her highness is awake…."

Rose cut her eyes to him in a glower as she stood and resisted the urge to smack him.

"I thought we could try some new weapons."

"Train with you?" She asked. "Now?"

"Unless you've somewhere else to be, your highness?"

Rose huffed a sigh inwardly. She didn't, and he knew it. "Lead the way."

Aaron chuckled again, and Rose did slap him hard on the shoulder that time, but he led her out of the warm and bright room. It took some walking before they were finally on the other side of the castle in the lower levels. He led her down the main corridor, around a corner, through a room, and down another hall. Rose glanced into a room, the door flung wide, as they passed and spotted tables, some chairs, and lounging guardsmen. Finally, Aaron stopped at a closed door at the end of a narrow hall.

"This is where we practice and train," Aaron said and opened the door. "Most of the guards use the training fields out on the grounds, but the Shields use this."

Rose turned in a circle as she looked around the giant room. There were racks with weapons lining the nearest wall, most with edged weapons and very few wooden practice swords, rolled mats along another wall, and benches scattered throughout. On the floor, various sparring rings were drawn out. Candle stands and sconces lit with dozens of candles illuminated the space, casting dancing lights along the walls.

She wrinkled her nose when the musty smell of sweat and man hit her.

Aaron walked toward an unoccupied corner ring and pointed at a stack of mats. "Unroll one of those."

Rose grunted but did as she was told while Aaron selected two blades from one of the racks.

"Now these," he said as he held them out to her, "I think you'll like better."

Rose took the blades, more like long daggers, and weighed them in her hands. They were light, well-balanced, and easy to handle, barely longer than her forearm.

"They're a type of dirk."

Rose slashed the air with one and spun the second around in her hand, reversing the grip. "An assassin's blades," she said with a small smile in her voice. She liked these.

"It will be more work to learn two blades together. You'll have to learn more technique and coordination, and you'll need to train your non-dominant arm."

Rose smiled, already liking these more. "Let's get started then."

Aaron nodded and took the blades back. He placed them back on the rack and selected two wooden practice swords. After handing those to her, he selected his own and turned to face her.

Slowly, Aaron started taking her through footwork drills and techniques with one blade at a time. Most were already familiar to her from working with Archie over the summer, but some were new. Aaron directed her in simple sequences until he proclaimed she was warmed up enough to begin.

Rose held back a few choice words. Warmed up? she thought, while puffing and sweat running down her temples. That wasn't even the real thing yet? Sweat rolled from her hairline and her arms shook. Fatigue and disuse had her shoulders aching. She rolled her shoulders. Her head pounded in time with her beating heart.

Aaron had her pick up both dirks and slowly started to work through a simple technique. He showed her how the two blades could move around each other, one being used as a decoy and the other as a defense while attacking. Rose sweat, concentration burned away any other worry or thought. Aaron worked with her, repeating and repeating the movements until they were smooth. Then he grabbed his blade and joined the bout. He attacked her slowly as she defended with the technique.

More than once, her two blades became entangled and fell clattering to the floor. Several times she forgot she had the other blade and was slapped with the flat of his blade for her mistake. When her blades clacked together and fell to the floor for the fifth time, Rose growled.

"This is deceivingly more difficult than I thought."

Aaron nodded and passed her a towel. She hadn't noticed the sweat pouring down her face and along her back. She rubbed her sticky face with the towel and tried not to grumble again. Her arms shook and even holding the towel up to her face was difficult. Her left arm was significantly weaker than her sword arm, and the scarred burn on her shoulder was stiff. She'd earned that burn before the throne room coup, when she'd been hit with wild, unknown magic. It had burned away her skin and poisoned her blood. Only the castle's magical healer, Daymon, had been able to undo most of the damage, but a thick, stiff scar remained.

"This is the first time you've needed to pay attention to what both of your arms are doing and the first time you've used your weaker arm. You're doing much better than I thought you would."

She glared at him. "I've dropped them more than anything else."

He chuckled and shrugged.

While Rose was sweaty, her work tunic sticking uncomfortably to her, he was clean and crisp in his loose-fitting tunic and trousers. He wasn't even a little out of breath, the ass. She glared at him and rotated her shoulder, trying to loosen the tight muscle and ease the ache.

She leaned against the cool stone while her heart hammered in her chest.

"Have you given any more thought about serving?"

"Serving what?" she asked, her voice dropping into an angry droll. She knew exactly what he was asking.

"The king. Joining a service."

She pushed off the wall and picked up her dirks again, giving them an angry twist through the air. "Not really."

"Should you want another option to consider," Aaron said as he faced her again with his sword. "I'm sure you'd fit in very well with the Shields."

She waved him on with her knife. "Not sure I have the patience to stand around and watch people all day."

"I've watched you. That's all you do; watch people."

Rose snorted and met the first blow. "I don't have the patience to watch people and not sell what I see, then."

"I don't think you'd ever do that."

Rose glared at him and struck back with a little too much force. Anger made her movements sharp and jerky, inaccurate. She swung again but missed. "You don't know me."

She'd become very good at finding and selling information before running from her father. Very good.

"You'd never sell what you learned of the king thus far."

No, she silently agreed. She wouldn't. Not with him. Though why Aaron thought that was a mystery to her. What had the king told him? How could they know her? Pretend to know her? She ground her teeth in frustration. They didn't.

"You have the determination."

"Aaron," she snapped and reversed her grip on her right blade. "I can't fight and talk. Pick one."

Aaron nodded and then started to attack her in earnest. He took her through bouts until her breath came harsh and fast, and her feet stumbled. He kept pace with her, his breathing steady and even. Only when her arms failed to lift and her stiff shoulder refused to move did Aaron call it an end. He took her blades from her as she stood there panting and sweating. He handed her a small towel. Rose turned toward the door with hopes of a long bath.

"You have the loyalty for it," he said to her back.

She stiffened but didn't let her feet slow. She'd only agreed to help during the summer, to stop an assassination on the king, because he'd promised to pay her. She had no loyalty. Her fingernails bit into the palm of her hand as she clenched her fists.

"What do you know of my loyalty?" she asked and kept walking, not really wanting to hear his answer.

"LOYALTY.... " Rose grumbled to herself as she rocked and swayed atop Starlit hours later. Starlit was her giant beast of a horse. She'd been bred to be a war-horse from the king's personal stock, but she'd been too ill-mannered for anyone to ride. Rose had just arrived at the castle and had been lost and confused about her place... only slightly more than she was now, and she'd spent many of her afternoons with the angry, solitary beast. Maybe she'd seen something of herself in the horse, tossed from rider to rider, and unwanted.

Starlit had taken to her, and King Micah had entrusted the mistreated horse to her care.

The horse jerked, and Rose was jarred from her thoughts as she rocked sideways in her saddle. She grunted and reseated herself.

"Don't be an ass." She pulled her hood tighter around her face. She nudged Starlit with her heels, and she clopped faster into town.

Rose needed a change of scenery from the castle. Something about Aaron's words, his assumption of her character, set her teeth on edge.

What did Aaron know of her? A few months at the castle, and suddenly everyone thought they knew her. She was loyal to herself and to the coin she could earn. *Hells*, she grumbled silently. *I wouldn't even help the king stop the coup until he paid me.* Just because she'd stayed, Aaron thought he knew her.

Rose pulled Starlit up to an empty post at the tavern, the Witch's Pit. Inside, the heat from the fire was enough that Rose was soon stripping her coats off as she settled at a table in the corner. The barmaid brought a pint of ale in exchange for the raised coins in Rose's fingers.

The tavern was quiet this early in the evening, and most of the tables were empty. The rickety tables were old and scratched, their tops gouged and marked from years of use.

Rose sipped the warm ale and let her eyes wander through the room. *It would be easy to leave,* she thought. Her past had already found her once here. How much longer did she want to risk it? She sucked down more ale. What about her magic?

She'd stayed, had told the king she'd stay, because answers about her magic seemed close. Closer than they'd been before, but months after D'ray's attack and Gerik's reappearance, everything seemed to have stalled. No more answers seemed to be coming. But...

In the corner of her vision, two red eyes hovered in the dark corner of the room. She could feel their stare, their weight on her as she ignored them. Even when her eyes weren't there, she knew they were watching. They were always watching.

Rose growled a sigh and turned away from the glaring corner. She didn't know what they wanted from her.

Rose sighed, finished her ale, and waved more coins in the air.

She was too conflicted. Too confused. She wanted to stay, to try to make this place her home. She hadn't had a place that felt like home, felt safe since the time before her mother had left. That had been so long ago. She could barely remember it. Her. Rose couldn't remember if she'd done something to anger her mother, something to disappoint her. Why else would her mother leave without her? She must've done something, but it was lost to her memory. Rose wasn't sure if she remembered what home felt like, if she'd know how to see it if she found it.

By her third mug of ale, her thoughts were more muddled and mood even more sullen. Aaron thought her loyal.... She wanted to leave in the night just to show him how wrong he was about her.

"Rose." A mug clanked on the table as Sam slumped into the seat across from her. "You look terrible. What's wrong?"

Rose sucked her teeth as she held back a groan. Sam was too gentle and soft to take the brunt of her foul mood.

"Sam," Rose said in a sigh, "unless you're bringing more ale, I'm not in the mood."

He twisted his lips in a grin and slid his mug to her. "Why such a foul mood?"

Rose took the mug and gulped half of it down. She waved his question away. "What're you doing here, Sam?"

He shrugged and leaned back in the uneven chair. "My family lives in town. I came in to visit and thought to stop in here on my way back."

Family. The word made Rose cringe and suck down more ale.

"It was good to see them again. They'd heard what happened with the coup and were worried," Sam rambled on, oblivious to her increasing glower.

"Do you think you'll go visit your family? They must be worried too."

"I don't have any family," Rose bit out and hunched over the tabletop.

A mother that abandoned her and a father that only wanted her magic as his personal doing of whatever needed to be done did not make a family.

"Oh," Sam stuttered and his eyes went wide and sad. "I'm sorry."

Rose dropped her elbow heavily onto the table and propped her chin in her hand, although it did little to help stop the sway of the room.

"D-did they die?"

She snorted. "Gods, it'd be better if they had."

The barmaid passed with a laden tray of drinks, and Rose plucked one.

The bitter taste of anger and ale on her tongue seemed to fuel her reckless words. She was in too many cups to be talking; should know better, but she let the words come. Part of her wanted them to know. Wanted them to see who they'd welcomed into their home with these grand delusions.

"No. No, my father tried to trade me to settle a debt he couldn't pay. That man," she gulped down her drink, "tried to rape me. I killed him instead. His partner thought it was funny. Funny that this 'little flower' could be so deadly. The nickname stuck, and my father learned just how useful I could be." Her words came too freely, too bitterly.

Sam's eyes were wide, and if Rose wasn't so deep in her ale, she might've noticed. Might've cared.

"I-I'm sorry. I can't... " he paused and frowned at her. "Little Flower? I remember hearing that name but -but it was the name of a mercenary. An assassin. That's a weird coincidence," he said with an awkward, forced laugh.

Rose held his eyes, unblinking, and slowly, Sam's grew wider.

Let them see, she thought grimly as she finally looked away and gathered her coat. Let them see what she really was.

She stood and pulled her coat back on. The room spun, and she wobbled on her feet as she walked past Sam. She stumbled out to her horse and managed to get up into the saddle after a try or two. Wearily and dejected, she headed back toward the castle. While she didn't know if she belonged there or not, she had nowhere else to go and she was just selfish enough to admit she wanted the comfort they offered.

CHAPTER 5

*T*hese forests were dense. Much thicker than the ones Goron was used to. Spruce and pine trees were packed next to each other, blocking out most of the sunlight. The ground was littered with dried-out pine needles and frost. Not much snow made it past the canopy here.

The world was so different from his time, so many years ago. His last memory had been laying down on a stone slab and trusting his commander and friend to wake him in a few weeks. A month or two at the most. Not nearly five hundred years. It was supposed to be the saving maneuver for their army. One last trick to outlast the bastard king and his forces. Instead, he'd woken up to learn everything he knew was dead and gone. The war was lost. His friend in the body of another.

He walked quietly through the trees, ducking around the low-hanging branches. The forest was quiet except for his soft footfalls. During his time, this forest had been impossible to find. Shademakers had lived here in numbers so vast they kept their forest hidden, secret. Their clan home was here, somewhere, but everyone who searched for it, found themselves wandering aimlessly through these woods only to leave them without realizing they'd been turned around. The fact he was able to enter these woods and not be turned around and lost within minutes... maybe they were all dead. Maybe once their Shadowstalker had died, they'd all followed suit.

He grunted, a smile curving his lips. One could hope.

Goron kept walking, the dried leaves and pine needles crunching beneath his feet. He knew the land, the familiarity of the earth was part of his blood, and these lands were ancient; the earth was seeping with a miasma of magic. Old magic. Unknown magic. The more he probed at the power in the earth with his own, the less he seemed to know what he was feeling. The power in these lands was too old, too intelligent to be called a simple magic.

"What is this?"

The birds stopped their chittering. Goron cocked his head as he noticed the stillness of the forest. He turned slowly, drawing his curved blade as he did. A slim woman leaned against a narrow aspen tree. He stared into her hard eyes. She didn't blink or look away. Her scarf and hood obscured much of her face; her hands shoved into the pockets of her long coat.

"What are you doing here?" she asked in a stern voice.

Goron shrugged but didn't sheath his blade. "Who are you to ask?"

"You trespass on our lands," she spoke, her deep voice rolling through the forest. She pushed off the tree and stood straight, her feet wide and planted. "So I ask again, why are you here?"

Not all dead then. He sucked his teeth. "The magic here feels old, odd. Is that the magic you Shademakers touch?"

"You don't know what you're touching." She slowly walked toward him. "That is the power of a god."

Goron scoffed. "Gods are tales meant for babes."

"Tsk. You know better than that." She stopped in front of him and tilted her head back. "Why are you here, Goron Velra?"

He jerked when she said his name. No one here should know his name.

"Oh yes, we know who you... were. But now you're back from the dead, it seems. How is that?" She pushed the hood off of her face. "Where have you been, Goron Velra?"

The woman's face was older than he had expected. Crow's feet sat at the corner of her eyes. Her graying hair, once a rich chestnut brown, was pulled into a loose braid.

Goron watched her, and wariness made him readjust his grip on his blade. This woman didn't look like a fighter. She stood with the confidence of someone used to being listened to, not a fighter. But.... He quickly glanced around the woods. These Shademakers had other ways of fighting. "Away."

She hummed and stepped back. "What are you doing in our woods?"

He strode close to the woman, who held her ground even as she had to tilt her head back to maintain his gaze. "I was starting to think no one was still here to claim them."

"Leave these woods. You've no place here."

Goron tilted his head at her and glanced around the forest. He'd spent years searching for the Shademakers in these woods, and now, he had one of them standing in front of him. Was it worth the fight? He glanced around the woods and noticed the mist thickening, the shadows darkening. His hand twitched toward the hilt of his blade as the forests darkened further.

"I would've killed you any other day," he said matter-of-fact. He had orders. He needed to remember that. As much as he wanted the fight, as much as he wanted to watch this woman's blood run for her clan's actions against his, he needed to remember his priorities.

"We know. We have a history that tells us exactly what you would've done. But I'm telling you," and the mist thickened further, "to leave."

He looked around the forest again and noticed the weight to the shadows that hadn't been there before, the otherness to it.

"Leave."

He brought his eyes back to her. "You should do a better job hiding it then." The shadows pressed against him, growing darker than the time of day should allow. "Or is that because you can't? Is the Shadowstalker the one responsible for hiding you?"

The woman didn't answer, but the narrowing of her eyes told him he was right. The Shadowstalker wasn't here; hadn't been. Maybe he will destroy this place and take her clan away from her like his had been.

A second set of footsteps sounded in the eerie stillness of the forest, and Goron glanced over his shoulder at a tall man, who stood with his hands in his pockets. Goron flipped his blade in his hand.

A growl sounded through the forest, low and gravely. He paused to listen. The sound grew, and as he watched, in the darkness, red eyes appeared. The shadows pressed further, and the hair on the back of his neck stood on end.

"The Shadowstalker isn't here," he said.

"Hmm, no. They're not," the woman said. "Which means no one is controlling them," she said and pointed at the glowing eyes in the darkness. "They're not always predictable, but they always protect their own. Do you want to risk it?"

Goron sheathed his blade and stepped back, his hands in the air. "Fine. I'll leave. But don't think this is the last we'll meet."

He turned and walked. The two Shademakers didn't follow, but he felt the eyes of the shadow beasts on him. Their eyes followed him in the darkness the entire way out of the forests. When he finally reached the edge, the large plain opening up ahead of him, he turned around and looked at the dense trees. He knew he wouldn't find his way in there again. Even if the Shadowstalker wasn't there, the beasts would keep him out now that they knew him to be a threat.

He sighed. Gerik had sent him with a mission; he depended on him. Goron needed to find the Anchor and finish this. He would have time for revenge later. Then he could come back for the last of the shadow clan once their queen was dead.

CHAPTER 6

"*H*ow many did you say are here?"

Micah glanced over at Lord Tyman, standing to his right. His salt and peppered hair was combed back from his forehead and cut short, the style of long-term military men. The lord had previously served as Micah's Captain of the Guard at his home estate before accepting the posting as his royal advisor. He'd known the man from childhood and had been trusted with guarding his family estate. This would be his first time acting in that new role, but Micah had no doubt he would succeed.

"Three, Sire. Lord A'amith and Farthin and Lady Sephrita."

"Sephrita was at the Atron Ball last summer, if I remember correctly," Captain Mariah Sayla said from her position on his left. "She was the head of the delegation."

The captain was also new to her role as advisor, though it was the title only. She'd previously been unofficially serving in that capacity since his ascension to the throne several years prior. Now that he'd finally removed his father's advisors, he was free to appoint his own advisors. Mariah had been telling him for years that he needed to build his own court; she had never expected him to appoint her to the position when he finally did listen to her advice.

"Yes." Micah nodded and watched the doors to the throne room. "These are some of the most senior members of the B'leakon Council. They have never had this many senior members in Rhivony at the same time before."

"And they said nothing of the purpose of their visit in the missive?" the captain asked.

"No, but we can expect they'll want D'ray returned to them," Micah murmured, "as if I would give him back even if I did know where he was."

The B'leakons. The native people of the Black Hill Islands. They were a strange people, nearly reclusive in their desire to avoid others. They controlled the trade from their islands fiercely and traded in items ranging from ores and metals to teas and textiles. D'ray had been a member of their delegation last summer when he'd been responsible for the coup on Micah's throne. He'd inadvertently freed the mind of Gerik, who had in turn taken over D'ray's body. How much of D'ray's mind remained was a mystery, but Micah suspected the B'leakon was dead.

The doors finally swung open as Ben, his steward, preceded the three B'leakons into the room. He looked like a child leading giants; their height so much greater than his. Micah remembered Lady Sephrita from the summer, her sharp, hawk-like features pinched in a scowl. The other two stood nearly a head taller than her, which was impressive given she was nearly four heads taller than Micah. Her companions had glowing orange eyes while hers swirled an inky, dark blue. He wondered at the difference, but some instinct had him thinking the dark blue was more dangerous than the orange or red colors. He knew the colors of the B'leakon's eyes changed based on their mood and emotions, or at least that was the simple explanation he'd been given.

Ben stopped in front of him, his eyes a little too wide. His faithful and hard-working steward had seen much in the past few months. More than he'd probably ever expected to see or experience, but he'd remained a dedicated worker. As organized as ever. He turned to glance over his shoulder but seemed to catch himself in time.

"Sire, Lords A'amith and Farthin and Lady Sephrita of the B'leakon Council, Black Hill Islands."

He gestured first to the B'leakon with raven black hair pulled up in a tight top knot, then to the male with hair so blond it was nearly gold. All three wore high-necked tunics decorated with elaborate embroidery and long, tight sleeves.

With Ben's announcement complete, he turned and left the room as quickly as decorum would allow. Micah needed to remember to thank his steward later. Standing with your back to beings that looked and felt like predators couldn't be easy. Micah looked over the three standing in front of him, their eyes nearly equal to his even as he sat on his raised dais. With their height, too wide eyes, otherness they extruded, it was hard not to see them as predators.

"Welcome to Rhivony," Micah said. "Welcome back, Lady Sephrita. It must be important indeed for you to brave the recent storms and leave your island."

The male with the glistening black hair, Lord A'amith, stepped forward. "It is. We demand the return of Lord D'ray, immediately."

"He has not returned to the island and has not made contact with any of us since the ball," the second, Lord Fathin, hissed, his accent the thickest of the three.

Micah slid his eyes to Sephrita, expecting her to say something as well, but she stood silent. Something about her stillness, her silence made his hands sweat.

"Even if I did know where the brigand is, I wouldn't return him to you." Micah forced his voice to be low and steady, despite the anger thumping in his chest. They thought to demand anything from him? After what one of theirs had attempted in his court? "Your council member helped to organize a coup against me and my court. When he is found and captured, he will be held accountable for the uprising he nearly started."

Lord A'amith hissed, low and long. "He is a member of our court."

"And he interfered with mine."

Lord A'amith's eyes swirled red, almost like a fire raged within, and pulled his lips back from his teeth. Lord Farthing hissed a string of words in their own tongue and stepped forward next to A'amith.

"We will deliver punissshment for his actions," Farthin said.

Lady Sephrita cut her eyes to the two males.

"But he must be returned to us," Lord Farthin continued.

"Again, as I said before, I don't know where he is. He's fled the capital. For all I know, he's fled the country. We searched for him throughout the fall and have had no luck. His cowardly actions have driven him into hiding."

"Yesss," Lady Sephrita hissed. "Tell us more of those actions."

Her two companions glanced back at her and whatever they recognized in her eyes caused them to step back until she stood ahead of them.

Micah looked at her with a raised eyebrow.

"I've heard strange tales from your humans about what happened during the attack. Perhaps you could confirm which are rumors and which are facts."

Micah leaned back in his chair, and Lord Tyman glanced at the captain. Mariah turned back to look at him before stepping up the dais step and leaned close.

"Sire, we should keep those details to ourselves," she whispered.

Micah nodded and turned to whisper in her ear, "yes, but she knows something or she wouldn't be asking." Mariah turned to look at him, a question in her eyes. "You never ask a question you don't already know the answer to."

Mariah nodded and resumed her position on the lower step.

"His specific actions don't matter. What does matter is he led forces into my castle and killed my people. He tried to kill me."

Lady Sephrita cocked her head to the side in a way a bird of prey would, and shivers shot down his spine. "But did he... have help, perhaps?"

Micah frowned at her. She definitely knew more than she was letting on. But how much she knew, and how she'd learned it, were the bigger questions. "He was in league with one of my lords if that's what you're alluding to."

She smiled, but there was no warmth or humor to it. "It was not."

Mariah stepped back up to him and leaned down close. "Can she know about Gerik?"

"I don't know how," he whispered back.

"Enough of this," Lord A'amith snapped and stepped forward.

Sephrita turned on him with a hiss so loud it was nearly a growl. Lord A'amith flinched and hastily stepped back. Lady Sephrita held the sound a moment before staring down the other B'leakon. Lord Farthin, although he hadn't been the focus of the reprimand, stepped further back, his eyes turning from orange to a swirling pale green.

Micah held his breath, his hands suddenly clammy in his lap. He'd once seen a cougar leap from the bush and land, snapping and growling, on a hunting dog when he was young. He'd been sure the cat would turn on them next and had nearly wet himself with the primal terror he'd felt. Forcing his breath out evenly to calm his frantic heart, he felt that same fear looking at the B'leakon slowly turn around and face him again. Only years of court training and willpower kept him in his seat to face her eyes.

Lady Sephrita rolled her shoulders and let out a soft breath. Her eyes had turned such a deep blue they were nearly black, and Micah again wondered at the meaning behind that color.

He swallowed and found his mouth had gone dry.

"Has D'ray's actions threatened the trade deal our courts have?" Sephrita asked.

Micah tried to swallow again. "I am inclined to believe his actions were his alone. Yes?"

Lady Sephrita nodded, and behind her, the two males slowly nodded their agreement as well.

"As long as his actions were truly his own, then no. They have not threatened the trade deal. However, if you continue to demand his return and deny us our retribution, then I may begin to believe his actions were endorsed by your council."

Lord A'amith spoke rapidly in their own tongue, hissing and growling sounds, and eventually, Lord Farthin joined him. Lady Sephrita listened, never taking her eyes off Micah. She tilted her head, listening to them further, before shifting and straightening. The two males ceased speaking as if that had been some silent cue.

"We cannot allow a member of our court to be punished by another. However, we will be satisfied with being present for any... *shylarlyc*.... " She turned and looked at Lord A'amith.

"Trial," he murmured.

"Ah. Trial. You find him and capture him. Give him a trial. Allow representatives of our council to be present, and we will be satisfied."

Her two companions' eyes turned deep red and Lord A'amith pulled his lips back in another silent growl but they made no other motions.

"Are you sure the council will be satisfied with that?" Micah gestured to the other two lords. "They do not seem pleased with the offer."

"Continued trade matters more to the council than the feelings of two hysrelyc males. The council will be satisfied. Are you?"

Micah watched her a moment longer and silently reevaluated his assumptions of the group. He had initially believed Lord A'amith to be the leader; clearly, that was incorrect. He looked at his two advisors, and when he saw no disagreement in their eyes, he nodded.

"Yes, assuming we ever find him."

"*Ashyryk*. We will return to our island then. May we be permitted a day's rest before setting out?"

Micah nodded again. *Tell the guards to watch them until they leave the gates,* he thought, knowing Mariah would hear his thoughts with her magic. He waited until he saw Mariah's subtle nod before saying, "yes. I will have my steward arrange rooms."

Lady Sephrita nodded and turned on her heel in a fluid movement without another word. The two males quickly moved to follow her out. Once the door closed behind them, Micah let out a loud sigh, his heart jumping into his throat and hands clammy. The captain slumped and rubbed her head, and even the stoic Lord Tyman shook out his hands.

"Anyone else feel like they just escaped fighting a giant beast?" Aaron surprised everyone by asking quietly from his spot against the wall.

Micah chuckled dryly. "We escaped something. Captain?"

"Yes, Sire." She moved to the throne doors. "I'll speak with Ben while I'm at it."

Lord Tyman glanced at Micah.

"She's telling the guards to tail them while they remain in the castle," Micah answered Tyman's unasked question.

"Lady Sephrita knows more than she's saying."

"Yes." Micah agreed.

"Let's hope that when we find D'ray it is in such a way that a trial will be unnecessary."

Micah grunted with a dry smile forming. "Yes. If we bring him back alive, that will lead to questions we won't answer."

Lord Tyman turned to leave but the doors of the throne room swinging open again stopped him. A Light Horse Officer, Micah tried to remember his name, hurried into the room.

"I apologize, Sire," he said while dipping in a hasty bow. "Officer Fiben, Sire."

Yes, right. Sam Fiben. The fire wielder. "Go on, Officer."

Thank the gods Sam Fiben's control over his magic was getting better. He'd had far too many reports from Mariah of burned and ruined rugs and tapestries because of young Sam. Not that he was worried about the cost of repairs, he did, however, worry about burning down parts of the castle. While it was mostly stone, there were plenty of wooden supports.

"While on my way back from my latest errand, I saw… well—"

"On with it, boy," Lord Tyman snapped tiredly.

Officer Fiben jumped. "Sorry. Sire, the ground was torn up. Destroyed. A few towns east of here, there used to be a large ridge bordering a river. It's gone. Flattened."

Micah's heart started to race. "Flattened?"

Officer Fiben nodded. "I spoke with several people in the Mantar Province. They reported seeing areas of land just… changed. It's almost like…. " he trailed off, his fingers twisting nervously.

"Like what, Officer?"

"It's almost like the old stories about Earthmovers, Sire. The rare, powerful ones."

"Are you saying there's an Earthmover running around the country-side, rearranging the landscape?" Lord Tyman asked, his voice incredulous.

"I'm saying it sounds like there is one, yes."

Micah rubbed the space between his eyes and held back a sigh. "Earthmovers haven't been seen for hundreds of years. Their magic has all but died out."

"I'm aware, Sire, but.... " Officer Fiben shrugged. "What else could it be?"

Micah let out a deep breath. Gerik was still missing. No doubt he was behind this.

"Whatever it is, it is not," Lord Tyman said, "Earthmovers."

But what else could it be? Micah sighed again, having no answers.

"Thank you, Officer Fiben."

Young Sam bowed again and hastily retreated.

"Lord Tyman, make sure Captain Sayla is updated on this, and all officers and soldiers are made aware to report anything similar."

"Yes, Sire." Lord Tyman nodded his head and followed Officer Fiben out of the throne room.

"Shit," Micah swore and made his own way out and to his office. Winters were supposed to be easy.

CHAPTER 7

*R*ose had heard there were B'leakons in the castle and they had met with the king. It was all anyone wanted to talk about, and the castle was abuzz with the gossip. She'd had her fill of B'leakons during the summer and was content to never talk to another one. She grumbled to herself and nibbled on the salted meat she'd snagged before leaving the dining hall. All she wanted was to eat breakfast in peace. She turned another corner, intent on making her way to the dining hall for breakfast, when she came face to face with the very thing she wanted to avoid.

Three B'leakons were striding down the corridor, right toward her. One she recognized from the ball, Lady Sephrita, but the other two were new to the castle. Based on the various shades of red in all their eyes, Rose decided it best to avoid all interactions with them. She stuck to the wall as she tried to pass them. The male with shining black hair glanced down at her as she passed, only for his arm to crash into her shoulder as they passed. Rose grunted as she spun into the wall.

"Sor—" Her words were cut short by a terrifying hissing sound right before the collar of her shirt was fisted in a slender hand as she was hauled up against the stone wall.

In the next heartbeat, she'd pulled her dagger from her boot and had it pressed against the B'leakon's ribs, angled right for his heart. His face dipped low, his eyes red and swirling.

"Move even a little bit, and I'll be wiping your blood off my boot."

The B'leakon smiled, all teeth and edge and hunter. The wolves sensed the fellow predator in him and pushed close against Rose's mind. They wanted in, wanted to hunt, to rise to the challenge of this other predator.

"If that was where my heart was... I might care," he said, low in his throat.

"A'amith." Sephrita growled, her eyes a deep, cold blue. She pressed close to them, her own hand extended and resting against his chest, her fingers tipped in lethal-looking claws. "Let the human go."

Sephrita pushed even closer, her chest pressed against Rose's side, and gripped his wrist as he pulled against Rose's shirt.

He hissed a string of words before letting go and stepping back. Sephrita dropped her hands, which looked like normal, slender hands once again. Rose kept her blade clenched in her hand while the two male B'leakons glanced at Sephrita before turning back down the hall.

"I apologize for that," Sephrita said, turning her cold, too wide eyes to Rose. "It couldn't be helped."

Rose nodded stiffly, breath in her throat and heart hammering, as the three of them continued down the hallway and around the corner. She let herself gasp a breath, and her heart thundered in her chest as she shakily put her dagger back in her boot.

"They have claws?" she said to herself. "Claws."

She shoved her hands in her coat pocket to hide their shaking, only to pull her hand back out, clutching the small rolled note that she'd found. Rose looked at the note, then back down the hallway. Unrolling it, she looked to the bottom for a signature and choked when she saw Lady Sephrita's name.

"It couldn't be helped," she repeated and looked down the hallway. "I nearly get eaten by giant clawed people just so you can pass me a note... "

Then she read the note, a hastily scrawled thing.

· · ·

I know the Earthmover is alive. I know he seeks
   a device for his master believed lost to time. If
   it does exist, all is lost. You'll need me. I can't afford
   to be seen talking with your leadership.
   I'll contact you again when it's safe.

Her breath caught in her throat, and she wildly looked back down the hallway they'd disappeared down. How, in all the hells, did this B'leakon know about the Earthmover?

Shit. She heard the chuffing growl from the shadows. She couldn't keep this to herself, not anymore. She moved quickly toward the captain's office. When she stopped at the captain's door, she knocked in short, hard knocks on the old wood.

"Come."

Rose slipped inside and promptly sat in the stiff, old chair across from the captain's desk.

"What happened to you?" Captain Sayla asked, barely looking up from her papers. "Your mind is a mess."

"A B'leakon tried to eat me."

"Well, the soun—" Captain Sayla snapped her head up. "What was that?"

Rose huffed a laugh and told the captain about her interaction with the B'leakon party. "I found this," she held out the note, "in my pocket once they'd left. It is signed by Lady Sephrita."

Captain Sayla leaned forward to take it. "How are you always the one getting pulled into these things?"

"Just lucky," Rose murmured, wishing she was anything but.

Captain Sayla's eyes pinched, and her brow furrowed as she read over the words, again and again. She looked up from the scrap of paper with a frown. "What in the nine hells is that supposed to mean?"

Rose frowned. "Aren't there only four?"

"The B'leakons deserve extra," the captain said. "Do you know what this means?"

"I… might," Rose hedged. At the captain's steely-eyed glare she quickly swallowed and continued, "The shadows have been restless, angry. They told me an Earthmover had appeared. They want me to do something about it."

"Like?" Captain Sayla glanced over the note again, a frown creasing her forehead.

"They haven't been clear on that."

"You haven't bothered to learn." Their growl reverberated from the shadows.

Rose flinched at the seething anger in the words that burned along her skull.

The captain, eyes too focused on the note, missed the flinch.

Rose shifted in her chair and tried to roll her shoulders at the sudden ache in the base of her skull. She wanted to learn. Didn't she? But she hated to admit to herself that a larger part was afraid to learn more. Afraid of what her magic might become. She'd spent so much of her life learning to accept what it was, and now she felt she didn't have any idea what it could be.

"You look more concerned than I thought warranted for the note."

Captain Sayla sighed before dropping the note and fixing Rose with her hazel gaze. "Yesterday, Sam reported seeing destruction across the Mantar Province. Destruction on a scale that could've only been done with magic. Like that of the Earthmovers of old. It seems Sam was right about it being the doing of an Earthmover."

A sinking feeling settled in Rose's gut, and she tried to swallow but her mouth had gone dry.

"You need to stop hiding," the shadows hissed and Rose clenched her teeth.

"So, my questions are," the captain continued, her eyes hard, as she held up her fingers and ticked off her questions. "How does a B'leakon know about an Earthmover when we're just now getting the report, and why," she paused, and Rose worried this next question would be directed at her, "you are just now telling me about this revelation of the Earthmover?"

She squirmed in the hard chair under the captain's gaze. Rose didn't have a good answer for her. She barely had an answer for the shadows.

The captain sighed, her eyes softening as she no doubt heard the confusion rattling around in Rose's mind.

"I'll give this to the king. They're due to leave tomorrow. If Gerik is looking for something... " She trailed off with a sigh. "Was there anything else about the B'leakons?"

"Sure," Rose said with false enthusiasm. "Did you know their hands can turn into claws?" She held her hands up and curled her fingers to demonstrate.

The captain shook her head at her.

"That should bother you more. Claws. Actual claws."

The captain chuckled. "Says the girl who talks to shadows."

She grunted, "Fine. That's fair."

Rose sighed as the captain went back to the note again before tossing it aside with her own sigh. She didn't like this feeling, feeling afraid of her own magic. She didn't like how it was moving and changing on her.

"I remember you saying you'd written to a friend of yours at the college," Rose said. "Have you heard back from him?"

Captain Sayla blinked at her before slowly shaking her head. "No. But that really isn't strange. The man is... he's an odd one and correspondence never really ranks high on his things to remember."

The captain paused before settling her hands on her desk. "Why?"

Rose rubbed her scars again and shrugged. It was a sharp, jerky movement. "Because I need answers, and I'm not finding them here. I'm just... " She shrugged again and let out a breath. "I'm just here. If there aren't answers for me there, then maybe I need to move on."

Captain Sayla was quiet for a long time, and Rose had to look away from her piercing gaze. With a jerk, she tucked her hands into her pockets to stop herself from rubbing the scars on her wrists.

Finally, the captain nodded. "Perhaps you should go to the college and seek out Professor Elias."

Rose nodded.

"I do not think, however," she continued, and Rose looked up to meet her hazel eyes, "that you are finished here. You should put more thought into joining a corps."

We'll see.

Captain Sayla hummed softly. "Rose, your shadows exist in a world between things, but you cannot. Eventually, you must make a decision. Eventually, you must take a stand and stay there."

"I know that." She sounded petulant, even to her own ears.

"Do you? I hope so." The captain sighed. "Think about it."

Rose ducked her head but nodded. "Yes, ma'am."

"The college is in a large town south of the capital, Alavra. It shouldn't take you more than a day or two. Give the roads a few days to settle from this latest storm before you leave."

She nodded and stood to leave when the captain called softly behind her.

"I'll hold your room, just in case."

The simple words made her eyes sting with tears, and her throat tighten. She nodded stiffly and slipped from the room. The captain expected her to return. Hoped she would. Somehow that simple sentiment nearly undid her. It was a new feeling and not, she quietly admitted, an unwelcome one.

The captain was right, which irritated Rose. She was just... existing here. Not living. If she did come back, she couldn't continue as she was.

She wandered to the Light Horse common room, with every plan to drink and feel sullen for herself. She searched the room for any ale or wine, only to find it already gone. With a sigh she plopped herself into the overstuffed armchair by the fire.

"You look like shit."

Rose looked over at the couch, where a sullen-looking Erik sat. She'd missed him in her search of the room for drinks. Erik, the sandy-haired, freckle-kissed young man was the newly appointed lieutenant of the Light Horse and most senior officer. He'd been the unknowing target of a spy sent by D'ray. Rose had been the one to reveal that secret, something they still hadn't talked about. She'd been avoiding him, truth be told. She'd seen the anguish in his eyes when he'd learned he'd fallen in love with a spy, that everything had been an act. Rose was afraid of that pain being directed at her.

"Thanks," she drawled at him. "You look drunk. Is that where all the ale went?"

"Well," he slowly sat up, "it may be."

"I support excessive day drinking more than anyone else, but for you, this is a little much."

Erik sighed and dropped his head in his hands. "I wanted so badly to be mad at you. I wanted to hate you."

Rose eyed the door. Should she just leave? Go back to her room. Hiding sounded good right now. She was good at that.

"But I can't," Erik continued. "No matter how hard I try. I can't make this your fault."

She sighed. The spy, Sasha, had situated herself close to Erik and the information available to him. She'd become intimately close to Erik and had revealed herself during the battle in the throne room, in front of Erik, Rose, and the king. "I'm sorry, Erik."

"Did you use people?" He snapped his head up and glared at her. "Did you do this to people too?"

Rose sucked her teeth and took a deep breath through her nose. "No. I never did what she did."

"You never used someone for their access to your target?"

She ground her teeth. "No, I did that all the time, but I never made someone fall in love with me."

Erik let out a long breath and rubbed his eyes. "I'm sorry. That wasn't... I didn't need to do that."

She tucked her legs under herself.

"She used me to get access to the king. I'm to bl—"

"No one's to blame but Sasha," Rose cut him off with angry words. "She did this. She chose this. She used you. She betrayed you. None of that is your fault. Don't take the blame that belongs to her."

Erik slumped back onto the couch. "How could you do what she did? How do you live with yourself?"

The words cut into Rose, and she grimaced. She didn't know either.

"How could you use people? How do people like you sleep at night?"

I don't. Rose felt her eyes tighten against tears and her throat went dry. Part of her knew he was talking about Sasha, that he wouldn't have said that if he wasn't drunk, but that didn't stop the pain. She and Sasha were the same in every way but one: Sasha enjoyed what she did.

"You said you're different from her." His words were softer, and his eyes slipped shut. "But are you? Really?"

Rose sniffed and stood from her chair, Erik's snores filling the room. "I don't know," she said softly as she passed him. "Probably not."

She was a fool to think she could belong here.

CHAPTER 8

The earth squeezed Goron as he moved through it. It pushed him beneath the surface at speeds faster than the fastest race horses. The earth was dusty and dry. As he moved further and further southwest the dirt grew wet. Fertile. Soon, the dusty lands of the plains were far behind him and he was in the swampy, rotten-smelling earth south of Rhivony. Further south and the mud of the swamps would dry out, the lands would rise out of the flat lands, and the deserts of the Southern Territories would emerge. Full of cliffs and canyons and dead earth.

Gerik would be calling back all the An'thila from the border. Getting them ready to move onto their next plan. Things were moving smoothly. The An'thila were the primitive people of the Southern Territories. Well, he had to admit, not so primitive now. Five hundred years had done their people good. They had backed Gerik in his war against the king. They had guarded his sleeping body. They knew how to fight and were wholly underestimated by the men of the north.

He wanted to travel further south, but his magic began to lag. The pull started to sting. This land. This time. So much had changed. The magic of the world had disappeared. Thinned. It took him longer to do less. Once, he'd been able to travel from the eastern coast with the sandy beaches and warm waters all the way to the western coast with its cliffs in a day. Now he could barely make it through a province before he was winded and tired.

With a sigh that echoed in the earth, he rose from the ground. Dirt fell from him in a cascade of mud and rocks. He shook out his coat and ran his hand over his smooth head. With one last shrug, the remaining mud fell from him.

He needed to find the Orthalen. That was the main goal now. Without it, Gerik was limited and still unable to use much of his magic. The Orthalen would speed up many things for Gerik.

Except, he couldn't sense it; couldn't feel it in his bones or the earth. Anything he'd made, crafted, he could sense. He could find. He should be able to find this. That he couldn't.... It could be hidden. Shielded in some way. It could be destroyed. He hoped it wasn't destroyed. That was a much larger problem.

As he walked, slowly with stiff limbs sore from the magical use, the sounds of hooves crunching on the frozen earth reached his ears. He turned and looked over his shoulder at the horse and rider approaching him.

The rider neared him, slowing the horse. He turned and faced them and planted his hands on his hips. Now that she was close enough to see, the rider, a woman, frowned down at him. Her black hair shined in the sun. His eyes roved over her uniform. The deep blue color didn't look familiar to him.

"Do you need help, sir?"

Her voice was firm, sure of herself. Used to being respected. He recognized the lilt to her vowels that those from the southern swamps of Salva Province had.

"No." He turned to walk away.

"Are you sure you're alright?" she asked again.

He stopped with an angry huff and slowly turned back to her. He looked again at her uniform.

"What uniform do you ride under, girl?"

Her lips pursed and brows creased. "I am an Officer of the Light Horse, messenger for the king."

"The king," he sneered, derision making his words sharp. "Is this king one of Jonas' get?"

The woman straightened in her seat, her anger pulling her spine straight.

He laughed at her indignation. All these king's men. Before and now. They were all so loyal. So sure of themselves. So self-righteous.

There was a bridge he headed for. It was a main thoroughfare for trade between the north and south and the only easy way to traverse the river and he was meant to destroy it, but... he shrugged and pulled his lips back in a feral grin. Why not start a little early to prove a point? This king's man, with all her self-assured authority, needed to learn that was nothing.

Goron threw his fists in the air, pushing the last of his magic. The ground around them exploded up in a blast of rock and mud and snow. He heard the woman and horse scream over the roar of the earth around them. The animal's panicked screams were cut off short, and the air was quiet save for the thuds of rocks landing.

He chuckled darkly to himself and turned away as the last of the rocks settled and started walking.

CHAPTER 9

*M*icah watched as the young lord left the audience room, Ben following behind. As Lord Isaac left, Ben turned to Micah after glancing down at his ever-present schedule book.

"Captain Sayla and Lord Tyman next, Sire?"

Micah nodded, his finger tapping against his chin. Lord Isaac was a quiet man, still very young to be lord of a province. He had to give the lord some credit, not only braving the storms to come in person but also to ask for Amora Province at all. He was the nephew of Amora's previous Lord Governor, thus making him the next in line to inherit the land. Micah wasn't sure about allowing the man whose uncle had committed treason and raised arms against him, but the northern lords still supported Damian's family. And Micah needed the northern lords. They controlled trade that came from the Invius Mountains. It was the main source of root vegetables traded throughout the country. He needed them to be cooperative. Tensions were bad enough as it was.

Ben knocked on the audience door, breaking him from his thoughts, as Captain Sayla and Lord Tyman entered and approached the dais.

"Sire," Lord Tyman greeted him as they bowed.

"There are several things I wanted to discuss with you two."

The captain raised an eyebrow at him. "Is one of them Lord Isaac? I saw him leaving."

"Yes. He is one. He requested to meet with me about Amora. He thought meeting with me personally to make his case would be beneficial."

Lord Tyman let out a breath that sounded like a cough. "Did he hope begging for forgiveness in person for being members of such a traitorous family would keep you from taking Amora from them?"

Captain watched him with narrowed eyes. "You're not going to, are you?"

"I'd thought not to, no."

"But Sire—" Lord Tyman spread his hands wide. "His uncle tried to take the throne from you."

"Yes, I was there," Micah said with a soft chuckle and leaned forward onto his knees. "However, Lord Isaac had nothing to do with that. When I sent Gregory to interrogate Lord Damien's remaining family, he was cooperative. His short time as lord of his household has been quiet, problem-free."

Gregory's reputation as the crown's interrogator and torturer had preceded him into the province and probably helped to ensure the severity of why he was there settled into their minds.

"I don't know if it's wise to let such a large province stay in that family, Sire," Lord Tyman said. "A lot of power sits in that land. Damian might've been a right fool, but that whole family echoed his sentiments. They haven't been happy with the throne since they lost it in the first great war."

"To a degree," Micah relented and agreed. "Yes. However, I need the northern lords' support, and right now, they still hold Damian's ilk in high regard. They are an independent lot and have never settled well under the crown rule. But they fall in line, most of the time. If I take Amora from the oldest family in the north, I may very well lose all the northern lords. Which means they can block trade, food. Much more."

Captain Sayla sighed, seeming to realize his decision had been made. "So, what is your plan?"

"Isaac will assume the mantle of Lord Governor over Amora. I will send one of your officers to Amora to watch and report on everything that happens there until we are satisfied Isaac does not pose a problem."

"Does Lord Isaac know this is going to happen?" Lord Tyman asked.

"He suggested it," Micah said.

Isaac was young, but he was smart, and he was ambitious. He was also a hard worker; having grown up working the beet fields until his older brother's death meant he was the new lord of the household. Of those in the Penish family line, Isaac might be the most level-headed among them.

"It was always my intention to do so," Micah continued. "But he suggested it before I could. I think that should speak to his character."

"Alright." Captain Sayla nodded. "It's smart, I'll admit. Even if I don't like it."

Micah smiled at her. "Good thing you don't have to."

"Now that that's been settled, I would like to address something," Lord Tyman said with a glance over at the captain.

That glance, and the one the captain gave the lord in return, told Micah he wasn't going to like what was coming and that they'd planned this together.

"Alright," he said hesitantly.

"The captain has informed me there are several marriage proposals you've yet to read."

Micah glared at his friend. *Traitor*, he thought at her. She met his gaze, but he caught the small twitch of her shoulders.

"With no queen, no heir, and potential conflict brewing with the Southern Territories, not to mention whatever is going to happen with Gerik's plans, I think it's time we start addressing the lords' proposals." Lord Tyman spoke softly but firmly, "picking the right wife could ease a lot of the tensions with the crown. You look weak, even though you defeated Lord Damian and secured your throne. You need to reestablish your control, or others may think they can challenge you as well."

Micah sighed heavily and looked away from his advisors.

"Lady Daniella, for example," Captain Sayla said softly. "Her father has made many overtures. Not to mention the dowry that would come with someone from the Ponditt family."

Micah continued to look out the far window. His advisors were right, he knew they were, but he couldn't seem to bring himself to entertain the thought. Maybe he was naïve, despite what Rose had said. Naïve in thinking he could marry for more than power and money, more than the title someone had.

"You stepped out with Lady Daniella during the summer ball, if I remember correctly," Lord Tyman said into the silence.

"Yes," Micah relented and turned back to them. He'd stepped out with her because he was expected to do so. She was a nice enough young woman and had been managing her own house since her mother's death. It wasn't a bad idea. But he loathed it so.

"She would be a good match, my lord," Lord Tyman continued. "And her family has strong ties with the northern lords, even though they're from the plains. Aligning yourself with the Ponditts could help with that. Not to mention she's the heir to the Mantar Province."

"I'll consider it," Micah said softly, wishing for just a moment he was free of his title to do as he wished. He knew he wouldn't be able to put them off for long, but for now, he would.

Captain Sayla narrowed her eyes at him and pursed her lips. He sighed again. Micah knew that look. He would be hearing from her later.

"I had rather hoped for a more resounding answer," Lord Tyman said, if a little hesitantly.

"I said I'll consider it," Micah snapped, making sure his sharp tone left no room for misinterpretation or rebuttal.

Lord Tyman bowed, and Captain Sayla ducked her head. She was like an older sister to him, a mentor and a friend since he'd been small at the castle, but sometimes she forgot herself. He had no doubt this conversation had been her idea.

"Captain, please have an officer ready to set out for Amora before the storms make that impossible. Now, I wanted to go over the arguments the merchants are having with the builders in town."

Captain Sayla frowned at him harder but allowed her monarch to move the meeting along. Lord Tyman bristled, but eventually, even he settled in for the remainder of the meeting. Micah was able to move through it quickly, handing most of the issues brought to him during the last public audience to someone else. They argued about taxes, and Micah solidly put that aside until spring. By the time it was over, Micah's stomach was growling loud enough for Aaron to hear it from his post behind the dais.

Lord Tyman left quickly, but the captain stayed, like he suspected she would.

"Lunch?" she asked.

"Yes, I'm starving." Micah stood and stretched his arms above his head. His back cracked, and he sighed happily.

Mariah fell in step with him as they walked in companionable silence to the small dining room they often ate in. Soon they were seated with a small meal of salted meats and cheese laid out before them, a steaming pot of tea at the center.

"It is a good idea about Isaac," Mariah said around her tea cup.

"Thank you," Micah said dryly but with a smile. "There is the potential for more bloodshed if the ordeal of Amora isn't settled carefully."

Mariah hummed in response and sipped her tea. "The events of the throne room were bloody enough."

"How are your people faring? Are they returning to normal lives?"

"Well enough," Mariah said with a sad glance. "They are adjusting. They're all handling it differently, some better than others."

Micah nodded and poured more tea. Maybe he was lucky, and Mariah would leave him alone for his meal.

"Micah," Mariah started.

Not that lucky, it would seem.

"Are you delaying choosing a wife because of Rose?"

Micah stilled at her words and slowly, deliberately, set his glass down. He looked up at Mariah, his jaw clenched hard enough to make his teeth ache. "You forget yourself. You should know better than to ask that."

"I'm speaking as your friend. I know she's fond of you." Mariah continued in a soft voice, "and I know you are as well. Do not let some tryst become a mistake of your rein. Nothing can come of this, and in the end, you'll only end up hurting her."

Micah ground his teeth. "There is no tryst. There's nothing for there to be an end of." His voice started to rise, and he struggled not to shout. "Would you begrudge me this friendship? Would you take that from her as well?"

Mariah took a breath to speak but Micah cut her off with a sharp cut of his hand through the air. "Enough."

"Yes, Sire," she murmured.

Micah picked at his food, but he'd lost his appetite. Eventually, he'd have to choose a wife. He knew that. He also knew why he was stalling. So did Mariah. He was lying to himself if he didn't admit that, but that didn't mean he couldn't put it off... for just a little longer.

CHAPTER 10

*R*ose curled her legs under her, the sun from the window bright and warm on her face. This solarium offered her the peace she needed to try to sort out her thoughts. The sun warming her skin meant the wolves and their angry words couldn't reach her. They had gone oddly quiet several days ago, offering no information as to why, but she could feel their simmering anger in the shadows. She hated to admit it, but she was afraid to ask.

The roads should be clear enough to travel in the next day or so, and she planned on leaving soon. She didn't know which she was more nervous for: possibly learning something about her magic from the professor or the decision she'd need to make when she was done.

A hand landed on her shoulder, and her heart leaped into her throat as she reached for the dagger in her boot.

"Easy, dear," the king said gently, with laughter in his voice.

Rose panted, her heart racing, and shoved her dagger back in her boot. "Sorry, I didn't hear you."

"Clearly." The king came around and sat next to her on the lounge. "What is it that has you so engrossed?"

She shrugged and looked away. "Nothing important."

"Ah," the king said softly. He rubbed his chin, his short, trimmed beard rustling in the quiet room.

"Has your sleep improved any since our last meeting?"

Rose clucked her tongue and looked out of the windows. Erik's words came back to her, sharp and cruel: how do you people sleep at night? She didn't. That was how. "I manage."

The king nodded slowly, watching her from the corners of his eyes. He didn't seem to believe her. "I'm sure Rita could help with a draft."

She hummed. "Perhaps."

The king watched her quietly, and Rose refused to meet his gaze. They fell into a silence, and it felt like it had during the summer, when they would sit together in the garden and talk, or more often, sit quietly. A companionship had developed out of that shared silence. She still didn't know what to make of his looks and smiles, but she wanted the ease found in these moments.

She kicked her feet out in front of her and crossed her ankles. "Is there more or less for you to do in the winter?"

The king shrugged as he said, "usually less. Not many bother to travel through the storms to air their grievances. Those that do, do so by letter and can usually be addressed the same."

"You said usually?"

He sighed. "Yes. Usually. After the failed coup, the tensions with the lords have increased. Not to mention the raids by the An'thila from the Southern Territories."

"I remember. They had been raiding Lord... Lord Mott? His lands." Rose struggled to remember the various lords. She'd never bothered to remember names before.

"Yes, Lord Mott. I've had several reports back now. They are concerning."

"Why?"

"The An'thila continue to gather at the border." He kicked his own feet out, mirroring Rose. "Once the soldiers arrived, they pulled back into their lands, but they haven't dispersed. The An'thila have been content to leave our people be at the mines, but now they seem to be posturing there as well."

"Why would they do that now? Have they asked for anything?"

"I think they're gathering for a rebellion." He shrugged. "I don't know. I don't know why they would. We outnumber them and are far superior in weapons and fighting ability. The only time they've fought us was during the civil war with King Jonas. After their defeat and King Jonas took the land as a territory of Rhivony, they fell back and haven't been a problem. While I can't think of a reason they would want to start a conflict, I can think of no other reason for their actions."

"Have you asked them?"

The king watched her from under his brow. "Yes," he drawled. "Neither of my emissaries have returned."

"Sorry." She breathed and looked away. "What are you going to do?"

"I don't know." He sighed, and he sounded tired. "My soldiers are still stationed along the south to help secure Lord Mott's border and an increased presence at the mines. My father would've already marched across and settled the whole thing in one bloody assault, put them back into their place. He would reinforce his rule and would take away the relative freedom they've had."

"But," she prompted.

"But," he sighed again, "I am not my father. If I attack them in response to them attacking us, then I could be helping to perpetuate a cycle that could go on for years. I could speed up a full rebellion. I will wait to see if this can be resolved peacefully first. Do you think that makes me naïve?"

"I think it makes you hopeful," she said with a glance at the Taspa figurine beneath the palm tree across from her. Hope. This room was full of it. There were far more Taspa figurines than any of the other gods. Had his grandmother built this place as a hopeful refuge?

"Aren't those the same?"

Rose glanced around the room while she gathered her thoughts. "No," she finally said. "Because I don't think you're foolish enough to believe peace is the only solution."

He nodded slowly and seemed satisfied with her answer. They fell into a silence again and Rose started to doze. Her head fell back against the lounge, and her eyes drifted shut.

"Captain Sayla wants me to join her Light Horse," she said softly. "Aaron wants me in the Black Shields."

"And you?"

Rose shook her head, rolling it against the back of the chair. An assassin should not be a guard, she thought to herself. She still didn't know if an assassin deserved a home.

"What do you want to do?"

She sighed, weariness making her bones hurt. "To sleep without dreaming."

Rose let her gaze move over the plants in the room rather than look at him. Her stomach fluttered. Erik's words seemed to haunt her. "Captain pointed out recently that I can't stay here and not do anything. Rather put me in my place about it." She paused and huffed a breath. "I don't like being put in my place."

"I know." He chuckled softly. "Why are you fighting the idea so hard?"

"Why do I resist anything?" she murmured. Rose sighed and shrugged. "Putting down roots is hard. Staying in place is hard."

"Running will not stop your past from finding you."

Except her past had found her once already. Would more people from her past find her? The Seer had implied as much.

Rose cut her eyes over to him in a glare. "That's not what I'm doing."

He stared at her with a raised eyebrow and a challenge in his eyes.

"I'm not."

"What are you doing then?"

She huffed a breath and threw her hands in the air. "I don't know. That's the problem."

He smiled at her gently, and it took some of the sting out of his words. "She'd be pleased if you joined the Light Horse; if you stayed and made a home here. I'd be pleased," he added softly.

She didn't know what to do about that proclamation, and she glanced away again. His words from the throne room came back to her: she is mine. What did he mean by that? Did she want those words? She didn't want to be owned, tied to anyone but a part of her she didn't want to acknowledge, knew he didn't mean it like that. She glanced over at him but darted her eyes away when she caught him staring at her. Micah let the silence grow while she chewed her lip.

Knocking interrupted the strained silence and her need to come up with an answer.

"Sire?" Ben came into view. Micah sighed softly.

"Yes, Ben?"

"Lord Mathias has just arrived. He was quite anxious to meet with you right away."

Micah sighed again and said under his breath, "if only the snow would keep them all away for a time." He stood and pulled his coat straight. "Thank you, Ben."

"Lord Mathias?" Rose asked softly.

"Lady Daniella's father."

Oh. The words added a heavy feeling in her chest she didn't understand.

"Until later, Miss Trewin."

She nodded at the king. "I leave for the college tomorrow since the storms have passed. Captain Sayla has a contact that might be useful for me to talk to. About my magic." She told herself the only reason she told him was because she'd promised him not to disappear, because she wanted him to know she wasn't disappearing.

Micah hesitated, looking down at her. "How long will you be gone?"

She opened her mouth to speak, but the words were stuck in her throat.

"You are returning, aren't you?" His words were so soft, so hesitant.

Rose licked her lips and nodded even as the words leaving her lips were, "I don't know."

He nodded, his face downfallen. Ben cleared his throat somewhere behind a flowering rose bush, and Micah turned away. He glanced over his shoulder just before he moved out of sight, like he wanted to ask more. Instead he nodded once at her and slipped away.

Rose sunk back onto the soft lounge, softer than anything in the Light Horse common room, and curled her knees to her chest. She felt the need to run after him to apologize; she just wasn't sure for what.

CHAPTER 11

*K*ing Micah watched as Lord Mathias retreated from the room. The lord was impatient, bordering on angry. He wanted an answer, felt he was owed an answer. Lord Mathias was many years Micah's senior and, in many ways, his superior. He was an accomplished fighter, a strong rider, and a fine leader. The elder lord believed, along with Micah's advisors, that his daughter, Daniella, was the best match for Micah. The lord didn't feel the delay in an answer to his marriage proposal was justified.

Lady Daniella's dowry was no small matter either, and while Micah would rather not make this decision any time in the near future, the decision might be taken out of his hand. Mathias had braved the snow and terrible roads to remind Micah not only the size of the dowry but also the number of northern lords he could bring around to support Micah. The unspoken veiled threat had been loud enough for Micah to send the lord on his way with angry words of denying his request of marriage simply because of the insult the man risked.

He sighed at the closing door, his anger still bubbling in his chest. He hated being forced into decisions, and he hated being threatened into them more.

Just as the door was about to close, Ben slipped in and walked briskly toward Micah and his desk.

"Ben," Micah asked hesitantly. His steward was the example of decorum and proper etiquette. It never bode well when he rushed.

"Officer O'Rayn is outside. She needs to report to you."

Micah nodded at Ben and straightened behind his desk. At the end of the fall, Micah had sent O'Rayn south to Lord Mott's land. He had wanted eyes on the situation with the Southern Territory, and the soldiers gathered at the border. More importantly, he'd wanted a representative and presence that wasn't a soldier; wasn't someone associated with warriors and fighting An'thila. He hoped that difference would make those around her more willing to talk and share information.

Ben retreated to the door and opened it wide enough for the woman to enter. She hobbled in, her blue uniform covered in mud. She limped heavily, favoring her right leg, and a large yellowing bruise covered her cheek and chin. Her black hair, usually shiny and pulled high on the top of her head, was dull and dirty, falling in a mess around her shoulders.

His chest ached at the sight of her. He had yet to grow accustomed to the risks, the responsibility of sending his officers out. He knew each mission could very well be their last. He knew they risked torture for the messages they carried. Mariah continued to tell him he'd get used to it, that he needed to, and to stop taking each injury so personally but looking at his battered woman, how couldn't he? He'd sent her on the path that caused this. He would again and they all would go, without complaint.

"Officer O'Rayn," Micah addressed her when she stopped and dipped in a shaky bow. "What has befallen you?"

Her hazel eyes were hard. "I have two things to report. I was on my way back to report developments when I encountered a man." She hesitated, and her eyes grew distant, as if she was seeing something from the past. "His clothing did not fit the weather, which is what made me pause. I thought, perhaps, he needed help. Instead, he attacked me with magic I've never seen."

Micah's mouth went dry, and he nodded for her to continue.

"He had control of the land, over the earth. He... I can only think of explaining it as an explosion. He exploded the earth around me. My horse, Raven, didn't survive the fall, and I injured my ankle when we landed."

"Did he leave you after the initial attack?"

Officer O'Rayn frowned and shook her head. "I played dead. Which wasn't that hard, honestly, Sire. He hit me hard enough I wasn't sure where I was. He just... left. It took me several days before I found a village willing to lend me a horse to finish my journey here. I have the name of the family for compensation."

Micah nodded absently and rubbed his face. Gods. "And the report from the border that started you on this journey?"

Officer O'Rayn, Luci, he believed her first name was, took a deep breath. "The soldiers gathering along the border have disappeared."

His spine straightened with the shock of her words. "What?"

"During the night, they disappeared. They abandoned their camps and left. The sentries posted, Lord Mott's men and yours, both reported no one made attempts to cross into Rhivony. Scouts were sent into the Territory, as far as the Ember Plains, and none were found. The scouts were pulled back at that point, rather than risk a confrontation."

Micah nodded. It was smart. Even though the desert to the south was a territory of Rhivony, the crown hadn't imposed its rule on the citizens there in generations. Aside from the iron mines, it was sparse in resources, far too hot for most of his people and the territorial indigenous people made the Southern Territory not worth most of the trouble. But where did they go? Why did they move?

"Officer," Micah asked, thoughts and theories already swirling in his mind. "Do you believe they've simply returned home?"

"No, Sire." Officer O'Rayn said firmly and without hesitation. "They had been steadily gathering in numbers over the fall and into the winter. They'd started smithing weapons. Wherever they went, it wasn't home to their fields."

"Something changed."

She nodded. "We just don't know what."

Shit. Micah breathed a deep breath and leaned back. This changed things. This escalated everything. There was no doubt a war was coming. Either a rebellion or something worse planned at the hands of Gerik.

"Sire," she interrupted his thoughts softly. "One more thing you should know."

He nodded again and took a deep breath. He saw the slight shift in her eyes. She was nervous.

"Lord Mott is growing impatient with the... stagnant feeling of the troops. The hunters in the south, Lord Mott especially, are very proud people. They feel personally victimized by the raids from the fall. They crave revenge or at least payment. They will not be stalled for much longer before they take action into their own hands."

He held back a sigh and nodded. He'd chosen Officer O'Rayn for this assignment over someone with more experience. She was from the swamps of the south, not Lord Mott's province, but she knew the people and the culture there. He'd hoped that familiarity would help her with gauging the moods of those in the south.

"I can't blame him," Micah said softly. Unfortunately, the lord's need for revenge needed to wait. Something was brewing in the south, and it was more than simple raids on alligators and farms. "Thank you, Officer O'Rayn. You've done well."

She nodded and dipped in another bow.

"Go see Madame Rita about your injuries and rest."

She turned, and he called after her softly as she limped away.

"And Luci," she turned, eyes wide with shock, and looked over her shoulder at him. "I am glad you were not injured worse."

Her eyes softened, and after a pause, she resumed her small trek out of his office.

He let out a long breath, too long to be called a sigh, and dropped his head into his hands, elbows braced on his desk. Micah heard Ben walk up to his desk, but it took him several more deep breaths before he could lift his head.

"Get Lord Tyman, Captain Sayla, and Archie."

"Uh," Ben started and frowned. "Archie?"

His slip made him snort in a small laugh. "Archibald. The Sword-master Trainer."

"Ah," Ben said softly with a shift in his eyes before he turned. "Yes, Sire."

"And bring some tea back with you, please," he called to his steward's back. He needed tea. Well, he needed a stiff drink, but that'll have to wait. He knew, was willing to admit, that he didn't know enough military planning to even begin to start with how to handle this new information. But, as he'd been reminded by Mariah plenty of times, that was what advisors were for.

CHAPTER 12

$\mathcal{R}$ose pulled her coat tighter against the wind as she walked down the dirt road. The dark clouds above her were nearly black, and the nip in the air told her another storm wasn't far off. The weather had held during the last two days of her trip, even if her toes were numb. How badly she wished she had Starlit. She'd been sad to say goodbye to the giant horse, pressing her face into the beast's cheek as she'd slipped her one last apple. She couldn't very well take the horse on the trip to the college if she wasn't even sure she was return- ing. The king, in all his allowances, would frown on horse theft, and he would absolutely notice if his favorite horse was missing.

Rose hoped she'd make it to the cover of town before the snow fell from the black clouds above her. Even with her great overcoat and wool short coat underneath, the wind chilled her to her bones.

She nuzzled her face deeper into the scarf and pulled her hood tight over her ears. The captain had narrowed her eyes at Rose when she'd spotted her in the deep blue Light Horse coat as she was leaving, but she didn't have cold weather clothing yet and as she'd bartered for these coats... as far as she was concerned, she was entitled to wear it a little. Even if it made her cringe.

I hate, she grumbled as her teeth chattered, *the cold.*

Her teeth chattered hard enough for her jaw to ache. In the distance, she could see the shapes of buildings and the faint outline of a monstrosity that must be the college. If she hustled, she should make it by early evening.

She made it to the town just as the winds shifted. They were cold and wet, the promise of snow in the air. She moved through the town quickly, following the main cobblestoned road, and watched for any inns or taverns she might find a room in later. The town was small, which surprised her. She'd expected a larger, more bustling city with something as large as the college in it, but instead, she found small bakeries, a tea house, and several merchant shops. Eventually, she passed a large tavern set just off the main square. The building had the same brick and wood frames and shingled roofs as the rest of the town. In the center of the square was a fountain, its water frozen with the cold of winter. At the center of the fountain stood the god Pethan, god of scholars and growth. His long robes pooled around his feet where the water had iced over. In his hands, he held an opened book.

Rose stepped close to it and peered at the hole at the top of the book. Ah, so water flowed from the book when it wasn't frozen. She snorted and looked away. No doubt it was meant as a metaphor for knowledge. *Little bit on the nose, isn't it?*

By the time she was reaching the college gates, the snow had started to fall. Large, fluffy-looking things that stuck to everything it touched. As she neared the giant double doors, Rose ran the short distance and darted inside and out of the wind. She brushed the snow off her shoulders and pushed her hood back. Pulling her scarf from around her neck, she slowly walked through the silent entry hall. Her boots echoed in the empty room as she walked.

She wondered what her life would've been like if she'd been the sort of person who would've attended studies. Her eyes were drawn up to the large entry room. The ceiling towered above her, covered in painted murals. She spotted a few gods she recognized among the figures painted along the dome.

She'd never been to the college before. It nearly rivaled the castle in looks, if not in size. It felt odd to be walking through these tall curved walls with elaborate paintings of deans and professors glaring down at her. Her footsteps echoed through the room as she walked, and the sound seemed harsh to her ears. She'd been to boarding school for a year when she was much younger before her father had learned how useful she could be. She was smart. At least Rose believed so. She knew her letters and numbers, knew how to run a merchant train, but she wouldn't consider herself a learned person. She wasn't someone who... studied, like the people here did.

After a little meandering through the large room and a peek or two into some other rooms that appeared down small hallways leading off the main hall, she finally found a door with the dean's offices marked on the wall at the back of the hall.

Rose slipped inside and looked at the red-haired woman sitting at the small desk along the wall.

"Hello?"

She looked up from the ledger, and Rose was met with the greenest eyes she'd ever seen.

"Oh, hello. I didn't hear anyone come in." She stood and smoothed her simple skirts as she came around the desk. "I'm Ella, the dean's assistant."

Rose nodded to her. "Afternoon. I'm Rose Trewin."

Ella smiled and looked over Rose's uniform. "How may I help you?"

"I was hoping you could direct me to Professor Elias."

Ella smiled again, professional and detached. "Of course. Was he expecting you?"

"Uh, no," Rose said. "But I was hoping to speak with him."

The assistant nodded. "Of course. His office is in the archives. The access stairway is in the Historical Wing at the back of the Everett Building."

Rose blinked at her. She was sure those instructions meant something to someone, but not to her.

"Ah, have you been to the college before?" Ella asked, her voice polite as ever.

Rose smiled a close-lipped smile. "Would you mind directing me?"

"Not at all," she said as she stepped around from her desk.

Rose fell in step behind her and tried to quell the irritation burning in her chest. She wasn't sure why she was so annoyed this woman had assumed she knew anything about the college. Maybe she was irritated because in a different world, she might've attended here. Learned trade. Grown to become a master tradesman with a fleet of her own ships.

She rolled her eyes at such an impossibility.

Ella strode back into the main hall, which was now teeming with students, many clutching piles of books. The silence of the hall was gone, filled with the chatter and poorly hushed voices of students. Their scholar robes flowed around them as they rushed and ran from one hall to another, crossing the large room. Rose had a moment of shock before shoving her way after Ella as she turned into a side hallway and continued on. And then, just as quickly as the crowd of people had appeared, they'd disappeared. She heard a faint bell chime from a clock tower somewhere, and with it, the last of the students vanished.

"Professor Elias' office is down in the archives, like I said. It's a bit gloomy, sorry. Not many students go down there unless they've been punished with research."

Rose chuckled and pulled off her gloves, stuffing them into her pockets. A pair of students scurried past them, one muttering about being late.

"Better hurry, boys," Ella called after them. "He's in a mood today."

The boys cursed and picked up their pace.

Ella turned to Rose as they continued down the dim hall. "Professor Elias, he's... a bit odd. Nothing to worry about, but he is a little to get used to."

They reached the bottom of the staircase, and Rose shivered. Her coat was damp, and the hall was cool. It made for an uncomfortable chill as it settled into her bones. Oh, how she wanted nothing more than to sink into a steaming tub and soak until her skin wrinkled.

Instead, she followed Ella further down the dank hall. The stone surrounding them had changed at some point in the stairwell. Gone now were the brick and mason stones. The walls here were smooth stone. No seams. Rose ran her hand along the wall and gasped at how fluid the stone felt. What magic had made the rock feel like glass?

Ella reached a pair of double doors and shoved one open with her shoulder into a cavernous room. Rose was greeted by a roaring fire in the corner of the room, its light illuminating the rows upon rows of shelving and bookcases. Blackness hid the rest of the room, but Rose could feel an immenseness coming from beyond.

Ella shivered and hedged closer to the fire. "His office is through there," she nodded to the far wall. "I must be getting back. Send for me if you need anything."

Rose nodded her thanks, shuffled toward the small open door, and poked her head inside. She knocked lightly on the door frame when the man sitting at the desk failed to notice her.

The wizened man snapped his head up, and storm gray eyes met hers with a wide smile. "Oh! A visitor!"

Rose smiled and let herself into the cluttered office that reminded her of the captain's. The large office was stuffed with piles of books and papers. The large desk, its varnish dull and aged and scratches covering most of what was visible, was covered in stacks of books. The visitor's chair held piles of parchments and… she frowned down at the chair… a sock? She hummed and looked around the room more. There was a couch against the far wall, or a thing she assumed was a couch, but most of it was covered in more scrolls and papers.

She glanced nervously at the large fire stove and the papers placed far too close.

"What can I do for a King's Light Horse Officer?"

Rose brought her eyes back to the professor and slipped her pack from her shoulders to let it rest on the floor at her feet. "Captain Sayla had written to you last summer. Did you receive that letter?"

"Oh!" Professor Elias stood with fierce vigor and knocked over a pile of books. They crashed to the floor with an alarming thud, and the professor wrung his hands in his long, white beard. "Yes, yes. I remember now. Caleb!"

"Professor! Professor, are you alright?" someone shouted from the large cavern behind them.

"Yes!" Professor Elias shouted back, and Rose held back a cringe. "Yes, Caleb. I'm fine. These blasted books got in my way again."

"If you'd stack them where they belong, and not on the floor that wouldn't happen." Rose jumped as the voice belonging to Caleb spoke right behind her. "I apologize for startling you."

Rose looked over her shoulder at Caleb, a man she guessed to be a little older than herself, who was dressed in a worn but nice suit. "It's alright."

"I'm Caleb Harven," he said, "and your name, Officer?"

"I'm not an officer," she mumbled. "Rose Trewin."

The young man wore a clean and decently made shirt. A glance at his shoes showed an expensive pair of leather boots. They were old and worn, but the quality was there. He had money or at least access to it but didn't seem to flaunt it. She dropped her eyes to his hands and saw they were clean and soft looking. He was a man of books more than labor, it seemed. "Are you a student of the professor's?"

Caleb smiled a dimpled smile and nodded crisply. "His apprentice."

"Assistant."

Caleb flicked his eyes over her shoulder to the professor and grimaced. "His assistant-apprentice."

She chuckled and tore her eyes away from his dimpled cheeks and back to the professor, who was re-stacking the pile of books. "Professor, I was hoping to follow-up on the captain's letter. She thought you might know something of magics... odd magic."

"Yes, yes. I remember. Please sit. Caleb, clear a spot for the lady."

Rose waved Caleb off and moved the papers to the floor before sitting in the chair and dragging her pack over next to her. Caleb leaned against the door and folded his arms over his chest. If there was other seating in the office, it was well and truly hidden in the chaos.

"That was an interesting request from your captain," Caleb said. "We weren't sure what to make of it at first."

"Yes," Professor Elias crooned. "I want to hear all about what led Mariah on such a line of questioning."

"I'm sure the captain explained when she sent her letter last summer," Rose said and tried to keep the bite out of her words.

"Yes, yes. But I know Mariah. There was more she didn't mention. Why did she actually want to know about the shadow magic?"

Rose pursed her lips. "Did you find anything or not?"

Professor Elias leaned back in his chair with a glance at Caleb. "Just as rude and impatient as Mariah."

"You have no idea," she said coolly.

Professor Elias eyed Rose before glancing back at Caleb. "We'll table that for later then. Yes, in answer to your question. I did find some things at first. What most people don't realize about the college is it was built over the archives. We were here first. The histories used to reside at the castle, but King Jonas, after the Great War, decided to move them, so they weren't in danger of destruction if the castle ever fell. Great Earthmovers were hired to create the cavern that's behind this room, and in it, are the most important histories this country has."

Oh. Rose thought back to the cavern walls. Their magic did that.

"Of course I found something," Professor Elias finished

"Then why didn't you write back?" Rose asked with exasperation.

"I did." He blinked at her and looked at Caleb. "Didn't I?"

Rose twisted in her seat, ready to glare at the man, only for him to shake his head. "No, sir. I don't believe you ever did."

She stopped herself from dropping her head into her hands, but only barely.

"Well, what sort of assistant are you!" Professor Elias exclaimed, his face red.

Caleb breathed a heavy sigh, and Rose slid her eyes over to him. That sound had so much patience and frustration in it she had to hold back a grin of sympathy.

"I'm your apprentice. Apprentice."

Elias waved Caleb's words away with an irritated hand.

"Same thing." The professor cocked his head as though listening to something, and Rose faintly heard the sound of bells. They had an echoey quality, a little metallic, and as she glanced up at the ceiling, she saw a small grate. Did the sound travel through pipes down to the archives?

"I've a meeting that will take the rest of the evening. We'll meet tomorrow, and I'll show you all I've found about the Shademakers."

Her breath left her in a whoosh, and she saw stars at the edges of her vision. "What?" she asked, her voice so faint it was a whisper.

Elias stood and dusted off his dull suit, threadbare and patched. "The Shademakers. The ones who worked the magic of the shadows."

––––––––––

ROSE HAD LEFT the cold and dank office of Professor Elias in a haze after that. She'd walked back to the tavern in the town center, the Scholar and Wine, and secured a room with the money paid to her by the king last summer.

She sat on the edge of the bed, mind still in a daze. She hadn't expected anything like that. She'd thought she'd find a few stories. Maybe a myth or a legend that had been written down throughout the ages. Or a long theoretical talk about what it might be but nothing as concrete as a name: Shademakers.

He'd called them a people. She used to have a people. She couldn't get her mind to wrap around that.

A shiver wracked her body and it seemed to help snap her out of her stupor. Chiding herself, she found the flint stick on top of the wood stove along the wall and built a fire in it. Eventually, the heat started to warm the room and she felt like her limbs were starting to melt. She unpacked her items, shoving them in the small armor in the corner in the room, and laid her overcoat out in front of the stove.

Grabbing her dry, short coat, Rose headed back downstairs to the tavern for a warm dinner and ale. Tomorrow, she would get answers.

CHAPTER 13

*R*ose stared at the low ceiling, watching as the shadows from the small bedside candle moved around. A slight breeze snuck through the shutters and pulled on the flame, changing the length of the moving shadows on the walls. Her tired eyes had stopped seeing any patterns or shapes hours ago. She suspected the sun would be rising soon, and when she glanced at the shuttered window, she saw a faint pink glow. Sleep had eluded her most of the night. How could she sleep when so much had happened? Try as she might, drink as she might, she'd been unable to quiet her racing thoughts long enough to settle into sleep.

Glancing again at the window, Rose saw the sun was even brighter. Sleep had not come last night, and it appeared now, it wouldn't at all. She abandoned any hope of rest and kicked off the covers. She stumbled over to the small vanity and dunked her face unceremoniously into the ice-cold water. She straightened with a gasp, her skin burning from the cold, and wiped her face dry. She leaned heavily on the stand and suppressed a yawn.

"Glad that worked." She pushed off and went about getting dressed. With a groan, Rose slipped on the blue coat and headed down for tea.

The small dining room of the inn was empty; it was still too early for most to venture down here. Feet shuffling, Rose helped herself to tea in the kitchen and settled at a table near the fire. She propped her head on her hand and watched the steam rise from her cup.

Her eyes grew heavy. A throat being cleared roused her and Rose blinked, trying to orient herself.

"Ma'am?"

She blinked at the man standing expectantly at her elbow, a pot of tea in his hands.

"Yer tea's gone cold, ma'am."

She looked around the room and saw several others sitting quietly at tables eating.

"Was I asleep?"

The man nodded. "I do believe you were," he said with a chuckle. "That's a trick to sleep sitting up like that."

Rose grunted and pushed her cup away. "Thank you, but I didn't ask for more tea."

"All the same, ma'am. It was sent by a mutual acquaintance." He set the steaming pot down, a folded piece of parchment under the edge. He quickly retreated back behind the bar before she could form more words or protest.

Rose eyed his retreating back before slipping the paper out. She dropped her senses into the shadows, looking for anyone hiding in the dark corners of the room. There was nothing. A few patrons quietly ate their breakfast. A grump cook in the back. A stable boy in the larder stealing some cheese. She pulled back from the shadows, a dull ache behind her eyes, and glanced at the paper. Unfolding it, she read the slim scrolling letters.

THEY WILL NOT BE STALLED for long.

Your king must find an answer for D'ray's death.

. . .

ROSE BREATHED HARSHLY through her nose as she looked around the room. That damned B'leakon. She pressed her lips together. What was she doing here, meddling here? Her eyes searched the room again. How did the B'leakon know where she was?

She needed to tell the king. Which meant returning regardless of wanting to or not.

"Miss Trewin?"

Rose jerked at Caleb's voice and glanced up at him.

"Professor Elias sent me to get you. He wants to continue yesterday's conversation."

Rose hastily folded the note and shoved it in her pocket as she gathered her coat. "Alright."

The walk to the college was cold, bitterly cold as the wind seemed to cut straight through to her bones. Snow had fallen more during the night, and the roads were covered in a layer of snow. The few people they passed on their way through town glanced at her, at her jacket. People here knew what the emblem on her coat meant. Unfortunately, that meant far too many eyes were on her, too many curious faces looking at hers. It made her skin tight and her shoulders tense.

"Do you know of any decent clothing shops in town? I need a new jacket."

Caleb glanced at her new, crisp coat. "Uh, yeah. There are a couple. What's wrong with this coat?"

Rose sucked her teeth. "The color is off."

They walked up the large steps of the college, and Caleb was still giving her odd side glances.

"How long do you expect to be at the college?" he asked as they headed toward the archives in the back.

"I don't know."

"Oh, okay." Caleb let out a breath.

Rose glanced sideways at him and continued into the professor's office.

Professor Elias stood when they entered and offered her a cup of tea. She sighed inwardly in relief and gratefully accepted it as she sat. She sipped the tea as she glanced around the room and noticed the haphazard stacks of books had been tidied, and a second chair was brought in, which Caleb sat in after taking his own tea.

"Tell me," Elias started while stirring an impressive amount of sugar into his tea. "What has sent Mariah on this search? Ever since she took that post with the Light Horse, she seems to be surrounded by different magic folk. Much more than you'd normally find. Has, perhaps, a Shademaker found their way into her ranks?"

"I couldn't say." Rose bit out.

"Can't or won't?"

She sipped her tea and defiantly held his gaze.

"Stubborn like an ox," the professor said while leaning back with a sigh. "You're worse than Mariah."

Rose smiled at him. Being compared to the stalwart woman, strong and intimidating, was not the insult he thought it'd be.

"Fine, we'll get to the bottom of that later. For now, Caleb, why don't you explain what you found."

Next to her, Caleb cleared his throat. "There was an old reference in one of the mage books dating back from the Clan Years."

Rose frowned. "Clan Years?"

"Yes, sorry. The years before any monarchy when there were dominating clans throughout the areas," Caleb clarified and then continued, "It was written in the Old Tongue so I had to get it translated first. But once I did, it talked about a balance that needed to be kept. I'm not sure if it meant literally or not, or if it was a translation error."

Rose nodded for him to continue as her heart pounded in her chest. At the edges of the room, she felt the weighted stare of the wolves.

"It talked about a person dwelling in the shadows, I'm assuming a Shademaker, who stood out from the rest, and that their role was to enforce the... balance, assuming that translation was correct. A word was used to describe this person, and we struggled to translate it, but we think it's something like a shadow watcher. Or they thought it might translate to shadow—"

"Shadowstalker," Rose said with a flat voice. The shadows had called her that during the battle in the throne room. They hadn't explained what it meant, only that she was one.

"Um," Caleb said and frowned. "Maybe. That wasn't one of the translation options they found, though. Anyway, from the way the passage was read and translated, it very well could be talking about some sort of ancient god. We're not sure. I think it's an old tale that predates the current story of the god of magic. Maybe even what was the original inspiration."

Unlikely. Her eyes drifted to the darkened corner, where two red eyes stared back at her. Gods they are not. Pains in the ass, more like. The eyes narrowed into a glare. She pulled her eyes away from the corner. "And you've only found one account?"

"So far, yes," Professor Elias spoke. "The manuscript Caleb found is extremely old, extremely fragile. Large parts of it were unreadable, and we have to proceed very slowly to save what's left of it."

"I can show it to you if you'd like?" Caleb asked with an eager smile.

"Caleb!" Elias snapped. "I just said it's fragile and delicate. We can't just go showing to anyone who bats their eyes at you!"

Caleb's cheeks flamed red. "I'm not going to let her touch it."

Rose managed to hold back her laugh at Caleb's flaming red cheeks, now moving to his ears. "No, thank you. That's not necessary."

"My word," Elias muttered under his breath but loud enough everyone could hear, just as Rose was sure he meant it. "I do want to show you something. If you'd follow me."

She gulped down the last of her cooling tea and followed Elias out and into the archives behind the office. He grabbed a lantern from the narrow table at the end and, after swiftly lighting it, turned down another hall that led away from the stairs to the main college. She followed slightly behind and let her senses stretch into the darkness, letting her sight drop into the shadows. Her heart stuttered as her vision dipped into the blue-grey tones of the shadows.

Their footsteps echoed through the darkness and reverberated through the shadows to her ears. She heard the scurry of a few rats as the light disturbed them. She sensed a vast space beyond her. As they rounded a corner, cold, musty air hit her face and made her wrinkle her nose at the smell. Then she saw the cavern they had entered.

"Oh my… " Rose didn't have the words for what she saw.

Elias' light illuminated the first few feet, but Rose could see it all in the darkness. She dropped her sight fully into the shadows and saw rows upon rows of stone shelving. Each wall of shelves stacked to capacity with rolled manuscripts, vellum books, and ancient pages.

"You can't really see because of the darkness, but this is one of the main archive halls. It holds several thousand scrolls and books," Caleb was explaining as they walked.

Rose stepped further into the darkness, away from the circle of light cast by the lantern and stretched her senses further into the hall. She felt through the shadows and saw this room extend several dozen feet, larger than the king's throne room. There was an age to the shadows in this room, a weight she hadn't felt before. Almost as if the age of the parchments had seeped into the shadows. Or perhaps, the age of the shadows had bled into the scrolls. The vastness of the room made her feel small, and she quickly moved to catch up to the others.

"You said this is only one of the archives?" she asked as she caught up to them.

The lantern's light burned her eyes as her vision went hot white. She pulled back from the shadows with a hiss and squeezed her eyes shut.

"Are you alright?" Caleb asked.

"Yes." Rose blinked away tears from the sudden change. "I just stared into the dark too long."

Elias watched her for a moment, then turned down the rows to the left.

"Yes. This is probably the largest. Off this room is another antechamber nearly this size, but not quite, and from there, there are three other small chambers," Caleb said.

"Are they all full?"

Elias set the lantern on the small table in the alcove at the end of the aisle and started lighting several lanterns standing along the wall. Soon the whole aisle was glowing with warm light.

"I don't think any of them are full. Maybe the smallest of the antechambers is, but there's room still in all the others."

And she thought the libraries at the castle were large.

"This place was created just after the Great War ended. King Jonas wanted to anticipate many, many more years of history being stored here and had the Earthmovers build it accordingly."

"This," Elias cut in before Caleb could offer up more of a history lesson, "was what I wanted to show you."

He gestured at a portrait hanging in the alcove. It showed a woman; her black hair was woven into a complicated set of braids with bright ribbons throughout. Her angular eyes, as black as her hair, stared down at them in what seemed like angry judgement. Her sun-bronzed skin seemed to shine in the painting. A thick silver armband adorned one bicep, and Rose marveled that the painter had painted the sharp lines of the woman's muscles. He hadn't turned her into a gentle feminine figure. The painting was complete with the woman's other hand gripping a short sword, dressed in an ancient style of armor. She was a fighter, whoever she was.

"She's beautiful," Rose whispered. "Who is she?"

"She," Elias breathed in awe, "was J'Teal. The last documented Shademaker we've found. Although, that," he grunted, "was damned hard to uncover. She was very close with King Jonas before he was king. She fought in the war as one of his trusted generals and advisors. The histories were pretty open about them being lovers. Eventually, I was able to find one really old diary entry from the king just before he died that mentioned her as a Shademaker."

"Diary?" Rose wrinkled her nose at him. The idea of ancient kings keeping a diary didn't fit her mental image. She turned her eyes back to J'Teal. This woman once had the same magic Rose did. What I wouldn't give to just talk to her.

"King Jonas was a prolific writer. We've found many of his journals. He was always writing things down, his thoughts, hopes, plans. In another life, I think he would've been a poet."

"And instead," Caleb said, "he became our first high king."

She glanced at Caleb and couldn't help thinking of King Micah and his battered sketchbook. "I'd wager he'd have rather been the poet," she whispered.

Elias continued with a glare at them for interrupting his lesson. "I was able to track down several historical references to J'Teal throughout the war. She died during a battle with some mage... historical records weren't precise about who or what he was. He appeared to have multiple magics, something that's never been seen before or since."

Gerik. The shadows growled softly, and she knew she was right.

"They fought and in the course of the battle, a relic was destroyed. Something they called the Orthalen. It may have been what gave the mage his abilities. However, someone went to great lengths to erase almost all mentions of this man or the item. I found books and histories with literal sections of the text crossed out or pages torn from the bindings."

"He was afraid," Rose whispered while staring at J'Teal's portrait.

Now that she looked longer at her, she didn't think the woman's eyes were angry. They were sad. Sad and determined. Like she was resigned to her fate. What were her thoughts as she stood there for this portrait so many years ago? Did she grieve? Was she afraid? Or did she know exactly what to do and how she was going to do it? Did she understand her place? Rose hoped she was as strong and confident as she looked.

"Why do you say that?" Caleb asked, and she turned to him.

"A man with magic no one else has, no way to control or stop him and the final battle to destroy him killed the woman he loved?" Rose turned back to J'Teal. "He was afraid it would happen again. That it all would've been for nothing. His country was tearing itself apart. I remember stories of the civil war. The landscape was changed. We now have a lake where an ancient city once stood. Mountains where before there were valleys."

"It makes sense," Elias said. "This relic, this Orthalen. Whatever it was, wherever it came from, they had finally destroyed it. The rebellious lords submitted to the king's rule. I'd want to hide all knowledge of it too."

And now it seemed to be starting over again.

Rose sighed and turned away from the portrait with the eyes of a defeated woman, feeling defeated herself. She'd sacrificed her life to end this, and Gerik was back. Seemingly to finish the war he'd started. How was she supposed to stop him when the warrior woman behind her had sacrificed everything and still failed?

"I haven't been able to learn much more than this. Records are... " Elias shrugged and picked up the lantern again. "The years following the civil war were thick with fear and suspicion. The dark times were hard for everyone, especially the magic folk. There isn't much in the way of records and documentation that survived those years."

Rose nodded. She knew about the ten-year period following the king's death. Fear had continued to plague the country. Fear and distrust of magic. The citizens had seen their lands destroyed and reshaped in front of them. Years of war left many broken families. The king that arose after Jonas had been a mistrusting, bigoted man. He'd sanctioned the hunt of nearly all magical users. He'd blamed all the famine, disease, and death on them. Even those that had fought for the king. It had shaped the country a second time, in ways no one would've understood then.

Magic seemed to have disappeared after the Dark Times. Sure, some people had magic, but nothing like what the stories had said there'd been before.

Rose felt the stare of the wolves on her back, and she turned around to see their red eyes watching her from the dark alcove from across the room. An anger simmered from them in the shadows, almost as if they were angry about that loss.

We are.

Slowly, a wolf formed in the darkness of the cavern. Rose glanced over her shoulder at Elias and Caleb, who were slowly making their way back to the professor's office. Turning back to the wolf, it blinked at her and turned further into the cavern. She turned to follow it, dropping her eyes into the shadows as she did. The archives shifted, from black and dark, to shimmering in blue-grays and silver tones. It came alive with details. Anywhere the darkness touched was hers to see.

She caught up to the shadow wolf, who turned to look over its massive shoulder at her, and turned down another row. She followed it down several more aisles, deeper and deeper into the maze of alcoves of the archive room. The wolf moved past rows and rows of scrolls, and as it moved, the air got colder and wetter; mustier. A sneeze crept up her throat, and the sound echoed in the quiet space. The wolf continued to move, weaving in and out of stacks of crates and around aisles.

She could hear the professor and Caleb shouting for her in the darkness. Their voices echoed as if through a tunnel.

"Well?" she whispered at the shadow. "What's going on?"

The wolf continued in silence.

"Gods above and below," she muttered. "Back to this?"

It didn't even turn to look at her. She shoved her cold hands in her armpits and followed.

Finally, when they reached a far wall, Rose shivering from the chill, the shadow stopped. It stood in front of a trunk shoved against the wall between two built-in shelves. It seemed forgotten in the far reaches of the room, covered in a thick layer of dust. The trunk was old and cracked along its seams, the leather straps broken and crumbled on the floor. She could barely make out what was once a crest on the lid of the chest; time had long since rusted the metal beyond recognition.

"What's this?"

The wolf blinked its red eyes at her. "Why should we tell you when you will only ignore us?"

Rose clenched her teeth. "Maybe if you told me more about what was going on, I wouldn't ignore you."

The wolf growled; its lips peeled away from its sharp teeth. "It is not our place to teach you. Not our place to interfere. We interfere too much, but the Balance must be kept. You must learn! We do your duty enough as it is."

With that last growling shout, the wolf disappeared with a crack in the Undertunnels.

Rose flinched at the sound, at their furious words. The king's words, so gentle, echoed back to her with new meaning. She needed to stop running. She just wasn't sure she knew how to. She grunted away the feeling of shame burning in her belly. Shame and inadequacy.

With a sigh, she gingerly eased the lid open. It creaked as it moved and one of the hinges fell away, causing the whole lid to slip to the floor. Inside were several old vellum papers scattered along the bottom; a few battered and broken books. In the corner sat a leather pouch that made the hair on the back of her neck stand on end. Slowly, she reached for it.

"We have protected it from time," the shadows spoke. "We knew it would be needed."

"Are you Seers now, too?" she asked, voice thick with bitter sarcasm, as she lifted the bag into her hand.

Silence met her question.

"Ass holes," she muttered, though she knew she deserved at least part of their anger. But only part. They didn't need to be so fickle about everything.

She pulled open the drawstring bag and found a lump of metal ore inside. It had a weird sheen, a coloring she wasn't familiar with. Whatever it was, the wolves wanted her to have it. That was the only thing she could think about why they would've led her here. She pulled the strings tight and stuffed the little bag into her pocket. Sorting through the remaining papers, she found nothing else of relevance. Old papers about mines, many that looked to be spent and closed up. Most were faded past the ability to read.

With a growing ache in her eyes, she closed the ancient chest and started the long trek back. When she finally reached the front of the cavern, the soft glow of the professor's office lights leaking into the space, her nose was dripping from the cold. Rose pulled away from her magic, letting the room fall into blackness again. As the magic left her, a pounding headache replaced it. She pinched the bridge of her nose and held back a groan.

She knocked her knuckles softly on the open door to interrupt. "I just wanted to let you know I'll be heading back to my room now. I didn't want you to think I'd gotten lost in there."

"Did you find... whatever you were looking for?" Caleb asked as he stood.

"I wasn't looking for anything."

"Then what were you doing? In the dark?" Professor Elias asked, his eyes narrowing.

She smiled thinly. "Walking. I hope you didn't mind."

"Not at all," Caleb said.

"A little," the professor said as he tugged on his beard.

Her smile stretched a little thinner at the older man. "Thank you for all your assistance. I'll be sure to pass everything onto the captain."

"How did you see to get back?" Professor Elias pressed.

She bared her teeth in a smile. "Good night vision, I guess." She left before he could pry anymore and hurried up the stairs.

Once she was outside, the brightness from the sun and glare off the snow made her squint. Her head pounded even worse with the brightness of the sun, and she walked quickly through the courtyard toward her inn. As she moved, she pulled the mysterious bag out of her pocket and drew it open. It wasn't even smithed ore. It was still impure, with chunks of rock and stone.

"Why... " she trailed off as her feet stopped. Why had the shadows led her to this?

"Don't let—"

Rose spun, one hand going to her small dagger at her waist and the other grabbing the stranger's coat in her fist.

"—the professor see," Caleb finished breathlessly.

"Gods," Rose swore and released her grip on Caleb's coat with a shove. "Don't sneak up on me like that." She shoved her dagger back into its sheath and pulled her coat over it to hide it from Caleb.

"My apologies," he murmured as he bent and retrieved the bag from the snow. He held it, almost reverently, with a deep frown etched into his face as he stared at the ore.

Rose watched him, his mouth falling open into a soft 'o' as he stared at the stone. He shook himself, mouth snapping close, and blinked at her. His eyes were pinched in a frown.

She took the bag back from him with a frown pinching her own eyes. What was that about?

"What were you saying about the professor?"

He gestured to the leather pouch as he rubbed his fingers together. "What is that?"

Rose glanced down at the leather pouch and then up at Caleb. "A rock. Why?"

He continued to frown at it before shaking his head and saying, "Don't let him see that you took anything from the archives."

She raised an eyebrow at him and tucked the bag into her breast pocket. "He's welcome to try to take it back."

Caleb chuckled nervously and raised his hands. "I'm not going to tell him."

She glanced at him and nodded, continuing her walk through the courtyard. "Did you need something, or were you coming to warn me about stealing?"

"Uh." Caleb hurried to catch up to her. "Yes, no. I was going to warn you but also thought we might share some lunch."

She stopped and turned back to him. The word 'no' was already on her tongue when he held up his hand again.

"Nothing untoward. I just thought you'd like some company, and we could talk... about... history."

His cheeks warmed, and the tips of his ears turned pink. A giggle worked its way up her throat at his nervousness, but she clamped down on it. No need to be an ass, she reminded herself. He was nice enough, polite, and in the few interactions with him, Caleb had seemed an honest sort.

She glanced down at his soft hands, stained with ink and the smell of parchment that clung to him. Besides, I can take him in a fight. It would be nice, she realized, to have a simple conversation over food. She hadn't noticed how much she'd missed talking with people. How much she was missing Sam or even Luci with her sharp tongue remarks. How much she missed talking with the king.

"Sure. I'd like some company."

They walked quickly to her inn, both eager to be out of the cold. Inside, she directed them to a table in the back corner of the room. It was near the large hearth, but it was also in view of the door and stairs to the rooms. Caleb pulled out a chair for her, but she ignored it and sat with her back to the wall. She smiled at his confused look and how he quickly sat in the chair himself, trying to pass it off as if he'd been pulling it out for himself.

Rose smothered another laugh and held up two fingers at the barrel-chested man behind the bar counter. "Soup please?"

He nodded at her and disappeared into the kitchen.

"Are you enjoying the college?"

"I didn't really come for an exploration, but the little bit I've seen is nice," she said.

The innkeeper quickly arrived with their bowls of stew, and Rose wrapped her frozen fingers around the bowl.

"You should explore some before you leave. It is quite amazing; nothing else really like it."

Rose grunted noncommittally and sipped the broth. The food was so much better at the inn than she was used to. The people in this town, she shook her head, they knew an ease and privilege she marveled at.

"The food here isn't as good as the college. They use lesser cuts of meat from the market. To keep the prices down I'm sure–what are you laughing at?"

She leaned back in her chair and took deep breaths to try to quell the laughter. "You think this is bad?"

Giggles burst past her lips again. "Oh, what a world you live in. The vegetables aren't rotten. I mean, the fact that there are vegetables is amazing."

Caleb stared at her, his spoon hovering over his stew.

"Oh, I'm sorry. I'm being rude." Rose took another deep breath. She was mostly sorry. "I don't mean to be. I'm just used to a much different quality of food."

"Even at the castle?" Caleb asked, disbelief coloring his voice.

"Oh... sure, the food there is just fine. But I haven't been there long."

Caleb nodded and took a heaping bite of soup. "What were you doing before you were an officer?"

"I'm not an officer," she reminded him again. "I was traveling."

Close enough to the truth.

"But you wear the officer's uniform," Caleb pressed.

"The coats are warm." She shoveled more soup into her mouth.

"And you're from the castle."

"Mh-hm."

"You're not going to tell me, are you?"

Rose grunted, but she had a smile on her lips. "It's not an exciting story."

They were silent for a moment, and Rose finished off the last of her lunch. As she pushed the bowl away, Caleb looked up at her.

"Looks like a storm is moving in. You should stay a few more days."

Rose hummed and pushed her hair out of her eyes. "It still looks a ways out. I think I'll make it."

"Don't you want to stay?" Caleb asked. "We might learn more about your magic."

His words froze her spine. Rose slowly straightened from the table. "What's that now?"

Caleb set his spoon down. "I'm sorry. I didn't mean to offend you. I just thought... Well you have to be a Shademaker. Why else would you come all this way asking about such a forgotten and obscure magic? And then you just walk off into the pitch-black like it was nothing. I just—"

"Enough," she snapped with a hasty glance around the room. "You should be more careful about airing other people's secrets."

"You're right, yes. I apologize."

She sighed heavily through her nose and glared at the young man. "How quickly did you figure it out?" she finally asked.

"Pretty quick," Caleb said with a hesitant smile, his cheeks dimpling.

Rose shook her head. Her time at the castle had made her reckless. She was too careless in her magic use today.

"Keep that bit of information from your professor. I don't like the way he looks at me. Like I'm some sort of puzzle to figure out and then prize to keep."

She stood from the table, and Caleb hastily stood with her. "Thank you for the company."

She retreated up to her room. Company was one thing. Young men with too many questions was another and something she didn't want to deal with. No matter how easy it was to tease a bright red flush out of him. She chuckled to herself. He was too easy to tease. Worse than Sam.

Once in her room, she added another log to the small stove in the corner and yanked her boots off. Pulling the rickety chair over to the stove, she propped her feet up as close as she could without burning them and pulled the rock from her pocket.

She rolled it around in her palm, big enough to fill it, and watched the firelight dance off it. The parts that weren't covered in rock and dirt were iridescent in the light. It glittered and shone, black and purple in the light. The fire was warm and with no sleep the night before, her eyes felt heavy in the warmth.

She was more frustrated now than before and she dropped her head back against the chair. Now she had a name for what she was. A name for the clan that had once been, but it was all useless information. The clan was gone. The last Shadowstalker that might've helped her had died hundreds of years ago.

She groaned.

Rose had answers, just not to any of the questions she asked.

CHAPTER 14

*R*ose woke with a start, blindly reaching for her dagger. Her eyes cracked open, and she would've screamed if she could get any air into her lungs. Her small room at the inn was gone, and instead, she sat on the gray, dusty ground of the Shadow World, the place the wolves lived, deep beneath the layers of the world. Dead, spindly trees dotted the barren landscape, and an unnatural fog swirled around her.

"Gods... " she moaned and stood. How.... She turned in a circle. "Not here. Not again." This was her nightmare. This was the dream that kept her from sleeping. Waking up and finding she was still trapped here. Only this time, she wasn't dreaming. Her breathing sped up, and her palms started to sweat.

"Calm down."

Rose yelped and spun toward the voice. A ghost stood in front of her. In the dense weight of the fog, a figure stood. Too transparent to make out any features, Rose could see the vague shape of skirts, the fall of hair. The mist and fog swirled and moved as if driven by an unseen wind, and it constantly distorted the shape of the person.

"What in the hells is going on? Who are you? What are you?" Her voice was quickly becoming a shrill shout. This voice from the mists was too similar to the whisperers that haunted her nightmares. The voices she heard when she went too deep into her magic or lost control.

"Do you know where you are?" the ghost asked.

Rose tried to take a deep breath. "The Shadow World. I've been here... before."

The ghost woman spoke in a thick, clipped accent. "I brought you here this time. And I've no time for your hysterics."

"What?"

"Things are happening. Old things from the past are waking. You must steel yourself for hard times." The figure of the woman solidified a little, and Rose could make out more of her features now. She paused and looked over her shoulder. "You must start listening to them."

Rose looked past the ghost but saw no one.

"You must find Goron Velra," she said, turning back to Rose. "You must stop him. He can't be allowed to gain power again."

"Who is Goron Velra?"

She turned again as something caught her attention. "The Earth-mover the shadows have warned you about. Damn," she cursed. "I'm out of time. We must speak again."

The Shadow World started to fade, and Rose reached out to the ghost. "What! Who are you?"

The woman smiled and finally stepped out of the mists. Her face came into sharp focus as the fog fell off of her. Rose gasped as she recognized the black eyes of the portrait staring back at her.

"My name was J'Teal."

ROSE'S FOOT thumped to the floor, sending a shock through her that had her bolting upright. Her head pounded, and she instantly folded in on herself, clutching her forehead.

"Shit." She breathed and eased upright. The ache in her head protested the movement and throbbed behind her eyes. She looked around for the rock and found it under the narrow bed. She wondered at the rock and why the shadows thought it was so important, but Rose was more concerned with how J'Teal had managed to pull her into the Shadow World or why J'Teal was even there as a ghost.

"What in the four hells... " Rose huffed and looked around the room. The shadows were quiet and benign. She swallowed another curse.

"One of you, get over here." She put every bit of demand in her voice as she could and felt power behind her words.

Slowly, reluctantly, the shadows formed into a wolf that turned narrowed red eyes to her.

"J'Teal?" she asked, eyes wide and breath coming too fast. "How?"

The shadow wolf sat on its haunches and languidly blinked at her.

Rose peeled her lips back in a silent snarl, her jaw clenched tight enough to ache.

"What," she held out the chunk of metal and rock, "is this?"

Its red eyes blinked again.

"What," she asked again with that same power behind her voice, "is this?"

The wolf growled. "A metal that can focus magic."

Rose looked down at the rock in her hand. "How?"

"We are not Earthmovers," they said with a dismissive huff.

Rose huffed and glared again at the wolf. "And Goron Velra? The Earthmover?"

The wolf chuffed and disappeared, the shadow along the wall returning to normal.

"Fine," she muttered to the empty room and threw another log onto the dying fire. She settled on the bed, sure she wouldn't sleep now, and prepared to wait out the night.

The few bits of sleep she'd managed were terrorized by nightmares of dead trees and thick fogs, running and searching for something only to end up lost in that shadow mist. When morning finally came, Rose was exhausted and cranky. Her eyes ached from no sleep, and the headache persisted. Groaning as she moved, she packed up her few items and trudged down the stairs for a quick breakfast before leaving.

After two cups of tea, Rose shouldered her pack with a sigh. Gods, how she wished she had a horse.

She glanced once again at the frozen fountain of Pethan before turning away.

"Miss Trewin."

She turned toward Caleb's voice as he approached her through the town square. His eyes went first to her pack.

"You're leaving so soon?"

"Unless you've a reason for me to put off my travel," Rose raised an eyebrow at him until he slowly shook his head no, "then yes. I want to try to beat the storm."

Caleb nodded, his hands twisting around themselves as he stood there.

"Was there something else you needed?"

"You're a... " he paused and looked around at the still empty square before lowering his voice, "Shademaker. That is amazing, and I just don't understand why you won't talk to the professor about that."

"Because," Rose spoke as she turned to continue walking, Caleb falling in step next to her, "it's not his secret, and I'm not something to be studied."

"He's the archivist. He'd want to write down everything you know. We thought the Shademaker clan was extinct."

"One person is not a clan. It's an oddity. Oddities are collected. By people like your professor," Rose snipped. "Trust me. People pay people to find and collect oddities."

They used to pay me, she thought darkly.

"You're right. I'm sorry. Sometimes I think I spend too much time with the books, and I forget."

Rose sighed. "Maybe one day. But not now. Now, I really need to be leaving. The clouds are promising snow, and I want to be at the castle when it falls."

"Yes, of course." Caleb stopped, forcing Rose to stop and turn toward him. "Maybe I'll find a reason to visit the castle and we can speak again."

"Sure." Rose smiled softly at him, ignoring the pang in her chest. Would she still be there? "Thank you again for your help."

He nodded and turned back toward the town square. Rose watched him for a second before turning away herself and starting the long walk back to the king.

CHAPTER 15

*C*aleb trudged down the stairs, his footfalls echoing softly against the cold stone. Years of walking these steps meant he rarely bothered with a light as he headed down each morning. He knew every nook, every crack, every bit of raised edge of stone. He wanted to look for more journals of King Jonas, but he might be pushing his luck with the professor. The man was like an odd uncle, but at his core, he was still the Archivist, and Caleb was starting to fall behind in his own duties in the days since Rose had left. But he wanted to look! A great number of the king's journals and writings had already been located and preserved, but the private ones that talked about the Shademakers were still missing. There must be more.

Caleb argued his search for more writings as a way to preserve the king's private life, something that was mostly a mystery to historians, and to uncover more about the elusive Shademaker clan. That was what he argued to the professor anyway. Caleb was willing to admit to himself he was doing it so he'd have a reason to travel to the castle.

He continued down more stairs into the cold of the catacombs and smiled to himself. Rose was a mystery and he wanted to discover more. She wasn't like any other woman he'd met at the college or his small town east of here. She was bold and sharp and... he felt his ears burning again. She was gorgeous. He particularly liked the little quirk the corner of her lips did when she tried not to smile. He was willing to take a few barbs at his expense if it meant the little lip quirk appeared.

As he reached the landing of the stairs, Caleb heard voices coming from the professor's office. He rarely heard anyone else down here this early in the morning. When he heard the angry voices echoing through the cavern, Caleb paused. Something about the visitor's voice made him pause, made him hesitate in revealing himself. It was too cold, too angry. His words had an odd lilt, not quite an accent but a way of pronouncing the words that felt old.

"Yes, Earthmovers built them. The archives were commissioned by King Jonas after the war," the professor was saying. "Why do you ask?"

"I can feel the power of my ancestors in these walls." The stranger's voice seemed to fill the room. "But I cannot sense The Orthalen."

Elias started to say something, but his words were cut off by the stranger's angry words.

"I sense the remnants of another's magic here."

"Sense? How can you feel magic?" Elias' voice was excited, eager. He didn't seem to notice the seething undertone in the man's words that made Caleb sink further into the wall's alcove.

"If you know what you're looking for, you can always sense it."

Caleb frowned at the man's words. Did that mean all magic users could sense one another?

"Where has the Shadowstalker gone?"

Shadowstalker? Caleb nearly moved out of his hiding spot to look at this stranger. Was he talking about Miss Trewin? Caleb frowned. He couldn't be? Could he? Could she be a Shadowstalker? Caleb missed the professor's response and peeked around the corner just in time to see the stranger, clad only in a leather long coat and trousers, lift his hand and bring it down in a rush.

The shelves around him collapsed as he did. The ground started to shake and books and scrolls started to fall off shelving. The history of the country began to crumble under the weight of the falling stones. It felt like a rock was in his throat as he choked on his scream, and he looked up quickly at the cracks spreading along the ceiling. Too much. Too much weight was up there to withstand the cracks.

Terror like he'd never known flooded his veins. Caleb's heart beat so fast and hard it felt it would break through his ribs. Professor Elias' scream was cut off by the deafening roar of stone and dirt collapsing. A billow of dust and debris whooshed into the cavern from his office.

Professor Elias screamed, but the words were lost in the deafening roar of stone and dirt collapsing against each other.

Earthmover, Caleb thought and scrambled up the stairs. He's an Earthmover.

A crack loud enough to make Caleb duck and cover his ears thundered overhead. The walls shook, and the ceiling started to cave in above him.

"Gods," he cried and ran up the stairs as they started to crumble. Dirt and rocks rained down, pelting him as he ran. He reached the main level, and students were running and screaming.

"Get out!" he screamed and pulled people toward the main doors. "The archive's collapsing!"

Cracks were spreading up the walls, spreading faster than his eyes could track, and large chunks of rock fell. The whole building trembled as it started to fall out from under itself. They ran for the doors, the dust and rubble so thick it was hard to see through. Caleb burst through the doors, coughing and gasping. The crowd of students and teachers were gathering in the courtyard.

"Keep going!" he screamed at them and continued to run. "Run!"

The Earthmover was bringing down the archives, and they extended several meters past the school foundations and into the courtyard. They weren't safe yet.

The ground started to tremble as the college collapsed behind them as they ran. Centuries of knowledge and history were buried beneath the rubble. They kept running as the courtyard started to splinter and crack. Large gaps appeared as it fell into the gaping chasm.

They ran to the far courtyard wall, where the archives didn't extend and watched as the grounds disappeared. Eventually the tumble of rocks stopped, the last of the building collapsed into a pile of stone and brick. Caleb wiped his forehead and his hand came away with blood and dirt. He didn't know when he'd been struck, and the sight of the blood broke away the last bit of shocked calm he had. His hands shook and his breathing came too quick. A bitter taste was in his mouth, and when he swallowed, his throat was clogged with dirt. Looking around at the bleeding and terrified students, he didn't even want to guess how many were missing.

"We have to look for survivors!" someone shouted.

Who could survive that? Numbly, Caleb followed the mass of people and started to shift through the layers of rock.

CHAOS ENSUED for the next several hours as the people who could looked for survivors. Those that couldn't, tried to set up a triage area for anyone they did recover. They didn't find many. Caleb dug well into the night before the temperatures, and eventually the soldiers called it off until daylight.

He sat huddled under a rough spun horse blanket with a group of other survivors near a hastily erected tent. He stared out over the gaping chasm that used to be a college. Now the building, the court-yard, the outlying buildings were gone. The space the archives had extended beyond the school into the gardens and surrounding fields were also gone. Nothing but the gaping hole remained.

They hadn't been able to dig deep enough to reach the professor's office. The rubble filled most of the space. His mind was blank. Empty as he stared at the destruction. If his hands hurt from digging, he didn't feel it. Nor did he notice the burning that must be there in his shoulders and back from lifting the rock. His home was gone, and as he stared at the pile of where some of his best memories were, he couldn't feel anything.

"Lad?" the stable master Larik asked. He looked pale and gaunt, just like everyone else did. When the people had started shivering in the cold winds, he'd started passing around the horse blankets. "Are you alright?"

Caleb looked at his feet. He didn't know where to even begin to answer that question. They needed help. More help than the few soldiers stationed in the town could give. They needed aid and shelter for all the people who now didn't have anywhere to stay. They needed to tell the king. The country's history was destroyed. All of it.

Caleb's blood went cold. Someone needed to tell the king an Earth-mover was looking for Rose; an Earthmover was roaming the lands.

He looked up at Larik. "I need a horse."

CHAPTER 16

*R*ose slowed her steps as she neared the long winding path leading to the castle. The high walls stretched up into the cloudy skies. The long, switchback walled road was called the King's Lead. It was a narrow cobblestone road meant to force any marching army to a two-horse abreast attack. It slowed any approach and, with the battlements at the top of the walls, allowed for arrows to be rained down on them.

Looking up at it, all Rose could think was how long of a damned walk it was. Her feet ached, and her shoulders burned from the weight of her pack. With a huff, she started up the long path.

By the time she was passing the large, shiny castle gates the first fluffy snowflakes had started falling. Made it.

Rose adjusted the pack on her shoulders and started through the large courtyard. The sound of horse hooves crunching on the cobblestones echoed through the yard. The weather had driven most people inside, but the few in the yard all stopped to watch the incoming rider. Only bad news came on galloping horses through the gates.

She glanced over her shoulder at the incomer only to turn around, her mouth dropping.

"Caleb!" Rose shouted as the young man directed his horse toward her. She reached out and grabbed the animal's bridle and pulled the heaving beast to a stop. "What happened? What happened to your head?"

Caleb frowned at her and raised a shaking hand to the large gash in his hairline. It was crusted with blood and bruising, an ugly, harsh purple and green color. He had a hollow look in his eyes that worried her, one she recognized.

"I need.... There was an attack... I just... "

"Alright," Rose interrupted his string of words and pulled the horse by its bridle. The beast puffed great breaths through its nostrils, and its sides heaved and quivered. She pulled the horse along toward the stables.

"After you left, late yesterday evening, an Earthmover came looking for you. He destroyed the college. Collapsed it. The archives. Everything. It's all destroyed."

Her mouth opened, but she didn't have any words. "How many dead?" she finally asked.

"A lot," Caleb said, his voice flat. She knew the flatness in that tone. "We need aid. We need... help, and I need to tell the king and—"

"Right," Rose cut in again to stop the start of his ramble. "No need to tell everything twice. Come with me, and we'll get everything sorted."

Caleb nodded, his eyes haunted. The king needed to know. There were people who needed aid and the dead needed to be recovered.

Her mind stuttered when she thought of the destruction of all those books and scrolls. All the information. History. Lost.

And why now? The weight of the ore in her pocket seemed to increase. Was this her fault?

"Did he," Rose swallowed, "did he say what he wanted?"

Caleb was silent, and she looked up at him. His eyes were hollow and sad, rimmed with tears. "He was looking for you. For you," he paused and frowned, "and something else."

Oh, gods. She wanted to vomit. Her stomach rolled and quivered enough she thought she might. A bitter taste settled on her tongue, and only deep breathing through her nose kept her stomach where it belonged. This was my fault.

She led Caleb to the stables on shaking legs and a nauseated stomach.

The stable master, Boris, greeted them at the doors. "Looks like you just beat the storm."

Caleb's horse, knowing a stable when he saw one, moved slowly on his own toward the doors. Caleb swung off of the saddle stiffly, with a quiet groan.

"He'll need a cool down," Rose said. "He ran hard to get here."

Boris grabbed the bridle with a frown but nodded. Rose pulled Caleb by a grip on his sleeve through the courtyard. He stumbled after her.

"Let's find the king."

"You can do that? I don't need to make an appointment or something first?"

Probably, she thought and ignored him as she pulled him toward the doors of the castle. Caleb limped along with her. Once inside, the many layers were stifling. She slipped off her pack and handed it to Caleb while she pulled off her gloves. She stuffed them in her pockets while she walked before she pulled off the great overcoat. Reluctantly, she took the heavy pack from Caleb and shoved it over one shoulder. Caleb was silent as they moved through the halls, whether from nerves or exhaustion, Rose couldn't tell. Both perhaps.

She steered them toward the public audience room, and she glanced over her shoulder at the young student. His eyes were wide as he stared at tapestries and paintings on the walls; the guards as they passed.

"I knew it was larger and much grander than the college, but I didn't really appreciate what that meant until now."

As they neared the public audience room, she finally found Ben, his nose buried in his schedule book, walking down the hall and away from the closed doors.

"Ben," she called to him, out of breath from her rush through the halls. "I need to speak with the king. Where is he?"

"Miss Trewin, you really need to learn to schedule these things.

Or," he glared at her and snapped his book closed, "learn what court decorum is."

Rose clucked her tongue and held back a smart remark that probably would've gotten her in trouble. "It's important."

"It always is," he muttered. "In his study. But he's not taking visitors the rest of the evening."

Rose pulled Caleb down the halls, dismissing Ben and his warning with a look over her shoulder. Maybe she was too sure of herself. Maybe she was overstepping. She'd worry about that later. She strode toward the king's study, Caleb hustling to keep up with her. Several more halls later, they neared the study doors and found Aaron standing outside.

"It's important," she said as she reached for the door latch and pushed the door open.

Aaron shoved his hand in front of her to stop her from rushing into the study. She glared at him and readied a sharp retort when the king called from inside the room.

"Let her in, Aaron."

The Shield rolled his eyes at her but removed his arm.

"Miss Trewin," the king schooled his face quickly as she entered, but Rose saw the surprise in his wide eyes before he did. "You've returned to us."

King Micah's eyes moved past her to Caleb before returning to her. "What appears to be so important?"

"I'm sorry for intruding. Something's happened at the college, and Mr. Harven needs to brief you."

Caleb remained tucked behind her shoulder, and when he didn't step forward, she grabbed his coat lapels and pulled him forward.

"Right, sorry. Your majesty," Caleb paused, and Rose could hear him swallow. "A man came to the college a few days after Miss Trewin had left. I didn't hear all that was said, but I heard him ask Professor Elias where the Shadowstalker was. He also asked about some... something else, but I forgot the word he used."

Rose's heart stuttered again at Caleb's words. King Micah's eyes bounced from Caleb to Rose briefly.

"I assumed he meant Miss Trewin. Professor Elias doesn't... didn't know about her magic, so he had nothing to give this stranger. This man, he... " Caleb took a deep breath before continuing, "he brought down the college on top of the archives. He's an Earthmover, a powerful one, and he destroyed all of it. Everything. The archives are gone. The college is gone. There are... a lot dead."

The king's mouth dropped before he remembered himself and pushed back from his desk. "Aaron!" he shouted. "Aaron, and find Ben!"

A moment later, the Shield entered silently, with Ben on his heels. Rose had a moment to wonder if the steward had followed them before the king was shouting orders.

"Aaron, I need you to take this message to General Arboh. He needs to get a squadron of soldiers ready to go to the college. Ben, this needs to go to Madame Rita." King Micah was hunched over his desk, hastily scribbling across several pieces of paper. "The college has been destroyed, along with the archives. Ben, after this is delivered to Rita, head to the quartermaster and tell him to start getting together supplies for the injured."

The king sealed the orders and handed them to the two waiting men, who promptly left the room for their various tasks. King Micah turned to Caleb. Rose saw the young man flinch under the king's gaze.

"When you say 'destroyed' how badly do you mean?"

Caleb took a shaking breath. "We haven't been able to unbury much, but so far, it's a total loss. Everything came down."

Rose looked away with a deep breath. All that destruction and death was on her soul. She had many deaths on her soul, many she'd caused with her own hands, but never before had she caused such destruction. Rose thought of Baener, the goddess of forgiveness and redemption, and wondered if she would ever be able to do enough to earn any. Of all the gods, she was the one Rose feared to pray to the most; she hadn't earned the right to yet.

"Gods," the king swore softly under his breath and ran his hand over his face. "And the Earthmover?"

"I don't know what happened to him or where he went," he said with a shrug.

The king nodded and glanced at Rose. "And nothing else was said about the shadow magic?"

Caleb shook his head.

"You look exhausted. And injured. See to your injuries in the Mending Wing. They can help find you a room for the night. We'll talk more later."

Caleb breathed a sigh of relief and nodded.

"Can you find the way?" Rose asked.

Caleb was already turning away. "It can't be that hard. I'll figure it out."

She waited for the doors to shut behind him before turning back to the king.

"This is not the first report of an Earthmover. Though this is the worst report yet."

"The others?" Rose asked.

The king waved his hand. "Fields, roads. A few bridges. Nothing like this."

"Oh," Rose sighed, her stomach threatening to empty itself again. She pressed her lips tightly together in an effort to not vomit all over the king's lush carpets, and breathed deep through her nose.

"Are you alright?"

She shook her head. "I'm fine."

He watched her before finally nodding. "He knows about your magic?" he asked with a cautious voice.

She was reminded that while this was her secret, her magic, he was uniquely connected to it. In the months since they'd learned he was her Anchor, a role they still didn't fully understand, he'd come to guard her magic almost as closely as she did.

"He's more observant than I gave him credit for."

"And who is he, exactly?"

"He is," she stopped and corrected herself, "was an assistant in the archives."

"Ah," Micah said and glanced away before turning back. "You weren't gone as long as I expected you to be."

She blinked and wasn't sure what to make of that. Had he missed her? Part of her hoped he had, but the louder, more logical part of her remembered that was foolish thinking.

She cleared her throat softly. "I've another thing to tell you from my trip."

He waved his hand gently to stop her.

"Let's talk over dinner. I'm interested to hear what else you've learned on this trip, and I'm sure you'll want to freshen up and are no doubt hungry."

"But–"

"I'm hungry," the king said with a soft smile. "And I'm sure we'll have much to talk about."

Her soul hurt. She wanted to cry and vomit. She wanted to drink. But she found herself meeting his small smile and nodding.

"Alright."

"Excellent. Later tonight, then. Eighth bell."

Rose nodded and slowly retreated from the room.

CHAPTER 17

*R*ose soaked until her fingers were wrinkled and the water was cold, but she'd finally been able to thaw out her frozen bones. Back in her room, the captain hadn't lied when she said she'd keep it for a time, she yanked her plain, straight hair into a tight braid and rummaged for any clean clothing. At the bottom of the chest, she managed to find a cleanish pair of trousers and a pale blue tunic. After wrapping the one decent belt she had around her waist, she was moderately presentable. At least she wasn't dressed in more uniforms.

A glance at herself in her small polished mirror and tired brown eyes stared back. Her petite nose and plain brown hair didn't stand out; too plain to be cute or pretty. Even if someone was inclined to call her pretty, the exhaustion clear in the lines around her eyes and the tug at her lips would chase that away.

As she approached the study doors for the second time that day, a new guard greeted her with the slightest of nods. He knocked twice then opened the door for her. Rose slipped inside and approached the king at his desk. He sat staring down at his desk and didn't look up until she stood right in front and cleared her throat softly.

"Rose," he stood up and stretched. "I didn't hear you I apologize."

She nodded and noted the tired bags around his eyes. He'd seemed to have aged years from when she first saw him in the summer. He wasn't as carefree anymore. Wasn't as relaxed.

The king stepped out from behind his desk, and Rose fell in step next to him. They walked silently for a time, the Shields following just far enough away to give the illusion of privacy. The king slowly steered them further and further away from the more populated ends of the castle. As they walked, the tapestries grew more ornate; the statues of armor older. The bustle of servants running about the halls quieted. Rose cast her eyes around the halls and realized they'd entered the royal wing. The crests adorning the walls were all from the various royal family lines.

"Tell me," he said as they walked, "about your trip."

Rose sighed. "I feel like I'm left with more questions than answers. We'd hoped to gain some information on Earthmovers, but now.... "

The king turned and led them into a small and unassuming dining room after what seemed like near-endless halls. A sideboard was set against the far wall with decanters and glasses. A small sitting area was wedged into the corner of the room near the large fireplace that heated the whole room. The simple table, already set, was at the other end of the room. Papers and books were scattered across half the table as if the king often worked late into the night while eating.

"Pardon the mess," he was saying as he hastily stacked the papers into a reasonable pile at the end of the table. "Mariah and I were arguing last night about—" he cut himself off with a sharp shake of his head. "It doesn't matter. Would you like some wine?"

She shook her head at the odd familiarity, domestic feeling. A distinct lack of servants. This didn't feel like dining with the king, or even a noble.

Like I'd know. She had to stop herself from rolling her eyes at herself.

"Rose?"

"Sorry. Yes. Wine would be nice."

The king poured two glasses, and after handing her one, sat at the table.

Rose sipped the dry wine and sat opposite him. "Why no servants to pour your drinks?"

He grinned at her over his glass. "I am capable of pouring my own drinks, and the servants have more important tasks than standing by to fill my cup."

Rose chuckled softly and nodded to his point.

"You mentioned something else you needed to tell me?"

"Lady Sephrita may still be in the country. Or," she tilted her head as she thought, "more likely her spies are."

His eyes grew hard as he watched her. "How do you know?" His voice was low and angry.

"She had a man at the inn I stayed at slip me a note."

His eyebrow twitched. "Another?"

She grumbled. "It simply said they wouldn't be stalled for long and that you needed to come up with an answer for D'ray's death. I guessed she meant the council."

The king looked away, his face drawn in a frown. "What is her goal? Why is she helping us?" He looked back at her. "What does she want?"

Rose shrugged. "Maybe it's a trade deal. The B'leakons only interact with people off their island when it involves trade."

"Yes, but to interfere this much without the knowledge or support of the rest of her council?" He shook his head. "There is something more here."

They fell into silence; Rose not having any helpful words to offer him. She poked around her plate of salted pork and beets. She sneaked a thick cut of bread, the white, fluffy stuff melting in her mouth. The whole-grain breads served in the kitchens wasn't bad, but this stuff was nearly decadent in comparison. Those breads were simply something used to shovel soups into your mouth, but this… she tried to hold back a moan as she ate more. This was something you ate and enjoyed.

"You said you went to the college to learn about your magic," the king said, and Rose quickly swallowed the gulp of spiced wine. "Did you learn anything about the Anchor?"

"No," she said softly, and he nodded. That was the biggest question of them all. What was the Anchor, and why was it the king? He had no magic of his own, yet he was able to pull her out of the shadows and ground her when her magic became too much.

"I did learn my magic used to have a clan. A whole group of people used to have the same magic as me. They were called Shademakers and one was different, called a Shadowstalker. The wolves called me a Shadowstalker after... what happened in the throne room, but I didn't know if that was the name of the magic or something else." Rose sighed. "But it doesn't matter now. They're all gone."

Not.... quite, she reminded herself. There was the mystery of J'Teal's ghost.

"Mariah explained to me once that magic often runs in families. Is there no one you could seek out for help? Your mother?"

Rose huffed a sardonic laugh. "My mother abandoned me when I was six, and my father..." She gulped down more wine at the memories threatening to open. "I don't know any relatives on my father's side. My mother never spoke of any, or if she did I was too young to remember."

"I'm sorry."

She looked up at his soft words and stared into his dark eyes. She had to look away from the sympathy in them. She stood from the table, unable to sit still. She wandered away from the table toward the fireplace. The wine swirled in her belly and glass.

"To awful parents," she said while raising her glass in a mockery of a toast.

Micah joined her at the fire and raised his own glass to meet her toast. She eyed his wrist, and the small marks she knew were beneath his sleeve. He'd mentioned once something about knowing cruel parents too. She turned back to the fire, confused. She didn't want his sympathy, hadn't liked seeing it in his eyes when he looked at her, but she was glad he'd followed her. He knew her secrets, not all of them, but so many of them, and he hadn't turned from her. He hadn't betrayed her. She didn't want his sympathy, but she found she was starting to want his presence.

She glanced again at his wrist, covered in fine fabrics. "What happened?"

He glanced at her before following her gaze to his wrist. "Nothing profound. I'm sure the same thing happens to hundreds of children."

"Humor me," she asked softly. "Please."

He met and held her eyes. He seemed to hear what she was thinking: she'd told him too many of her secrets and needed something in return.

"My father was not a loving man. I wouldn't say he was cruel, just not very kind. I remember he was angry at something a servant had done; I forget what. He was hitting him with a crop. I stepped in and tried to stop it, which only made him angrier, and I got the whipping the servant had been getting."

Micah pulled his sleeve up for Rose to see the small, pale lines criss-crossing his forearm. "He only did it one time. I think mother yelled at him for hours when she learned about it. He was cruel in other ways, though. Luckily, I had my grandmother and much of my time was spent with tutors."

"Sounds lonely."

He met her eyes and pulled his sleeve back down. "Not any more than many other childhoods."

She grunted and turned back to the fire. They stood in silence for a time, the cracking of the fire enough sound to fill the room. Soon, Rose found herself leaning her shoulder into Micah's, and she couldn't bring herself to pull away. It was calming, and grounding.

A log breaking apart on the fire was enough to startle Rose out of her stupor, and she straightened with hot cheeks. "I should go. Thank you, sire, for the meal."

"Of course, Rose."

She turned, more than a little wobbly on her feet, cheeks burning and confusing feelings swirling in her head.

CHAPTER 18

$\mathcal{M}$ariah poured herself another cup of tea and turned back to the pile of officer paperwork covering her desk. It was pay week. Which meant balancing the accounts: her least favorite task. Rose had been doing this for a time, but with her indecision, Mariah decided to take the task back. Lest they go forgotten once again.

She would rather face down an entire court in her dress uniform for a week than deal with this. Normally, her Chief Officer would deal with this, but she barely had a lieutenant and he was overworked as it was.

Adding to the mess, she'd spent all morning with the king and Lord Tyman learning about the loss of the college. Several dozen soldiers had left early this morning, bringing medical supplies and food from the castle's larder.

Normally the number of soldiers going to the college wouldn't have mattered, but combined with the amount being sent south to the border... they were starting to become thinly spread. Add to that the destruction of the trading bridge in Rosemand.... Mariah pinched the bridge of her nose to stave off a headache. Trade from Hostal's Dock will take nearly twice as long now to get to the rest of the country.

That bridge was the fastest and easiest way to cross the Althus River into the northern part of the country. Without it, trade will be forced either south into Salva before the roads connect north, and the raids will make that unlikely or east around the lake into Saron, the farthest northeastern point in the country. It wasn't the only trade port, but gods... it was the largest one.

The roads being destroyed by the Earthmover were only making things more difficult. Trade will be crippled. The thought made her hands shake, but she'd faced down insurrections and assassinations. She would face this. Her king would face this.

She sighed as the numbers on the paper blurred together. "Dammit," she groaned and reached for her tea. She looked up, however, at her closed door when Rose's turbulent thoughts were already breaking into the quiet. She'd heard whisperings through the Light Horse Wing that she'd returned yesterday. Honestly, she was surprised. Mariah had hoped she'd return but hadn't expected her and certainly hadn't expected it this soon.

Knocking sounded on her door a moment later, and Mariah braced herself for whatever trouble the girl was going to start up this time.

"Yes?" she called through the door.

Rose let herself in with a young, tired-looking man following her. Rose promptly sat in the only chair her office would allow, and the young man stood awkwardly between the door and her desk.

"You've returned to us."

Rose nodded, her thoughts a swirl of messy sounds.

"How can I help you, Rose?"

"I have an idea."

Gods help me, she thought to herself before nodding.

"This is Caleb Harven." Rose pointed over her shoulder to the man. "He's from the college."

Her eyes snapped to him, his eyes clouded with painful memories. She had to focus hard to stop the barrage of images: falling rocks, walls collapsing, the screaming students. It was a fresh and painful memory. Those thoughts were always the hardest to block out. Her hand unconsciously raised to cover her ear against the explosive sound of stone striking stone before she was able to raise the wall of water that blocked out the young man's thoughts. He'd barely escaped.

"Caleb was apprenticing under Professor Elias in the archives. Until he finds where to go from here," Rose glanced at Caleb, "I thought we might put his skill with libraries to use."

"How so?"

"The castle has several old libraries and an even older one in the abandoned section. We need to learn more about the Earthmover, and maybe there are more books in the libraries that could help with that." Rose shrugged. "Maybe not everything was lost in the archives."

Mariah nodded and cautiously lowered her wall of water. Caleb's thoughts were under control again, and she let out a small breath of relief. "It's a good idea, Rose."

Rose smiled at her, a soft, hesitant smile that reminded Mariah of the fragile girl Rose really was... if you dug deep enough. A fragile girl wanting approval. She just needed to keep trying to reach that part of Rose. Maybe with enough time and coaxing....

"I have a name he can search for. The Earthmover's name is Goron Velra."

"How did you come by that name?"

Rose hesitated across from her, her thoughts a swirling mess. "A source told me," she finally said while locking eyes with her. *The shadows told me.*

Mariah blinked as the direct thought echoed from Rose. She gave a small nod, glancing at Caleb.

"Alright, I'll bring it up with the king. We'll need to see about clearing the collapsed stairway to the old library."

I miss him.

The thought burst through so sharply Mariah flinched at the forcefulness. It had the force of forbidden thoughts, ones buried deep and never acknowledged. She glanced at Rose and gently probed just a little at the thought, hoping she was wrong and it wasn't what she thought it was. Longing and loneliness streamed from the thought, and Mariah followed it deeper. So many thoughts and emotions and conflicts were tied to this thought. And peace. A peaceful stillness was buried in that tumultuous mess of thought and emotions about the king.

Mariah shuffled papers into a pile, buying time as she pulled back from Rose's mind. She sighed, a long breath through her nose. She wished she'd been wrong, but she'd seen how close they'd gotten over the past few months. For Rose's sake, she hoped Micah put a stop to whatever was starting soon. Nothing good could come from this pairing.

"Mr. Harven," Mariah said once she'd gathered herself. "I will speak with the king about some sort of stipend for the work you'll be doing, assuming the king agrees. We'll need to have you moved out of the mending wing and probably into one of the empty rooms with us, however."

"That's fine, ma'am. I just want to be useful."

"Yes," she said softly. "It'll be good to keep busy. You may go. I'll have someone find you once the rooms have been sorted."

The young man slipped away, and she hoped he was going back to his room to sleep. When the door shut behind him, she turned back to Rose. She wanted to tell her to walk away from whatever feelings were starting with the king; find someone else. That young Caleb, for example. He even seemed to like her. However, Rose might finally be feeling comfortable here and was starting to think of it as home. The last thing Mariah wanted to do was push her away. No, she'd set Micah right first. Besides, he should know better.

"Will you be staying?"

Rose slowly brought her eyes up to meet Mariah's.

"It seems," Rose said slowly while looking away again, "that whenever I try to leave, I find myself needing to return."

"That doesn't sound like a decision." Mariah folded her hands on top of her desk.

It's not. Rose's thoughts whispered. The girl shrugged and finally dragged her eyes back.

Well, Mariah sighed to herself, *she's getting there.*

"For the extended future, at least, it sounds like you'll be here with us?"

Rose nodded, and Mariah smiled.

"Perfect." She pushed the large book of accounts toward Rose. "You can get back to these then."

Rose glanced up at her from under her lashes in a glare that would've made other people step back. Mariah smiled wider.

She was not other people.

"Fine," she muttered and took the book. She was still grumbling as she retreated from the office.

CHAPTER 19

*R*ose changed into a worn work tunic and a patchy pair of trousers before making her way to Archie. Despite the cold and the snow, Archie still insisted on training outside on the grounds. He either didn't know about her trip and potential exit from the castle or didn't care. He still demanded she attended training.

So, Rose made her way outside into the snow. She grumbled about it, but she liked that he expected her to come. She liked the rhythm and routine they'd established. And, she needed to hit something.

She stormed across the grounds, the wind freezing as it blew, and Rose just became angrier. The wind cut through her clothes and to her bones, and it pulled her hair loose from its braid. Rose steered toward the small structure at the edge of the training field. The simple building housed trainees during the cold or bad weather. As she stormed inside, Rose eyed the racks at the back of the single-room building with training blades. The ground was covered in hay to keep the mud and dirt down. Several small groups of soldiers were already working, some moving through warmups, others sparring, some halfheartedly sparring while glancing at the door. Rose stripped her greatcoat and threw it into the corner.

"Brought yer temper, I see," Archie said, standing next to where her rumpled coat lay. "Pick that up, Tiny. This isn't your room to do as you please in."

Rose glared at the red-head, all too ready to pick a fight. "Don't start with—"

A large hand thwapped into the side of her head. She stumbled, and it felt like her eyes were rattling in her skull.

"Ow!" she yelled and held her head. "What was that for?"

"Pick up," Archie growled at her, "yer coat."

Rose watched him hesitantly before deciding she didn't want to risk a second smack to her head. She bent and picked up her discarded coat and daintily laid it across the stack of hay serving as benches along the walls.

"You're in my space. Respect it. If you want others' respect, you better start giving it. And that means no more backtalk."

Rose raised an eyebrow at him.

"Fine," he relented with a huff. "Significantly less backtalk."

She grunted but nodded. He made a point. She didn't like the point, but it was a point. Archie tossed her a wooden practice sword, and she caught it with ease. Without any further words, Archie grabbed his own practice sword and started into the basic swordplay movements. He moved her through the forms until sweat dripped down her back and her hairline was soaking.

"Good," he finally said and set his sword aside. "Now that you're warmed up, we can begin."

Rose grunted, wanted to snap something witty, but was too out of breath.

"Here." He pointed to a wooden strike dummy. "Use the weighted sword."

Diligently, Rose traded her sword for the heavier, lead-weighted sword and approached the dummy.

"Work through the forms. Pay attention to your footwork. Go."

She held back a curse, barely. Slowly, trying to focus on the forms and her footwork, she moved through the basic movements. The weighted sword sent painful shocks up her arms on each impact with the dummy.

"So, why such an attitude today?"

Rose glanced at him from the corner of her eye as she continued. "It's just—" She paused for lack of breath and words. "I may have been responsible for something bad."

Archie kicked her ankle when she missed a step, and she grunted as she corrected her stance. Some of the burning anger that had disappeared while working returned, and she hit the dummy with more force.

"What'd you do?"

"I didn't do anything." Rose beat the dummy. But it was her fault all the same. Her arms were starting to go numb from the impacts. The musty smell of the training rings mingled with the damn smell of the hay covering most of the ground. Rose ground her teeth together and focused on the pattern of the swordplay, the smell of the room. Perhaps Archie saw something on her face because he stopped asking questions and pushed her through the forms. Forewords, backwards, starting midway.

"Hawk strike," Archie shouted at her.

Rose moved into the technique, her sword cutting swiftly down at an angle.

"Parry, Hawk Strike and riposte."

She followed his command, moving through the movements against the dummy.

How do you sleep at night? Erik's words came back to her and they seemed to settle in her chest with a new weight. So much blood was on her soul. Very little of it was innocent, but the college…. They weighed heavily on her. Their weight made her bones ache. Was she allowed to find peace? Happiness? Or was that her punishment for the things she's done?

"Don't let your footwork get sloppy!" he shouted when she stumbled. "Again."

She groaned, sweat falling into her eyes and blisters burning on the palms of her hands. But she continued. She let herself fall into the rhythm and focus of the movements. Archie would shout techniques at her. She'd follow through. The simmering anger receded beneath the calm and focus of the fight. Even some of the heart-stopping sadness disappeared. There wasn't any room for it in this calm. Rose lost track of time as she beat her sword against the dummy until Archie called out for her to stop.

"Why?" she panted. Her hands stung, and her breath came in loud pants.

"You're well past your time, and your hands are bleeding."

Rose dropped her sword and looked at her bleeding palms. She hadn't noticed when the sting turned to pain or when the hilt had gone sticky with blood instead of sweat. Archie's large hand engulfed her smaller one as he gently started wrapping her hands with bandages.

"What happened?" he asked while he worked. "I haven't seen you train like this before."

Rose watched him wrap her hands. She could feel his eyes on her, but she couldn't make herself look up from her hands to meet his eyes.

"You're improving," he finally said. "Working with Aaron has helped your form, even if you do keep forgetting your footwork."

"Thank you." She dropped her bandaged hands and finally looked up at him. "Why do you keep training me? I'm not paying you."

"Wish ye would," he grumbled softly before he shrugged and fixed her with his hazel eyes. "Because you need it."

She felt there was more meaning to his words than he said, but her mind was too tired to try to figure it out.

Now that the focus of the fight was fading, and her heartbeat was slowly receding, Rose could feel the throbbing in her hands and the tremor of her muscles. She would be sore tomorrow, but her mind felt clearer than it had before. She felt like she had a level of control over her emotions she didn't before.

"I hope this helped," Archie said, and she finally brought her eyes to him. "Whatever you're facing, I hoped this helped."

Her mind was quieter than it had been in days. That or it was too tired to worry. "I think it did."

"Eventually, you're going to have to move past hitting things and talk."

Rose snorted softly at him and went to retrieve her long coat. "You and Aaron both say that. Never going to happen."

"One day," he said to her back.

Clara, Archie's redheaded daughter, skipped past her. She was a smiling, boisterous girl that spent much of her time watching her father train. When Archie finally did chase her out from under his feet, she was running simple errands for her aunt, Captain Sayla, around the castle.

Snow was gusting on the wind, and she felt calmer than she had in days. Sometimes talking is overrated. Rose trudged toward the baths to wash the smell of sweaty hay from her.

———

SHE STAYED in the baths until the water grew cold, and only then did she reluctantly leave. If she were ever to leave the castle and stay away, she would sorely miss the baths. In her room, she pulled out the mysterious lump of ore. The light glimmered off it in strange colors and hues. Rose tossed it gently in her hand before sighing and shoving the thing into her pocket. Until she knew what this thing was for, it was staying with her.

Next, she eyed the deep blue Light Horse overcoat with a grimace. Her coin purse sat on the nightstand, not as fat as it had been before the trip to the college. She needed clothing that wasn't blue. Rose wasn't sure if she was staying at the castle, but she did know she wasn't joining the Light Horse. At least, she thought as she eyed the coat again, she was mostly sure she wasn't.

"Damn it all," she muttered and grabbed up her coin purse and coat.

She searched out Caleb's room down the hall, where the captain had put him until other arrangements were made, and knocked hard and loud. The quiet scholar had been too quiet in the few days he'd been here. She knew the haunted look in his eyes, knew it personally. He needed careful distraction, or that kind of pain would take hold and rot.

She knocked again when there was no answer.

"Hey."

Rose turned toward Sam's voice as he walked up to her.

"I was just coming to find you." Sam held out a slip of paper as he neared. "Kid's stayin' in some inn in town. Left last night. Here, he told me to give this to you."

Rose took the note with the name. "Oh, thanks."

"Sure." He waved and returned the way he'd come.

She looked down at the note again with a frown. Why was Caleb in town? She shoved the note in her pocket and headed to the stables.

It didn't take her long to saddle and tack Starlit, thought the giant horse snorted and stamped the whole time. The horse nearly burst from the stables before Rose had even managed to get up into the saddle. Starlit tossed her great head, her mane billowing in the wind as Rose directed her out of the castle.

Starlit's ears flicked, her breath puffing in great white clouds. A freezing cold had settled over the area. The sun, so bright and deceiving in the sky, did nothing to warm the day. Rose stared at the hanging wooden sign for the inn, her horse standing obediently at the post by the doors. It was definitely not as rowdy as the Witch's Pit, and she raised her brow at the sign. She'd heard this place was much nicer than her regular inn and tavern. Staring at the tidy, painted door and decorative sign, she knew it was. For one, she was pretty sure it was a tea house and not a tavern at all.

Why did he pick this place? She sucked her teeth, and Starlit shifted on her feet enough that she was rocked to the side.

"Moody," she said and swung out of the saddle.

She strode to the door, coat and scarf wrapped tightly around her. Inside, a soft bell jingled at her entrance. Instantly, the smells of baked sweet things and the deep, earthy smell of good tea hit her nose. The good, expensive kind from the southern hills of Catven. The kind the king drank, and Rose savored each and every time she was able to sneak a cup. She tried to hold back a moan of envy.

The dainty tables and fine cloths covering them were clean and crisp. A lady came to the front of the room from what looked like a larger parlor in the back. Her hair was coiffed perfectly atop her head; her dress a simple but fine cut with expensive-looking cloth. Eyeing it, Rose suspected the dark and even purple color came straight from the Black Hills. The B'leakons had amazing dyes, but only they had that shade of purple.

The woman looked Rose up and down and then slowly back up again. No doubt her leather boots and simple trousers poking out from beneath her long uniform coat did not meet the standards of her regular clientele.

"Can I help you?" she asked stiffly, most likely wishing very much that Rose would just turn around and walk away.

"I was meeting one of your tenants," Rose pointed her gloved hand to the ceiling. "If you'll just show me the stairs... "

The guardian of nice and pretty things raised an eyebrow at her before daintily gesturing to her left. "Through the door, stairs on the left."

Rose cracked a smile at her, full of teeth and bite, and turned to the mentioned door. She was itching for a fight. Her sparring with Archie had done little to quiet that desire. She took the stairs slowly, on shaking legs, and walked down the quiet hall until she reached the door number scribbled on the note.

She knocked on the door and heard shuffling before Caleb pulled the door open. His face was worn and drawn. Red rimmed his puffy eyes. He cracked the smallest smile when he saw her, his dimples appearing briefly.

"Miss Trewin."

She pushed her way into the posh room, looking widely around. The room had soft curtains thick with embroidery. The carpet was lush, her boots sinking into the weave as she walked. To the right was a small sitting area, complete with full tea service on the table. To her left was a wide bed.

She draped her coat over the back of one of the chairs and turned to Caleb with an eyebrow raised. "Castle isn't posh enough for you?"

He blushed, the tips of his ears going pink again, and Rose smiled at the sight. He wasn't beyond help then.

"No, no. It's not that." He settled himself in the other chair.

She joined him at the table and noticed the ill-fitting tunic and vest he was wearing. He noticed her frown, and with another blush, fingered the clothing.

"A young Light Horse officer was nice enough to lend me some of his older clothing items. Sam? I think his name was Sam. All of my clothing… " His words trailed off, and Rose realized he didn't have anything. He had even less than she did, but where she chose to travel light, his items had been ripped from him.

She glanced at the room, wondering how much it cost him a night and why he hadn't bought new clothes yet.

"Your captain was kind enough to put me up here until I figure out a more permanent solution." He shrugged. "An advance on my pay for the research I'll be doing."

"Why are you here?" Rose asked again.

He stared at the tabletop, his hands clutched around each other. "It's too similar," he finally said. "I… It's too similar to the college. That first night I woke up thinking I was back home."

She kicked herself for not realizing it sooner. His voice was so broken, so sad. The guilt came roaring back tenfold, and she had to take a deep breath.

"Well," she started with more cheer than she felt, "let's go find you some clothes then."

He looked up at her with a frown. "I don't have any money. I'm already going to owe for staying here."

Rose pulled out her coin purse, the money she'd earned for spying last summer, the money she was going to use to buy her own clothing and finally be free of this uniform, and dropped it on the table.

"There should be enough in there for a few decent things." She stood and slipped the Light Horse uniform coat back on. "Come on, the weather's not even half bad."

He stood, though his face was drawn in a frown. "I don't want to owe you too!"

"You won't," she said softly and pocketed the coins. "Grab whatever coat Sam gave you. It's not bad weather, but the wind is shit."

He obeyed, though Rose thought it was mostly out of habit than actual understanding of his actions, and followed her back into the tea room. She remembered a draper was near the market square and she pulled Caleb out onto the cobbled street.

"Why are you doing this?"

The wind stung her cheeks as they walked. Because she needed to try to repay the damage she'd caused. Because he was too gentle a soul for such suffering.

"Because I can," was what she finally said.

CHAPTER 20

*H*ours later, they sat in the dimly lit tea house parlor with plates of smoked fish, potatoes, and some sort of cream sauce that Rose fully intended to lick off the plate. On the floor next to Caleb sat several paper-wrapped parcels of new clothing. Nothing fancy, nothing like the suit he'd worn at the college, but clothing that was his and that fit.

The man across from her looked better than the one that had greeted her at his door earlier this afternoon. She didn't think it was enough to repay what had happened, but she felt it was a good start.

The innkeeper watched Rose with wary eyes from her place by the kitchen door. She allowed Rose the meal since Caleb was her tenant, but she hadn't been happy about it. Rose smiled sharply at the woman.

"Thank you," Caleb said, and Rose pulled her gaze away from the haughty glare of the woman. "For today. You didn't have to do that."

Rose hummed and poked at the last of her potatoes. "I did."

Her coin purse was so light she thought it was empty now, but it had been well worth it.

He nodded absently. "Do you know what it is?"

"What what is?"

Caleb gestured toward her coat with his spoon. "The ore, rock thing."

Rose shifted in her chair, pushing her hip against the armrest, feeling the shape and weight of the ore sitting there in the pocket. "How'd you know I had it with me?"

He frowned at her. "Didn't you pull it out today?"

"No."

He frowned harder at her before shrugging. "I must've seen it at some point."

Rose watched him, knowing damned well she'd never pulled it out or let anyone see it at all today. "I don't know," she said and slowly reached into her pocket and put the ore in front of him. "What do you think?"

Caleb's eyes were drawn to it as he stared at it and slowly reached his hand to lift the ore. He held it near the candle on the table, and the golden light danced off the iridescent surface.

"It looks like a metal, but I couldn't name which one." He turned it around in his hand. "Why do you still have it?"

Rose held her hand out for it, and reluctantly Caleb dropped it into her palm. "I don't know. I think I might need it."

She re-pocketed the mysterious thing as the innkeeper came over to remove their plates. Rose struggled to hide her yawn, and Caleb laughed at her.

"It's been a long day."

She smiled at him. "I should get back."

They stood, and Rose re-donned her blue coat. It was warm, even if she hated everything else about it. Caleb made his way back up the stairs, and after one more parting smile at the innkeeper, her perfectly pressed skirts swishing as she moved toward the kitchens, Rose retreated from the tea house.

A SLIGHT TWINGE in her chest made Rose frown and open her eyes. Instead of her dark room with a glowing stove, she stared at the thick, rolling fog of the Shadow World. She sat up, heart beating fast in her throat, and looked around. The pale, moonless and sunless sky. The dead trees. She stood on shaking legs, the nightdress she wore to bed fluttering around her ankles. The clearing she was in was thick with mist and fog. Her skin prickled at the cool dew.

"Girl."

Rose whipped around at the Shadowstalker's clipped voice. "Why are you doing this!"

The woman stepped forward into the clearing, her skirts bringing a cloud of mist with her as she moved. The harsh lines of her face were made worse by the glare she directed at Rose.

"Because you are the Shadowstalker, and you are ignoring your duty!" The woman shouted back at her, and the dark mists in the woods quivered.

Rose stepped back but held her back straight. "How do you know that?"

"Because I was one!" she shouted. "Can you not feel how angry they are? How they fume?"

She glanced over the ghost's shoulder at the dark and swirling woods. "I sort of thought they were always like that."

"This is not a joke!" J'Teal planted her hands on her hips, her words a crisp clap of sounds. "You have a job to do."

"And who's around to teach me this job, eh?" Rose snapped, harsh and loud. Her lips started to tingle, and she had to remind herself to slow her rapid breathing. She took a breath, held it, and forced herself to let it out slowly.

J'Teal frowned and dropped her arms. "Why haven't the elders been teaching you?"

Rose turned away with a harsh laugh. "What elders?" she asked as she turned back to face her. "Hm?"

Her heart raced. She could feel the heat in her face, and all her previous careful breathing evaporated. Her breathing came in angry puffs and the mists started to growl.

The mists grew and swirled around her legs. Memories that weren't hers started to work their way into her mind. People and places she didn't know flashed through her mind faster than she could recognize.

Stop, she told them, panic starting to swirl in her chest. *Stop*.

The wolves were angry, annoyed. They wanted her to listen, and this was how they were going to do it. They pushed against her, demanding her attention.

She ground her teeth, hands fisted, as she pushed against their will. The fog grew to her knees.

"Stop!"

Her shout shook the shadows, the darkness wavering like smoke in the wind, and even the wolves were quiet. Her breaths came in giant gasps that rattled her throat. Slowly, she calmed her breathing.

Stupid, she chided herself, her breath puffing in her chest. Stupid. Of course the wolves would be stronger in their own lands.

"You are untrained," J'Teal whispered shakily.

"No shit," Rose puffed.

She watched as J'Teal's mouth dropped, her harsh black eyes slowly widening. Rose waited. She held J'Teal's eyes and waited.

"Where... where are the elders?" J'Teal's voice was soft, but Rose heard the shake in her words. "Where is the clan?"

"Dead." Rose shrugged, too angry to pretend to be sympathetic. "For all I know."

"How can that be?" J'Teal whispered and turned her back to Rose. She was silent for a long stretch, and Rose started to feel a little sorry for the woman. Even if she was dead, somehow, she was here. And she'd just learned her people were gone. All of them. Rose had let her temper get ahead of her again.

"The world does not know anything of this magic," Rose said, her voice softer than it had been before, "nor of any people who once had it."

When J'Teal turned back around, she was pressing her hand to her mouth. With a deep breath, she dropped her hand. "Your duty will be all the harder then."

She dropped her head back with a sigh. Around her, the world started to fade. She dragged her head back up and met J'Teal's disappearing form. "And what is that, then?"

"The Balance," her voice echoed as the Shadow World faded. "You must right the imbalance caused by Goron's return."

Rose bolted upright in bed, her heart pounding in her chest and thumping in her ears. Her stove had burned down to embers and an uncomfortable chill in the air. The sweat coating her skin and making her sleeping gown cling to her made her shiver in the cold room.

With a groan, she leaned forward, drew her knees up, and pressed her face into the bedding. Her head pounded enough to make her stomach roll. Her body was wracked by another shiver, and with an angry huff, Rose dragged herself out of bed to throw more logs into the stove. She dove back into her bed and curled into a tight ball under the bedding.

"Dammit," she muttered. J'Teal, Goron. Shademakers. Who was next?

CHAPTER 21

*B*y the time sunlight was shining through, her pounding headache had dwindled to a dull throb behind her eyes. As Rose cracked her eyes open, the room looked fuzzy. Her eyes felt like they were covered in sand. She pushed herself into a sitting position with a huff and groaned only to drop her head into her hands.

She didn't know what to do. What was going on with J'Treal? Why was she appearing? How was she supposed to handle any of this?

With a deep breath, she sat up and combed her hair back from her face. She shouldn't, but she wanted to talk to the king. He always seemed to push her toward answers or shape her chaotic thoughts into something that made sense. She shouldn't.

Rose chewed her lip. She knew she shouldn't. He was the king, and she already had a problem with boundaries.

"Bugger it," she said and pushed herself off the bed.

She changed quickly into a simple tunic and trousers. She sent her eyesight through the shadows of the castle. Rose floated through the dark hallways and corridors. She searched out the royal apartments first. It was early enough in the morning she doubted many people were awake. There were servants hustling back and forth in the corridors, lighting fires and waking the castle.

As she sent her eyesight into the solarium, the hazy sunlight harshly limited what she could see. She dipped and weaved under the plant leaves and tables throughout the room. The soft sounds of pencils moving across paper drew Rose into the alcove, her alcove, and saw the faint outline of the king.

Rose took a deep breath and dropped the rest of her body into the shadows. She settled into the shadows beneath a large sta'aka leaf before stepping out of the shadow. She fell to the ground from the leaf, her knees landing hard on the floor with a grunt.

"Ow," she murmured and stood stiffly.

"Rose?" The king stared at her, half standing from the settee he'd been sitting at.

"I'm fine," she muttered and brushed dirt from her pants. "It's been years since I've done something like that."

"Something like?"

Rose huffed and dropped into the plush armchair next to the sta'aka. "Trip as I come out of the shadows."

The king quirked a smile at her and reached over to the small table at his elbow and picked up the tea cup. Rose followed the movement of the cup and tried not to drool at the idea of tea.

"Was the door too difficult?"

She chuckled and looked away. Too many servants were roaming the halls early in the morning. She didn't want rumors circling. She may be foolish, but she wasn't a total moron. She shoved her hands into the pockets of her short coat. Before, she was so sure of herself and confident, now she was rethinking her actions. It was obvious, with the tea and plate of biscuits, that she'd interrupted his breakfast.

"Are you alright?"

Rose turned back to him with a raised eyebrow.

"You just popped in here in the early morning hours. I assume something has happened."

She couldn't stop the smile. "Am I that predictable?"

"No," but he was smiling.

Rose leaned forward to steal a biscuit. She munched on it, chewing on the sweet bread just as much as her thoughts.

"I'm stuck," Rose finally said and slumped in her chair. "The shadows are angry with me. Pretty pissed, actually."

"What is upsetting them?"

She let out a long breath. "The Earthmover. He's out of place. Out of time, somehow. The Balance is broken, and they are not happy about it." She took another breath and shrugged. "They're angry with me and how I've behaved. Apparently I'm not standing up to their expectations."

The king leaned forward onto his knees.

"And now," she slumped further in the chair, "now I have a dead Shadowstalker talking to me in my dreams, and I still don't have any idea what I'm supposed to do."

Rose glanced over at him, expecting to see shock or disgust on his face, but instead, he simply watched her.

"I'm not crazy."

"No," he held out his hand and straightened up. "You talk to shadow beings and have a magic no one understands, but you are not crazy."

She held his eyes a moment longer before nodding. He held out the plate of biscuits, and Rose quickly grabbed a few more.

"This Shadowstalker," Micah said after biting into his own biscuit, "can you not get answers from them?"

She sighed around her biscuit. "I can try, but she doesn't know anything after her death. She didn't know the Shademaker clan was gone. She doesn't know how the Earthmover is back. She was the last Shadowstalker, but I don't know how many answers she'll have."

"But she could help you with your magic."

She shoved another biscuit in her mouth. But how much could she learn in short, unpredictable dream conversations? J'Teal might be her past, the last great Shadowstalker, but she needed something more. Someone more. She wanted more answers.

"When your past looks you in the face, you will need me."

The words whispered through Rose's ear like the Seer was right there speaking them. Her mouth dropped, slowly forming an 'o'.

"Rose?"

She pulled her eyes to him and snapped her mouth shut. She remembered a conversation from long ago, almost forgotten with a Seer in an alley.

"We aid our voice," the shadows said with chuffing laughter in their voices. "Since you will not think."

"Shit," Rose swore. "I need to find Ode."

She stood and paced the small space, the morning sun warm on her skin. Ode. She couldn't believe it. That crazy woman with the stupid riddle in a dingy alley. She could not believe that was coming back.

"Rose."

She stopped with a jerk and forced herself to sit back down. "Sorry."

"What's happening?"

She shook her head. "I didn't think anything of it. Last summer, I ran into this woman, this Seer. She told me a riddle, and I forgot it nearly as soon as it happened. This woman, Ode, told me my past would return, and I would think she has the answers. She said when my past looks me in the face, I would know I need Ode."

"And you think this Ode to be a true Seer?" Micah asked. "That your 'past' she spoke of is this old Shadowstalker."

Rose shrugged. "She had a power to her that felt real. And just now, it was as though she was right next to me, whispering the words in my ear again."

She stood and paced in front of Micah, her ability to keep still failing.

"There's an Earthmover roaming the lands, and we don't know why," she continued, her mind moving too fast for her to organize her thoughts. "She's a Seer. We need answers about what's happening. I need answers about... so many things."

"You think the Seer will provide answers."

She shrugged as she passed him in her pacing but didn't stop. "I think she'll have something. The shadows pushed the memory of Ode to me. I ignored them when they tried to warn me about the Earthmover. They're very angry with me for ignoring them. I don't think I should ignore them on this."

"For being keepers of the Balance, sworn not to interfere, they sure seem to be doing that a lot."

Rose barked a harsh laugh and folded her arms tight against herself. "You've no idea."

"What do you think we should do?"

"Me?" She finally paused in her pacing. "We?"

"Yes, you. Us."

Rose eyed him. Us? We? She wasn't sure where the 'we' was coming from.

"I'm not a member of your court. I haven't taken a position. I'm just... here until I leave," Rose protested.

"Regardless, I count you as a member of my court. I value your input and advice... and your company."

She blinked at him and frowned. "But this doesn't... this isn't your problem."

"Stopping Gerik and whatever he has planned is. Stopping the Earthmover that is destroying my country is. If finding Ode is the way we solve those two problems, then so be it."

She eyed him. "You have much more faith in these beasts than I do."

He grunted a small chuckle. "Perhaps not faith, but I'm willing to admit they might know more than we do."

The shadows cackled at her from the dark edges. She resisted the urge to bare her teeth at them, but only barely.

"So, how do we find Ode?" he asked.

She cleared her throat, pulled her eyes away from the shadows, and turned to him. "I know she's from the north, across the mountains, but I don't know if she returned there before winter or not."

"How can we possibly find her, then?"

She took a deep breath and jerkily shoved her hands into her coat pockets. "Michael can track almost anyone. If she's to be found, he can find her."

Michael. The clan chief of the Tracers. A small, rare magical group capable of tracking anyone as long as they had a piece of you: hair, a scrap of clothing, something. And for the right amount of coin.

Micah watched her, his eyes blinking slowly. He stood from the chair, and Rose was forced to look up at him as he stepped closer. "If I remember correctly, the two of you made a pact. Something along the lines of promising not to kill any of his people."

"Any more," she muttered. "Yes, we parted badly, and we struck a deal: he wouldn't look for me, and I wouldn't kill anyone else. That was a long time ago. He won't agree to meet with me, and I have nothing he wants badly enough to force him to the table. Without Michael, I don't know how to find Ode quickly."

Micah rubbed his chin, his eyes losing their focus. "This Michael, you had said he is the clan chief, unofficially? Would he be interested in being recognized, officially?"

Rose jerked at his words. "Recognize the clan? The Tracer Clan? You can do that?"

"King, remember?" Micah smirked. "I will check some things, but I see no reason I can't. Would that be something that would keep him at the table?"

She took a deep breath but nodded. "Yes, but..." She let out a long breath. "A magical clan? There hasn't been a crown-sanctioned magical clan since the Dark Times."

A period of years right after the civil war that crowned the first High King. So much damage had been done during the war, much of it by magic users, that they'd been hunted down. The Dark Times saw the end of many magical families. Whole clans disappeared.

"Perhaps it is time that changed," Micah said, his voice soft like he spoke a secret.

"Why would you take this risk just for one Seer?" Rose asked, her voice matching his in an almost whisper.

He studied her, his eyes wary. She was surprised when he didn't answer her. Instead, with a blink and a breath, he asked, "will he be able to look past whatever happened between the two of you to meet with us? To do this for us?"

Rose sucked her teeth and looked away as she thought. Maybe, she thought to herself. "There are very few things he wants more than being recognized by the crown. I think he will. As long as we don't lead with me." She dragged her eyes back to the king. "Are you going to ask me what happened?"

Micah breathed and watched her with a look she didn't understand. "No," he finally said.

Rose eyed him, and when he met and held her stare, she finally nodded. She nodded again, mostly to herself, before turning away with a sigh. She felt the king's eyes on her back as she retreated from the warm, quiet room. She wondered what else he was thinking, being so willing to offer the Tracer chief clanship. She'd read stories, heard the bards tell tales, of a time when there were just as many magical clans as there were tradesman clans now. A time when those who could touch magic had order and protection, respect granted by the kingdom. Those times were long gone. A nearly forgotten era. Something else was going on. There had to be, to take a risk like this. Rose just wasn't sure what it was.

CHAPTER 22

"*G*irl."

Rose jerked awake at the voice and grabbed the dagger on her nightstand.

"That won't help you."

She dropped her eyesight into her shadows as she eased herself upright. Looking around her room, she finally found the faint outline of the ghost woman, who came to stand in front of Rose. Her pale skirts swirled silently around her feet. Rose set her dagger back on her nightstand.

"Again? What are you doing here?"

"We need to talk," J'Teal snipped. "You have too much to learn."

Rose snorted. "So everyone seems to be telling me lately."

"There is a tale you must know, and I don't have the time to tell it."

Rose dropped her bare feet to the floor. "What does that mean?"

J'Teal reached out her pale, ghost hand, and before Rose could flinch away, touched her finger to her forehead.

SHE RAISED HER BLACK SWORD, and shadowy tendrils drifted off the blade. She leveled it at the thin chest of the man in front of her, several meters away.

"You cannot continue, Gerik."

"You can't stop me." His baritone voice rumbled through the ruins of what was once a bustling village.

The buildings lay in ruin around them. Few still stood. Carrion crows circled in the skies, their shadows covering the ground. J'Teal wished she could say the smell revolted her, but it didn't. Not anymore. That time had long gone. Now, the only time she noticed the smell of rotting things was in the few places it was absent. Ironically, the last place she had been that hadn't reeked of dead things and war had been the castle tombs. All those bodies of fallen heroes entombed because of this forsaken war, and the only thing she'd smelled was dust.

Gerik took a step forward, and she let out a short, sharp whistle, and instantly, her shadow beast was beside her.

"We will stop you. We must."

Gerik growled at her and swept his long arm toward her. A shadow leaped up from his hand and flew at her. She flicked her sword across it, and the errant shadow was gone. Her arm shook with the effort to keep the Shadow Blade in this world.

She nodded toward Gerik, and her giant catamount padded forward. Its ears flattened against its head; a low growl echoed over the barren street.

"You've betrayed your duty! The shadows will end this, Gerik. They will end you."

He ignored her words. She wasn't surprised; he always did. She didn't know why she kept trying. Maybe she hoped one day he would see what he'd done. What ruin he'd brought. Instead, he raised his hand. A red glow started to pulse from it, and J'Teal stepped back.

The shadow lunged, and Gerik spun his fist, striking the shadow across the face with his burning fist. The giant cat disappeared, but J'Teal heard the whimpering whines in the Undertunnels. She ran screaming at Gerik, sword raised over her head. Gerik flicked his hand at her as she neared. The ground bucked and rolled under her. Her legs buckled and she fell hard on her side, but years of fighting had her rolling back to her feet within seconds.

"You must do better than that," she yelled and swung her sword at him.

The ground continued to shift and buck around her, but she was used to it. It was an old trick. She leaped through the shadow cast by the looming wall of rock as it crashed over her and emerged running on the other side of it.

Gerik met her blow with his staff, sparks flying off the two as they clashed. J'Teal gripped his staff and pulled him close to her.

"J'Teal," Gerik hissed, his nose nearly touching hers. "You will lose this fight. You should've just let me take it."

She tightened her grip on his staff. She could feel the wrongness the Orthalen emanated from being this close to Gerik. He twisted in her grip, and his elbow slammed into her eyes. She cried out as the pain blinded her more than the blow. She fell with a smothered grunt and felt blood slip down her face. Anger made her quick as she surged back to her feet and rammed her shoulder into his stomach, knocking them both to the ground. They rolled, each trying to gain the advantage.

J'Teal lost the grip on her Shadow Blade, and it disappeared back into the Shadow World. Gerik wrapped his arm around her throat from behind. She tucked her chin to her chest, desperate to protect her airway as he tightened his grip. Dots appeared in the edges of her vision as she struggled to breathe.

She rolled her arm behind her and gripped the back of Gerik's neck as she pulled her head under and out of his hold. J'Teal followed her grip on his neck down and pushed Gerik into the muddy earth. She spun and sat on his back, using her legs to pin his arms. Her heart hammered in her chest, and she could taste iron on her tongue.

"You never did listen when we trained," J'Teal said through gasping breaths. She gulped down air, tried to breathe as her heart raced. She pinned her own arm around his neck, securing the headlock he couldn't. "You always thought you were too good to grapple in the dirt."

She pulled the leather book from her inner pocket and shoved it next to his chest. So many had died securing this item. He clawed at her arm, and it burned as he drew blood, it burned as he broke her skin, but she didn't stop. Couldn't stop. She pushed the throbbing pain to the back of her mind. With her free hand, she grabbed the Orthalen around his neck, its strange, swirling black color stark in the daylight. This blasted thing that started it all. She screamed as her hand burned, steam and smoke rising. She ignored the pain and pulled it close.

Gerik seemed to sense her plan, or at least part of it, and his struggling increased. He bucked and twisted beneath her, but her end was in sight and she would not yield.

Please, she begged the shadows. *Now, before I lose my strength.*

The shadows answered her, as they always have, and they raised the Shadow Blade and leveled it at the book clutched against Gerik's chest.

"This will kill you," he choked.

"I was never meant to live past this."

Now.

The shadows plunged the black Blade through the book and through his ribs. J'Teal screamed as she focused the magic into the book and Gerik, all while pulling on the essence of the Blade. Gerik screamed and arched against the magic yanking his soul away. The magic that pulled his soul into the book.

J'Teals scream joined the air as the red, pulsing magic spread from Gerik and into her veins, taking her life force as it worked. It burned as it traveled, working its way to her heart. She held on with her last breath because this was their last chance....

***

ROSE FELL BACK onto the bed screaming, clutching her head. She curled in on herself and whimpered, her head pounding as if it were about to split in two.

"What did you do to me?" she whimpered. Tears streamed down her cheeks, nausea rolled in her stomach, and her chest burned with the phantom pain of the ancient battle.

"Hush, it'll pass. I gave you my memory. You needed to know. You needed to see what it took. You needed to see how bad it was."

Rose gasped and tried to ease herself out of the ball she'd curled into. "Someone could've heard me scream."

J'Teal tsked. "No one heard anything. I may be dead and lost to them, but the shadows still obey me a touch."

The agonizing pain in her head eased enough for Rose to drop her hands. She opened her eyes to glare at the ghost woman, but her vision was hazy and dark. She held her hand in front of her eyes and blinked.

"Your vision will return."

"I know," Rose sighed and dropped her hand. "If I overuse my magic, I go temporarily light blind. It'll fade."

"For now."

Rose snapped her head up at J'Teal. "What does *that* mean?"

"It means," J'Teal sighed again, "it means that as a Shadowstalker, our cost is our eyesight. Eventually, you will go blind. The more you use your magic, use the shadows, the faster it happens. Those Walkers with the ability to look through the shadows can also go blind. All magic has a cost. This is ours."

What? Her breath caught in her throat. She gasped and her breath came in uncontrollable heaves. Blind! She holds her hand over her mouth, trying desperately to slow down her frantic breathing, only to gasp behind her fingers.

"But you are young and just starting your life with the shadows. That will still be a long time in the future."

Rose swallowed and bit her lips. Deep breaths through her nose, and slowly, she was able to control her breathing. Focus! She needed to focus. She could panic about going blind later. But first, she needed more answers from J'Teal before she disappeared again.

"You said that was your memory?"

"Yes… " J'Teal's voice was soft and sad. "My last memory."

"And you're a ghost now? I don't understand."

J'Teal chuckled, but it was bitter and angry. Rose shrank back on the bed. "No, I am no ghost. But that is a tale for another day. You needed to see what happened between Gerik and me. What it took to contain his mind the first time. We had thought, hoped, that it would contain him forever, or at least, long enough for his mind to fade from existence, but instead, all that happened is that my war is becoming yours."

Rose shook her head and tried to speak, but J'Teal cut her off.

"I am out of time. I don't know if I'll be able to speak to you again. They're angry with me for this."

"But... wait."

J'Teal turned, but then she was gone.

Rose stared dimly at the empty spot, her mind whirling too fast for any rational thought. She wanted to talk about everything that just happened but didn't know who to go to. There was too much change, too many surprises happening, and she didn't know if she had the strength to handle it.

Part of her wanted to seek out the king, but she knew that was a bad idea. Not now. She mustn't be a fool. The bells tolled softly in the distance. It was early morning. Very early, but, she thought, maybe not too early for the captain. She'd sought her advice before.

Rose pulled on clean trousers and a long overcoat on top of her night-shirt and pulled it tight. Shoving her feet into boots, she moved silently down the hall and around the corner to the captain's room. It was early enough that the only people about were the scullery maids. She raised her fist to knock on the door when it swung open.

A tired-looking captain, her long blond hair pulled in a loose plait over her shoulder stared at her.

"What?"

Rose blinked at her and slowly lowered her fist.

"Girl, I heard you coming from down the hall. Your thoughts are a mess. What happened?"

Instantly, guilt burned her belly for waking the captain. How exhausting must her life be, constantly hearing every thought and panic. She shouldn't have come. She opened her mouth, could find no words, and closed it with a clack.

Captain Sayla looked at her up and down and sighed. "Alright, come in then."

Rose breathed a sigh of relief and followed the captain inside the small room, although it was the tiniest bit larger than her own. Large enough, anyway, for at least another chair next to the writing desk.

"Yes, I'm captain. I get the grand accommodations," Captain Sayla drawled while lighting a lamp on the nightstand.

Rose squinted at the light and shrunk away, curling up in the chair near the stove.

"So, what happened?"

She squinted, the room fuzzy and dark even with the lamp. "Do you believe in ghosts?"

The captain tucked her legs under the sheets and pulled a shawl around her shoulders. "Hm, I don't know. The gods do strange things when it suits them and I've seen my own fair share of it. It wouldn't surprise me."

Rose hummed.

"Why, have you seen one?"

"She said she wasn't a ghost. But I don't know what else she'd be. She's J'Teal, the last Shadowstalker. She's been dead for," Rose shrugged, "hundreds of years."

"And you've seen her?"

"Had a rather long chat with her just now."

Captain Sayla grunted but didn't say anything else. She didn't call her crazy or try to convince her otherwise.

Taking a deep breath, Rose launched into what had happened, what she'd seen. And the other times she's seen J'Teal.

"It was like I was there, like it was me. Like I was the one that died," Rose said once she'd finished. "J'Teal knew what she was doing, and she couldn't destroy it. How can I? I don't have any idea what I'm doing!"

"Gods, how many people from the dead are we going to have to deal with?" Captain Sayla asked in a mutter. "Best to look at problems one at a time, sometimes."

Rose sighed but nodded. She didn't have any better answer. She thought she was finally starting to understand her magic, and it turned out she wasn't even close.

"Rose," Captain Sayla said, pulling her from her thoughts. "Most of the time, none of us know what we're doing at all. Especially in life. What matters is how well we try."

She nodded. "The shadows, the wolves… they keep," she fluttered her fingers around her ear. "They're like gnats. Just buzzing and buzzing. They won't leave me alone, won't stop bothering me about how much I'm failing."

Rose turned tired eyes to the captain. "You said you learned how to block out the voices. How do I do that?"

The captain let out a long breath, too long to be a sigh. "Rose. I have no idea how our magic works, but I do know you can't block them out. They are, however so, a part of you. You need to accept that."

She ducked her head, and she could feel her cheeks burning.

"It's clear you have a role you are meant to play in this. Perhaps you start acknowledging that."

She nodded slowly and shifted in her seat.

"How did you learn to control your magic?" Rose asked in a small voice. She didn't know who else to ask, who else she could turn to.

When she looked up at the captain, the woman was smiling softly.

"Archie. When I was young, my magic nearly cost me my sanity. He started teaching me swordplay to distract me. He could see it was starting to wear on me. The constant thoughts. All the fleeting words that went through a person's mind. It was so loud."

Rose nodded and brought her heels onto the chair, wrapping her arms around her legs.

"Archie kept making me duel with him. He hounded me about it. Forced me into a sweaty mess every day with the blasted sword. I finally asked him why he was doing this; why he was bothering with this. He just stared at me and said, 'because you need it'. I finally realized that when I focused on the swordplay, the voices stopped. Swordplay taught me how to focus, how to silence everything but my focus on the sword."

Rose chuckled softly to herself and felt tears gathering in her eyes. Archie had said the same words to her. She sniffed and tried to force back the tears that closed her throat and made her lips shake. She didn't know what it felt like to have someone care, but she thought it felt like this. She had once wondered if she would ever have someone miss her if she disappeared, and she realized these people would miss her. The realization made tears slip silently down her cheeks.

"I told you," the captain said with a smile in her voice, and Rose dragged her watery eyes back to her. "Archie is all gruff and growl, but he's good people."

"Yeah," she murmured. "He is."

The clock chimed the breakfast hour, and Rose slowly uncurled her legs while wiping at her wet face. "I'm sorry. I didn't mean to keep you all morning."

"Not to worry, Rose. Don't forget, we have a meeting with the king later."

She nodded and retreated from the room, a little embarrassed to have stayed as long as she did, but, as she was walking back to her own room, she felt lighter than she had in days. Maybe, she thought, she'd finally found something more than just a home. Erik's words still sat uneasily in her memory, but Rose was starting to realize that her past would always be part of her. Maybe it was time she started living, despite her past.

CHAPTER 23

*R*ose knocked on the door just as Captain Sayla walked up.

They entered the office, Rose's eyes moving over the man already sitting at the table, with papers scattered in front of him. She watched him, his bright eyes watching her, as she sat several chairs away. This was the king's private office; the walls were covered in drawings of horses. Many were ones King Micah had drawn.

"Rose, I don't think you've met the king's newest advisor, Lord Tyman." Captain Sayla gestured at the lord, who nodded at her. "Lord Tyman, this is Rose Trewin I was telling you about."

Rose glanced away from the newest drawing, one of Starlit running through the paddock and over at the captain. Telling him what about me?

"Now," the king said as he entered the room. "I have brought Lord Tyman up on the most recent developments. He is aware of the details involving Ode and Michael."

"Yes," Lord Tyman spoke with a surprisingly soft voice. "I checked the law books for specifics on recognizing clans, and I couldn't find anything saying you couldn't recognize a magical clan. The standard paperwork and charter for clanship will suffice."

The captain made a choking sound. "I'm sorry, did you say clan-ship? For a magical clan?"

Rose shifted. "We need Michael's help to find Ode, and the only way Michael will help us is if he is offered a clanship."

Captain Sayla glanced from Rose to the king and back again. "This will set a whole new precedent. This will have unknown repercussions."

"Quite possibly," the king agreed. "But this is one way to start change and to shift ideas. For too long, an entire section of my people have been living in the shadows and ignored by the public. This offers a chance at true change."

What change was he hoping for? Had he searched out what life for his people was like? When she first met the king, his view and knowledge of his country was pretty limited. She remembered telling him, and she cringed now thinking how boldly she'd chastised him, that he didn't know the country he ruled. Had he taken her words to heart more than she thought?

The captain nodded slowly and glanced back at Rose. She opened her mouth but seemed to rethink whatever she was going to say and closed it with a clack. "How do we proceed then?"

"We need to set a meeting with Michael." The king looked to Rose.

"He won't come to the castle. He'll think it's a trap for something. He's too cautious and too protective of his people to come here. Not all of his deals are on the wrong side of the law, but enough of them are."

"He can't be that protective of them if he cuts them out of his graces," Lord Tyman said.

Rose slowly turned to look at the lord and clucked her tongue. "You catch up fast."

He nodded, not flinching under her gaze. "I've read the reports."

Tyman was talking about Simone, the Tracer bounty hunter that had captured Rose last summer. Simone had been captured in turn and exiled to the Mercian Islands to live out the rest of her miserable life as a servant and caretaker to those Shields who trained and retired to the island.

She grunted softly and started to turn away when he said, "you never answered the question."

"I didn't hear one," she snapped, not sure she liked this lord yet. "But to answer your unasked question, if someone put the others at risk or disregarded his rules, then yes, he would cut them out. Loyalty means the world to him. More than family."

Lord Tyman nodded and seemed satisfied with the answer. He turned back to the king, and when Rose looked away, she was met with the glaring look from the captain. Archie had said less backtalk. This was less, Rose told herself.

"So, we go to him." The king asked, "where is he?"

"He keeps a house in the city."

"Finally, something easy." The king heaved a sigh. "Will he be receptive to visitors?"

Rose held back a sardonic laugh, though a rough snort did escape. She could only imagine what Michael would do if she showed up at his door, if she even made it past the gates. "It may be best if we meet him somewhere. Neutral ground. One of the local taverns would do nicely."

The king nodded and cast a wary glance at the two advisors. "Then, we shall send him a message to meet. Miss Trewin, I assume you know the best location." He waited for her to nod before continuing. "Good. Then once the meeting is set, we shall go."

"When you say 'we', Sire, who do you mean?" Lord Tyman asked.

The king got a glint in his eye, a slight tick to the corner of his lips, that made Rose worry just the slightest.

"Myself, Miss Trewin, and I suspect a few guards."

Clamoring broke out instantly. The captain broke her stoic demeanor and started shouting, and Lord Tyman tried to shout over her. They both were yelling how insane the plan was and how out of the question it was. Rose watched, mouth slowly hanging open, as the king simply smiled and looked damn pleased with himself. He is out of his mind.

"As king," Lord Tyman was saying after putting a hand on Captain Sayla's arm to stall her shouts. "You cannot be making deals with people in the darkness of taverns."

Rose glanced at the captain, who was red in the face and breathing heavily.

"A king doesn't deal with people who refuse to come to the castle. You don't stoop to their demands before they've even made them."

"Why not?" King Micah asked Lord Tyman. "Why can't I? We need this man's help, and I have something he wants to ensure it. I have been repeatedly reminded how cruel the world can be to magic wielders. Why should I demand Michael come here when he has no reason to trust me? What do I actually lose by going to him instead?" His voice had gotten harsher and harsher. By the time he was finished speaking, the king was leaning across the table.

Rose was reminded he was a king, and while he was a quiet-spoken man most of the time, he commanded armies.

"Your safety," Captain Sayla spoke up, her voice softer than Rose had expected it to be for how red her face was. "You will risk your safety unnecessarily. I can appreciate what you are trying to say to Michael by going to him, but I don't think the message is worth the risk."

"We can send someone else," Lord Tyman said. "One of us to relay your wishes to him and arrange for him to come to the castle to speak with you then."

"No, Lord Tyman," King Micah said, "I will go. Aaron will ensure my safety, and in case everyone has forgotten, I'm a trained swordsman in my own right. Captain, send one of your officers with the invitation to Michael. I plan for this to happen within the next several days."

She nodded stiffly. "Yes, Sire."

"Aaron already knows to prepare a detail for when we leave. I will inform everyone once the officer returns with Michael's response."

Rose stood with everyone else, avoiding the captain's eyes as they retreated from the room. Once the door was closed behind them, Rose let out a long breath. Lord Tyman grumbled something and stormed off down the hallway.

"Did you know about this?"

Rose snapped her head to look at Captain Sayla. "No! Did the look on my face imply I knew anything about this? Did my thoughts?" She shoved her hands into her pockets and started down the hall. "I knew he wanted to offer the Tracers clanship, but I didn't think he'd go all—" She shrugged and looked over at the captain next to her. "Stupid!"

Captain Sayla was quiet as Rose's words seemed to sink in. "Ah," she finally said. "I had thought this might've been your doing."

"Why in all the hells would I tell the king to go meet with the Tracer leader, who only sometimes acts above board, in a tavern?" Rose hissed.

"Because," the captain hissed back as they walked, "he told me you are always telling him to go out among his people."

"I meant for a walk!" Rose shouted and was hushed by several people walking by. "I meant," she continued quieter once the group had passed, "to go out for a ride. Or to visit the market. Or the theater. Something normal. Something safe."

Captain Sayla sighed and rubbed her forehead. "Alright, well, fine then. I'll get the address information from you once I have an officer ready to go out with the king's message."

Rose nodded and slipped away down another hallway. She worked her way through the halls to the Light Horse Common Room. Her hand found the lump of ore that sat in her pocket. She'd forgotten about the mysterious ore in the chaos of Caleb's arrival. It had sat forgotten in her pocket until her fingers grazed over the smooth ore in between the rough lumps of rock and dirt.

What in the hells is this? Luckily, she knew someone perfectly set for research.

She turned into the Common Room and did a cursory look around for Erik. She told herself she wasn't afraid to face him again and didn't care if he was here. But she knew she'd be lying. Instead, she was surprised to see Caleb sitting on the battered old couch with a pile of books and papers taking up the entire couch.

The rest of the room was empty, and Rose moved to sit across from Caleb in the old armchair.

"What're you doing in here?"

Caleb looked up at her, startled. "Captain said I could use the room. The old libraries are... "

"Yeah," she said softly when his words stopped. "Have you found anything interesting?"

He shook his head and moved the current book off his lap. "No."

"I was wondering if you might look into something else for me while you're in the libraries."

He watched her with tired eyes and nodded.

"That rock I nicked from the college, I don't know what it is."

"I was actually thinking about your weird rock." Caleb rubbed the back of his neck. "I don't know why... "

Rose kicked her feet up onto the small, scratched table between their seats and crossed her ankles.

"It's a weird color, right?" She nodded at him, and he continued, "but it has the same sort of shimmer that Cirkus steel does. That steel was forged by a specific family of Earthmovers, the Revasts."

Cirkus steel was a rare metal, and the knowledge to forge more had apparently died with the Revasts. It repelled magic. Blocked it. Rose glanced down at the marks circling her wrists from where the Cirkus steel had burned her.

"Do you think it could be a similar type of metal?" Caleb asked, drawing her back into the conversation. "The world is full of opposites. It likes to balance itself out."

Rose couldn't stop rolling her eyes. Balance. It all came back to the blasted Balance.

"When I was reading for more information about–" he glanced around the room, and Rose smiled, "about Shademakers I stumbled across an old mage book. It was saying how one of the basic principles of magic is that it repels each other, but like magic pulls toward each other."

Rose pulled out the lump and held it up to the firelight. "You think this thing is the opposite of the Cirkus steel? The balance to the metal that repels?"

Caleb shrugged. "Just an idea. I'll keep looking, though."

She moved the ore around in the light, watching as the orange glow from the fire danced off the iridescent surface. It shimmered purple, nearly black in the light.

The memory hit her hard and fast, so fast she dropped the rock into her lap with a gasp. It's the same material Gerik's old necklace was made of. That odd, strange metal that had burned J'Teal's hand when she grabbed it.

"You alright?"

"Caleb," Rose picked the rock back up and leaned forward, dropping her feet back to the ground. "Have you found anything in the old histories around J'Teal mentioning a thing called the Orthalen?"

He blinked at her and glanced over at the pile of papers. "Only that it was that relic she destroyed. Should I be looking?"

"Maybe," she murmured and looked again at the shimmering metal.

She was missing something, some key element. Why was Goron roaming around the country? He was destroying things. Things that would make travel and trade difficult, yes, but that couldn't be his only goal. His movements seemed too random. What if he was looking for something? What if he was looking for the Orthalen? She glanced at the rock. Or something to make a new one?

"Hear me out on this," Rose said and pinned Caleb with her stare. The young man sat forward, matching her stance. "Let's pretend this," she held up the rock, "is the opposite of Cirkus steel, and instead of blocking and repelling magic, it channels it; hones it. What would someone be able to do with an item made from this? Would they be able to use all magic?"

Caleb shrugged, his wide eyes going to the ore in her hand. "The mage book I found was missing a lot of pages, but everything I was able to read said a person can only use one type of magic. Would something like that be able to override magic's natural aversion to itself?"

Yessss, the shadows growled through the shadows. Their growl was angry, bitter. It made her head hurt, and her skin crawl. It sounded like the promise of death.

Twisted. Defiled. Made wrong, but yes. He broke the Balance. Betrayed his duty!

Rose groaned and held her free hand to her head, rubbed against her temple. "Alright, alright," she murmured. "Settle down."

"Huh?"

She waved him off. "Not you." She breathed through her nose at the relief in her skull as the pressure receded. "Trust me when I say we're onto something. Add looking for any reference of an Orthalen to your list of things."

"Did they just talk to you?" he asked quietly, his eyes darting to every darkened corner in the room. "The gods in the shadows?"

Rose laughed, loud and boisterous, full of snorting and gasping breaths.

"What!"

She wheezed, trying to stop her giggles. "Gods," she scoffed and took more breaths. "Whatever they are, they are not gods. Pains in the ass, sure."

A growl echoed through the shadows.

You are a pain in my ass.

The shadows chuffed at her.

And I think you enjoy it.

"There is an old god, rarely talked about and mostly forgotten. But there is one. The name for this god has changed over time, many times. But he was the god of magic and creation. Destruction."

"And you think the beasts in the shadows is this god?" Rose asked, her voice incredulous.

Caleb shrugged again. "Who knows?"

She grunted and eyed the shadow along the wall, cast by the fire's light being blocked by the hearth. Who knew?

"I'll look for anything about the Orthalen. The old library, much of it is still inaccessible because of the fire damage. Your captain said workers are trying to clear it, but," he shrugged again. "it's slow going. Much of the support for the floors above have been damaged so they have to replace them before they can remove things. But I'll look.

From the things I've found so far, it looks like most of the items are from several hundred years ago. The chances are good."

She nodded and smiled at him. He echoed her smile, even if it didn't quite reach his eyes. The dimples were back, though.

"Thanks. Now." She stood and held out her hand to him. She knew he was too polite to ignore it and smiled to herself when she was right and he took it. She pulled him to his feet. "Let's find some food."

CHAPTER 24

*M*ariah strode down to the Shield's training rooms, her blood pounding in her ears as she did. The Shields she passed must've seen the rage in her eyes and wisely left her alone. She didn't often venture down to this section of the castle, much preferring to train in the fields and the clear air over the sweat stink of their hall. How could he be so stupid? She clenched her hands at her sides. As she neared the training room at the end of the corridor, the sounds of swords clashing together became louder, and eventually the grunts and shouts could be heard through the thick doors.

The two Shields standing guard on either side of the door glanced at her, then at each other, before taking a step away. Smart boys, she thought with a glance at them before pushing her way into the training room.

She found him, training with Aaron near the far wall, and her blood started to boil all over again. She stripped her uniform jacket off and tossed it at a nearby trainee as she stormed toward Micah and Aaron. As she passed a rack of training swords, she pulled one at random, spinning it until it rested in the palm of her hand. Aaron glanced at her over Micah's shoulder and ended the sparring match. He jerked his chin at Mariah, and Micah half-turned over his shoulder to look at her.

Shit, I'm in trouble. She looks mad/furious/scary. Micah's thoughts tumbled at her as he turned and wiped his sweaty forehead on his loose sleeve.

"Aaron," she spoke low, her eyes never leaving Micah. "I need to have a word with the king. I'll take your spot for now."

Aaron glanced between the two of them and backed away. Mariah spun the sword again in her hand, flipping it up and around.

"Am I going to like what this conversation is about?"

"No," she snapped and swung her sword. It was lighter than her normal sword, and the balance was off, but a sword was a sword, and she could handle any of them like a master.

Micah met her blows and soon they fell into a give and take of strikes and parries. Her anger made her blows sharp and quick. Micah's eyes grew pinched, almost as if he had forgotten she'd gained Swordmaster status long before he had.

"Are you out of your mind?" she asked him with a sharp swing at his ankles.

"Excuse me?"

Mariah's sword caught his, and she spun their blades until he was forced to step back to free it. "Clanship."

"It's a good idea!" Micah snapped and thrust his sword at her.

Mariah parried it away easily and slapped the flat of her blade hard on his exposed arm. "It's reckless, dangerous. You can't know the consequences of this to act this rashly."

Micah shouted with the sting of the hit and stepped back. "I'm not being rash."

Mariah sensed anger coming from his thoughts at that statement.

"What planning have you done?" She thrust, hard and fast, and forced Micah to stumble back in order to deflect it. "What conversations have been had?" Thrust. "Have the lords been consulted?" Thrust. "No!" Her last word was punctuated with a hard swing that had him crashing against the wall with the force of her strike.

"You're being reckless."

"I don't need this lecture." Micah clenched the hilt of his sword. "I made the decision. What I believe to be the best course of action."

"You do need this lecture," she hissed at him. "Because you seem to have forgotten you're the king of these lands, not some boy to run around doing as he pleases. You need to start acting like it. And that means picking a wife." Micah opened his mouth, but Mariah slapped the flat of the sword against his chest and held it there. "A wife... who is of noble birth."

Micah glowered at her, and it was almost enough to make her step back, but dammit, she'd faced down angrier men than this in her career. "There is potential war in the south with the tribes. Gerik is planning we-don't-know-what. There is a madman running around destroying the country. And you're risking even more conflict with the lords by offering clanship to magical clans. There is a time for this," she tapped his chest again, "and it is not now."

"I have a plan."

Mariah let the sword tip slip to the ground. "Oh? Tell me this plan." She feared she knew his plan but hoped she was wrong.

No. No. I don't know. Haven't thought it through/it's going to work. "I need to secure a partnership."

"Preferably with the northern lords," Mariah muttered. "Daniella comes to mind."

Micah sucked his teeth but Mariah continued. "No. Securing the loyalty of the magical clans. Finally uniting the two halves of my country."

Mariah blinked at him as the pieces slowly fell together. "Are you," she growled at him, "out of your gods-given mind?"

No/Yes/Maybe. It'll work. "No one has partnered the magical clans in nearly a century. They haven't aligned with anyone."

"Because the magical clans were hunted to near extinction during the years that followed the civil war. Why do you think they'll align with you now? Because of one clanship? How do you plan to align with—" Her teeth clacked shut so hard she felt it in her eyes. "Does Rose know you want to use her like this?"

"Use?" he shouted, and Mariah took a step back at the fury that hit her with that word. "You think I want to use her? You misunderstand me. I want to secure a partnership with the magical clans. The

first step of that is clanship for the Tracers. After that, moving...
slowly... to approaching other clans. Gaining their trust. Further
clanships."

"And what? Marry some lord's daughter who has a secret magical
ability?"

He shrugged, and Mariah felt her blood boil. "Something like that.
This will take time. Many careful conversations need to happen. A lot
of watching and waiting."

She caught just the quietest of whispers coming from him: wait for
Rose. He better not be planning what that sounded like. His thought
was so quiet she almost missed it, but she didn't. And with it, she felt
all the trepidation, loneliness, and hope in that little thought. Gods, he
was just as bad as Rose. Her heart ached for them suddenly at that
moment.

"You think I am being rash, that no thought has gone into this.
You're wrong." Micah heaved a large breath. "This is only the first
step, testing the waters. Any further steps will be determined by this
one."

Mariah planted the tip of the sword on the floor and planted her
free hand on her hip. She was breathing fast, but it had nothing to do
with the little bout of swordplay and everything to do with the idiocy
coming out of his mouth. Her blood was starting to boil again.

"You can't be serious. That'll never work. You can't repair generations of hate and mistrust with one clanship and a marriage. The lords
will destroy you."

"You forget yourself, Mariah," Micah snapped, and Mariah took a
step back. "I'm not such a fool. I know this will take time. Many, many
conversations need to happen. Many things need to go right. I know
this. I'm still working on many of the details, but I know the clanship
for the Tracers is the first step."

She probed his thoughts just the slightest, pushed into the raging,
confusing thoughts of this ridiculous plan, and felt the utter conviction
in them. He didn't know how this was going to work, but he wouldn't
be swayed from it. Another thought struck her as she watched Micah,
his eyes cautiously watching her, and her sword. Last she spoke with

Rose, she was still very confused about Micah, about what she was feeling for him.

"And what does Rose have to say about this plan?" She watched his eyes narrow. "You haven't even talked to her about it, have you? You might not think you're using her, but you are. You're using her connections, her magical ability. Have you even told her any of this?"

Can't ask her.

Too afraid.

She's afraid.

Nonono.

Mariah grunted and stepped back from the chaos coming from Micah. The distance did nothing for the sound bombarding her, but it did help her center herself and quiet the stream of thought. "You're a fool if you think she won't see what you're doing, eventually. You risk losing her entirely if you don't talk to her."

"It is hard," he started and had to unclench his jaw, "to broach some conversations. She is learning to trust and trust me, but she is still very hesitant about her magic and her past."

She continued softer, feeling for him and the confusion that was in his thoughts. "You have to talk to her. If she finds out this is your plan before you tell her yourself, she will feel used and cheated. You'll destroy any trust she has in you, in us, in this place."

"I know. I have a plan."

She sighed deeply through her nose. His naivety, his wish, and his belief that people were better than they were was part of what made him a great king. If only he wasn't always so optimistic. Micah was sometimes too much like his grandmother. Most of the time, that was a good thing. But his heart was a gentle, fragile thing, just like his grandmother's had been. She might not be able to outright stop him, but she could help to urge him to the right decision.

"This is a long play," Mariah said while looking around for the trainee who had her jacket. "If you're going to pursue this, you need to take precautions." She finally found her jacket, clenched in the hands of the young trainee who stared at her with eyes so wide she worried they might fall out. She held out her hand and curled her fingers at him, and with a jerk, he ran over, depositing her jacket into her waiting hand.

"Yes, ma'am," Micah said softly behind her. "I am appropriately chastised."

"Good. You needed it."

"I'd forgotten how great a fighter you are." He came forward and added his sword to the rack. "It's been so long since we've sparred; I'd forgotten."

"I can tell," she quipped. "You got sloppy."

"I wasn't expecting my friend and advisor to attack me in such a way."

"I was angry."

"No!" he guffawed. "Were you? Couldn't tell."

Mariah chuckled to herself despite her apprehension. "How is Rose?"

"Why do you think I would know?"

She grunted. "I know what happens in my wing, to my people. Even if she's still fighting the idea."

"Quite right," he murmured and nodded. "She is… tired. I think weary might be a better word for what she's feeling. She won't tell me, not really, but I see it in her eyes. She talks of nightmares plaguing her sleep. Something about the college's destruction is bothering her more than she'll say."

"I thought she'd gotten over her sleeping problems." At least, Mariah had stopped hearing the nightmares at night.

"No," Micah was shaking his head. "She'll sleep for a time in the Solarium while I'm drawing. I think that's the only time she manages a peaceful sleep."

She grunted softly that she'd heard him and slipped her jacket back on. A mess… the pair of them, she sighed to herself. A mess in love. She sighed again, her heart clenching. They needed to get their mess sorted out before they both ended up with broken hearts. It was a pain she wouldn't wish on either of them. A loneliness they couldn't understand. Her mind drifted to Nico, just for a second, and the blinding loneliness that came with that thought. She hoped these two never had to feel that kind of pain.

"I'll let Aaron resume his training with you. Listen to me, Micah, listen to what I've said. You are playing a dangerous game. Please, please think about what you are doing."

"Always," he said and laid a hand on her shoulder. "If this is a fool's plan and no hope will come for it, I will accept that. I will not ruin my kingdom over this. I remember our history. I know what happened to King Edmeyerz."

The disastrous king who'd chased his mistress into ruin and had nearly fallen into another civil war in the process.

Mariah took a deep breath and hoped he was right.

"Let me see if I can start to repair the damage done during the Dark Times. If not," he shrugged, and Mariah could see the sadness in his eyes at the thought, "then so be it."

Mariah smiled at him and patted his hand on her shoulder. "Good."

She dipped her head in a small bow and retreated from the training room, although much slower than she had arrived.

CHAPTER 25

*R*ose was curled in the overstuffed, beaten armchair in the Light Horse Common Room with a warm cup of tea in her hands. The fire was large and warm. Luci was sitting against the far wall. The two still didn't get along or talk much. Her ankle was healed, luckily it hadn't been broken, but storms had stalled her return to the south. Luci would never say it, but Rose suspected she was impatient to return to her assignment. She'd told Rose what she'd seen and experienced on her trip back to the castle. The destruction Goron had caused, was continuing to cause, was terrifying. Rose was beginning to doubt they would be able to stop him. He was from a time when magic was prevalent and people understood and knew magic. What chance did they have now?

Caleb lounged on the couch across from her, his nose buried in another book. Most of the time the quiet scholar kept his nose buried in books. It must've been familiar. What he knew. She couldn't blame him. Losing your entire world could shatter you. She'd know. She'd lost hers enough.

Rose stretched her foot out and poked Caleb's knee with the toe of her boot. "What are you reading?"

He jerked and looked up. Rose sipped her tea and curled her leg back under her.

"Uh," he shifted and closed the book. "It's a history of King Jonas. I thought it might be good to know more about the first High King and the victor of the civil war." He shrugged.

Rose hummed and nodded. "Anything interesting?"

Caleb shrugged again. "He was smart but also sad. This covers his life after the war, and he never seemed like a happy man. He married, had children. His son inherited the crown and was the start of the Blackmer reign. But he never seemed happy."

She nodded and curled around her warm cup.

"Are you getting used to the castle?" she asked when he fell into silence again.

Caleb looked around the dark room, lit mostly by the giant fire and a few splattering of candles. "It reminds me a lot of the college. I am getting used to it. Slowly. Being able to leave each night helps, I think."

The door to the common room opened. Rose glanced at the door, only to look away as Erik limped in. She'd tried her best to avoid the man after his angry words. She knew he wouldn't say those things to her when he had a clear mind, when he was aware of his words, but ale made your tongue loose against the worst of words. Many times they were truthful.

"Erik?" Luci asked from her corner. "What happened to you?"

Erik sighed, his shoulders hung as if under a weight, and he trudged into the room. He sank to the ground in front of the fire, his body shivering. "I was visiting my family, my aunt. She lives a few days' ride north of here. On my way back, I had to divert several days east to avoid all the damaged roads."

"Roads?" Caleb asked.

Erik nodded without looking away from the flames. "So many roads are destroyed. Some are completely washed out; others are covered in so much rubble it'll take weeks to clear them. The Earth-mover," he paused and sighed, though the sound was harsh, "is ruining roads. It'll make trade impossible in the spring."

Shit. Rose met Caleb's worried eyes.

"But that's not even the worst part."

Rose turned her eyes back to Erik. "What is?" she asked quietly, wanting to know but not wanting his attention.

He turned and looked at her over his shoulder with sad eyes. "The refugees."

She frowned and glanced at Caleb and back. "From where?"

"The south."

Luci's sharp intake of breath pulled everyone's attention.

Erik continued, his voice softer, "I spoke with a few of them on the road. Many are moving north, fleeing their homes. The tribesmen from the territories are attacking. Nothing like what they did in the fall. These are planned and organized war parties. They've taken several smaller towns near the border."

Caleb muttered a prayer, and Luci surged to her feet, vibrating with anger. Her hands clenched at her sides, and she turned, took two angry steps to the door only to turn back and collapse back into her chair with a harsh curse.

"I just came from briefing the king. He's sending more soldiers to the south. They have orders to drive them back, to take the villages back, and hold the border. Luci, you're being sent south as soon as you can, regardless of the weather, to update the orders of those at the border."

She nodded, once with a sharp jerk of her chin.

"Captain Sayla will be speaking with you soon to give you the orders."

"How many dead?" Rose asked quietly.

Erik shrugged. "I don't know. I don't know if what I heard was true or an exaggeration from many times of being retold. Either way, King Micah is acting swiftly and harshly, finally."

Rose held her tongue even as she wanted to snap at him. He didn't know what the king was thinking, didn't know the stress he was under. But she held her tongue. It wasn't her place.

The common room door opening again brought everyone's attention to the door as Captain Sayla looked in.

"Luci," she said, her eyes hard. "I assume Erik's already talked to you."

"Yes, ma'am."

The captain nodded. "Good. Follow me to my office. We have things to go over."

Luci was already up and walking toward the door before the captain had finished. Rose wasn't surprised. She'd heard Luci was from the south. This news must be very personal to her. She half wondered how she would feel if her home was attacked, and she found she was indifferent. She hadn't been to her home province in years, and even when she was living at home with her father, she'd never really had an invested interest in the area. It was land. An area. The small valley her home was settled in grew juicy peaches and sweet corn. But it was never a place she held dear.

The thought of soldiers coming north to the castle, to the city of Haven that the castle overlooked, brought a tight grip of fear to her chest. She had people here, people she wanted to keep safe. Archie, who she still teased relentlessly about his nickname, and Clara, who was thriving around her father. Sam, Luci, and even Erik, all the other Light Horse Officers, were important. She had somehow, without trying or even wanting to, surrounded herself with people she cared about and who cared about her. She started to build a home here, and now that the idea, the thought, and the possibility that it could be in danger, brought a new type of fear to her belly.

Erik pushing himself off the floor brought her attention back to the room. He stopped in front of her, and Rose dragged her eyes to his. *Shit.*

How was she supposed to avoid him if he stands right in front of her?

"Rose," Erik started, and she saw him swallow, his throat bobbing. "I think... I need to apologize– "

"No," she cut him off. "No, let's just... pretend that never happened." She didn't want an apology, didn't feel she deserved one. His words had been harsh, they had been almost cruel, but they hadn't been wrong.

He watched her carefully before nodding. "Okay."

She nodded, feeling awkward and too aware Caleb was watching her and Erik.

"So, yeah… " Rose said slowly, and he nodded and stepped back jerkily, retreating from the room.

"What was that about?" Caleb asked, his eyes wide but a small smile tilting the corner of his lips.

"Don't you worry about it," Rose said and tucked her legs under herself in her chair.

"Can I ask a different question?" Caleb asked softly, and Rose narrowed her eyes at his tone. "About magic?"

Rose watched him a moment longer before shrugging one shoulder. "You can ask. I can't promise to answer."

He nodded like he'd expected that answer. "I was working on a little project before… " he trailed off before shaking himself and continuing. "I was working on trying to categorize the magics and their side effects. I wanted to see if each type of magic had the same side effect or if it was dependent on the person." He shrugged again and met her eyes. "While reading today, one of the books mentioned something about the magical cost and I was wondering what yours was."

"Why?"

He shrugged again. "No reason now, I suppose, aside from my own curiosity and three years of destroyed research. I never found a reason why it happens."

Rose turned back to look at the fire, a chill going down her spine as she remembered J'Teal's warning. She didn't want to think about going blind. She didn't want to have to face that. Not yet. "I don't know why. Maybe because nothing comes for free in the world."

"Balance," the shadows hissed from the Undertunnels. "Everything must have it's balance. We give, we take. The world must have order, or else chaos will reign."

Rose thought about that for a second and was starting to understand why the shadows were so focused on the Balance. She was starting to see how everything was so carefully managed, each side with an opposite. The shadows managed it all. Ruled them all in that Balance.

Maybe they are gods, she thought with a small, weary smile. She expected them to chuff or growl at her, but they remained oddly silent.

She sighed. She didn't want to talk about it, but he'd lost so much. She remembered he was a scholar without a school and couldn't bring herself to deny him this bit of familiarity. "Generally, it makes me tired, like a physical drain on me. But it can also give me headaches and make my eyes hurt," she paused, unable to shake off J'Teal's words.

"Eventually," she said softly, almost too softly to be heard, "I'll go blind."

Why had she told him that? Her thoughts drifted to the king and how she hadn't told him. She didn't want him to know. Not yet. She didn't know if she could bear the pity in his eyes.

Caleb took a sharp breath and leaned back.

"I'm sorry."

She shrugged and hooked her legs over the arm of the chair, sitting sideways. "You're not doing it."

"You're very… calm about it."

Only on the outside. "I've had many things taken from me in my life. What's one more?"

Caleb smiled tiredly at her and stood with a stretch and a yawn. "I'm going to head out to bed. You should too."

Rose grunted, knowing she was still in an argumentative relationship with sleep, and poured the last of her tea. How could she sleep now, knowing the missing warriors had resurfaced only to attack with a new vengeance?

She watched Caleb leave and turned her attention back to the flames. It would be some time before she could attempt to sleep, only to toss and turn the rest of the night.

CHAPTER 26

*H*e couldn't sense it. As an Earthmover, a Revast, Goron should be able to sense any item crafted with their magic. The magic seeped into the stone, the earth, and it left a miasma that could be sensed. The fact that he couldn't meant it was being hidden. He doubted it was destroyed; only another Earthmover could destroy the Orthalen.

But who would be hiding it? Had Jonas hidden it at the end of the war? Why couldn't he find it! His jaw ached from clenching his teeth, and he had to remind himself to relax his jaw. He had two tasks: find the Orthalen and find the Anchor. And he couldn't do either!

Had the years asleep stolen some part of him? His hands clenched into fists at his side as he stormed up the hill. This damned time, this place, had stolen his magic. Made him weak. He hated it here.

As he approached the small town, he knew it as Maytar, he sensed the spicy, tingling power running down his spine. His clan had settled this mining area years before his time. His grandparents had molded the stone in the area into great longhouses for his clan members. It was those houses he sensed now, and knowing they had survived time, warmed his cold insides. Not much from his time had survived. This land was foreign to him now, strange. It wasn't his home anymore, but perhaps this place was still as he remembered it.

He moved through the dense trees to crest the edge of the valley. Down the hill, the trees were sparse from the years of mining in this small, sheltered valley. The area was rich in Falkus ore, and even in his time, there had been extensive mining done. It showed in the landscape.

Goron made his way quickly down the hillside and started moving through the newer buildings. The design was different, the building materials were different. He glared at the wood buildings, the stacked brick homes, and shops. These were not the homes of his people. Where was the carved stone? The beautiful fluid rock of the Earthmovers?

"Oi," a middle-aged man shouted at him from his shop door.

The man, his beard long and wiry, walked quickly over to him. The man wore a blacksmith's apron, the thick leather marred by black stains and burns. His hands were a worker's hands, covered in calluses and scars.

"What're you doing wearing only that?"

Goron glanced down at his simple trousers, worn leather boots, and his beloved leather long coat. His body didn't feel cold or heat. No Earthmover did. His breath puffing in front of his face and the snow covering the ground told him it was cold, but he would never feel it.

"I'm looking for the mine foreman," Goron spoke, his voice a low counter to the blacksmith's.

The man looked Goron up and down before frowning. "Which mine, lad? The tin or the quartz?"

Goron felt a shiver of panic move down his spine, and he quickly looked around the buildings surrounding the small alley. "The Falkus mine."

The blacksmith frowned and took a step back. "What rock have you been living under? Falkus hasn't been mined here for…" he trailed off with a shrug. "Gods, I don't know. Decades."

Goron ground his teeth, his hands fisting at his sides.

"I'm surprised you even know what that is," the smith continued.

"Did your ancestors also settle this valley looking for that magical ore?"

"Are you saying there are no Falkus veins or ore in this valley?"

"Lad," the smith spoke softly but firmly, "there isn't any Falkus in Rhivony. It's practically a forgotten item."

Goron turned away and retreated from the small town and the blacksmith's confused calls. The ore was gone. He couldn't smith a new Orthalen. Goron let out an angry huff of breath, his hands clenching and unclenching at his sides. He had to find the Orthalen now. Replacing it wasn't an option.

As he climbed the hill, he turned back to look down at the town, the abandoned longhouses, and his forgotten life. Anger filled him. The burning, rage-filled anger at how much had been taken from him, how much he'd lost in this war.

He reached down in the earth, his magic flaring to life. He reached with his magic down to the maze of tunnels and shafts of the mines, new and forgotten. They stretched out and across the entire valley. Some moved deep into the mountains at the northern border. Goron weaved his fingers into all those tunnels.

Then he flexed his hand into a fist.

His magic curled and writhed, and the vast network of mines collapsed as his anger pulled them down.

Dust clouds puffed above the few open shafts first, then a rumble filled the air. The screaming started as the ground shook and the valley fell in on itself.

Goron turned away as the sounds of stone crashing and screams being silenced echoed through the trees. He needed to find the Anchor, and to do that he needed to find her. Gerik had told him she was at the castle last summer. He'd start there.

Then... then he'd search anew for the Orthalen.

CHAPTER 27

*J*n the days waiting for Michael, the king received two additional notices of destruction caused by Goron. This time a town was destroyed; a small mining town deep in the mountains and most of the valley it sat in. Now a sheer rock face where a mountain range had once been. Caleb had been tasked with looking for any possible significance to the town. It seemed out of the way from all the other destruction caused by Goron.

When Michael finally did respond, the message had been simple. No room for assumptions or guessing at any intentions. He agreed to meet. Nothing more. Rose still couldn't believe he'd responded at all.

The captain had informed her of the plan: Aaron, the king dressed as a commoner, Rose, and Caleb would travel into town and meet Michael just after sunset. More Shields would go into town hours earlier to check the area and find strategic positions in the event of an attack at the tavern. It sounded insane. She couldn't believe the king was actually going into town to meet with Michael, someone who didn't have the best of reputations, and that he was going with the offer of clanship. She wondered how much of this was because of those conversations she'd had with the king, berating him for not going among his people.

She wasn't sure how she felt about that and how much influence it meant she might have. Influence wasn't something people like her had. She hadn't meant to start anything. She'd spoken without truly thinking.

She worried her lip between her teeth while she waited at the stables. The horses were ready, Starlit snorting and ears flicking. The sun was starting to drop behind the mountains, casting a red glow across the sky. Caleb joined her in the stables not long later, his eyes wide and a little pale. He joined her near the stalls where she was leaning.

"Why are you coming again?" she asked.

Caleb shrugged and thrust his hands in his pockets. "The king wants me to be the scribe for the meeting since my apprentice at the archives covered transcribing."

Rose grunted and folded her arms. She wasn't sure if the king was having him come along as another way to keep him busy or if his scribe skills were really that in demand. She wasn't sure she liked Caleb being this close to one of her bigger secrets, but she had to admit he was nice company. He had a gentleness to him that seemed to settle even her worse moods.

"Why does everyone seem so worried about this? Captain Sayla seemed... " he paused. "She seemed upset with the plan."

Rose grinned. Oh, the captain was upset. Very upset. "I think everyone is worried about the king going into such a public place with so few guards. Michael is... well, he's not harmless, but he won't be the one to worry about if things go badly."

"Who are we worried about, then?"

She huffed a breath. There were a number of Tracers who were more than a little furious with her still. "No one."

"No one?" he asked with a quirked eyebrow.

She let out a loud breath through her nose. "I have a history with Michael and his people."

Caleb started to say something else, but the king walked up in time to stall whatever the words were. Rose turned to greet him but stopped when she saw what he was wearing. She stared at him, a frown creasing her forehead.

"The captain said you'd be dressing the part of a commoner."

King Micah looked down at himself then back up at her. "What's wrong with this?"

"Everything!" Rose yelled.

The clothes were plain, at least he got that part right, but everything was far too fine. The trousers were too clean and the embroidery too neat on his breast pocket. It had embroidery! The quality of clothing was enough to mark him as different from the other workers and common men.

"Don't you have anything without embroidery?" Rose asked as she circled him. "Gods, even your boots are new."

"And the problem with that?" Micah's voice started to sound defensive.

Rose stood in front of him and crossed her arms over her chest. "You look like you haven't worked a day in your life. You look like a noble. You look like money. Tan colors and simple cuts aside, you'll stand out."

"What did you want? For me to borrow clothing?"

"Yes," Rose nodded for extra emphasis, "that would've been a great idea. Do you know how I spotted Nico as a king's man? His clothing, while dirty and old and torn, had fine stitching. The dyes were deep and even. The quality was good when it was new. Others might not know what they're seeing, but they'll notice it all the same."

"Oh," the king sighed and looked at her dejectedly.

She drummed her fingers on her arm where they were crossed. "I can fix this."

She turned and glanced around the stables at the various guards standing around, the stable workers.

"You," she pointed to a stable worker who was pretending to muck out a stall while watching the goings-on. "Come here."

The young man jerked and dropped the rake before running over. Rose pointed to the king. "Stand next to him."

"But, ma'am—"

"Just," she waved her hand at them. "Stand."

The young man glanced at the king before shakily bowing and standing, back stiff, near the king. Rose eyed the two men. The stable boy was thinner and taller than the king but only barely taller. The young man's clothing was rough spun and faded in color. The brown trousers were stained and had an old patch on one knee. They were perfect.

"Yeah," Rose nodded as she looked at the clothing. It would be a little ill-fitting but that would add to the look. "Switch."

"Excuse me?" King Micah asked, his voice higher than she'd heard it before.

A harsh snort came from behind her, but she ignored it.

"Switch clothing. You're supposed to look like a working man to avoid unwanted attention." Rose planted her hands on her hips. "Here's a working man that's about your size."

"But... but ma'am... " the stable worker stuttered.

She glared at the young man, who promptly stopped talking. "Consider the really expensive clothes payment for your troubles."

"You're giving away my clothing now?" Micah asked even as he pointed to some empty stalls and directed the quivering stable worker over.

Rose clucked her tongue and glanced over her shoulder at Aaron while the two men switched clothing. The guard's face was red with his efforts to hold back his laughter.

"What's so funny?"

He gestured to the king, who was diligently handing clothing over the stall wall. Rose felt her cheeks burn and quickly looked back to Aaron even though the most she saw were some bare shoulders.

"You just ordered the king–" he stopped to gulp down air around his halting laughter, "to change clothes with a servant, and he listened."

Aaron continued to wheeze as he tried to control his giggles.

"I didn't know Shields knew how to giggle."

"No," Aaron gasped and finally managed to smother his laughter. "There was no giggling."

Rose giggled as she looked away. "Alright. If you say so."

The king stepped back out of the stall, looking much more like a worker. Somehow, seeing the king dressed in simple clothing, no embroidery or fancy dyes, shocked her to stillness. He looked so different. She wasn't expecting it. The regal bearing was still there. If you knew to look for it, you'd see the confident and powerful way he stood. The way he held his shoulders back and cast his eyes around with authority. But... Rose cleared her throat and gripped Starlit's reins. It was a different look. It wasn't a bad look.

"Shall we?" she asked in a small voice.

She slipped past the king and mounted Starlit. Caleb followed suit, and soon they were all riding down the steep and narrow path of the King's Lead. No one spoke as they rode. The path was too narrow for more than two horses to ride abreast; Aaron took up the rear of their party. Somehow Caleb had found himself at the front with Rose and the king in the middle.

The king's gray horse nickered next to her, and Starlit flicked her ears. Rose studiously kept her eyes forward and tried to ignore the king riding next to her.

"I'm sorry—"

"I suppose—"

They both stopped, and Rose fiddled with the reins in her hands.

"Please," Micah said.

Rose cleared her throat and started again. "I'm sorry," she had to pause as the words seemed to get stuck in her throat. "I'm sorry for demanding you change and... for giving away your clothes."

Micah chuckled. "You achieved your aim."

She wasn't sure if that was a good thing or not.

"I was going to say that I suppose I don't really know how a working man dresses. Whenever people come to court, they are dressed in their finest. I don't know what the common man wears to the pub."

"Have you ever been to one?"

Micah was silent for a long time, and Rose finally looked over at him. He was frowning and worrying his lip between his teeth. "I have been to some gentleman's clubs and shared drinks with different noble-men after dinner. But I'd wager that's not the same."

"No." Rose laughed. "Don't you ever eat and drink with... friends? People who don't want anything from you?"

"The captain. A few others I would count as friends, but even they want something from me at some point. Except you."

He turned and looked at her. Rose met his stare and felt a flutter and some of that tension from the summer. That burning, building tension seemed to be moving toward something.

"Me?" She chuckled, disbelief coloring her voice. "Surely you have better options for company."

"None that would dare to order me about in such a way," he said with a smile.

That made her look away as she hid her smile. She wasn't sure why it made her smile, but it did. "Well," she said after a deep breath. "A tavern is not like any of those dinners. And it is not likely to be quiet."

Caleb turned in his seat ahead of them. "I've heard of this place. There's always the best bards and music."

Rose nodded at him. It was why she'd suggested the Witch's Pit. The music was loud, and it was almost always full. It would be very hard to overhear conversations.

"I don't know if this is the best time," Caleb said, "but I found something about the town that was destroyed."

The king nodded at him to continue.

"It used to be the home of a large number of the Revast Clan. They used to mine in the mountains."

"For what?" Rose asked, her breath coming a little fast. Were they mining for that strange ore?

Caleb shrugged. "It didn't say. Only that the mine was depleted some several hundred years ago, and the Revasts moved on. They mine tin and some quartz now.... used to mine."

Goron was looking for more ore. Ore that seemed to be gone. Was the lump in her pocket the last of it?

Caleb turned back around once the king had said his soft thanks.

"Does that mean something to you?" Micah asked softly.

"Maybe." She sighed and pulled the ore out and showed it to Micah briefly before shoving it back into her pocket. "I think he's looking for more of this. Whatever this is. The shadows said this will focus magic. Gerik had a necklace made out of this metal and used it to control all the magics. I think Goron is looking for more ore to make a new one."

"How do you know this?"

She chewed her lip and tucked her coat collar tighter around her neck. "J'Teal told me."

Micah met her eyes and nodded.

"What is likely to be Michael's reaction when he sees you?"

Their plan was for the king and Caleb to meet and sit with Michael first, then Rose would join them. Hopefully, Michael would remember decorum and control his reaction to seeing her. It had been a long time, but time doesn't heal all wounds despite what the bards and love poems say. Sometimes they fester and grow.

"I don't know. Hopefully, he'll be civil."

She slowed Starlit, adding distance between herself and Caleb. King Micah matched her speed and stayed even with her, and cast her a curious glance.

He deserved to know, she thought. He deserved to know why Michael was so unlikely to help them, why they had to go to this length.

Rose cleared her throat and spoke in a hushed voice. "I killed his brother."

Micah's reaction was subtle, like all his reactions were, but she saw his eyes widen, the small breath he took, the tightening of his hands. "I didn't ask."

"You deserve to know." Rose stared squarely ahead, too afraid to meet his eyes.

"Why?" Micah asked. "You don't do anything without reason. Why?"

"It doesn't matter. I still killed him."

"It matters." The king was insistent.

She growled and glared at him. She didn't want to talk about it, didn't want to relive it. But she told him anyway. "I was hired by

Michael's brother, Waylen, to help recover some items. Waylen told me some items had been stolen, but they couldn't retrieve them without my help. I didn't find out until later that it was all a ruse."

She ground her teeth at the memory, at how betrayed she'd felt. How used.

"I met Waylen and several others. That's when he told me what he really wanted me to do. Waylen is Michael's younger brother and he wanted to run the clan. He thought he could do it better, make more money than Michael."

"He wanted you to kill Michael." The king spoke for her when her words wouldn't come.

"Yes. I told him no. I didn't want to kill my friend. I didn't want to be some... some kind of king-maker." Rose sighed. "'But you're an assassin,' he'd said. Like that was all I was, all I was good for. I should've left. I should've turned down the offer and left, but Waylen said Michael was dead regardless of who did it, so I might as well make some money off it."

"You killed Waylen to protect your friend."

"No," she snapped. "I killed Waylen and his four friends who were there. I killed five men that day when I should've left. It wasn't my business. It wasn't my clan, but I killed the five of them anyway."

"You were still protecting your friend," Micah said softly. "Why does Michael hate you for saving his life?"

"Because that's not what I told him. It would've destroyed him to know his own blood had wanted him dead. It was easier to tell the lie: Waylen wronged me on a deal, and I killed him for it. It was an easier lie to believe." She shrugged. "That's when I learned people really did see me only as an assassin. I hadn't expected him to believe it so easily."

The king was silent, but Rose couldn't bring herself to look at him. She didn't want to see any pity in his eyes and didn't want him to see the shame in hers. She stared at the back of Caleb's head and listened to the crunching of snow beneath the horse's hooves. The glow of the town lights could be seen in the distance. They were nearly there. Soon Rose would need to break off and continue on her own, approach from a different angle, just in case Michael had people watching.

"You carry burdens that aren't yours to carry," Micah finally said in a soft voice, and Rose turned to him. "Waylen's actions are not yours to bear."

His eyes were soft, and Rose found herself unable to look away.

"Perhaps," she said. "But his actions lead to their deaths, and those are mine to bear. You try too hard to absolve me of this when it is my punishment. These aren't the only deaths I have on my soul."

She glanced again at the town, finally breaking away from his gaze. "I'll meet you inside the tavern." She pulled Starlit away before he could respond and nudged her sides. The great beast leaped at the slight pressure and darted off into the tree line. All the memories had a headache building behind her eyes and around her temples. The sooner this was over, the sooner the memories could go back to that dark part of her, the part she tried to bury and hide.

Rose directed Starlit away from the small group and through the trees. She went deep into the woods, angling her approach to the town. She rode until she couldn't see the road. She wanted to distance herself from the king, from the conversation they'd just had. From how much she'd accidentally said.

With a shake, she cleared it from her mind and focused on what needed to be done. She pulled on her magic, and the shadows answered. She willed herself to sink into the Undertunnels. The shadows resisted letting Starlit, but Rose pulled them around the horse, and with a soft pop in her ears, they were in the dark tunnels, mist swirling around her long legs. She'd managed with much less resistance than the last time she'd tried to bring another into the shadows with her.

Rose guided Starlit, whose eyes were wide, and her breath came in great, harsh puffs, through the tunnels toward town. She planned on coming into town from the east, giving the appearance of completely arriving separately from the king's party.

Red eyes appeared next to her, and soon a large wolf was walking alongside her, its head nearly even with Starlit's shoulder.

It walked alongside her, silent as it stared at her. Rose glanced at it quickly before returning her attention to the paths ahead of her. Starlit nickered but continued walking, and Rose wondered if the wolves were exercising their control over Starlit like they had before with Taspa. For how calm the beast was with the giant shadow wolves walking so close, she guessed they were calming her mind. The wolf followed along, not speaking, for the rest of the short journey. Rose came to a window opening that led to a deserted back alley. She hesitated before stepping out of the shadows, glancing once more at the wolf. "What do you want?"

"For you to learn." The words reverberated through her head, and the wolf disappeared into the mist.

Rose thought about the captain, Archie, and all the others that wished she'd figure out what in the hells she was doing. "You're at the back of a long line," she muttered to the darkness and guided Starlit out of the shadows.

Starlit let loose a large breath, and her side quivered. Rose patted her neck, slick with sweat. "You're alright."

The horse puffed again and glanced back at Rose as if to say she was out of her mind. Maybe she was. Rose patted her neck one more time before nudging her toward the tavern. It was early enough in the night that once Rose came upon the main street, there were still several people about. Soon, she was able to hear the faint sound of music echoing through the darkness. Rose glanced through the shadows and found the tavern several buildings away. Deciding she was close enough, Rose swung out of the saddle and tied Starlit off at a post of a closed tea house.

She pulled her hood over her head, shoved her hands in her pockets, and strode down the street. It was time she faced her past and Michael's wrath.

CHAPTER 28

*T*he music grew louder the closer she got, and soon she was slipping into the crowded tavern. The lute's notes filled the room, and even though the patrons were loud, the bard's voice could still be heard over the clamor. Rose glanced quickly around the large room, looking for the unmistakable white hair that gave every Tracer away.

When she didn't find Michael anywhere in the room, she headed over to the packed counter. She pushed through the crowd of people and held several coins up to get the attention of the busy barmaid. She quickly exchanged her money for a large mug of frothing ale and slipped away from the push of people. Rose weaved her way through the tables and people toward the far corner and tucked herself in at a tiny table. Propping her feet up on the table, crossed at the ankles, she sat and sipped her ale.

She willed the darkness to listen to her and tugged it around her. She pulled the shadows cast by the many candles and lanterns to become the tiniest bit darker, to obscure her just that little bit more from the eyes of those in the room.

Her magic obeyed, and as the corner darkened, as Rose stepped just that little bit into the Undertunnels, her senses heightened. Her eyesight took on a grey hue, and the clamoring voices sounded distorted. Whispers in the dark became louder and clearer. Being hidden like this felt comfortable and safe.

She sighed softly and sipped more ale. Her eyes continued to roam over the room, stopping on as many faces as she could. Rose quickly spotted the other guards scattered among the crowd. They were dressed in simple clothes and looked like regular folk. No one would know the difference, but Rose could see it. She could see the stiffness to their movements; could see the sharpness and attentiveness to their eyes that gave them away.

They'd done better than the king, anyway, she thought to herself with a small grin.

Almost as if they were summoned by her thought, King Micah and Caleb walked in. The king's eyes scanned the room quickly as he steered Caleb toward an empty table near the far wall. His eyes passed over her before snapping back and looking right at her. His stare seemed to jolt her bones and rooted her to her spot. How could he have noticed her, seen her, hidden as she was? Everyone else was passing over her, ignoring or missing her presence. Micah nodded once then settled next to Caleb.

The wolves were so adamant that she learned; she wondered what they would do if she tried something new. Rose dropped further into the shadows, just the smallest amount, and whispered through them. Willed them to carry her voice. She could hear through them, see through them. Why shouldn't she be able to speak through them? He was her anchor. Maybe that meant more than just being able to pull her out of her magic.

"Can you hear me?" She whispered, sending her voice through the shadows to him.

Micah jumped, and his eyes snapped to her. Caleb looked over his shoulder before turning back with a frown. Micah nodded once at her.

She smiled. "Good."

She drank more of her ale and checked the door one more time. Her eyes went back to Caleb and the king, sitting there, in a tavern, with no drinks. Gods help them.

"Get drinks. You're at a tavern," she whispered. "Act like it."

Micah glanced back at Rose, and his sigh echoed back to her. Soon Caleb was up and trying to push his way through the people waiting at the counter. Micah leaned back in his chair, balancing precariously on the back two legs, his broad shoulders resting against the shadowed wall.

"Anyone ever tell you you're bossy when you want to be?" he whispered. The shadows carried his words to her.

She smiled into her drink. She liked this. This barbed back and forth. She wished it had been different. That she was sitting at the table next to him, laughing, drinking. Elbowing him sharply in the side when he got sharp-tongued. The thought and knowledge that it couldn't be, stole her smile.

"This is new, isn't it? Projecting your voice through the shadows?"

"I wasn't sure it would work." Rose gulped down the last of her drink as Caleb was returning with theirs. "Handy that it does, though."

Both of them barely touched their ale, and Rose couldn't stop the eye roll. She wasn't sure which was more painful: waiting for Michael or watching those two try to look natural. She was about to say something that would probably get her in trouble when a hush settled over the tavern. Everyone turned to stare at the newcomer pushing his hood back from his face, and the barb's cords slowly stalled. Rose instantly recognized Michael. His long, white hair pulled back in the same intricate plaits he'd worn years ago.

He looked the same. Years had added wrinkles to his face, but his eyes still watched the room with calm assurance. Her heart twinged. She'd once thought of this man as a friend. An elder brother.

"That's him," she whispered.

And now he thought of her as the woman who killed his family.

Michael moved further into the room, and slowly, the noise returned. A Tracer walking into any room always caused a momentary stir, but soon everyone was returning to their ale and food, and the bard resumed his melody. Rose saw Micah shove an elbow into Caleb's ribs, and he jumped up. Caleb pushed his way through the people to Michael, and Rose waited until they were seated back with the king before standing from her corner. As she moved, she let the shadows fall away from her.

She shoved her way to the front of the counter, ignoring the elbow someone jammed into her and held up more coins for the barmaid.

"Two this time, please." Rose dropped more coins than was required, and in return, got her drinks before anyone else. Sipping the foam from one, she steeled herself for what was about to happen.

The three of them were already deep in conversation when she walked up to their table. Rose set the full mug of ale down in front of Michael before taking the last chair.

"Michael," she said and took a long drink. She watched him over the rim of her mug as he turned his tawny eyes to her. Anger filled them instantly. His brows creased, and she saw the muscle in his jaw twitch as he clenched his teeth. She finally set the drink down, licked the foam from her lips. "You look the same as you did all those years ago."

Michael pulled his eyes away from her and turned to the king. "When you said one more was coming—"

"I meant Miss Trewin, yes. A lot of this was her idea."

"Her idea or not, if I'd known she was coming, I never would've," Michael said with a glare back at her.

"Obviously," Rose snapped. "Why do you think we went to all this effort? That doesn't change the fact that we are still here offering clanship."

"'We,'" Michael mocked. "You cannot offer me anything. What do you actually want with me?"

"I offered you the beer," she growled and leaned forward. "More than that, I offered the king your name and good character."

Michael sucked his teeth and glared at her a moment before turning back to the king. "Do you know what you're working with, dealing with her?"

"Do you?" Micah's words were cold, and Rose prayed he wouldn't tell secrets that weren't his to tell.

Michael scoffed again. "Oh, I know exactly how Little Flower works."

Rose saw Caleb jerk his eyes up in surprise before quickly returning to the paper he scribbled on. Micah took a long breath, his chest inflating slowly with it.

"You cannot trust an assassin."

Caleb's hand paused, and his eyes met hers over his papers for a heartbeat before returning to his notes.

She swallowed, well, tried to, but her mouth was dry. Her tongue stuck to the roof of her mouth.

"I upheld my end." Rose leaned forward and hissed in his face, "I kept my promise. Even when it would've saved me great pain and suffering not to."

Michael leaned forward to match her, nose nearly touching. Despite everything, despite her broken kinship with the man, Rose dropped her hand toward her dagger. She might miss his friendship, but she would not let him overtake her because of sentiment.

"You think that means you have honor?" he growled at her, and his body shifted. Just a slight movement, but she saw his hand drop to his waist.

"Don't," she said, and her own dagger pressed against his inner thigh an instant later. "You know that's a bad idea."

One little movement. A slice. That's all it would take. She'd have her blade back in her sheath before anyone even noticed the blood. He was stupid to think he could move first. He knew her better than that.

She sensed movement in the shadows and knew the guards were slowly gathering. Slowly moving closer.

"Sir," Micah leaned across the table, his hands clasped on the top. "If I wanted to kill you, there would've been a much easier way. If I'd wanted to imprison you, I would've. This invitation was sent in good faith with an offer of clanship, but if you harm a member of my court, I will watch you bleed out from her blade and spare no further thought to it."

His voice was so calm. So serene. She wanted to turn and look at him. She wanted to see his face when he said such things about her, but she kept her eyes on Michael's.

"Everyone step back and we can continue this discussion. If you truly wish to put a personal vendetta above the wellbeing of your clan, then so be it. But walk away. Any other movement will not end well for you, and I will go home with my people."

My people. My court. Mine. The words seemed to ring in Rose's ears, and it made her heart race. She held her blade to a man's artery, a mere wrist twitch away from death, and Micah still claimed her as his. His people. His. She wanted to see his face, see his eyes, but she kept hers focused on Michael's.

Michael's eyes shifted from hers and she leaned back. Just enough. Michael nodded, a sharp, jerky movement, and Rose sheathed her dagger back at her hip. Sweat ran down her temple and mingled in the wispy curls of hair at her ear.

"You really would've killed me too?" Michael asked as a shaky hand reached for his drink.

"I've never been one to lay down and die, Michael. You know this."

The man let out a harsh breath and nodded. He placed both hands on the table after a glance at Rose, who did the same.

"Back to the matter at hand." Micah pushed his drink away.

"You actually mean to offer me clanship?"

Micah nodded, his face harsh and stern. "Yes. I have a request of you."

"Why clanship? Why not offer me so much gold I couldn't refuse?"

Micah spread his hands over the table. "Would you prefer that instead? I'd be happy to come to a number if that's what you'd really wish. I had hoped offering clanship would bring a group of people with a very useful skill-set into the public, benefiting both of us. But I can spare the coin if that's what you wish."

"And if I refuse?" Michael asked. "If I still turn down whatever task you have for me? I walk away empty-handed. Or will you imprison me for my illegal acts, for the underhanded deals I make? I know you have a ledger with my name in it somewhere."

Rose cringed. She knew his name was in it. When she first arrived at the castle, and the captain had checked through their ledger, she was surprised hers wasn't in it.

"It would be very unfortunate if you refused, but not disastrous. We will find another means to find who we're looking for. I would still hope, however, that you would still consider the clanship."

His words were so simple. His tone never changed. He could've been talking about the quality of the ale for all he sounded, and yet he was offering something that could change their entire world.

Rose blinked and looked at the king, not sure if she'd heard right. Michael looked at Rose, the old animosity forgotten for just a moment, with wide eyes before turning back to the king. Rose looked harder at the king and started to wonder what she'd missed. She remembered the look the captain gave when she'd first heard the plan of clanship and now this....There was something more behind this offer of clanship. This was a step in something more, and her mind raced to try to find what she'd missed.

"You would offer me clanship even if I say no to whatever trade you're asking for?"

"Yes." Micah sat back and folded his hands in his lap.

Rose reached for her forgotten drink and took a large gulp. A means to an end. That's all she thought this was. Never would she have expected this, but now she knew something else was going on. A part of her wondered if the king had used her, used her connection to the magical clans, to get to this point. He had a plan for the clanship. He wanted to change things. She was the only one he knew with ties outside of the castle. Had this really all been a ploy? The thought made her throat tight.

But, she glanced sharply at the king. He'd just threatened to watch a man die if he'd harmed her. What if he was using her? Making her feel important? Being needed would blind her to a lot of things. She swallowed harshly. It had blinded her to this maneuvering.

She shook her head. No. Machinations were happening she didn't understand but she wouldn't let herself think he'd used her. No. It hurt her chest too much to do so. But he had some explaining to do, she thought while looking once more at his stern face.

He'd never taken his eyes off Michael, focused on the negotiation.

"Why?" Michael was asking. "Why offer me this?"

"Because," Micah leaned forward with such an intensity in his eyes, Rose was reminded he was a king and not just a young man dressed in finery. "There is a divide among my people. A hatred and suspicion left over from years of war and blame. My advisors tell me of a prejudice toward magic users based upon old myths and fear. I would fix that if I can. Because it will benefit me to align with magic users."

Rose nearly choked on her ale. She coughed into her collar to clear her throat, and when she looked over at Caleb, saw him feverishly writing on his small pad of paper.

So that was the plan. But why had the captain thought this was her idea? Why had the captain looked at her during that first meeting?

"So, when I say I want to offer you clanship," the king continued, "it is no small thing. Your clan must be above reproach. No more illegal doings. No shady business. Your clan must be the example of what can be."

Michael was stunned to silence. He swallowed, and though it was too loud to hear the gulp, Rose saw his throat bob. He glanced at her then over to Caleb, who was still writing at a furious speed.

"And this man's purpose?" Michael asked, pointing at Caleb.

"A historian. He's here to document what happens and to ensure it is recorded."

Michael rubbed his face and was silent for a long time. Caleb finally finished writing and glanced nervously around the table.

"Who do you need me to find?"

"Are you saying 'yes' to the clanship?"

"I need to think; to talk to the others. This affects them too greatly to not consult with them. But, as a show of good faith and to acknowledge the trust you have offered me, I will find this person for you."

Rose let out a breathy sigh that was almost a laugh. What in the hells? Too much. This entire meeting was too much. She thought she knew what was going to happen, what the plan was. There had been too many surprises, and her poor heart couldn't beat fast enough for all of them.

Micah smiled softly and leaned forward. "I appreciate that. We're looking for a Seer. Her name is Ode."

Michael let out a long breath. "A Seer? A true one?"

Rose nodded. "She's from the lands north of the Invius Mountains."

Michael's tawny eyes watched her before slowly turning back to the king. "I can find her, but I'll need to see her face to do so."

The moment Rose had been dreading. Michael could track anyone without any Tool, or without needing any part of them. But he did need to see them. Michael had explained it once years ago. The old Tracers, the powerful ones from before the wars, could track anyone they saw, and with a simple touch to one's forehead, they could see the person's memories. Rose had wondered if, over time, the magic had separated, leaving people like Nico and Sasha who could see memories at a touch of skin, and the Tracers who couldn't. Michael was different. She doubted anyone else like him left.

She knew at some point, for this to work, Michael would need to see her memory of Ode and risk being shown so much more. She licked her lips before pressing them together.

"I've seen her," she said in a voice with a little tremor.

Michael turned to her. "Are you ready?"

Focus, she told herself. Focus on Ode. Rose nodded and thought of the woman's face. Her dark skin seemed to glisten in the night. Her eyes, too bright with knowledge and the power that had emanated from her. Michael lifted his finger and tapped it against her forehead. It was fast, less than a second, and she hoped Michael only saw Ode.

"Got it?" she asked.

"Yes," Michael responded and closed his eyes, his head cocked slightly to one side. "Ah, yes. She's near. I can find her and bring her to you at the castle in a few days' time. Will she come?"

"Tell her I'm the one seeking her, and she will."

Michael snapped his eyes open to glare at her. "You are the one that seeks her? Not the king?"

Shit. Rose opened her mouth, but the king spoke first.

"We both do. Miss Trewin is the one Ode met and knows."

Michael heaved a sigh. "Fine. I am a man of my word. I'll bring her, and we can finish the conversation of clanship then."

"Very well." The king held out his hand for Michael, and after a tense moment of hesitation, shook it.

"One last question. Why here? Why not the castle?"

"Miss Trewin said an invitation to the castle would be ignored as you would think it a trap. Was she right?"

Michael stood and threw on his coat. "Yes," he finally said. He ignored Rose as he turned and made his way through the thinning crowd to the doors. Their meeting had gone longer than anyone expected, and the crowd had started to retire for the night.

Rose rubbed the space between her eyes and groaned. "Can we go home now?"

"Yes. Mr. Harven," the king turned to Caleb. "Did you get everything?"

Caleb nodded.

"Good. Then yes, let's go home."

The three of them stood and, after gathering their coats, returned to the dark and cold outside. Silently, they retrieved their horses, and the guards slowly exited the tavern, following behind. They rode in silence through town, the wind cold against their skin. Rose shivered in the wind, the cold biting her exposed skin. She pulled her scarf over her nose and settled in for the short ride back to the castle.

CHAPTER 29

*T*hey rode silently back to the castle. Aaron and the other Shields spread out in the darkness. Rose tried to bury herself deeper into her coat and scarf. Her mind was still reeling at what had happened in that meeting. Of all the ways she had pictured that going, what actually did happen wasn't even close. Rose was still reliving the deal struck and the implications it could have when she noticed something odd in the shadows. She dropped her sight into the darkness and saw a man walking on the road toward them. A man wearing a long coat, open and flowing. Simple trousers and boots. How was he not freezing?

The shadows started to hiss and growl.

What? she asked them. *Who is that?*

But she knew. Something in her bones, some knowledge that wasn't hers, told her who that was.

"Stop," she said, just loud enough to be heard. She felt the shadows gathering around them. The wolves were near, and only the darkness of night kept the others from seeing them.

"What?" King Micah asked as he stopped his horse.

Caleb came even with them, his borrowed mare nickering at the nearness of the shadow wolves. The king's horse pawed the ground and held his ears tight to his head.

"Goron is here," Rose said.

The king spun in his seat as he looked around. "Where? How do you know?"

Rose pointed ahead of them, at the figure now close enough to be seen in the moonlight and snow. "The shadows know him."

"Well," Goron yelled over the distance between them. "I've been looking for you."

The Shields started to gather and draw their swords. The wolves paced at the edges of her mind. They wanted in, wanted to hunt. This man, this thing was defying nature. She could feel the wrongness about him. He was a thing out of time, cheated death. It went against the Balance of nature.

"Who is it you were looking for?" Micah asked, his breath fogging the space in front of him.

Goron ignored the king, his eyes locked on Rose. "I have business with you."

Rose let the wolves in, just a little. She kept a tight grip on the boundary between her mind and theirs, but she slowly let them in. She felt that power she'd felt before in the throne room rush through her. Fragments of memories that weren't hers flittered through her mind. The wolves pushed. They wanted more, full control, but Rose tightened her grip.

"You should not be here." Her voice was deep with the growls of the shadows. "You cannot be here."

That wrongness made her stomach turn, and the shadows needed to correct it. She could feel that desire from them, the urge to repair the Balance of Life and Death.

Goron tsked. "I've no time for your judgement or proclamations."

He lifted his hand and slammed it into the snow-packed road, dropping to one knee as he fell. The ground rose in a wave around him and rushed out toward them. They were thrown from their horses as the earthen wave rocked beneath them. Air whooshed from Rose's lungs as she landed hard on her back. Starlit screamed as she fell hard onto her side, her long legs thrashing as she tried to right herself. Rose tried to force air back in her lungs, and through the ringing in her ears, she could hear the Shields shouting.

Protect the king, she commanded the shadows. *Hide him.*

She felt the shadows engulf Micah and hid him deep in the Under-tunnels.

"Rose!" Micah shouted. "Rose, let me out of here!"

Gingerly, she rolled onto her side and gasped air into her lungs. She didn't see the second wave of earth, but it flung her into the air. She wheezed, lungs too sore to scream.

Enough of this. As Rose fell, she fell into the shadows and slid through the mists of the Undertunnels. She gasped for breath and checked the others. A few Shields were down and not moving, but most were struggling to their feet and searching for weapons that had fallen. The king was still being held by the wolves, deep in the shadows.

She pulled a long knife sheathed under her coat.

"Come now," Goron said. "It's no fun if you hide."

Rose circled around in the shadows; she pulled her lips back in a silent snarl, baring her teeth. The wolves pushed against her grasp, but she kept them back, for now. She could feel her grip on them loosening, her control starting to slip.

She circled behind him, ready to jump out and strike while he was distracted. The Shields ran towards Goron, and with a flick of his fingers, the earth swallowed their legs. She rose from the shadows and sliced her blade across the back of Goron's knee before stepping back into them. He screamed as his leg collapsed beneath him. She didn't wait for him to recover as she stepped out again, this time aiming for his neck.

A wall of mud and snow met her blade, and Rose retreated deep into the Undertunnels.

"So, you know a trick or two," he growled as he dropped the mud shield. The moon was big, and the light reflected off the snow.

Rose circled him again, moving from one shadow to another. The wolves growled low and quiet. It was a sound Rose felt more than heard. She was about to drop out of the shadows for another strike when they hissed, "pack. Hunt like a pack!"

She sunk deeper into the shadows while she thought. The wolves worked themselves a little deeper into her mind. Yes. A pack. Rose sent a wolf after Goron. It appeared in the snow and leaped at him. A wall of mud rose and the wolf crashed into it. Rose ordered another, only for it to be stopped by the earth again.

"This the best you're capable of?" he shouted into the night. "Come on, girl!"

Rose growled and remembered what Caleb had said about magic; that they repelled each other. She needed to try harder.

She dropped out of the shadows behind him with her blade raised, ready to drive it into his ribs, when Goron spun and caught her by the throat. He fell with her as he dropped her hard onto the ground, his hand squeezing around her. The wolves growled and attacked in a fury, teeth snapping, but Goron raised his free hand into the air, and the ground went up with it, encircling them in a dome of mud and snow.

"J'Teal liked that trick too." He squeezed harder. "It didn't work back then either."

Rose kicked and tried to twist away from him, but a simple flick of his fingers and the frozen ground covered her legs.

"Your kind killed my brother. That wound is still fresh for me. I've promised not to kill you, but for what your kind did, I will still make you pay."

Spots were appearing in her eyes, and Rose clawed at his hand around her neck, her breath locked in her chest. Her lungs burned with the need for air as she gasped and fought to breathe past his grip. The ground suddenly released her legs, and Goron hauled her upright by his grip on her throat. She gasped the smallest bit of air she could, but then he tightened his grip so even that disappeared. Her ears started to ring and the shouting of the soldiers dimmed to a soft din.

He brought his face close to hers. "I will watch you die, eventually, but not before you've lost your mind. Not before I've watched every little bit of sanity be driven from you. Not before I've taken your Anchor from you."

Micah!

Something inside her snapped at the pure terror that drove through her. Rose felt a rush of power and pure fury push into her. Like a barrier had been broken and shoved aside, revealing holes and places meant just for the shadows. They settled into place, sharing their mind with hers. Something clicked, and for the first time, Rose felt whole. Complete. Like finally being able to scratch the itch you'd learned to live with. Or finally taking a full, deep breath without restraint.

Power filled her, over-flowed her. They were so strong, so much stronger than she had ever previously believed. She could sense deep down in the shadows that even more power lurked. This... mind-numbing strength she felt was only the tip of what was possible from them. The magic felt old. It tasted old, the way a room full of old books and manuscripts tasted. Dusty. Dry. She didn't know how old the wolves were, how old the shadows were, but they were older than anything else she knew.

A choked growl broke through her lips. Rose brought her hand up, now encased in a dark shadowed claw, and swiped at Goron's arm. He screamed and dropped her, the dome of mud crumbling around them. Bright blood leaked from the four long claw marks on his forearm. Rose coughed and gagged, forcing air back into her starved lungs. Then the fury in her drove her forward, and she lunged at him, her clawed hands outstretched.

She would have his blood!

He dodged backwards a step, but her claws still found purchase in his chest, and four new claw marks appeared in his skin. The wolves formed around her, their eyes glowing red in the moonlight. They were more solid than ever before.

Stop him, she commanded them.

Wolves darted forward while others circled behind. They nipped at his ankles, his arms, and leaped at his neck. Goron leaped back and threw waves of snow and mud at them, but they pushed through it. They were not simply shadows anymore. Now they were in this world, fully. She could feel the tether between herself and the shadows tightening, giving them the ability to be in this world. As the tether tightened, she felt her grip on her world slipping. Her thoughts started to feel overwhelmed by their memories.

Rose stalked forward, a low, deep growl coming from her throat. His eyes met hers, and she saw fear in them. Prey.

A wall of earth surrounded him, and when it fell, he was gone.

"NO!" Rose screamed, her voice echoing with the power of the shadows. It grated against her battered throat, but still, she screamed her fury.

The wolves pushed her. *We must follow!*

He escapes!

Hunt!

A growl slipped past her lips, and Rose took two shaky steps before stopping herself. Her identity was slipping. She could feel her strength slipping away, like the shadows were pulling her life with each second they stayed in the world. She didn't know what to make of this. She wasn't ready, wasn't prepared for this. The magic was too much.

"No," she said, her voice gravely and broken, but her own. "No, go back."

She pushed them away, fought to find the boundary between her mind and theirs again, and forced them back into their shadows.

They left her, more willingly than they have before, but one lone wolf stood and stared at her. His head was low to the ground as he stared at her. She could feel the demand in his eyes; to continue the hunt.

"Later," she promised him. "Later."

The wolf snarled but disappeared into the darkness of the night. The last of the shadows left her, and she sank to her knees as the power left. She felt hollow inside, like something was missing. Her limbs started to shake, and she could feel the cold seeping into her bones. The Shields ran over to her, past her, finally freed from Goron's magic.

Aaron approached her hesitantly, his steps slow and cautious. "Where did he go?"

She shrugged, throat too battered to speak now that it was just her and not the power from the shadows.

"Are you... alright?"

Again, Rose shrugged. She wasn't sure how to answer that question anyway. Caleb ran over to her, their horses pulled behind him.

"I... I," Caleb stopped and collapsed in the snow next to her. "I didn't know what to do," he said meekly. "I grabbed the horses and hid. I didn't know what to do."

She shakily patted his knee and tried to gulp down air. She wanted to stand but didn't think her legs would hold her.

Where was Micah?

Again that pure terror stilled her blood. He'd wanted to kill Micah.

At her thought, the shadows released their hold on him. The quiet cold echoed with his footsteps through the snow. She looked up at him as he neared, and Micah gripped her hard on her arms, pulling her to her feet.

"Don't you ever do that again!" His voice shook as he shouted at her. His face was pale against the dark sky.

"I—" Rose tried to answer him, but her throat burned, and she had to stop.

Micah released his grip on her arms only to grip her again when her legs started to buckle. Rose braced a hand on his chest, the other gripping his arm. Her limbs shook, and it was from more than the cold. Small dots started appearing in the corners of her sight, and Rose had to tell herself to slow her gasping breaths.

At the edges of her hearing, she heard the whispers.

Micah pulled her arm over his shoulder. "Can you ride?"

She nodded and reached for the reins in Caleb's hand. She had used the shadows in ways Rose never had before, and the cost of that was going to be high. She could feel her body pulling her towards sleep, toward unconsciousness. The whisperers were getting louder.

You will not pass out, she told herself as Micah pushed her up and into the saddle.

"Sire!" Aaron shouted as he rode towards them, now back on his own horse. "Are you—"

"I'm fine, Aaron." The king cut him off and swung into his own horse's saddle. "The others?"

"A few horses didn't make it through the fall of that first wave, but no one else is badly injured."

"Good. We must get back to the castle. Before or if he returns."

They rode quickly and quietly. Rose hung onto the saddle by pure stubbornness alone. Her only thought through that ride was to hold onto the small saddle horn and never let go. Her vision swarmed in and out as they rode, and her throat started to swell and close off. When they finally arrived in the castle courtyard, other guards were rushing to meet them. Rose sagged in her saddle, her breath wheezing. Sleep. She needed to sleep.

Someone tugged on her arm, and she slid from her saddle. Micah caught her, barely managing to keep her upright before looping her arm over his shoulder. He carried her toward the castle, her feet tripping under her weight.

The whisperers were loud. Demanding. Words on top of words that she couldn't understand. Rose covered her ear with her free hand.

"You'll be fine," Micah said. "Just focus on me."

She did. She tried. She focused on the feel of his shoulders beneath her arm and the feel of him pressed next to her. She tried to match her wheezing breaths to his, and slowly, the press of the whisperers started to fade. Just as they were turning into the mending wing, Rita running towards them, the last of her strength gave out.

"Shit," she croaked before falling.

CHAPTER 30

The barren landscape was back. Rose sighed and wearily looked around at the dead trees and fog. She felt the weight of a gaze on her back, and when she turned, J'Teal was standing between the trees, fog swirling around her skirts.

"Why am I here this time?"

"I didn't bring you," J'Teal said with a shrug.

Great, she thought. That meant she was back here because she was lost, her mind wandering somewhere in the shadow's realm.

Rose walked over to J'Teal and leaned on one of the thin trees. "Tell me something about the Anchor. Will I go insane if I lose mine?"

Goron's words... had they been a threat or truth?

"Yes, eventually you will. It depends on your ability to block out the Speakers and the shadows on your own, but yes. Eventually, you'll lose your mind, your ability to separate the two worlds. And then..."

"And then?" Rose prompted when J'Teal fell into silence.

"You'll end up trapped here. Trapped like me, with the rest of us who couldn't separate our minds from theirs. You'll forget everything you were before and become one of the Speakers."

A sour taste leaked into Rose's mouth. "The Speakers?"

J'Teal looked behind her at the soft whispering coming from the fog. "Those voices you hear when the shadows are too near. Those are the Speakers. They are the Shadowstalkers that were lost to the shadows."

"Why do you seem different, then?"

"Some are stronger than others. Sometimes not everything fades away. I refused to forget who I was. They cannot take that from me, but it is… " she sighed, and her shoulders dropped, "difficult to remember sometimes. There are times I don't remember anything. Others I can remember only a day, or a conversation, or a face."

The murmur of voices grew louder, and Rose turned to look. J'Teal must've heard it too because she also turned and looked into the fog rolling thick in the trees. "But only for a time. The Speakers always come back."

Rose could sense Micah near her, back wherever her body had ended up, and she wanted to go back to him. She tried to follow that… presence to him. It was almost as if a path had appeared leading back to where he was, and she willed her mind to follow it. The landscape started to fade, and with it, J'Teal and the Speakers' voices.

"Be careful, girl," J'Teal warned before she disappeared entirely. "Allowing the shadows control over your body is dangerous. I wouldn't toy with that."

Rose wanted to ask what she meant, but the Shadow World disappeared, and when she blinked next, she was opening her eyes in a room. She glanced around and realized it wasn't hers; the vase of flowers was missing from the nightstand. Turning her head the other way, she saw Micah sitting in the lone chair, his legs kicked out in front of him with his elbow propped on the arm of the chair, holding up his head.

"What are you doing here?" Rose asked softly, her voice gravelly. She winced at how tender her throat was and gingerly poked around it with her fingers. It hurt and ached with even the lightest touches.

Micah jerked and straightened in the chair. He cleared his throat and blinked. "I wanted to make sure the whisperers were gone when you woke."

"They are. How bad?" she asked, pointing to her throat.

"Bruised. Daymon was a little worried about the swelling but said he healed the worst of it."

Rose nodded and pushed herself upright. Her muscles were stiff and tight, and she groaned a little at how much they protested moving. "I don't need to be here."

She looked more fully around the room, and that's when she noticed how dark it was. She looked at the oil lamp on the table between her bed and the king's chair. It shouldn't be that dark for how big the flame was. Her breath caught in her chest for a moment, and she remembered what J'Teal had said about going blind... eventually. Rose sighed and brought her knees up, dropped her head onto the heel of her palm.

Blind. Insane. Which was worse? She shook her head against her hand. Tears built up in her eyes again, but she bit her lip and refused to let them fall.

"Drink this," Micah held out a cup. "It's probably cold by now, but Rita wanted you to drink it when you woke up."

Reluctantly, Rose took the cup and sipped the cold Supbulent tea. She cringed as the bitter liquid hit her tongue and made a face. She put the cup down without drinking more.

Suddenly, he leaned forward and reached a shaky hand toward her battered throat. Rose stilled as his fingers ghosted over her skin. She guessed he was following the bruising Goron's hand had no doubt left.

"Why didn't he kill you?" he whispered. "He came very close; could've."

"Because he wants to kill you," she whispered back.

His hand stilled on her skin. "Why?"

Her heart was beating so fast she could feel it fluttering against his hand where it rested on her skin. She didn't know what would happen if she moved, if he'd remove his hand or not. Or if she wanted him to. He was so close and she was so confused about how she felt about that closeness. His fingers were soft against her skin. She was close enough to him she could smell the dusty aroma of horse on his clothes.

"Because," she finally said, "if you die, I'll go insane. Eventually."

He sat back at her words, taking his hand with him, and Rose was embarrassed to admit to herself that she missed the touch.

"Insane?"

She shrugged. "If you're not there to keep me in this world, the shadows start to take over, and I'll end up as one of the whisperers. Or... I guess they're called Speakers."

"How do you know that?"

"J'Teal told me... because she is one. Though, her ability to separate herself from them is rare from how she described it."

"Gods... " Micah swore, his eyes shifting back and forth rapidly as he thought. "Does that also mean if we are physically separated for an extended period of time or over a long distance, you're also at risk?"

"N—" Rose stopped herself. The more she thought about it, the more uneasy she became. The Anchor's death wasn't the only thing that could drive her mad, it was simply the most permanent way. "Shit," she swore and dropped her head onto her knees.

"Well," Micah said, and Rose turned her head to look at him. "That just means you've got to stay here. No more plans for the plains." He had a tentative smile on his lips, like he wasn't sure what her reaction would be.

Rose couldn't help but smile back. "No, I suppose not."

He grunted a soft laugh.

Rose grunted back, immediately regretting the action, and groaned. The bells in the courtyard started to chime, and Rose groaned at how early in the morning it was.

"I really should leave. I was here much longer than I planned to be."

Rose nodded against her knees as Micah stood. He pointed at the cup of tea, forgotten on the nightstand. "Drink it."

She scrunched her nose at him but nodded. Without more words, Micah slipped from the room.

CHAPTER 31

e stared at the stack of marriage proposals, letters from Lords with promises of money and allegiances, dowries, and ego. Lord Tyman might be more of a hound about them than Mariah, and they'd both been bothering him incessantly about picking a wife. The attack by Goron several days ago had done nothing but increase their pestering. They liked to lord over him how close to death he came and left no heirs. He'd grumbled at them that he hadn't been anywhere near death, but the point was made, and they knew it. He knew he needed to focus on the future of his reign. He hoped, however, to have one more option if things played out the way he hoped.

He scrubbed his face with a sigh and tried, again, to focus on the papers in front of him. A gentle knock at his office door saved him from further failed attempts to focus.

"Come," Micah called and pushed the papers to one side.

Ben walked inside and after a quick bow, said, "there is a gentleman here to see you. Michael Torventon with a Madam Ode."

Micah sat up and waved Ben on. "Show them in."

He hadn't been expecting them so quickly. Michael had said Ode was close, but he still expected this to take weeks. This was good, though. He took a deep breath to ease his sudden anxiety. This meant they were one more step closer. Closer for Rose and her magic. Closer for him and his plans.

He stood as the white-haired man walked toward his desk with who he assumed to be the Seer Ode. The woman was much taller than the woman of Rhivony. He remembered Rose telling him Ode came from the lands north of the Invius Mountains and wondered if all their women were this tall.

"Sir," Micah said to Michael. "I thank you for your help."

Michael turned his tawny eyes to him and nodded his head. "We had a deal." He added almost as an afterthought, "Sire."

Micah turned to Ode, standing silently next to Michael. Her eyes cautiously watched the two of them. The whites of her eyes stood out against the darkness of her skin, her black irises. She brought those sharp eyes to him and smiled, her teeth bright white.

"Ode Balora," Michael said, gesturing to her.

"I hear you're looking for me." Her voice was soft, with a lilt to her vowels.

"Thank you for coming, ma'am." Micah settled himself back in his chair. "I have been looking for you."

Ode watched him with eyes that felt old with wisdom. How much did a Seer know, anyway? She smiled a close-lipped smile, and those old eyes looked over his shoulder a moment before turning back to him. "Aye. I've already directed one of the servants to bring me my things. They should be unpacked by now."

Micah was unsettled for a moment before words came back to him. "You've a room in town then?"

"No," she said. "The room you were going to offer me."

"Ah," Micah glanced at Michael, who was watching Ode with narrowed eyes. "I trust you know the way… then?"

"Aye, Sire." She smiled again.

He had to stop himself from shaking his head. "Thank you for coming. I'll send for you tomorrow so all interested parties can be present."

Ode smiled another close-lipped smile, full of secrets, and nodded. "Of course. I'll see myself to my room if you don't mind, Sire."

He shook his head and gestured for her to leave. Ode glanced once more over his shoulder before turning and leaving, her multilayered skirts swishing as she moved.

Michael and Micah watched her leave. He felt out of sorts after the short conversation with the woman. Like she knew more than she said and was humoring him the entire time.

"Seers," Michael grunted. "They know more than they ought and speak only in riddles and rhymes."

Micah couldn't help but agree even after such a short experience with one. "Have you thought any more about my offer?"

Michael nodded, his white hair coming free of the complex braids, and a few strands fell into his eyes. "I have."

Micah took it as a good sign that Michael sat down across from his desk.

"What, exactly, would it mean to have Clanship?"

"It means you'll have the crown's protection. You could bring slights or arguments about clan business before the crown for mediation. It means you must have a charter that is granted by the crown for conduct of your clan. You will have to pay taxes. You'll be a recognized group just like the leading merchant clans."

Michael nodded slowly, steeping his hands beneath his chin. "Would it require a registry?"

"Yes, but not for the reason you will suspect." Micah leaned forward. "A registry of your members is needed for many reasons. So we may keep track of members when they misbehave, for census purposes, so on. But I do not wish to keep track of the magic-users, if that is what you are thinking. Every clan must keep an up-to-date record of the clan members."

"That is what I expected, but I promised my people I would ask all the same. And other magical clans?"

"You're the only one I know of with the numbers to justify a clanship. But that doesn't mean there isn't the possibility of others in the future."

Michael nodded slowly. "My people are hesitant to put their names on a list. They are afraid of what will happen to their safety."

"Luckily," Micah said softly, "part of the charter is protection to your clan members."

Michael straightened. "Then I think I would like to look at this proposed charter."

Micah smiled as the first piece fell into place. "I'd hoped you would say that." He reached down into his drawer, pulled out the document he had prepared earlier and handed it to Michael.

"You're rather sure of yourself, Sire."

"No," Micah said. "Just prepared."

Michael grunted but took the document. "I'll look this over then and speak with you before I leave."

Micah nodded and watched as Michael slowly stood, watching him with a cautious eye.

"Rose..." Michael started, and his hand clenched against the document.

"You needn't ever involve yourself with her again."

"You shouldn't either," Michael said, anger coloring his voice. "Little Flower will betray you when it best suits her."

Control. Micah clenched his own hands. Control, he told himself. "I advise you to consider that you don't know all the facts of the story."

Michael grunted and turned, letting the argument fall. Micah watched as he left, the door shutting softly behind him. He didn't know why the Tracer's words left him with such anger, but they did. He felt as if he should've done more, said more, something.

A plan was forming, a long plan that would take time and very careful maneuvering.

CHAPTER 32

*R*ita finally released Rose back to her room with a strong caution against using any magic until she'd rested fully. Her eyes ached, and her throat felt tight, but she was fine. She kept telling Rita that until she finally agreed that she was. She took the bright outer corridors back to the far wing her room was in, the large windows streamed in a harsh light as it bounced off the stone and snow-covered courtyard. It was a slightly longer walk, but these public halls were near empty with the storms keeping even the most determined courtier away. The servant halls were too full of gossiping women, and the bruise on her throat was far too visible.

She squinted against the light, her eyes ached like sand had been rubbed in them, and she hurried through the halls until she was in the far eastern wing. As she turned down the hall to her room, Sam nodded at her as she passed. He paused, his eyes widening as they settled on the mottled bruise. Word had no doubt spread through the officers and guards of the attack.

Rose waved him off with a small smile.

"It's nothing," she croaked.

"Doesn't look like nothing," he protested. "Nor sound like nothing."

She harrumphed. "I'll survive."

He smiled softly at her and clapped her gently on the shoulder before continuing on. Rose watched him leave with a soft smile. She wasn't sure she belonged here yet, but she was starting to feel that she liked it regardless. She turned back down the hall.

She entered her room, letting out a soft sigh at how much relief she felt to be back in her small room. She pulled out the chair from the desk and perched it in front of the stove. After building the fire up, she slumped in the chair, the heat from the stove warming her. She let her head fall back against the backrest, content to simply rest in her own room.

"Oi, girlie."

Rose jerked out of her chair, hand pulling her dagger from her boot as her eyes settled on the Seer standing just inside her door. How in the hells had she not heard the woman open her door?

"You going to stab me or invite me inside?"

She tried to calm her racing heart as she eyed the tall woman. The woman's eyes were bright and searching, the whites so bright against the dark of her face. Those eyes seemed to know so much, too much.

"When did you get here?"

Ode grunted and swished her skirts around her long legs as she walked to sit on the bed.

"I hear you've been looking for me. I knew you'd need ol' Ode, didn't I?"

Rose bristled and slowly re-sheathed her dagger. "Why? What is it you know?"

Ode chuckled again and tipped her long finger against her lips. "Hmm. Yes. I only know what I'm supposed to know when I'm supposed to know. Must not be time yet."

Rose ground her teeth. "You said I'd need you."

Answers. She wanted answers, and over, and over she's been denied answers.

"Aye." The Seer's voice was deep with power. "I did."

Ode hummed and tilted her head at her. Her eyes seemed to look through Rose. "The air around you feels broken and disjointed. Well," she chuckled and reached out to grip Rose's wrist, "more broken. Something is brewing around you. So many paths seem to be circling you but not settling. You've decisions facing you, hm?"

Rose tried to yank her arm free. "What do you know of them?"

Ode squeezed hard enough that Rose yelped. Her grip only tightened and Ode pulled her close.

"We're talking about the secrets hidden by death and sought by those who should be." Ode's voice was deeper than it was a second ago, and it seemed to move through the room.

Rose's mouth went dry even as a tingle started up her arm.

Ode tilted her head before letting go of her wrist and leaning back in her chair. Rose rubbed the numb spot on her wrist, the strange tingle slowly subsiding.

Rose sat there, mouth hanging open, staring at the strange woman watching her with calm eyes. "That's all? That's all you're giving me?"

"Girlie," Ode drawled at her, voice back to normal, "I'm a Seer. Not a god. I'm not all-knowing, and I only know what I'm meant to know."

She growled to herself.

Ode tilted her head again. "I don't think it's you the information is meant for. I feel like I'm still waiting."

"For what?"

"Oh, I don't know. Perhaps we'll find out when we meet later."

Rose sighed, so bone-weary she couldn't bring herself to be angry anymore. She wanted answers. Easy answers. Not more riddles and half spoken sentiments. She wanted just one thing to be easy.

Ode stood, her head cocked to the side.

"Why did you come?" Rose asked.

Ode chuckled softly as she looked around Rose's small, barren room. "I wanted to see who you are." She glanced down at Rose, and Rose felt the look go through her bones. "But I do not think even you know."

Rose wished she had something smart to say back, but she couldn't find any. Ode turned away from her.

"Girlie," Ode called softly, her hand on the door handle. "You've a role to play that you've not yet discovered. That doesn't mean others won't try to mold you to their needs all the same."

She let out a long breath, and Ode left the room just as silently as she'd arrived.

CHAPTER 33

The king called everyone to his small audience room the morning after Ode's surprise visit. Rose's eyes fell on Ode, sitting in front of the king's large desk. Caleb stood against the wall to her left, the captain by the king's shoulder and Lord Tyman on the other. Ode turned those bright eyes to her with a tight smile. She was surprised at Caleb's presence and wondered why the king would include him in such a meeting.

She eyed Ode and stood behind the empty chair next to her. "Are the people who need to be here, here now?"

Ode humphed with a shrug. "Who's to say?"

Rose rolled her eyes and looked away as she sat in the empty chair.

"We were told you had vital information for us," Captain Sayla spoke into the silence.

"Hmm, yes, I very well may," Ode said with a dismissive wave of her hand. "I won't know until I know. I have a question, though." She leaned forward to peer past Rose at Caleb. "Who is the boy wrapped in despair? The air around him is nearly as broken as yours, girlie."

Rose sucked her teeth. "Caleb Harven, from the college."

"Ooh. Such destruction." Ode leaned back in her chair and tilted her head. "Hmm. You're important. I just don't know why yet."

Rose closed her eyes again and hoped for patience.

"Madame," the king spoke, and Rose forced her eyes open. "We need information about Gerik and Goron. About their plans. Are any of those things something you can help us with?"

Ode blinked, her bright eyes almost shimmering. "So many threads hover in this room, so many lines to emerge."

"You told Miss Trewin she would need you. Is that no longer the case?" King Micah asked her, his eyes hard. "If so, speak. We have no time for games."

Power shimmered through the air, made the air on her arms stand on end. When Ode spoke, her voice had a power and deepness to it that hadn't been there before. "In the Forest of Shadows, a battle paused by time will begin again. The search for lost and forgotten things will end. The true battle will start. A ruler will come home. One leader will awaken. Another will be quieted. The threads of history meet."

The room was quiet in the wake of her statement. The words played over and over in Rose's mind. What ruler? What leader? Her eyes landed on the king and locked with his. Was he the ruler? She pulled her eyes away from his. There was too much she didn't know.

"What is that supposed to mean?" Lord Tyman asked in the growing silence.

Ode shrugged, her movement smooth and dainty. "It means nothing to me. You must find the value."

Anger started to burn in Rose's chest. So many riddles. Too many. Answers. That was what she wanted. Needed.

Ode looked over at Caleb, standing still and silent, his eyes wide. "The broken boy must go. Things broken may be repaired and forged anew. I know this to be true."

Caleb's eyes widened, his face paling. The king rubbed his face, his eyes looking sunken. The captain let out a sigh so full of defeat it made Rose's face flush. She'd done this. She'd brought Ode here because she was supposed to have the answers, had said she had the answers.

Rose dragged her face up to look at Caleb, his eyes wide and a little panicked. She just wanted a straight answer. Why couldn't she just get one straight answer?

"Seers are creatures between things," The shadows whispered at her and Rose dragged her eyes back to Ode. "Between things are yours to command."

Between things? Rose watched Ode, not hearing the questions flung at her by the king or the captain, ignoring the stare from Tyman. Between time and place. That's what a Seer was. Someone who saw between time and place. Shadowstalkers had control over the beings that lived in the between spaces. Things that fell in the layers between layers were hers.

"Tell me," Rose demanded and pushed what power into her voice she could. She focused the anger and frustration she felt into the demand behind her words. The shadows in the corners of the rooms darkened and grew. "Tell me what you know of the Orthalen. Does Goron plan to make another one?"

Ode turned angry eyes to her. "You dare order me–"

"No!" She silenced her, and the wolves rushed in. They melded into her, and she let them, her anger making her reckless. They settled into their places, the gaps left for them after whatever had happened in her confrontation with Goron. Memories of powerful women ordering the shadows, commanding the denizens in the between places, of being powerful filled her. She knew, as their memories bled into hers, she could order her. And she knew Ode would obey.

"You dare defy me? Tell me what you know. *Look* and tell me!"

Ode's eyes shimmered, and Rose felt a push back against her order, a small shove against her mind, but she growled her dominance through the shadows at the edge of the room. Ode flinched, and her eyes turned white.

"Tell me," her voice echoed with the voices of the shadows, "of the Orthalen."

Ode's sightless white eyes stared ahead and the last of her resistance faded. "In the shroud of death and the cold of time, it lays." Her voice still had its powerful weight. "In the crypt of the sacrificed, it lays; hidden from time and protected from the searchers."

Rose felt her breath catch in her throat. Protected? Did that mean it wasn't destroyed?

Ode blinked, and the white faded from her eyes. Rose slowly released her grip on the shadows. Her breathing came in fast, shallow breaths and sweat was trickling down her temples. Slowly, the shadows receded back to their corners and edges, leaving a pounding headache in its wake. The room was eerily quiet, and when she turned her eyes away from Ode, everyone was staring at her. Tyman and Captain Sayla watched her, their mouths agape and faces pale. Caleb hunched his shoulder inward, like a small child waiting for a beating. Even the king, so steadfast, watched her with scared eyes.

"You are more than you think," the shadows whispered to her in the silence. "But you must stop running to claim it."

Rose glanced over Ode's shoulder at the shadow falling along the wall and floor.

Ode stood from her chair fast and hard, making it fall backwards with her momentum.

Her mouth opened, closed. Her normally ebony skin was ashen and pale. "No one has ever commanded a Seer through magic."

Rose stared up at her, the memories of her forbearers still fresh in her mind. A memory, old and frayed from decades, flitted through her mind. A woman, tall and regal looking. A face like Ode's but eyes such a bright blue they looked like a lake. This woman, in an era nearly forgotten, had bowed to a Shadowstalker's command. "You know that's not true."

Ode's eyes narrowed even as her breath continued to come in harsh gasps. Color was slowly returning to her ashen cheeks. She pressed her trembling lips together as she stared down at Rose.

"Perhaps you do know who you are."

Rose slowly unclenched her hands. Ode glanced around the room before turning and striding from the room, the bells tied into her dark hair clinking with her strides. Rose turned to look at the rest of the room. The fear in their faces made her chest ache and her throat grow tight.

"Who is the sacrificed?" Rose asked, her voice feeling oddly small after the power she'd forced through it.

"J'Teal," Caleb's voice seemed to echo in the room. "She sacrificed her life to try to destroy Gerik and the Orthalen. Her last act brought about the end of the civil war."

"Do you know where her tomb is?" the king asked.

Caleb shook his head with a shrug. "The answers would've been in the archives. Maybe," he shook his head again, "maybe there is another record here?"

"She said it was protected from the searchers," Captain Sayla spoke up from her post at the king's shoulder. "What do we think that means?"

"Goron has been searching," Rose said slowly as she tried to form her thoughts into something that made sense, "for something since he appeared in our lands. I thought perhaps he was looking for more resources to make another Orthalen. A... a relic that seemed to have focused his magic. It was destroyed when J'Teal fought him last. But what if it wasn't?"

She met the king's eyes and watched as they slowly grew wider.

"What if he's been looking for the thing that made Gerik so powerful it took a martyr and a civil war to stop him so he can finish whatever it was he started?"

The room was silent, silent enough she could hear the chatter of the guards outside in the hallway through the thick doors. The air seemed to thicken, and the king's face grew pale. Finally, the captain swore, a soft, barely heard sound on her breath, and it seemed to break the spell on the group.

"If that's the case," Tyman said after clearing his throat, "we must find it before he does."

"So, we just need to find J'Teal's tomb," the captain said and rubbed her forehead before dropping her hand and locking her eyes on Rose.

Rose nodded. I'll try to ask.

The captain nodded again.

"If we do find this Orthalen," Lord Tyman said into the silence. "Perhaps we can use the Orthalen as a trap to lure Goron."

Rose turned to him with a glare. The king raised his hand to stall the angry words bubbling up her throat. How could he suggest a thing?

Rose fumed silently in her seat. The Orthalen was too dangerous, too important to use as a trap. What if they lost it?

"Lord Tyman, Captain, work with Archie and start coming up with some ideas. We'll revisit this in a few days. Thank you everyone."

Rose stood, the dismissal clear, and the room cleared out.

CHAPTER 34

*R*ose paced back and forth in the warm garden room. She ran her hands through her hair, yanking it roughly from her braid as she did. She didn't know how to get to the Shadow World on her own. She wasn't sure she wanted to. Every time she ended up there, it was because she was either pulled there or got lost.

She collapsed onto the couch, her hands shaking and legs weak. Her breath wavered. The statue of Taspa, the priest's hands held up in benediction seemed to almost mock her. She snorted at the little statue hidden mostly by a fern. She needed more help than a simple wish of hope.

She dropped her chin into her hands, covering her lips with her shaking fingers. The Shadow World scared her. Scared her more than she wanted to admit, and now she had to purposefully look for it. She pressed her lips tight against the wave of nausea.

Somehow, without her knowing or realizing, she sat there long enough for the sun to start to set. The room was dipped into a soft orange glow, and she blinked and straightened, finally noticing the new darkness. Her back cracked as she straightened.

"Shit," she whispered.

"Rose." Micah's voice startled her as he came into the sitting area and sat across from her. He watched her with soft eyes and slowly leaned forward to lean his elbows on his legs. "You look tired."

She huffed and pushed her hair back from her face again. She yanked it into a knot at the base of her neck.

"I need to talk to J'Teal, but I don't want to do it."

"Why?"

She sighed and rubbed her lips again. "I don't want to go to the Shadow World. I don't want to get lost. I–"

"What is the Shadow World?"

She shrugged a jerky movement. "The deepest point in the shadows. The world where the wolves and whisperers live. It's where I end up, where my mind ends up, when I get lost in my magic."

The king leaned back into the couch, crossing his ankle over his knee. "Is this a physical place? Or mental?"

She shrugged and resisted the urge to pull her knees to her chest like a child. "I think it can be both."

He nodded slowly, his eyes locked on hers. She watched him, unsure of his motives or thoughts. Suddenly, he leaned forward across the small gap and held his open hand out to her. She eyed his hand, her heart in her throat and hands suddenly clammy.

"I know how you hate to ask for help," he said, his hand not wavering.

Rose unclenched her own hand and slowly slid it into his. Her heart hammered in her chest, but the feeling that washed over her wasn't fear or anxiety. A calm settled over her. He knew her. Knew her ticks and bad habits. Knew them and offered his hand anyway. She wasn't sure when or how she'd allowed him close enough to see, but he had. Rose found she cared less than she thought she would've.

His hand was warm and dry in hers. She could feel the rough calluses on his palm and fingers. She liked that his hands were as rough as hers. They weren't the fine and gentle hands of a lord, and that made her happier than it probably should.

Micah gripped her hand firmly as if he was worried she'd pull hers back.

"I don't really know what I'm doing."

"I know," he said with a soft smile.

"No encouraging words?" she said with a huff.

"I don't think you particularly like the speeches and pomp."

"Hmm," she hummed and laid down on the couch without breaking their clasped hands. "No, I guess you're right."

Rose let out a long breath and tried to keep her heart from jumping back into her throat.

"Just don't–"

"I won't let you get lost."

She looked over at him and nodded. He wouldn't. She believed that. She closed her eyes and focused on the darkness in the room. She wasn't sure how to find what she was looking for but knew it was deep in the shadows. She let herself settle into the shadows and felt as she fell into the Undertunnels. As she opened her eyes, the dark fog-filled world greeted her. She looked down at her empty hand but could still feel the king's in hers. Rose wiggled her fingers and felt a squeeze back in response. Rose smiled, and a bit of peace settled in her. She could do this because, for the first time in her life, she wasn't alone.

She rolled her shoulders back and took a deep breath as she looked around the Undertunnels. The mist swirled gently around her knees, and the darkness around her was filled with openings into the gardens. She turned away from those and looked into the darkest area of the Undertunnels. Deep in the mists, almost hidden in the fog, was a path of nearly complete darkness.

The more she stared at it, the more the path seemed to solidify in the fog. The path was too long and too dark for her to see more than a few paces into the darkness.

A wolf formed to her right and Rose looked at it with a raised eyebrow.

"Well?"

The shadow dissolved in a huff of mist and darkness.

"Ass," she said and turned down the dark path.

Rose hoped it was the right path. She didn't actually know where it led. If it had existed before now, she'd never noticed it. How could she? She'd never bothered to explore the Undertunnels. Her magic.

She sighed. She should've tried harder. She learned the bare minimum to work her magic and had stopped. Her fear had stopped her.

A squeeze on her hand and Rose shook her head. Fluttering her fingers once more, she turned down the dark tunnel. The fog grew thicker as she walked, the darkness became denser. It was almost as if it was becoming a physical thing and pressed against her. She forced herself to walk further down the darkness, surrounded by grey mists that dampened her skin. The darkness pressed further against her, and her chest grew tight. She squeezed her hand into a tight fist as her breaths became pants against the weight of the darkness against her chest.

Micah's squeeze on her hand helped. It helped remind her that the shadows were her place. Even as they threatened to squeeze the air from her chest, she knew they wouldn't. Rose gripped his hand in hers as it shook and grew clammy and continued on.

The further she went, Rose could feel herself stretching from her body. Like a pull at the back of her mind. She tried to swallow, but her mouth had gone dry. Sweat started trickling down her temple, and her muscles ached. An exhaustion started to settle in her muscles.

Rose could just make out ahead of her, a barrier of some kind. In the near-complete darkness, broken only by the swirls of fog and mist, she saw a moving mass of shadow. She stopped just in front of it, her breath erratic fast and hard. Her limbs shook, mostly from fear but also from the heavy weight of using so much magic. How far had she come? Was distance even something that could be measured here?

Tentatively, she reached out a hand toward the writhing mass of shadow. With trembling fingers, she touched the thing and gasped a small breath of surprise when she felt a soft, smooth texture. It moved under her fingers, undulated and rolled. It had a mass that she hadn't expected, and when she pushed against it, she was met with resistance.

Many scholars believed in an edge to the world. That somewhere there was a cliff where the world ended, so sheer and high you could see no ground. A place where the oceans ran off the map and into the abyss. Was this where the world ended? Had she reached the edge, and this was the barrier to the abyss? Were the gods waiting on the other side?

A wolf formed beside her again, and Rose jerked at its sudden appearance. Micah squeezed her hand again, and she returned the pressure. The wolf watched her with glowing red eyes before turning away with a huffed breath. It walked into the shadow wall and disappeared.

"Well, shit," Rose wiped the sweat from her forehead.

She placed her clammy hand against the rolling shadows once more, and with a deep breath, pushed.

It was like pushing through sand. Firm, but it eventually gave way to her, and she pushed herself through the barrier. Panic flooded her chest, and her breath grew tight as the shadows squeezed her harder and harder. What if she was lost? Would she be trapped here? Her breathing grew fast and short, and she started to wave her hand wildly through the darkness.

A firm grip on her hand, almost enough to hurt, brought her attention back from the panic, and she forced herself to stop. Slow down. She took a deep breath. Reminded herself that panic makes mistakes. Reminded herself that he wouldn't let her get lost. Another deep breath, and her heart didn't feel like it was about to burst from her chest anymore. Blowing out a long, slow breath, she stepped forward again.

She made three more steps through the darkness before suddenly the ground fell out from beneath her. With a startled gasp, she fell a short drop before landing awkwardly, her heart in her throat, in the ashen woods of the Shadow World.

A laugh burst from her, and she shoved her clenched fists into the air. Her laughter echoed through the woods, and the eerie silence quickly stopped her giggles. She looked around, the spindly white trees surrounding her. Above her, the orange-tinged sky was cloudless and strange.

"J'Teal?" Her voice was small, and she cleared her throat before trying again, with less of a shake. "J'Teal."

Silence.

"Well, shit," she muttered again and walked through the trees.

Deep in the mists, through the thick trees, Rose heard the Speakers. Their words were unintelligible, a murmur in the distance. She licked her dry lips and wiggled her fingers. Micah's presence in her hand helped to calm her, but her heart still quickened as their voices moved around her. Knowing they were the voices of dead Shadowstalkers and Shademakers only added to the anxiety making her gut roll.

J'Teal had told her she was part of the Speakers. Rose stopped her slow wandering and turned to the loudest of the mists. Could she command the Speakers? She commanded Ode. Speakers were even more between things. These beings were her between things, lost between death and life. Locked in the form of shadow.

She licked her lips again. She should be able to command them.

"J'Teal," she called toward the darkening mists. "Send me J'Teal."

The Speakers shouted in a flurry of voices and words. She winced at their sudden volume but forced herself not to flinch. Not to cover her ears.

"J'Teal," she called again.

This time the Speakers silenced, and in a whoosh of fog and dew, a transparent J'Teal walked forward. She stayed in the mists, not quite as clear or present as she had been before. The edges of her were blurred and seemed to weave in and out of the fog. She looked like the shadow wolves.

"You are learning much faster than I expected you to." J'Teal's voice had an edge of otherness to it. It echoed like she hadn't quite separated from the Speakers, and they spoke with her. "It usually takes years to learn how to find the Shadow World on your own."

Rose shoved her hands into the pockets of her short coat. *Oh.*

More sweat ran down her temples, and she started to notice the trail down her back. A steady ache was building behind her eyes.

"I need your help."

J'Teal folded her arms and stared at her.

"Where are you buried? Where were the Clan Lands?"

J'Teal's form flickered, and when she reformed, she was clearer, firmer than before. Rose could see more colors to her skirts and hair than before.

"Why?" This time her voice was sharp and clear. All traces of the Speakers were gone.

Rose sighed, and it was mournful. "Because," she paused and worried her lip between her teeth. "Because the Orthalen wasn't destroyed, and a Seer told me it was hidden with your grave."

J'Teal collapsed to her knees with a wail that shook the world. The mists roiled around them, and the Speakers seemed to echo her cry. Rose started and held her arms out to the fallen woman but didn't know how to help her. J'Teal beat her fists against the ground, and Rose stood there, helpless.

"Are you sure?" J'Teal demanded, her voice raw and broken as she looked up at Rose.

"No," she admitted and squatted down on her heels to look J'Teal in the eye. "But I'm pretty sure."

"It was all for nothing?" her voice was so broken, so defeated. Rose hesitantly reached out a hand and gripped J'Teal's arm. "It was all for nothing."

J'Teal dropped her head, chin nearly touching her chest, as her hair framed and hid her face.

"Goron has been searching for it. We need to find it before he does."

"Obviously!" J'Teal snapped her head up to glare at Rose, and she hastily pulled her hand back. "Of course you do, girl! Do you think I don't know! I died trying to destroy that abomination!"

Rose pressed her lips tight and stood up. She would not let this woman see her fear. "Then help me find it. The Seer says it's hidden in the sacrificed tomb. We think she means you."

With a deep breath, one the mist and fog seemed to match, J'Teal heaved herself to her feet. No tears fell down her cheeks, though Rose had expected there to be. She watched Rose with hard eyes.

"The Crown's Forest. Jonas did what he could to protect our lands. Within the Crown's Forest, hidden from the world, is our forest."

The Crown's Forest was a game preserve, private lands that belong to the royal family situated east of Haven Province. It was forbidden to hunt, fell trees, or live in those woods. Royal Woodsman patrolled them, ensuring it was protected. As far as Rose knew, that forest had always belonged to the crown.

Rose nodded and let out another breath.

"Do not let him win again."

She locked eyes with J'Teal. She didn't know how she could promise such a thing to J'Teal. This warrior woman in front of her had training. She had the benefit of an entire clan teaching her, helping her. How could Rose promise to do what J'Teal couldn't with even less?

She didn't have an answer. She didn't want to say out loud that she didn't know if she could. Instead, she gripped Micah's hand and released the grip she'd kept on her Shadow World. Her mind retreated from the misty forest, J'Teals hard eyes following her the whole way.

SHE BLINKED AND GASPED, returning to the world and her body with a throbbing behind her eyes. Groaning, she rubbed her forehead with her free hand.

"Are you alright?"

Rose grunted at Micah, trying to ignore the heartbeat in her head and focus instead on the warm hand gripping hers.

"I'll be fine," she mumbled and eased herself into a sitting position. After one last gentle squeeze, Micah slowly pulled his hand free of hers. She told herself she didn't regret the loss.

"Did it work? Did you find J'Teal?"

She curled her hand into a fist and slid it into her coat. "Yes. She said the Clan Lands were in the Crown Forest."

Micah leaned back in his chair and rubbed his hand over his short beard.

"J'Teal said King Jonas hid them, tried to protect their lands."

"He hid them so well even future kings would not know the value of those forests," Micah murmured and shook his head. "How much have we lost to time? How much of our past have we forgotten?"

"Too much." And with the destruction of the college, even more, they couldn't begin to understand yet. She thought about J'Teal and all the things she knew. All the things Rose wished to know. Could her ghost teach me? Would she be able to separate from the shadows enough to train me? Rose quickly disregarded that idea. The pounding in her head and exhaustion plaguing her bones from this trip was enough that she didn't want to make it again any time soon. The ache behind her eyes was a weary reminder of the potential risk she took every time she used her magic. Which was worse: going blind or ignorance?

Micah sighed and his shoulders slumped. There were bags under his eyes and a downward pull of his lips.

"At least now we know where to go."

"Yes," Rose said, "and Goron doesn't."

CHAPTER 35

He'd never been more frustrated in his life. Goron stood in the ruins of his home. The once great and beautiful stone buildings and statues were reduced to rubble and stacks of forgotten history. He sat on a pile of stone, the sun blocked by a new group of storm clouds, black and heavy in the sky. The snow and ice covered much of the remaining bits of his home. He hadn't expected anything to be here, but a deep ache settled in his chest at seeing the destruction.

He couldn't find it. He still couldn't sense it. Gerik seemed so sure, so adamant, that it hadn't been destroyed, but what if he was wrong? How could he return to his general as a failure in his most important task?

Goron dropped his head into his hands with a groan. It had to be here. Somewhere.

"How goes your search?" the voice whispered around him.

Goron jumped, a small twitch of his shoulders, at Gerik's voice. He hated many aspects of his magic, but the whispering through darkness was the one he hated most. It felt unnatural. Evil. Something about it felt contrary to nature.

"I cannot find it," he admitted with a rumbling sigh. "I cannot sense it."

The darkness was silent. Large, fluffy snowflakes started to fall from the dark sky. Dense and wet. He felt none of the cold as they settled about his shoulders.

"That is unfortunate."

Goron ground his teeth. "Perhaps you could join me in the search for it."

"My wound heals, but I still cannot travel."

Goron made a face at Gerik's whispered words. He damn well could travel. He just didn't want to risk a fight he might lose. Goron held no delusions on his friend and master's priorities.

"But," the darkness breathed, "perhaps I can still find a location for you."

"Good." He nodded to the empty field. He was always better with a goal.

CHAPTER 36

*K*nocking on her door woke her. Cracking her tired, sore eye toward her window, Rose saw the smallest glimmer of light.

"Gods," she murmured with a groan and rolled over. "Too early."

The knocking continued, louder and longer.

"Fine," she yelled just loud enough to be heard and rolled out of bed. The cold floor shocked her feet as she stumbled to the door.

"What?" she growled as she yanked open the door.

Aaron stared at her, lips quirked in a cheeky smile. He raised an eyebrow at her. "We're training this morning."

She blinked and tried to shake the sleep from her mind. "Now?"

"Yes. Get dressed. I'll be in the training room."

With that, he turned on his heel and marched back down the corridor. Rose stared at his back as he went before slumping back inside. Groaning and grumbling the whole way, Rose changed into an old tunic and trousers, shoving her cold feet into thick socks and boots.

She'd rather be sleeping, still be in her warm bed, but she knew the strain on her muscles and focus needed would help clear her mind. With the revelation of the Clan Lands location, the Orthalen.... She needed that. She wanted to start searching the Crown's Forest. She wanted to find the ruins of her people's home. She needed to find the Orthalen. The king had asked her to wait. He'd asked her to wait for a plan, and she'd reluctantly agreed.

The waiting was making her skin itch.

As she entered the training room, Aaron had already set up the space and gestured to her blades waiting in the stand.

"Why are we doing this so early?" Rose asked as she selected her blades and stepped into the marked circle.

"I've things I'm doing the rest of the day, and you can't let your training lapse."

Rose grunted and spun the blades in her hands. Aaron stepped into the circle with her, and they began. It felt good to have the sharp edges spinning around her, the control she felt over them. She dipped, dodged right around Aaron's thrust. Popping back up, Rose thrust her right blade toward his side while her left swung across his chest in a reversed grip. Aaron bladed his body past her leading feint and brought his sword in close to deflect her slicing blade. She pushed her advantage and jabbed for his chest with her right blade again. His sword met her blade, and in a swirl of movement her eyes couldn't track, he'd spun his around again to knock her left blade from her hand.

"Shit," she puffed and tried to step back, but the fist of his free hand, pounded into her forearm and her right blade clattered to the floor.

A second later, his sword was level at her throat.

"Dead."

She glared at him, her breath coming in puffs and sweat dripping down her temples.

"I almost had you."

"Almost doesn't count in life and death."

She ground her teeth. "Obviously." She strode over to her fallen knives and picked them back up with jerky movements. "You think I don't know that?"

"Then train like it. You fight like you train, and you train like you fight. Take it seriously. All of it."

She pressed her lips tight against the words she wanted to yell at him and instead faced him again with her blades raised. Aaron grunted and nodded. Rose rolled her shoulders and squinted against the headache behind her eyes. She turned to Aaron, her blades at the ready. Aaron nodded and raised his own long sword.

"Have you thought any further on joining the Shields?" he asked as he danced around her on light feet.

She humphed and watched his arms, waiting for the twitch of muscle before he struck.

"Not many have the strength for it, but I've seen that strength in you."

She jabbed a false strike that he ignored, and circled him as he circled her. When he finally struck, she barely saw it in time and had to jump back, her blades coming up in a cross to stop the downward strike. She pulled her knife free and sliced at his middle only to get clocked in the jaw by the pommel of his sword. Pain exploded in her jaw, and stars clouded her vision.

"Ack!" she grunted and stumbled away. She blinked and shook her head to try to clear her vision. She painfully rotated her jaw but was glad it moved smoothly.

"You're not usually this reckless. What's wrong?"

She rubbed her jaw, head pounding. Too many things, she thought with a shake of her head.

"Why do you want me to join your lot so badly?"

Aaron shrugged and leaned his sword in the weapons rack.

"I can see a place for you here. I think you'd do well with us."

He held a waterskin out to her and she slowly took it. His words shocked her more than she'd expected. He watched her with expectant eyes, clear of any misgiving. He meant what he said.

"You say that because you think you know me."

He huffed and tossed his hand into the air dismissively. "Everyone has a past. What makes you think yours is the only one important enough to matter?"

"Not everyone has a past like mine." She tossed the water away.

"No, but are you going to let it define you 'til the end of your days?"

Rose glowered at him but knew his point was too valid to continue to argue. Even if she didn't know what to do about it. She turned to set her dirks away when she felt a tug. She paused and put her hand to her chest. The sharp, hard pull had taken her breath away.

"Rose?"

"Something's wrong," she gasped.

She felt the tug again, harder and sharper, and she gasped at the pain. It felt like her very soul was being torn. The next tug felt like something snapped inside. Her knees went out, and her vision went dark before she hit the floor.

CHAPTER 37

*R*ose fell to her knees, clutching her chest. She would've screamed if she could draw any breath. Instead, tears fell down her cheeks, and she choked on gasping sobs. She looked down at her chest, expecting to see a gaping hole but found none.

"Gods," she gasped and finally managed to force air into her lungs. "What... "

Mist swirled around her knees, and when she looked around through blurry, tear-filled eyes, she saw the barren trees and flat-lands of the Shadow World.

"J'Teal?" Rose gasped and struggled to stand. "J'Teal, what in the hells?"

"That bitch still around?" hissed a familiar voice.

Rose turned and saw Gerik standing several paces away. It was the body of D'ray staring at her, the strange B'leakon eyes swirling orange and red. "How—"

"How'd I do this?" he asked while gesturing at her. "This was my trick that J'Teal stole from me. I taught it to her, and she acts like she's the only one who can work the magic." He scoffed. "Please."

Rose pushed herself to her feet, biting her lip to hold back the whimpers as she did. "What did you do to me?"

"The same thing J'Teal's been doing when she pulls you here. I just wasn't nice enough to do it while you were asleep."

Rose pressed the heel of her hand into her breastbone.

"Feel like your soul was ripped out?" Gerik asked with a sneer. "Because it was. Being asleep makes it easier, less painful. Your soul tends to drift while asleep anyway."

Gerik took several large steps and gripped her hard by her jaw. He towered above her, his eyes swirling red. "Now, where is the Orthalen?"

"How are you here?" Rose bit out past her clenched teeth.

Gerik sucked his teeth. "I am, at the end of everything, still a Shademaker."

"But why haven't they come for you?" The shadows were silent, the mists swirling around in the darkness. Even the Speakers were quiet.

"I am still weak, thanks to you, but I am not without some tricks. Now, last time I ask nicely. Goron can't find it, so I'm assuming the bitch had it hidden after she died. Where is it?"

Rose clenched her jaw and would've spit if she was able to open it against his grip. He shoved her away with a hiss, and she stumbled backwards. Before she could blink, Gerik gripped either side of her head.

"Usually, once I've tasted a magic, I can recreate it. To some degree," Gerik was saying. "Even without the Orthalen."

A sinking feeling settled in her stomach, and she tried in vain to pry his hands off. Rose screamed as burning pain seared through her mind. That same pain as that night in the throne room, that night he'd used and manipulated the captain's magic. She felt Gerik claw his way through her mind, memories. He burned through her mind and left burning chasms behind. He pushed through her thoughts, searching.

She screamed faster than she could draw breath. This was so much worse than last time. Fragments of memories flitted across her vision: the quiet night listening to Micah draw, Caleb's tired face, the captain watching her with a wiry smile.

He was so much stronger this time. Rose tried but couldn't control her thoughts or memories. The pain was so distracting, she couldn't do anything but writhe. She felt blood fall over her lips and drip off her chin.

More memories flew across her vision: the stone, the shadows found in the college. Jonas' writings about his lost love. The location of the Orthalen.

Gerik hissed and dug deeper into those memories before releasing her. Rose crumpled to the ground and lay where she fell.

"They buried it with her, hm?" Gerik was saying, but Rose barely understood the words. "And the king is your Anchor. My... that is interesting. I will send my warrior to destroy those fools." Gerik bent over her crumpled body, and suddenly, his face filled her vision. "I look forward to watching you die."

He faded from view, and with him, whatever magic he'd used to hide their presence vanished. The whispers started, loud and forceful this time. Wolves prowled the misty forest, growling and hunting for Gerik, though he was long gone. The fog swirled as if driven by some unknown wind. Rose tried to roll over, and after the third try, was finally able to roll to her side. The Speakers were yelling now, voices so loud and so numerous she couldn't make out the words, but the meaning was clear: a pack. She needed to join the pack.

She remembered that was bad, that she shouldn't listen to them, but she didn't remember why. Rose eased herself onto her hands and knees, whimpering as she moved. Blood dripped from her lips to the gray earth. She stared at the strange dirt, not sure where it was from or why she was kneeling on it.

The fog swirled around the drops, and she wondered, again, why she shouldn't listen to the whispers. She put her hand to her chest, to the ache that sat there, and wondered if she should be worried about what had happened. Something had. She remembered that much but couldn't remember what. Maybe the whisperers knew. Maybe they would help her remember.

MICAH HAD a sour taste in his mouth that hadn't gone away since the servant girl had told him Mariah needed him in the Healer's wing. Something in his bones told him Rose was hurt or in trouble. He didn't understand or know where the feeling came from, but something felt... off. It was like some part of him was pulled too tight and was straining against some great force.

Micah quickly realized he soon wouldn't be able to turn back from Rose and how she made him feel.

He turned the last corner into the Healer's Wing and found Mariah leaning her shoulder against the wall with a frown creasing her face.

"What happened?" he asked as he neared.

Mariah watched him with cautious eyes and pushed away from the wall. She glanced at the closed door across the hall. "She was sparring with Aaron and collapsed. She's breathing, but that's all. He sent word to me once she was here."

Micah's heart raced, and it made him a little breathless. He looked over at the room she must be in and again felt the pressure that had been plaguing him all afternoon.

"As her Anchor," Mariah said, and Micah snapped his eyes to her, "I thought it would be wise to have you here, in case this is related."

Micah nodded at Mariah. "It is."

"How do you know that?" she asked him.

"I don't know," Micah rubbed his chest again. "Something just feels... wrong."

It felt like his soul was being stretched across distances. Something was wrong, and he knew it. He just didn't have the words to explain why. He turned and pushed open the door to Rose's room, all decorum forgotten. He didn't care how it looked. He only knew something bad was happening. Mariah shouted something at him and followed closely on his heels. What he saw made him pause, bile rising in his throat.

Rose lay on the small bed, skin ashen pale. Her closed eyes were sunken. The bruise on her throat looked bright in stark contrast to the rest of her. He barely noticed Rita standing on the side, wiping away the blood that was running from her nose. Micah sat gingerly on the edge of the cot and brushed shaking hands across her forehead. Her skin was cold. Too cold.

"Sire," Rita murmured. "We're doing everything we can think of but... none of us have seen anything like this before. We still don't know where the blood is coming from or why."

The pressure in his chest increased, almost to the point of being painful, and it felt like whatever was being strained was nearing a breaking point. His breath caught at the sharp pain growing in his chest.

He gently cupped her cheek, shaking fingers brushing against her smooth skin. He'd seen her injured, seen her broken before. This was different. She felt empty, laying there, and all the fiery resilience he loved was gone.

"Micah," Mariah said softly somewhere behind him. "I can't *hear* anything."

"I think she's lost," he said softly as he brushed her cheek. He remembered what she'd said about going insane if she became lost in her magic. He didn't know what had happened, what she'd done, but he knew in his bones she was lost.

"How are—" Rita started.

"Be silent or leave," he snapped and turned his attention back to Rose.

"Come back to me," he whispered while tracing her high cheekbones with his thumbs. Her eyes twitched under her lids, but that was the only indication she'd heard. "Come back."

Mariah had explained to him once, years ago when he was a young, impatient man, that like kingdoms, magic was most often passed down through family lines. She'd also told him using and mastering it was instinctual. There were no more mages to teach people how to use their magic, and they were now left with trusting their instincts.

His instincts were telling him to imagine a chain. As her Anchor, it seemed their souls were bound and tied together. He imagined that bond, the tie, as a chain. It was bright in his mind's eye. Bright and glowing. He formed the chain around the pressure sitting in his chest and followed it with whatever intuition he had. He worked that chain until he felt it was stable enough, that it had formed and flowed all the way to Rose. Once it was there, once he could grip it in his mind, he focused on that pressure and *tugged*.

CHAPTER 38

*S*he could almost understand the words now. If she listened hard enough, she could pick out a few words here and there. She looked down at her hand and saw it smeared with blood. Why was that there?

She touched her other hand to her lips and felt something tacky and thick. When she pulled her hand away, there were smudges of dark blood. Ah, that's why.

The endless sky was getting darker, the fog getting thicker. She should go soon. Shouldn't she? Go where? She didn't know. She needed to go somewhere, but she couldn't name it now.

Come now.

Join us.

Join the pack.

The words were clearer now. She should go with them, but still, she lingered. The mists were cool on her skin as it swirled around her. Was that where she was supposed to go?

Hands ghosted across her cheeks, sending a jolt down her spine. She touched her hands to her face but didn't find the hands warming her skin. This was familiar. Why was it familiar?

"Come back to me."

She smiled, and tears filled her eyes. She knew that voice. Not the name or the face that came with it, but she knew the voice.

"Come back."

"How?" she sobbed, her voice gravely and sore. "How?"

A tug seemed to come from deep in her chest. It had the smallest memory of the painful rip that brought her here, but there wasn't the pain. The tug seemed to come from a chain that appeared around her, rooted somewhere deep in her chest. She gripped the chain, thin and dainty looking, and it pulled tight, no more slack in the links. There was another tug on the other end of the chain, and it pulled at Rose. She gripped it harder and pulled on it. Gently but firmly, the chain started to pull her, and she stiffly stood and followed it.

The whisperers shouted at her as she walked, but now she remembered she wasn't meant to go with them. She needed to go home.

"Rose?"

The chain pulled her home.

Rose opened her eyes and saw his face leaning over her. It was his hands on her face, and shakily, she raised her own hands to grip his.

"There you are, Rose."

She blinked at him and tightened her grip on his wrists.

"Do you know who I am?"

More blinking. She did. She knew she did, but the soft whispers in the room wouldn't let her remember. Tears rolled down her cheeks. She wanted to remember.

He stroked her cheeks with his thumbs. "Focus on me, Rose. Listen to my voice and tell me who I am."

The whispers slowly disappeared, and the more she focused on his face, his worried brown eyes, and the feel of his rough hands on her face, the more she could think.

"Micah," she hoarsely whispered.

Micah smiled and nodded. "Yes."

She felt a gentle tug somewhere deep in her chest, and when she followed the chain from the tug, it ended with Micah.

"Oh," she breathed and pulled on her end of the bright chain. "It was you."

He nodded again, and with one last little pull, the whisperers disappeared entirely. "Do you want to sit up?"

Rose nodded, and gently, Micah helped her to sit up. Her head pounded with the movement and her eyes watered from the pain. His hands fell away, and he started to move back. She reached out in panic and gripped him hard on the arm.

"No," she said and buried her face in his shoulder. "They might come back."

Micah eased her feet to the floor and tucked her under his arm. She curled into the space and rested her cheek against his chest. The sound of his heart beating helped to remind her where she was.

"Can you tell us what happened?" a different voice asked.

Her eyes went around the room and stopped on the two strange people staring at her with wide eyes. No. They weren't strange. She knew them. She just needed to find the memory.

"Rose?" the blond woman asked again.

She tried to think, but her head hurt, pounded, and she couldn't think. It was like chasing a dream just after waking up. She knew she had the memory; she just couldn't grip it. Micah gripped her chin and tipped her face up to meet his eyes.

"There aren't any shadows in your eyes," he said, a frown between his brows. "What's her name?"

Rose looked at the blond woman again and knew she knew, but there was nothing where the memory should be. She felt something warm pour down her lips, and she whimpered at the pain that flashed across her head. "I don't know."

"Get Rita back in here!" Micah bellowed, and Rose gripped her forehead as the pain built.

The blond woman held a cloth to her lips and wiped the blood away. Micah tightened his arm around her and pressed her head into his chest.

"What do you remember?" his voice rumbled in his chest.

Rose curled in on herself and curled into his lap. He'd done this to her, with his forbidden, stolen magic. He'd broken her.

"Rose?"

"*Gerik*," she whispered, tears rolling down her cheeks. "Gerik did this."

Someone else entered the small room. Her hair was short and stuck out in a curly mess. She looked familiar, but pain flared the moment Rose tried to think why. The curly-haired woman put her hand on Rose's forehead, and the pain receded under the warmth that spread from the woman's hand. Words were said around her, but Rose didn't have the ability to understand anymore. She clung to Micah, the only thing she knew or could remember, and ignored the rushed words spoken around her.

A cup was pressed into her hand and Micah helped her drink it. The liquid was too hot, bitter, and Rose recoiled from it. Micah shushed her and gently made her drink it.

"She needs to sleep."

Rose didn't know the voice, but she strongly disagreed with sleeping. If she slept, what's to stop the voices from coming back? What if she woke and didn't remember anything anymore?

"Are you sure that's wise?" Micah asked.

"Her mind needs to rest," the voice was saying. "Rita can watch her, but she risks more damage if she continues to try to remember things."

Another cup was pressed into her hand by Micah, and reluctantly Rose drank. It was the same bitter drink as before, but this time, it had a sweet aftertaste that she found she disliked even more. The voices around her had slowly quieted as though they'd run out of words. Her eyes, already closed, became heavier and hard to open. She fought against the heavy pull.

"Just sleep, Rose," Micah told her in a gentle voice and she lost the will to fight anymore.

CHAPTER 39

*R*ose had spent the last several days in and out of sleep. Whatever was put in her tea put her into a deep, dreamless sleep. She'd woken several times, not remembering anything. Sometimes she would remember a name, a face, a conversation only to wake up later in the day to have a pounding headache and no memories. The only thing that seemed to help, the only thing that kept her from losing her mind entirely, was the tender, reassuring tug at the end of the golden chain. Micah would tug on it gently, like a slight pressure somewhere under her ribs, and she'd tug back.

It became a familiar back and forth. When she was awake and in control of her mind enough, she would follow the chain in her mind's eye to the presence that was Micah at the other end.

She didn't know what to make of the new bond, the chain that ran between them. It was reassuring, familiar. Whenever she felt the shadows getting too close or her memories slipping through her grasp, she could focus on that bond and would ground herself; the shadows would be pushed back. Rose had enough wherewithal about her to wonder if she would be as calm and as accepting about this new, stronger bond being put on her if it had been anyone else. She hadn't liked the answer she found at the end of that introspective question.

Now, finally released from Rita's care with what felt like most of her memories intact, she walked hesitantly toward the meeting room. Now that Rita had deemed her recovered or recovered enough, they all were eager to hear what had happened, what Gerik had done to her. What he knew.

She shivered and rubbed her sternum, where the chain was coiled. She didn't want to talk about what happened. She felt invaded, wounded like she'd never been before. He'd ripped her soul from her and forced his way through her mind, her memories. He took what he wanted and destroyed the rest. She didn't know if she was ready to talk about that.

Rose arrived at the closed door and knocked gently. The chain buried in her chest twitched as Micah called for her to enter.

Tea sat on the table and chairs surrounding the small table. She hadn't been in this room before, but the drapes and plush rug made it feel cozy compared to the study or throne room. She looked around, realizing she was the only one there.

"Sorry, I didn't think I was this early."

"No," Micah said from his chair. "I told them to come later. I wanted to check—to talk to you first."

She nodded and settled herself in the chair closest to his.

"How are you?" he asked softly.

"My memories are back," she murmured. "At least, it seems like they all are. Sometimes it takes me a bit to remember, but I can."

"But how are you?"

Rose twisted her fingers in her lap and had to bite down the wave of nausea that rose in her throat. "I'll be fine. Eventually."

He looked like he wanted to press her further; his mouth opened and closed, and his eyes were pinched. But, in the end, he nodded.

"How did you do it?" she asked into the growing silence and rubbed her sternum. "How did this... how did you do this?"

"I don't know," his voice was soft, tentative. She'd never seen him speak with such hesitation before. "I am sorry, though, for... for binding you like this."

"Do not be sorry," she spoke quickly and quietly. "Do not. Without this grounding, I do not think I'd have come out of these last few days anywhere near as sane as I did."

Her life was chaotic and changing. She wasn't sure what she really wanted out of it anymore or where she wanted to be, but she knew she didn't regret or hate this new thing.

He watched her, waiting for her to change her mind, before nodding. "I'm glad of that, then."

"We will keep this to ourselves, though?" Rose asked.

"Oh, yes." He agreed instantly, and Rose felt relief that he felt as she did. This thing, this bond, was too intimate to share with others.

"Was it the whisperers that caused the memory loss?" he asked quietly.

"Some of it, I'm sure," Rose whispered, her eyes fixed on the wall ahead of her. "But not all."

"Are you ready to talk about this? We can wait."

"No, we can't." Rose turned her eyes to him. In her mind's eye, she saw the shimmering chain and gripped it. She gripped it so hard she could feel the links biting into her palms. "But I will be alright."

He nodded and pressed his fingers to his sternum. "I can feel that," he said softly. "Right here. It's very strange."

Rose smiled softly in apology and released her strangle-hold grip.

The knock at the door interrupted any response she might've had. Micah let out a soft sigh and called for them to enter. Captain Sayla and Lord... Rose frowned. She knew his name, but it escaped her now, and a rush of panic had her heart beating. Her frantic grip of the bond returned, and Micah shifted in his seat in response to her death grip.

She frantically searched her memory for this man as the three settled themselves around the table. He was an advisor. He was new to the castle. But his name...?

"Lord Tyman," Micah said firmly as he nodded to him. "Thank you for joining us."

Rose turned grateful eyes to Micah.

The captain was glancing between Rose and the king, and Rose wondered at the look. The captain almost seemed apprehensive.

"Now," Lord Tyman spoke up, and everyone turned their attention to him. "Miss Trewin. What has happened with Gerik?"

Rose turned her eyes to the advisor and wished she could remember if she liked him. Everyone turned their eyes to her. She took a deep breath through her nose and tried to quell the nausea that was starting. She rubbed her sternum and the phantom pain there. Their chain shook, and Rose turned watery eyes to Micah. She gripped the bond, running it through her fingers in her mind. She reminded herself that most of what happened wouldn't make sense to them, that she could keep the details brief and to the point.

"Gerik," she willed her voice not to shake, "was able to pull me... pull me to an in-between place in the shadows. There he— he was able to go through my memories."

"How?" the captain asked.

"Like before," she whispered, meeting her wide eyes. "Like in the throne room, but it was so much worse. I couldn't fight him. I couldn't do anything to keep my memories safe."

"What information did he get?" Lord Tyman asked, his voice too loud, too clear.

She cut her eyes to the lord, and regardless of how she might've felt about him before, she decided she did not like him now. "Every-thing." The word tore itself from her chest. "Everything. He knows where the Orthalen is. He's sending Goron."

Lord Tyman cursed quietly under his breath, and the captain rubbed her forehead. "So, what next?"

"Most of my soldiers are in the south, helping to re-secure the border. I cannot leave the castle and the capital unguarded, but I can send a small group of soldiers and Light Horse Officers. Lord Tyman, Captain Sayla," King Micah said. "How soon can your people be ready to leave?"

"Two days," Lord Tyman said. He glanced at Captain Sayla who nodded.

"Yes, two days."

"That is too long," Rose snapped. "We need to leave now."

Goron could travel through the very earth. He could be there at any moment. They didn't have the time to wait, to plan. She itched with the need to act. To do something.

Captain Sayla's eyes turned to her, and Rose had to look away from the pity she saw in them. She didn't want their pity. She wanted vengeance. Action. She wanted to make someone bleed for what was done to her.

"Rose, we are moving as fast as we can, but there are steps we need to take. People we need to outfit." The captain's voice was soft and smooth, and for some reason, it grated on Rose's raw nerves even more.

"The forest is large," Tyman said. "And as you've said before, Goron cannot find the Orthalen. This has narrowed his search zone, but it is still several hundred acres."

Rose clenched her hands tight enough that she felt her nails bite into her palms. She forced herself to nod, even if she didn't like his logic. Even if she knew he was right.

"Captain, Tyman," Micah took hold of the conversation as they settled into silence. "Begin forming your people. Be ready to leave in two days."

They nodded and filed out of the room. Rose stood on shaky legs. A soft touch on the back of her hand stalled Rose, and she waited until the room was empty, save for the two of them, before turning around.

Rose pressed, clenching and unclenching her hands. "We don't have time to wait."

Micah's hand wrapped around her fist. "I know, but you need to rest."

"No!" she shouted but didn't pull her hand from his. Despite the nausea, the pain, and the remaining terror she was feeling, she needed to get this over with. She needed to move. It was almost a panicked fury that was pushing her along. "No, we need to leave. Now. Goron could be there at any moment. We can't let him get the Orthalen."

Micah stepped close and thumped his chest with his fingers. "I can feel it, Rose. I can feel how close you are to breaking. Rest. This can wait a day."

Rose took a deep breath and tried not to gasp. Talking about what

Gerik had done, remembering it. She tried to push those memories back. She tried to bury them with all her other horrible memories, but she couldn't. Not yet.

She took another gasping breath and looked up at him. "He took everything." Her voice broke and shook. "Everything and left me with nothing."

Another deep breath, and Rose closed her eyes. The panic was rising again, and it was making her heart race. Her breathing came faster and faster. That dreadful feeling of not remembering anything, that emptiness....

Micah's arm slid across her shoulders, gently and smoothly, and he pulled her to him. His arm was lose against her shoulder, loose enough she could pull away if she wanted. But she didn't want to. She fell into his embrace, her cheek brushing against the soft linen of his shirt. His arm curled around her, and seemed to fold around her.

She felt so broken and hurt and alone and angry, she couldn't make herself step away. The tears she'd been holding back broke free of her in a harsh, gasping breath. Her free arm wrapped tightly around Micah's back, and she fisted the shirt. Rose gripped him tighter and sobbed. She wept for the violation she felt. For all the fear she felt. For the loneliness. She sobbed loud, ugly tears into his chest and clung to him. The bond between them pulsed, the sensation comforting.

Rose didn't know how long she stood there sobbing, but by the time her breathing started to slow, his shirt was wet, and her arm was stiff from her death grip on Micah. She shifted her cheek to some dry linen.

The bond between them seemed to thrum, and she sighed, letting the feeling settle her raw nerves.

"You said you could feel me about to break," she said, her voice a broken whisper. "What did you mean?"

"I don't know if I have the words to describe it," he whispered back. "It was like I could feel the tension in you. Like I had swallowed a rock."

"Hm."

Slowly, reluctantly, she pulled back and wiped her damp face on her sleeves.

"You'll be alright?"

Rose tried to smile but couldn't. "It's a good thing I'm stubborn."

He didn't respond to her poor attempt at a joke except to return the squeeze to her hand. Rose ran her hand along the chain and savored the peaceful, grounding feeling it gave.

"Thank you," she whispered, and hoped he felt how much she had needed him then, how much that had meant to her.

Micah nodded, and she slowly slipped from the room.

CHAPTER 40

*S*he tried to rest, she did, but she couldn't make her mind quiet enough to sleep. The silence scared her. The wolves were quiet too. Since the attack from Gerik, even they were distant. It was like he'd burned her magic out of her. Her magic seemed to be reduced to a small ember. She could feel it deep, deep in her chest and in the bond that told her it was still there. It was simply buried.

It left her feeling empty, vulnerable. The one thing she'd always been able to count on being there, to always fall back on, was silent. It made her feel small. And that... Rose took a shaky breath. That made her feel weak.

She sat with her knees to her chest, arms wrapped tightly around them in the stillness of her room. She'd lost track of the time of night long ago, but her eyes still drooped, even though she couldn't sleep. The embers burned low, a gentle red glow from inside the stove.

A tickling of awareness floated down the chain, this new thing. Micah was awake. She'd left him hours ago, eyes red and raw from crying. Part of her was ashamed she'd shown such weakness. That she'd allowed him to see it. But a larger part was begging her to go find him. To curl into him.

It was a bad idea. Terrible, really. She was a commoner at best and an assassin at worst. The rumors it could cause. The damage it could bring. She'd had horrible things whispered about her before, but did she want these things? When she'd finally found a place she wanted to be? To belong in?

In the end, she decided right now she didn't care. Rose shoved her feet back into her boots and took the quiet, empty servant corridors toward the royal wing. At this hour, even the castle workers were asleep. She slipped into the main corridors only when she had to and quickly into the solarium.

She knew he'd be here, and she didn't think it was the new bond that told her that. The garden was dark as she walked through the trees and plants; many of the blossoms were closed up. The reading corner, set against the stars of the night sky visible through the massive windows, was alight with a gentle flame.

She walked quietly into the corner, and Micah looked up from his worn sketchbook. His eyes were tired, hooded, and drawn. His hair was disheveled, and he wore a loose-fitting shirt and simple trousers. Simple even for him. A long, warm-looking robe was pulled and tucked around him.

Rose glanced down at her equally simple attire, old tunic and patched pants. This felt oddly intimate, and most of her didn't care.

"I can't sleep," she said into the silence as he watched her.

"I could tell." His words were soft, and Rose worried her fingers together beneath the cuffs of her coat.

"I didn't keep you up?" She gestured to the air between them. "With the... I didn't keep you up, did I?"

"No." He put aside his charcoal sketch book and folded his hands in his lap. "I also couldn't sleep."

She nodded, at a loss for what she was doing here and what it was she wanted.

With a gentle smile, Micah patted the space next to him.

"Sit, Rose."

She gathered herself and curled into the space next to him. Maybe it was the bond they shared now. Maybe that was always there, they just didn't realize it. Maybe it was letting him see her broken and vulnerable and trusting him to not trample on the pieces. Whatever the reason, Rose couldn't keep the walls up around him anymore. He centered her, grounded her. He chased the loneliness away.

She hesitated a moment longer before curling into his side, pulling her knees to her chest. He tensed but only for the briefest of seconds before dropping his arm across her shoulders and tucking her firmly into place. She sighed in relief, relief she hadn't known she needed.

This. This was what she'd wanted.

A tightly wound part of her started to relax.

"I cannot go with you this time," he said into the silence.

"No," she hummed. "No, you can't."

"Be careful. And come back soon."

She nodded and curled deeper into him. She felt like they were nearing some decision, some line they were toeing up to. Micah let out a long sigh, a deep one that shifted his chest against her, as he settled against the couch. She felt like they were about to cross something but...

The conversations with Michael. The glances and looks from the captain. His planning and scheming. She found safety here, a belonging. Gerik had broken her enough that she could admit to herself now she wanted that belonging. She wanted the security and happiness she found here. But she couldn't cross that line; she couldn't contemplate staying here, tucked into him like she belonged if she didn't have this answer first.

"I want to ask you something, and I need an honest answer."

She felt him shift above her, but she kept her eyes on the glassy sky.

"What are you scheming with the magic users? You're planning something. Michael was the start of it. Don't tell me that was all part of a plan to bring magic into a more favorable light. There's more to it. Whatever it is, the captain is nervous about it, and she thinks... she thinks I'm part of it. What are you doing, and why are you doing it? Why now?"

She felt the shudder that went through him. Rose sat up and finally met his eyes. He watched her with more apprehension than she'd expected, and she pulled further away so she could look at him straight on. He pulled his arm back and watched her wearily.

After a deep breath, he finally spoke. "I have an idea, a plan to rebuild part of my kingdom."

Rose tilted her head at him as the pieces started to fall together. "You want to gain the favor of magical users." His breath stopped short, and she frowned at him. "Did this idea come before... or after I introduced you to Michael?"

That shimmer of fear appeared in the back of her mind. Fear that he'd used her, used her connections for this plan.

He held up his hand, placating her to wait. "No, you were the one that gave me the idea. The longer I thought and the more research I did, the more I thought this could be the start. The Tracer Clan is the first."

Rose hummed that she'd heard. She wasn't sure if that eased her fear or not. "Why would you do that? Why the favor of magical clans? Surely there are other places to find support. Support that wouldn't be so... dividing."

It was his turn to hum and nod. "Yes. My advisors are not thrilled with my idea and would rather I marry someone like Lady Daniella, gain the support of the northern lords, and be done with it."

She nodded and dropped her feet to the floor. She shoved her hands into her cuffs to hide the tremor. Her chest tightened and ached at the idea. It was the logical, safe, practical choice, but it still hurt. How would the bond, how would they be, when he married? It was so new. They didn't know what it meant, what it would be. And how would the need to marry affect this line they were approaching? The ache grew in her chest. She hadn't thought that far ahead. She had just wanted to feel safe.

Micah touched her arm gently. "That is not my plan. If I am to align with someone, some group for my benefit, I would do so in a way my people can benefit."

She swallowed around the tightness in her throat. "Then some other noble-woman. One with magic, if such a woman exists, to gain favor and an alliance with the magical clans." The words left a bitter taste in her mouth. "I'm sure, with some digging, I could find some suitable potentials."

She wanted to be helpful, to show she still had a reason for being here even if part of her was weeping at what she was losing. She'd been foolish to think she could've ever had it.

"That is some time away, still. Right now, I must focus on whether or not such an idea will even be tolerated; by the people and the nobles. Was I right in believing many already knew of the existence of the Tracers? Were they the best choice?"

Rose nodded absently, her mind still wrapped up in the thought of having to share. This bond, this tie between them, shared so much. Over time, it would share even more; she could feel that potential. The thought that this intimacy, this privacy, wouldn't be something shared with just her, made the spot where the bond was anchored burn. What if what he felt for his queen was shared through the bond? The thought burned her chest.

"Yes," she murmured. "They are mos–"

She was stopped by a firm, almost painfully tight, grip on her arm as Micah dropped his forehead to her shoulder. His breath was hot and harsh as he breathed ragged breaths.

"Stop."

She put a shaky hand on his shoulder.

"Stop," he said again. "Please." He rubbed his sternum with his free hand, and Rose winced. She'd forgotten about that.

"I'm sorry. I didn't mean to hurt you."

He shook his head against her shoulder, his hair brushing her face. His breathing slowed. "I will not be marrying Lady Daniella nor any other noble-woman, magic or not," he said softly into her shoulder.

And with his words, Rose felt they crossed the line. Whatever it was, whatever decision they'd come to, they'd crossed it.

He eased the grip on her arm and slowly sat back. Rose nodded, words gone and tears threatening her eyes. Her hand fell away but his remained resting on her arm.

"I wouldn't do that to you; wouldn't make you do that."

When did she become so emotional? When did she become so attached?

"Do what?" she asked quietly, hoping to hide the quiver in her voice.

"Share," he whispered.

Rose had to close her eyes against the tears that wanted to fall. How did she come to this? What were they going to do? She knew she should reject the sentiment behind his words, that she had no place wishing what she did, but she couldn't. Whatever had been simmering between them, the bond had cemented it. She couldn't ignore it and wasn't even sure she wanted to.

This is a bad idea, she thought to herself as she opened her eyes. She met his gaze and nodded before curling back into his side. His arm fell back over her shoulders.

"This conversation isn't over," she whispered, eyes growing heavy.

A chuckle rumbled in his chest. "I didn't think it was."

Rose let her eyes fall shut and tucked her head into his shoulder. The bond rumbled in her chest: happy, content, safe. She wasn't sure if they were her feelings or his, but at that moment she didn't care.

CHAPTER 41

The freezing wind burned her cheeks as it blew across her skin. Rose pulled her hood tighter around her face and shivered in her coat. Starlit rocked beneath her, her strides long and smooth. Around her, the other horses snorted and puffed in the cold. It was a small group. Smaller than she'd hoped, but a larger number wasn't feasible. The captain had reminded her this morning as they prepared to leave that too many soldiers were south at the border and the castle could not be left undefended.

"Speed and stealth over strength," the captain had said as the sun crested the mountain tops.

Normally Rose would agree, but that was when she was able to sense things in the shadows, when she was the one capable of stealth. Now, with her magic still oddly muffled, she felt exposed and wished for the extra bodies. The six soldiers, two Light Horse Officers, Sam and Ty Reeson, a young man with flaming orange hair and a cheeky grin, recently returned from an assignment on the east coast, and Caleb made up their small party.

Caleb rode quietly next to Rose, equally bundled up in his coat and scarves. She hadn't had a chance to talk to him since their excursion to the tavern, and she didn't know what he thought about

Michael's ill-timed assassin comment. Somehow he'd settled into a spot as a friend she didn't want to lose. Maybe part of it was the guilt she still felt over his loss. Maybe it was the pure kindness he had.

He nudged his horse closer to hers, and Starlit flicked her ears at the small mare. Rose glanced over at him and shifted the reins back and forth in her hands.

"So," he started, his breath freezing in front of his face. "You alright?"

A harsh laugh burst from her, the simple question being the last she expected from him.

"Honestly, I've been better."

Caleb nodded, his eyes soft and sympathetic. "I heard you got your ass handed to you a little."

She chortled again, and it felt good to laugh. "A little."

"At least all the pain was worth it."

Rose looked over at him with a frown.

"Michael. He signed the charter for Clanship. The king asked me to record the charter in the records."

She jerked at his words and glanced sharply over at him. "When?"

"Yesterday."

She reeled, felt like she'd been hit in the stomach. She hadn't expected Michael to accept, let alone this quickly. She was honestly surprised by his decision and wondered how it would affect everyone's future.

Ty pulled his long-legged black gelding up to Rose's other side. Starlit still stood nearly a full hand taller than the leggy beast.

"I hear you're the one that knows why we're going to the Crown Forest." Ty leaned across the gap between the horses, and Rose eyed him, waiting for the young man to fall out of his saddle.

The chain shifted, and Rose resisted the urge to rub her sternum. The warm flutter still caught her off guard. "I doubt I'm the only one. I'm sure the soldiers know as well."

"Yeah." He waved off her words with a glance ahead of them at the black-clad men, broadswords strapped to their saddles. "But they're not the most talkative, and I want the real information. Not the dumbed-down stuff we get in the briefings."

Caleb snorted, and she turned to look at him.

"You'll have more luck with the soldiers," Caleb muttered with a grin at Rose. She chuckled softly and turned back to Ty.

"Was there a question in there somewhere?"

Ty's grin never wavered. "Any details you want to share that weren't in the brief?"

Rose's lips thinned, and she nudged Starlit. Her horse quickened her pace with a short jerk, her long legs easily out-pacing Ty's.

THREE LONG, cold days later, the small group slowed their horses at the edge of the forest. The grasslands leading up to the forests were covered in packed snow, the top frozen into a sheet of sharp, hard crystals. A few small, straggly trees dotted the desolate white land before the wall of woods ahead of them. As they neared, Rose could see the large trunks of the ancient trees so wide around she doubted three people holding hands would be able to encircle them.

At regular intervals along the tree line were large posts with old, weathered signs. The paint had long since worn off, and even the engraved letters had begun to blur. She stopped Starlit next to one of the posts and squinted at the old sign. A brand sat in the bottom corner of the sign she assumed belonged to King Jonas.

"By order of the king, none shall hunt, fell, or otherwise trespass upon these woods," Ty said as he rode next to her and glanced at her with another of his long side-eye looks. Something about the quirk of his lips or the squint of his eyes made Rose think he was up to no go.

"Oh?"

Ty nodded towards the nearly unreadable sign. "It's what it used to say. Some still do. Royal Woodsmen go through and fix up the posts periodically."

"And how do you know that?"

Ty grinned at her again, a crooked smile. "Used to be a Royal Woodsman."

Rose whispered a soft, "ah," and nudged her heels into Starlit's side. The horse moved forward, and thankfully, Ty followed behind.

As they traveled further into the dense woods, the snow thinned to a soft dusting. The canopy was thick overhead, blocking most of the bright afternoon sunlight, and making for a dappled, shadowed forest. The ferns and bushes were frosted with snow and covered most of the forest floor.

The group rode quietly through the trees. Rose saw more than a few of the soldiers grip the pommels of their swords. The crunching of frozen leaves and snapping of dead twigs under the horses' hooves was the only sound that moved through the forest. At the edge of her awareness, she could sense the wolves moving. Her magic was still dulled. Quiet. It felt just out of her reach in a way that left her feeling angry and frustrated.

"Where now?" a stern voice asked to her right.

Rose glanced over at the soldier, an older man with gray starting to show at his temples and in his beard. She thought she remembered hearing he was a lieutenant. Regardless of his rank, he was in charge of this little expedition. Something he'd made sure she knew every chance he could in the last three days.

It must chap his ass to have to ask her where to go. Rose held back a smirk. Barely.

Her amusement at the lieutenant's irritation was short-lived as she turned away from him and looked throughout the forest. She didn't know. The shadows were silent to her still. She'd longed for a day where her magic would disappear and the wolves would leave her alone. Now that they had, part of her felt empty. Missing. She didn't like it. It felt imbalanced.

"Well?" he snapped, and Rose jerked.

She nudged Starlit ahead and turned deeper into the trees. She could feel their stares on her back, but she refused to turn and look. She pushed further into the dense woods, the trunks growing larger, the space in between becoming smaller. Letting her eyes close, Rose puffed out a slow breath. She stretched her senses toward the shadows, toward the minds she could feel in the darkness.

It was sluggish, foggy. A throbbing started in the back of her head and a twinge in her chest. She stopped her efforts with a grunt and rolled her shoulders back.

Gods damn it.

The chain fluttered, a soft tug as if asking a question. She sighed and jerked it back harder than she meant to.

"I don't know the way," she whispered, barely audible even to her own ears. "I need you to help me."

The shadows thickened, the darkness deepened. The horses behind her nickered and whinnied. Caleb sidled his mare next to Rose as she watched a shadow wolf appear in the gloom.

"Rose?"

She canted her head toward him but kept her eyes on the wolf. The shadow blinked its large red eyes. No one made any note of the beast, not even Caleb as he looked directly at it. The wolf moved and swayed with the wind, like a wisp of smoke on the breeze.

Follow.

"Rose."

She glanced at Caleb with a small smile before nudging Starlit after the flickering shadow.

"This way."

Rose led the group deep into the forest. The soldiers whispered and murmured amongst themselves. The sun slowly moved across the canopy, the soft glow moving from east to west.

The further they went, the darker and thicker the forests became. Soon, the mutterings of the men stopped. Rose noticed the chittering of the forest birds quieted. Even the sounds of the horses seemed to fade. The sun vanished; when Rose checked the sky, she couldn't see the glowing orb.

"It's too early for the sun to have set," Caleb whispered behind her.

"It hasn't," Rose said as the gloom grew thicker and a fog appeared at the base of the trunks. "We're getting close."

The shadow started taking a firmer shape, and Rose could see more red eyes in the growing mist. She pushed further into the mist until soon it was dense and thick around them. Covering them. The soldiers crowded around her, their group now a tight knot of nickering horses and panting men. She glanced over at Caleb, his face pale and sweat-slicked. She turned her eyes back ahead of them, at the dense wall of mist surrounding them.

Finally, the shadows said softly, *you are home.*

The fog broke almost instantly, falling away behind them as they moved the last few feet in the forest. The men around her gave startled laughs, shaky and breathless, but Rose's eyes were trained on the group of people standing in the small clearing of oak trees and willows.

Their eyes were wide, faces afraid, but in the center of the five of them, a woman stood with graying chestnut hair and crow's feet lines around her brown eyes. Her mouth fell open as she recognized her mother's eyes staring back at her in shock and disbelief. A mirror, she was sure, of her own face.

Why? Rose snapped her mouth shut but couldn't pull her eyes from her mother. Years. It had been years. Why was she here? Why now? She finally pulled her gaze away and took in the others standing with her mother. They didn't look like travelers. Wearing only winter coats, with no packs or supplies, Rose knew they weren't traveling. *They've been here.*

The group of them stopped their horses in front of the five, and silence filled the clearing.

"What in all the damned hells are you doing here?" Rose's voice was sharp, angry, too loud in the quiet woods.

"I could ask the same of you," her mother said as she surveyed the soldiers before bringing those familiar hazel eyes back to Rose. "Looks like we have much to discuss."

CHAPTER 42

he flame from the lantern on his desk flickered. The fierce winds outside rattled the windows, and bone chilling strips of wind creeped through the room. King Micah sighed and rubbed a hand over his face. The pile of reports scattered across his desk made his head hurt. The weather had delayed a lot of them, but they all said the same thing. A strange man was destroying towns, fields, and roads.

A small village in Careen, the northeastern province, had been decimated. What was worse, unfortunately, than the lives lost and changed was the destruction of the fields just east of the village. The corn-fields and apple orchards stretched across much of the area and were the main supply for the eastern part of the country. Now, most of them were ruined. It would take much of the planting season trying to repair the damage, make the land plantable again, and by then, it was likely most of the season would be lost. There were other large farms in the southern end of Careen, but any loss would be felt in the region. A similar thing was detailed in another report, only this was throughout Mantar, the central most province, and their wheat fields.

It seemed that Goron, in his quest to find the Orthalen, was also on a mission to starve them. If the damage continued, if Rose couldn't stop Goron and his attacks, it was very possible there would be a large and unending food shortage in the spring. Micah had tasked his advisors to review the damage reports and meet with the head of the merchant clans to go over just how dire the current situation was.

Unfortunately, the B'leakon Council representatives were due again. Their patience had seemed to run out, and they were back to demand recompense for D'ray.

Another gust of bitterly cold wind made its way through the shutters. He groaned and shifted, pulling his short coat tighter around him. His head hurt, a dull pounding in the back of his skull. Rose had been angry about something earlier. Her sharp, almost frantic emotions bleeding up the chain had made his heart race before he'd realized she didn't seem to be in danger. He'd sent a thought of a question down the length of the chain, stretched so far, and he felt only a dim presence of her. He tried not to worry; he knew it wouldn't help, but he still did. She'd been so exhausted, the weariness making even his bones hurt.

The wind rattled the shutters again, and he grumbled. He should be working in his study, next to the fire, where it was warm, but if he moved from his office, he knew he'd sleep instead. And he had too much to do to sleep. Too much to read. He needed to think about how he was going to feed his people if it was as bad as he feared. To plan how to repair all the roads that were damaged, ruined by Goron. Trade would be hampered if not drastically slowed.

He couldn't sleep yet.

He dropped his head into his hand as Ben slipped into his office, closing the door quietly behind him.

Micah turned his head on his palm.

"It's late, Ben," Micah murmured, his head pounding. "Whatever it is, it can wait until there's daylight."

Ben stopped in front of his cluttered desk. "I really don't think it can, Sire."

With a sigh, he lifted his head and blinked at Ben.

"Sire, Lady Sephrita is outside."

Micah snaps his eyes to the door then back to Ben. "The B'leakon party is due in several days. She's here ahead of them?"

"She says it's imperative."

He nodded, unable to wipe the frown off his face, and quickly pushed the mess of papers and reports into some semblance of a pile as Ben rushed to the door. His eyes tracked as the tall woman, clad in a long, dark cape, strode across the floor toward his desk. She pushed the hood to the cape off her head as she stopped in front of him. Micah raised an eyebrow and nodded his head toward the chair.

"This is quite the surprise, Lady Sephrita."

She watched him with her wide eyes, swirling a dark blue with sparks of red and orange.

"I assume this has something to do with your very cryptic messages."

She stared, unblinking, and tilted her head. "I take quite a risssk being here."

"Let's start with why you're here, then." Micah leaned forward and rested his forearms on the table. "Why are you here?"

She breathed out a sigh, a hiss of a sound, and tilted her head. "Because I know things you need. I know an Earthmover was woken from his tomb in what you call the Southern Territories. I know he is looking for an item called the Orthalen."

Micah took a deep breath and tried to calm the racing in his chest. How, in the name of the gods, did she know this? "I know these things. How do *you* know these things?"

She smiled a lethal, cold smile. "You think humans are the only beings capable of spies? Do you think just because humans have no interest in the desert, we don't?"

He watched her, refusing to lean back even as every part of his being wanted him to run. His eyes narrowed at her mention of spies. He'd had enough of spies.

She hissed a breath. "None in your court, human." Her eyes swirled orange a second before settling back into her dark blue. "My heritage has long watched the doings of the *mylrishck...* the," she closed her eyes with an angry sigh, "the Southern Territory."

"Why?"

Lady Sephrita blinked, once, slowly, and her eyes swirled nearly midnight black.

The look in her eyes, the endless pool of that black color, sent a chill down his spine. His hands grew clammy nearly instantly, and he desperately tried to swallow around his now dry mouth.

"Have you found the Orthalen?" she asked, her voice crisp.

This time he leaned back in his chair and folded his arms over his chest.

"Why are you here?" he asked again. "Why are you slipping surreptitious notes to my people? Why do you care about Goron and the Orthalen?"

His pounding head and the dull presence at the end of the chain were distracting. He didn't have the patience to dance around this conversation, to play and lead and fence with the words.

She hissed and looked away. She rapidly muttered a string of words in her own language before turning back. "If the Orthalen exists, we are doomed. I know what it doesss."

"And what is that?"

"It focuses magic, channels all magic to the user. Are you familiar with Cirkus Steel?"

Micah nodded.

"The Falkus Steel is the antithesis to Cirkus. Where one repels, the other hones."

"How do you know this?" As far as he'd been taught, they were a magicless people and generally disliked it.

"Who do you think taught the humans, the Revasts, to mold it?"

Micah's eyes slowly widened.

"My family are master smithers. My great grandmother's mother first taught the skill of molding the Cirkus Steel to your Revast people, and during the war, my great grandmother knew the risk if your magic folk continued to torment the world."

"And she helped King Jonas because of that threat?"

Lady Sephrita laughed, a breathy, lyrical sound. "No. She lent her skills to smith the cuffs needed to contain your ancestor's captives in exchange for a trade agreement."

Gods above.... His mouth fell open the slightest. The trade agreement between the Black Hill Islands, the homeland of the B'leakon, was one of the most unbalanced trade agreements in the kingdom's history. No taxes were collected by the crown. No record of the imports were reported. All the money, the records, everything was sent back to the B'leakon council. He'd always looked at the accord and wondered what had gone through the first high king's mind when he agreed. Now he knew.

He was almost impressed. Micah knew Rose would've appreciated the skill needed to put King Jonas in such a position to accept such an agreement.

"That trade agreement gained my family the second-highest seat on the B'leakon Council. A seat I now hold."

So, what does she want now? Micah chewed his lip while eyeing her.

Lady Sephrita grinned, almost as if she knew where his thoughts went. Her eyes swirled, lightning closer to a sky blue.

"What does this have to do with the Orthalen?"

Her eyes narrowed and changed to red, a deep red with streaks of orange, almost instantly. "My great grandmother taught one to mold a different ore, the Falkus."

"Goron," Micah said softly. "Why would she teach him to mold the Falkus metal? Clearly, you believe magic should be restrained. Why would she teach him to focus it?"

She looked away again, and he could see the muscles of her jaw flexing. Lady Sephrita wrinkled her nose before turning back to Micah. "If the Orthalen is destroyed, Gerik will need another one made. And you will need the skills to smith more restraints if Gerik is to be caught."

Micah leaned forward again, his heart beating fast.

"I am willing to assist," her words drew out in a breathy hiss, "in molding these cuffs."

"For?" Micah asked simply. His palms were sweating, and he interlocked his fingers to hide their shaking.

Lady Sephrita smiled, and it was lethal.

CHAPTER 43

*S*he paced the space of the small room, her footsteps angry and heavy. A soothing tug came from the chain, but she shrugged it off. She was too angry. Too confused. Too disappointed. Rose puffed to herself, an angry huff of breath, as she turned at the wall and paced back across the room.

After the initial shock had worn off, they'd been brought into town. Not a pile of ruins and rubble, forgotten paths, or an overgrown forest. No. A thriving town. With people.

At the center was a small courtyard market, where a dirt road was lined with a few simple shops. At the peak of the town square sat a large house made of stone and timber. The stone had an age to it, the way it had faded color and gained new shades. Her mother briefly explained that it was the council house before directing the soldiers, Caleb and Ty, to the stable sat just off to the side of the council house. Rose had been dragged a different way out of the square and shoved into this simple home. She had just enough time to explain why they were there and what they were looking for before her mother disappeared again.

"Stay here," she'd ordered Rose as she disappeared out the door.

Had she been here the whole time? Rose had spent days wondering, imagining where her mother had gone when she was young. Time quickly burned that away, leaving her bitter and resentful. It had been years since she'd thought about her mother. Where she might be. What she was doing. She was far too angry to let herself go down that path. Only more anger and tears had been at the end anyway. But now. Now she was here.

She angrily huffed and turned to resume her pacing in front of the fireplace. Her mother had magic. She had to if she was here. The irony of that burned deep in her chest and made tears fill her eyes. Rose raised her shaking hands to her face and brushed wisps of hair away from her face. She didn't even know where to begin to understand what was happening.

I thought they were all dead.

The door clicked open behind her, and Rose spun around to face her mother as she entered. Iris looked tired, frazzled. Rose remembered her hair as a rich chestnut always maintained in orderly plaits or chignons. Now it was frayed, and strands fluttered around as if she'd run her hand over her head over and over. It was streaked with gray, the color dulled with age.

Iris wore long wool skirts, a tunic of thick cotton, and she could see well worn leather boots sticking out from the hem of her skirt. The items were simple but not homespun. They were too fine. They'd been made with care and knowledge. Rose pulled her eyes up to her mother's face. They'd traded for them.

"The other elders want to speak with you as soon as we're finished."

She sounded just as she remembered, and it made her throat clench. Memories she'd buried deep, hidden away from the light of day, started to surface.

"Other? You're an elder then?"

Iris raised an eyebrow and stared at her with a withering glare before moving into the room and removing her thick wool coat. That glare made her want to scream at Iris.

"Where am I?" Her voice trembled with anger and pent-up tears. She would not break. Not here. Not in front of her.

Iris moved to the roaring fire at the far wall, pulled a boiling pot from the kettle stand, and set about making tea. She raised her eyes from the table as she set a second cup down.

"My home."

Rose hesitantly accepted the steaming cup of tea. She sipped it cautiously and glanced around the room. The walls were covered in delicately woven tapestries, small and simple but fine construction. Some were starting to fade from their time in the sun. Nicknacks were scattered around the surfaces. A well-used armoire. Her home was simple, but it was a home. It felt like a home. Something Rose never felt before. She'd never had this.

It made her grind her teeth and set her heart racing again. The urge to hit something grew.

"What's happening to the others?"

Iris settled into a chair at the table with a sigh. "They are being cared for. They're being given food and bedding. They're out of the cold. We are not used to outsiders. It shocked a great many of the people, but we were able to situate them in the stables."

Rose shook her head. She took a deep breath, swallowing the lump in her throat and trying to quell the anger in her chest. She stripped her gloves, stuffing them in her pockets with jerky movements, before slipping the coat from her shoulders and draping it over a chair. "I didn't know you were here. That anyone was here." She had to swallow. "I have so many questions," she whispered.

Iris perched on the edge of the chair across from Rose. "As do I."

Rose took a deep breath and had to hold it to keep it from shaking. So much of her wanted to scream and cry, rage at the woman for leaving her, for leaving her alone. A small part, a part that Rose desperately tried to bury, wanted to throw herself into her mother's chest and never let go. Most of her wanted to rage. She'd been abandoned with a magic she didn't understand, and her mother had been here the whole time.

"How were you able to find your way here?"

She licked her lips and rolled her shoulders back, trying to ease the knot forming between her shoulder blades. "The shadows led me."

Iris scoffed, "you don't have magic."

Iris didn't believe her. Rose's blood started to boil, and she gripped the chain, buried deep in her chest, tight enough that it cut into her hands. She wrapped it around her fist, tightly winding it around and around. It wasn't enough that her mother had left her, left her with her father to beat her, left her alone with this curse of magic, but to not even believe her.

She heard a ringing in her ears.

She was left alone to figure out how to survive with it on her own when her mother could have taught her. Her clan could've helped her.

Behind her, she heard a low growl come from the far reaches of the room, where the evening sun didn't reach. Rose let a deep breath out through her nose. "How would you know?"

Iris watched her, fingers drumming on the table. "What are your limits, then? With the magic?"

Rose unclenched her jaw and snapped, "I don't know; haven't really bothered to find out."

Iris smothered a sigh, low and disapproving. Rose gripped the chain tighter. A wiggle, a little tug of a question came from Micah, and she tried to loosen her hold.

"The shadows call me the Shadowstalker." She relented with a shrug.

"Impossible," Iris scoffed. "Even if you do have some shadow magic, you're not the Stalker. You can't possibly speak to them, control them."

"I don't think anyone can control those beasts, but yes. I can speak to them."

Iris was shaking her head, leaning back in her chair and raising her palm as if to ward off Rose's words. "No. No matter whatever stories you might've heard, whatever you've experienced that makes you think you're the Stalker, it's not possible."

"Why are you so sure?" Rose bit out.

"I tested you!" Iris snapped, her voice rising. "Years ago, when you were young. You showed no trace of magic. None. If you had, I would've taken you with me!"

"You were wrong!" Rose shouted as she surged to her feet. She was going to show her mother exactly how wrong.

She bared her teeth and growled low in her throat: a wolf's growl that echoed in the room. The shadows surged into her mind, crowded against her, and in her anger, Rose let them in. She held her arm up, wrapped palm down. She whistled. That same long, low whistle that had come to her by instinct in the throne room. It resonated through the room, through the shadows, and the sound made her hair stand on end.

Come! She commanded and darkness gathered around her. The pull was sluggish, her magic still wounded from whatever Gerik had broken inside her, but her anger fueled it. They came, they listened, and obeyed without hesitation. The darkness became dense, thick, substantial around her, blocking out the light in the room. A large dark cloud rose from the shadows on the floor. It swept up and curled under her hand, a black mist taking shape. A snout, ears, and then red eyes solidifying out of the mass. The shadow wolf's head brushed itself into Rose's hand and turned its red eyes to Iris. She choked on a gasp as the wolf growled and then fell back to the floor. A pressure built up behind her eyes as she kept her grip on the shadows, and she could feel her pulse in her ears.

"You. Were. Wrong," Rose bit out, her voice deep with a timbre that wasn't hers. The room was dark, bathed in a darkness that wasn't natural. Mists started to swirl around Rose's feet. Memories that weren't hers started to work their way into her mind. She saw the face of Jonas, a much younger king than was depicted in his portraits. Another vision of the castle, only as a pile of stone and a partially completed tower.

Stop. She told them as they pressed further. The pounding grew in her ears and a pain spread across her mind. *Stop*.

But the wolves were angry, annoyed. They carried an anger that went deeper than hers. They wanted her to listen, and this was how they were going to do it. They pushed against her, demanding her attention.

"*The Earthmover is a threat. An abomination!*" they growled through her. "*You must act!*"

She ground her teeth, hands fisted, as she pushed against their will. The fog grew to her knees.

"Enough!" she shouted, her voice her own. Sweat had broken out across her forehead.

Her shout shook the shadows, the darkness wavering like smoke in the wind, and even the wolves were quiet. Her breaths came in giant gasps that rattled her throat. Slowly, she calmed her breathing.

"Not now," she told them, and with one last grumble, the shadows returned to normal. The preternatural darkness disappeared; the shadows were confined to the corners of the room once more.

A frantic flutter came from the chain in her chest as it was yanked and pulled hard enough to make Rose wince and rub her chest. She wiggled her end back, and Micah's frantic tugs stopped.

Rose collapsed back into her chair, limbs shaky. She hurt, and it seemed to be everywhere.

That was dumb. She rubbed her aching forehead.

Iris watched her with a pale face and open mouth, her eyes too wide for her petite face.

"You are untrained," came her shaky whisper.

"No shit," Rose puffed. "Whose fault do you think that is, eh?"

"You have no idea what you could've done. What almost happened."

Rose eyed her mother and wondered at the naked fear in her eyes. The shadows were dangerous. She knew this. She'd seen them kill, had ordered them to kill. They'd torn through the soldiers occupying the castle last summer, but so far, she'd only ever seen them do so one time. They growled and snapped and bared their teeth like a fighting dog, but until last year, they'd been silent from the world. Iris was a Shademaker, so why was she so afraid?

Rose breathed heavily and eyed Iris before turning her eyes slowly to the shadows along the wall. What else didn't she know?

"Nothing was going to happen," she said with winded words. "They're cranky. I'm cranky, and we have shit to do."

A chuff of laughter came from the shadows, and Rose quirked up the corner of her lips in response.

Iris shook her head. "You've no idea what you touch."

"No. I have no idea. I grew up thinking I was cursed. Maybe I am. But you left me to figure that out on my own. You don't get to be annoyed with how I've done so." Rose clucked her tongue and glared at Iris. "I was alone."

"You had no magic." Her voice had no apology, no remorse, and Rose had to swallow around the lump in her throat at her words.

"And? You just left me there. With him. Do I not matter if I don't have magic? Is that the only thing that gives me value?" The only thing that has ever given me value. Tears pricked her eyes again. She'd always thought her father was the crueler of the two, but perhaps it was just a different type of cruelty.

"I couldn't take you with me. You didn't have magic," she said again with a shrug of her shoulders. "It isn't allowed."

Iris' words were so simple. So cold. As if this hadn't been the most devastating moment in Rose's life.

She cleared her throat and shifted in her chair, using the movement to hide her hand wiping the tear from her cheek before it fell further. "Have you told the others why I'm here?"

Iris pressed her lips and set her own cup down. "Yes. The few fighters we have are running patrols now."

"Let the soldiers help. That's why they came."

Iris shook her head and waved the words away with a flutter of her fingers. "You need to tell the shadows to mind the border. We will have no need for your soldiers then."

Rose blinked at her.

"The border." Iris sighed again, and somehow Rose still managed to feel like a chastised child. "What you passed through when you arrived. The shadows maintain it. Prevent any from entering. As long as they're being guided to do so. Only the Shadowstalker has that ability."

Her words were stern and irritating. Rose resisted the urge to stick her tongue out. Iris already thought she was childish, no need to give her more reason to believe so. Rose glanced around the darkened room, looking for the glowing red eyes. She wished the shadows had a name, a way to call them. Something better than angrily shouting at them.

"We have had many names. All forgotten by time," the words whispered through her mind as the wolf appeared in the room.

Iris took a sharp breath but otherwise remained still.

The edges of the wolf were blurred, undefined, almost like dense smoke. The room was dim, the ambient light enough to disrupt the hard lines of the beast.

"How else am I supposed to call you, then?"

The wolf huffed and sat on its haunches.

"I still think you need names."

"Rose," Iris snipped, and Rose huffed her own sigh. "Be respectful. The beings of the shadows are older than the gods. They fear nothing and should be feared in return."

Rose glanced over at the wolf and knew the power they held. She'd felt parts of it when she'd let them in, let them take control. Even then, she knew... she knew that wasn't even the tip of their power. Older than the gods. She huffed. She'd bet they created the gods. Hells, maybe there were no gods, and it was just the shadows working their machinations.

The gleam in the wolf's eye made Rose think he'd overheard her thoughts and that she was closer than she thought.

"Everything has something to fear," the wolves whispered through the room, and Iris jumped, her face going dangerously pale. "Even gods."

Iris gasped another breath. "Bless the Sa'akil."

Rose frowned and turned back to Iris. "The what?"

"One of our names."

"The ancient god of magic," Iris said with shaky words.

Rose turned back to the shimmering shadow wolf with a deeper frown. Was the god named after the shadow, or were the shadows named after the god? Was there even a difference? And why the god of magic? A forgotten god, never spoken of or worshiped.

The wolf blinked, long and slow, and Rose felt she was on the tip of understanding something enormous. She would have time for theological debates later. Right now, she needed to focus. She'd let her mother distract her enough.

"Hide the town. Hide the town from outsiders," Rose said.

The wolf's ears twitched as he sat there, silently.

Her temper started to boil. Her heart jumped and started to race again. The urge to hit something crept into her hands. Slowly, slowly so she didn't throw it, she set the cup down and leaned forward.

"Hide. The. Town."

"You haven't earned our obedience yet."

Her face felt flush. Hadn't earned? She clenched her hands. Test after test after fight. They wanted her to lead, to be in charge, to command but when she tried she was met with this? Rose let out a rough, angry breath.

She reached out her hand and gripped the wolf by the scruff of its large neck. It lifted its teeth in a growl, its muzzle wrinkling. She fisted its fur, cool and damp from the mists, but real and solid in her hand.

"I'm getting really tired of you having it both ways. You want to muck around in my world. You want out of your Shadow Lands and to interfere in mine and demand my help to do so; you don't get to be pissy when I return the demands."

Iris squeaked, but Rose didn't look away from the shadow's red, furious eyes. She had a point to prove.

"Hide... the blasted town." She put every ounce of power and demand into her words. I'm trying, she thought to them, to be the person you say I am. Stop fighting me every damn step of the way.

The wolf chuffed and laid its ears flat, lips pulled back in a silent snarl. They were going to damn well listen. She was no one's tool to use or order about. If they wanted her to listen, they needed to as well.

Rose released her grip on it's scruff and sat back. Her heart was racing and her breath was erratic, but she sat still waiting for them to decide.

Iris' breathing was fast and short, and when Rose glanced briefly at her, she saw her face was ghostly pale.

"It is done," the words echoed through the room, and Iris flinched.

"Thank you."

"You do not fear us." The wolf cocked its head to the side, and Rose shrugged.

"I may hate you, be irritated beyond measure by you, and I may fear what you're doing to me, but you?" She shrugged. "I fear many things, but the shadows have always been my safety. Why would I fear you now?"

"Because they can kill you," Iris' words were a hoarse whisper.

Rose snorted. "No. They need me. It would upset their precious Balance." She turned her eyes back to the wolf. "But I'm tired of being tested and tried. And used."

The wolf stood and shook out its fur. "Good."

The shadow dissolved in the darkness of the room and Rose let out a long sigh. *That better be the last test*, she thought at the shadows she knew lingered in the room. *Or we're going to have words.*

A chuff of laughter echoed through the room.

"I think they like fighting with me." A small smile tilted the corner of her lips. "I think they think this is funny."

Iris gulped down a breath. "You cannot continue to behave like this is a game," she stood and stared down at Rose with wide eyes. "There is a decorum you must learn."

Rose stood and nearly touched noses with Iris. Her hands itched, and her fingers flexed. "I've never been one for decorum, but I do like a good fight."

She turned away before Iris could come up with the next thing to lecture her about and before she gave into her impulse to punch the woman's nose in. She paused at the doorway and glanced over her shoulder. She ignored the upheaval in her stomach, the headache sitting behind her eyes. "Take me to the elders."

Iris straightened her spine and nearly vibrated with anger, but she pushed past Rose and led her outside. Rose followed, squinting against the bright sun. As they walked back through the simple town with dirt paths nestled among the trees, Rose paid more attention to the buildings as she passed. Simple houses and huts were hidden among the massive trunks. Near the market, they passed what looked like a blacksmith.

Iris noticed her watching and searching the town as they walked. "A couple of us work small farms, and we have a great number of hunters. What we can't do ourselves, we'll travel to nearby cities to trade. We're not entirely removed from the world."

Just the memory of you, Rose thought as they walked further into the town center.

"What do you do?"

Iris glanced over at her with weary eyes. "I am an elder. I work with the other elders researching our history, maintaining the boundary as best we can, and preserving peace among our people."

"And they pay you for that?"

Again Iris glanced at her. "Yes. You must've worked prior to coming here. What have you done? Did you work with your father's trading company?"

Rose laughed, but the sound was bitter enough that Iris took a step away.

"Was your life so terrible?"

The sincerity in her voice made Rose turn back to look at where Iris had stopped walking. Her brow was pinched as she stood there.

"Yes," Rose said, her words cold. "It really was."

"One day, I would like to know."

Rose watched her and felt the sincerity of her words. Was she finally starting to see? Did she finally see the daughter she'd abandoned? She scoffed at her. It was years too late.

"If you cared to know, you shouldn't have left."

Rose turned away and continued through the square to the council building. As she stepped up onto the large covered porch, she spotted Caleb sitting on the floor against the building, arms resting on his bent knees.

"Oh, you're okay."

Rose let out a relieved breath, her eyes aching from the short time in the sun.

"That's relative," Rose chuckled and offered him a hand to help stand. "You waiting for me?"

He nodded, his eyes going from Rose to Iris and back again. "I snuck out. Figured you'd go here eventually."

"Well," she patted him on the shoulder. "Let's get this over with."

CHAPTER 44

"Strangers aren't welcome here."

Rose paused at the harsh words thrown at her.

"The boy will wait outside."

Her eyes found the speaker, an older woman with a hawkish nose and gray eyes. She sat on a chair, not unlike a small throne at the head of the room. Next to her sat three others, all with varying states of gray hair. Two men and a woman. The four of them watched her just as cautiously as she watched them. Rose wanted to tell the woman no, defy her and make it clear she wasn't here to be told what to do, but she also didn't want to spend every moment here in a fight. She didn't have the strength for that.

"Fine," she murmured and turned to Caleb. "I guess you're still waiting outside."

He nodded and hurriedly slipped back out. The wolves paced at the edges of her mind. They felt angry, annoyed, and she wondered why they were suddenly so upset.

Rose glanced over at Iris, who'd walked over to join the group. "These your cohorts, then?"

"We make up the council," the younger of the two men said. "Liddia is the matriarch and the leader among us."

He pointed to the woman with the hawkish nose. Liddia, apparently the leader, wore a fine necklace around her narrow neck. The one hand Rose could see was adorned with rings set with expensive stones. Liddia held herself with an air of circumstance and power. Liddia, Rose thought as she approached the table, came from money and was used to the privileges it brought; and the obedience it gave.

She glanced around the council room. Behind Liddia, on the wall, was a large tapestry with names and faces embroidered on it. It looked like a genealogy tree, but as she looked through the tree, she saw J'Teals' name and face. She wondered if this was a list of the Shadow-stalkers.

"Is this determined by age?" Rose asked as she sank into the open seat.

"By strength," Liddia said. "The wolves have been restless since you arrived yesterday. You've upset them."

Rose felt the quiet hiss from the shadows and their annoyance directed at Liddia. She reached out with her mind and tried to settle the beasts; tried to run a calming hand through their fur. They quieted a little. If Rose were to guess, she didn't think the wolves liked Liddia much, and she wondered why. She hadn't felt them express anger at anyone other than Gerik and Goron before.

"They're probably restless because Goron is on his way here; I doubt my arrival here has anything to do with it."

"Liddia," Iris started with a glance at Rose. "I should inform the council that Rose is the Shadowstalker."

Five sets of eyes turned to Rose. A few mouths gaped, but Liddia stared at her with a frown and pursed lips. Rose settled her gaze on the older woman.

"Are you sure, Iris?"

"Yes," Iris pulled her eyes from Rose to nod at her superior. "She is the Shadowstalker."

Liddia's lips pursed further, to the point Rose wondered if she'd swallowed a lemon.

Liddia cleared her throat. "Is that so? Hm. An outsider, no less.

And you seem to think you know where the Orthalen is as well, is that right?"

Rose clucked her tongue. "I know what a Seer told me."

"Well," Liddia hummed while looking around at the others. "A Seer... "

Rose fought to contain her eye roll and temper.

The shadows pressed against her mind, and they shared her irritation. She could feel their urgency. They needed to find the Orthalen. The Balance of the world would be threatened if Goron found it. They wanted to find it first. This need pressed on her from the shadows.

"Where is J'Teal's grave?"

"You honestly think it's in her grave, and has been the whole time? Absurd." She fixed her eyes on Rose in a withering glare. "And that we'd let you muck about in her tomb?"

"We may as well check it," the younger man spoke again.

"Mark," Liddia said in a warning. "You really want to entertain this nonsense?"

"I agree with Mark," the rounder woman, with a plump face and button nose, said. "What is the harm in looking?"

Liddia sighed and rolled her bony shoulders back. "Anyone else?"

Iris slowly raised her hand. "I also agree."

Rose glanced over at Iris, surprised. She hadn't expected her to agree and back her on this.

"Fine." Liddia let out a guff of air. "I am out-voted."

Liddia stood and jerkily pulled on her coat. The fox fur collar pulled tight against her neck. "Agatha can lead the way."

The short woman stuttered, "but, right now?"

"Do you have something else to be doing?" Rose drawled. "Or is making sure an enemy stronger than anyone in this room doesn't find the most powerful magical artifact of our history not that high on your list of things to do?"

"You have no idea the strength of this room," Liddia snapped. "We might not be a Shadowstalker, but the shadows have listened to us. To me. Do not think yourself our better simply because of a title you haven't earned."

Rose ground her teeth against the raging anger building in her chest. Her hands shook as they balled into fists.

"Listened!" the shadows growled at Rose. "We have allowed her to speak until the Stalker was found!"

Rose saw red. Her anger was deep and writhing, but the fury coming from the shadows was infernal. It was an old, smelting anger of a god. She let them in, let them into her to speak their fury.

"*You act with a mantle not that is yours and a power not given!*" Rose's voice was deep and grave. It echoed with the growls of the uncountable. The room darkened at the edges as the shadows pressed in, red eyes glowing. The mists of the Undertunnels leaked into the world and swirled around their legs.

"*You think we LISTENED TO YOU?*" she shouted, and it felt like the world shook.

Liddia's face turned ashen white, and the others, Iris included, fell to their knees.

"*We went along with your requests because it suited our needs. Do not begin to think your voice could be the voice for the Judges.*"

Liddia gulped and nodded.

Rose took a big step toward Liddia and pushed the wolves back enough to claim her own voice. "That'd be me."

She stepped back, and the shadows slipped from her with ease. Her head pounded, and her eyes ached, but they didn't fight, didn't struggle, or argue for dominance. She wondered if this was because they'd finally started listening to her. Maybe she was finally growing into her role.

They whispered their gratitude as they left, and Rose held back a smile.

We both had a point to prove, she thought to them as they retreated.

The shadows chuffed a chuckle before returning to their silence. She pushed back the growing headache and shook her hands out. "Shall we?"

The group jerkily moved back to their feet, and poor Agatha, red in the face, shuffled to the door. Rose waited for the group to pass before falling in at the back. As they walked back outside, Rose squinted as the bright sun radiated off the patches of snow. Through watery eyes, she gestured for Caleb to follow.

"Where are we going?"

"To J'Teal's grave."

Caleb nodded and jutted his chin out at the group ahead of them. "How'd your meeting go?"

Rose grunted, but her lip twisted in a half smile. "Interesting."

They walked out of the town and through the forest. A small path was visible, and eventually, they came upon a cemetery. It wasn't a large cemetery, but there were plenty of headstones dotting the fenced-off area. Near the back, nestled against a hillside, was a small crypt.

Agatha led them through the cemetery and up to the crypt doors. She gestured to the eldest of the men.

"I need your key, Collin."

Collin, who'd managed to be silent this whole time, sighed but handed a large wrought iron key to Agatha.

Iris stepped next to Rose while Agatha fought with the old, rusted lock on the door.

"Be careful around Liddia," she whispered while keeping her eyes straight ahead. "She is the strongest here, yourself notwithstanding, and she is brutal. Her family line is the oldest in the clan, and she has very good connections outside of it. She is used to being obeyed."

"I guessed she came from money and privilege. She's probably," Rose shrugged, and she eyed the woman's back, "what, sister of a lord?"

"Aunt." Iris turned and glanced at Rose. "How'd you guess that?"

Rose shrugged again. "I'm good at reading people."

"Well, despite your standing as Shadowstalker, she can make your life very difficult. We have functioned with Liddia as the clan leader for years. She's not likely to give it up easily."

"She's welcome to keep it," Rose said and crossed her arms. "I've no desire to take her position."

"Rose," Iris' voice was harsh, urgent, and Rose turned to look at her. "The Shadowstalker is the leader of the clan. You are..." she shrugged and shook her head. "There is so much you don't know."

Rose scoffed and folded her arms. "I'm no leader. I can't even keep myself out of trouble. No," she shook her head, "no, I'm not a leader."

Iris sighed, a deep, disappointing sound. "We will talk more about it later."

Rose shook her head again. No. No, she was going home after this. She grabbed the chain and gripped it. It was quickly becoming a habit, a reassurance, to run her fingers along the smooth thing. It hummed in the back of her mind and settled her nerves.

The lock on the door finally snapped open with a loud clang. Agatha looked up and around before her eyes fell on Caleb.

"You. Come push this door open."

"Yes, ma'am," he said and diligently shouldered open the heavy crypt door.

Rose started after him and slipped in through the door before any of the elders could. Inside was solid blackness. The filtered light from the outside only reached as far as the small landing before a narrow set of stairs descended into the earth. She dropped her eyesight into the shadows to see her way down, even as her eyes ached. Caleb clamored behind her, and after the second step, he missed, put his hand on her shoulder and followed.

The stairs continued down longer than Rose had expected them to, and as they descended, the air grew colder, crisper. She shivered under her coat and pulled it tighter around her neck.

"An earthmover made this," Caleb whispered behind her.

"How do you know?"

"I don't know," his whisper was so quiet she only heard it through the shadows.

Rose glanced over her shoulder at him, and even in the blue-gray hues of her magic, she could see his face was pale. Her fingers found the lump of ore in her pocket as she turned back around. A nagging feeling was starting to settle in her stomach.

Finally, nose numb and lips stiff, the stairs leveled out into a small room with a stone sarcophagus in the center. As the group behind them filtered into the room, Mark went around the room lighting the torches placed along the walls. With a soft sigh, Rose pulled her sight out of the shadows, a headache pounding and her eyes aching. She prayed to whichever gods were listening that Goron was slow to arrive.

Liddia gestured to the sarcophagus. "Here is our queen."

Rose cut her eyes to Liddia then to Iris. Was that a term of endearment, or had J'Teal been a queen? Was it a title that passed to others? Iris' shoulders tightened in a small jerk. Rose sighed heavily through her nose.

She approached the giant block of stone and ran her hands over the cut-outs and carvings. A sleeping woman lay carved in the stone on top, hands draped loosely across her chest. The carving resembled J'Teal so well the stonework was so delicate, it looked like it was her. Rose glanced at Caleb, who was staring at the stone with a deep frown etched between his eyes.

"Earthmover?" she asked him softly.

He nodded.

She pressed her lips against the budding idea that was building and turned back to the tomb. She resumed moving her hands along the sarcophagus, feeling for any loose sections, latches, hinges. The sides of J'Teal's tomb was engraved with giant cats, larger than any catamount in these lands. Their lips were pulled back in silent snarls, ears flat against their heads. She paused as she looked over the scene carved into the side of the catamounts disappearing into a fog.

She'd asked the wolves once why they were wolves, and they'd given her a cryptic answer about that being what they chose to appear as.

"When did you change to wolves?" she asked them softly as she continued around the tomb.

When she died.

"The histories note the shift in form happened soon after J'Teal was killed," Liddia spoke from her spot near the wall.

"Didn't ask you," Rose said without looking away from the sarcophagus and planted her hands on her hips as she stared at the tomb.

A loud sigh from Liddia put a small smile on Rose's lips.

Iris cleared her throat. "What are you looking for?"

"A hidey-hole," Rose said. "Secret compartment. But I'm not seeing anything. It feels solid. Let's look inside."

A collective gasp filled the room and Rose rolled her eyes. Through the shadows, she heard J'Teal's echoing sigh of annoyance.

"What am I going to do with my old bones, eh?" J'Teal whispered faintly.

"Does it make you feel better if I tell you she doesn't care about her remains?" Rose asked while grabbing Caleb and moving to one side.

"And we're supposed to believe you can also talk to the dead?" Collin guffawed.

"She's not dead," Rose said and braced her arms against the thick stone lid. "She's just not... alive either. It's complicated."

Caleb positioned himself next to her. "This is going to be really heavy."

"Yeah," she groaned but silently hoped her feelings about the quiet scholar were right. It might not be that heavy at all for him.

She nodded for him to push, and after a second of groaning and straining, the heavy lid started to move. Painstakingly slowly, with sweat dripping down her face and rolling down her back, they were able to inch the lid open enough to peer in the top half. They straightened, Rose's back aching and burning, and panted. She looked over at Caleb, who slumped onto the floor, breathing just as heavily, and frowned. Maybe not, then.

Rose grabbed one of the torches from the wall and brought it back to the tomb. Inside were dusty bones and threadbare cloth. It must've been nice garb when she was buried, but time had since turned it to tattered wrappings. The flesh was long gone, but most of her long black hair remained. Rose wrinkled her nose, even though there was no smell but dust and dirt, and peered closer.

Draped around the neck, resting against the ribs and sparse cloth, was an intricate metal necklace. There were three long points falling from the thick and ornate chain. The three points, nearly as long as her forearm, were a black iridescent color. It caught the light from the flame and seemed to dance, the colors moving and shifting from purple to black and blue. A wrongness emanated from it, and the shadows hissed.

Caleb pushed himself up and looked down at the Orthalen. "It feels... evil. I didn't feel this before."

The elders pushed in around the sarcophagus, their eyes wide and mouths open.

"The tomb insulated it, I think," Rose said. "Even the wolves couldn't feel it."

"But," Liddia stuttered. "Why didn't we know? Why wasn't this in the histories?"

"You can't give up what you don't know," Rose said softly and shivered as memories of Gerik's assault surfaced.

She reached out a shaking hand to grab the strange necklace, the same colored metal as what was in her pocket. Her fingers touched the cold metal, but she ripped them back with a curse. The tips were red and blistered, burned from that simple touch. She remembered, briefly, from J'Teal's memory of it doing the same thing to her hand.

Caleb reached out, and Rose quickly grabbed his sleeve.

"What are you doing?"

"I... " he shrugged but didn't look away from the necklace. Slowly, he reached in and gingerly picked up the Orthalen with a trembling hand. A gentle tug and the chain broke, the two pieces dangling down from Caleb's fingers.

"Why can he touch it?" Iris asked.

Rose cradled her burned hand. "Because he has Earthmover blood."

She eyed the quiet scholar, cradling the necklace gently in his hands.

"And his ancestors made this."

"I'm just a scholar," he whispered.

She put a soft hand on his shoulder and said gently, "looks like now you're not just a scholar. Can you guard that?"

She knew what she was asking him to do. So did he. She was asking him to put his life right in the line of danger. He wasn't just along for the ride anymore. Just like she'd been pulled into this a year ago, he'd found himself in the middle of something without meaning or wanting to.

He met her eyes and nodded, his hand curling around the prongs of the Orthalen. The metal clanged an eerie discord sound.

Rose nodded, unsure how much of the Earthmover's blood he had or if it was just an affinity for it. Either way, he was the only one able to touch it with ease. She looked back at the open tomb and sighed.

"Help me push this back, and then I think it's time for food." And a nap, she thought silently.

Eventually, after what felt like hours later, Rose and the troupe of elders emerged from the crypt. As they were starting the short walk back to town, Agatha asked the first question from the elders in a while.

"Shouldn't we have left it there? If the tomb was shielding it, shouldn't we have left it there?"

"Goron is coming here to look for the tomb regardless of it being shielded. Might as well keep it where we can see it."

She blinked watering eyes at the bright afternoon sun and was eternally grateful when Caleb silently offered his arm. One hand clamped over her sensitive eyes, the other tucked around Caleb's, they silently made their way back to town. As they neared the buildings, the sounds of people talking and working broke into the quiet of the forest, Rose pulled Caleb to stop.

"My people need lodgings. We're not going to sleep in the barn."

Footsteps sounded around her.

"You're not sending them back?"

Rose pinched the bridge of her nose and spoke in the direction she hoped Liddia was standing. "Goron is a threat to more than just you. We know he's coming here. We need to stop him while we have this chance."

"Fine," Liddia spoke, her voice harsh and bitter. "We have a few empty houses that have been kept up in decent condition. We will move your people into those."

Rose nodded and tried not to sag against Caleb. She didn't want this bitter old woman who thought herself better than anyone to see how exhausted she was, how bone-weary.

"Have whoever is in charge of your scouts speak with the lieutenant about coordinating your patrols. Caleb, make sure you either have a guard or me with you."

She heard Liddia sigh. "Fine. Why didn't you bring more soldiers with you for this battle?"

Rose sighed and pushed down the tide of confusing emotions that came with that question. "We didn't think there'd be people here to protect."

The second Rose saw people living here, saw the town, she knew they couldn't simply leave with the Orthalen. Whether or not Goron found it here, he'd destroy this place. She didn't know what to feel about this place, but she did know she wanted the time to find out.

More footsteps approached or left; Rose wasn't sure.

"I'll show you to the home you can use," Iris' voice was softer than Rose expected it to be. "And I'll bring some tea for your eyes."

She nodded, and soon Caleb was leading her after Iris and Rose was counting the moments until she could sleep.

CHAPTER 45

She had rested well during the night and had eaten more Subpulent berries this morning than she ever had before. Despite being bitter, nasty berries, they did help to restore and ease the hollow feeling left by her overusing her magic. She felt rested, more rested than she had been in a long time. The soft hum deep in her chest had helped to settle her into a deep and dreamless sleep. Although her eyes were sore like sand had been rubbed into them, she could see, and the soft morning light didn't blind her as it had before. The berries were helping. The rest was probably helping more.

The next few days were quiet and uneventful. Rose spent most of them sleeping, eating, and drinking Subpulent tea. She was able to convince – threaten – Liddia into giving Caleb access to some of the history books about the war, which he'd been feverishly reading in the evenings. She didn't know where he went during the day and figured it wasn't her place to ask. For her part, when she wasn't sleeping, she was training. She took to practicing forms with her dirks in front of the guest house, and she'd sparred with a few of the soldiers. She didn't think much of the coming fight would be done with swords and steel, but she felt better than if she didn't practice.

Liddia had reluctantly admitted the added bodies helped the

patrols. Even though they were few in number, they helped. A steady shift had been established to walk the borders and scout into the forest.

Liddie had tasked Mark, the youngest of the council members, to work with Lieutenant Samson. Caleb had been kind enough to inform her of the man's name. Together, Mark and Samson were helping to train the clansmen to fight.

Rose sighed as she thought back to last night's training session. More like Samson was trying to keep them from cutting off their own hands. Fighters these people were not.

They were farmers, craftsmen, and traders. Simple people. There weren't many who had any experience with fighting or weapons. Samson had sent Ty back to the castle with the urgent request for more men, but Rose had a feeling no matter how fast the Light Horse Officer rode, he wouldn't return with the help they needed in time. Rose didn't know what was making Goron pause in his attack, but she knew they were overdue.

She needed one question answered from J'Teal before everything went to hell. Her half-baked plan relied on it. One evening while Caleb was busy making notes in whatever new book he was reading, Rose retreated to her small bedroom and sunk down into the shadows. She pushed herself deeper than the Undertunnels, through the layers of the world until she fell into the bleak, barren Shadow World.

This time the path was easy. She found the dark tunnel without thought and felt no resistance as she moved quickly down the dark. Maybe it was her lack of fear, or maybe the wolves were upholding their promise to stop testing her. Either way, she made it to the Shadow World quickly.

The gray trees greeted her, and the cool mist moistened her skin. She kept a tight grip on the chain, just in case, and looked for the Speakers. The voices were quiet, had been since the chain was formed, and Rose walked deeper into the trees.

"J'Teal?"

A flurry of sound echoed through the trees and a breeze swirled the fog up and about as J'Teal stepped out of the trees. Her ghostly form moved by the breeze as it settled.

"You're getting stronger, gaining more control."

Rose nodded. Her magic seemed to be answering her quicker, easier since her argument with the wolf several days ago. She walked closer to J'Teal. "I wanted to ask you about something you said."

J'Teal crossed her arms and tilted her head.

"Before you said you hadn't messed with letting the wolves control over my body."

"It is so dangerous." J'Teal let out a loud breath and closed her eyes. "So much easier to lose yourself. As Shadowstalkers, we are the shadows. We're not simply human. Letting the wolves take over so much of you that you start to take their form... normally, I would say it is not reversible. We were taught to never let the boundary between you and them become that thin and absolutely never allow it to disappear."

Rose frowned. "I was able to push them back out."

"Like I said," J'Teal said. "Normally. You do not appear to be normal. You have had no training. Have had no support. Yet, you've managed things I trained my entire life to do. You have an ease with the magic I haven't seen before."

Rose chuckled. "It doesn't feel easy."

J'Teal hummed. "Yes, and imagine how it was for me. What does it feel like when you let them in, when you Speak for them?"

She shrugged. "It feels like... a puzzle clicking together. They fill their places and settle. Like they have places meant for them. I can see their memories, and I get a... like I gain knowledge that isn't mine. It's gone when they leave. I feel," Rose hesitated before she finally settled on the right word, "whole."

J'Teal laughed. "For me, it always felt like too many people in one room. We barely fit together. It was almost painful. And I most certainly did not get their memories." She took a deep breath. "You have no idea how powerful you can be. Just because it's doable, that you could push them out that one time, doesn't mean you shouldn't be careful."

She nodded, and J'Teal watched her with hard eyes. "Do not lose yourself in their strength."

Rose nodded again, her hand tight around the chain. It shimmered in her mind, and there was a little tug, like a question, on the other end. She wanted to go home. She wanted to ask to see what it was he drew all the time. Instead, she smiled and gave the chain two sharp tugs back. "I won't."

She called the shadows to her and stepped back into the Under-tunnels.

"Rose," J'Teal called just as the world started to fade. "I am so very glad you found our people."

Rose remembered the heartbreak J'Teal had suffered when she thought the clan had died out. She could only imagine what relief she felt now, knowing that a small group of them remained, but Rose wasn't sure they were truly her people. Not yet.

J'Teal and the Shadow World faded, and she rose up from the shadow. She stepped into the room and sat on her bed. She sighed as the bone weariness started to settle in her limbs. Her head hurt. It seemed to be an almost constant ache behind her eyes. When she got home, she was going to rest, actually, rest for a long time.

Caleb was still in the small common room; his soft words as he read to himself seeped through the door. She gathered the ore from her pack on the floor and walked into the warm room.

"Where'd you go?" Caleb asked once he looked up from his book. "It was silent for so long I checked on you," he said with a shrug.

Rose sat in the chair nearest the fireplace. "Needed to have a chat with someone."

He nodded and closed his book. He propped his feet up and angled them toward the fire. Rose tossed him the lump of ore, and he caught it easily.

"I think it's safe to say our theory was right."

He rolled it between his hands. "Seems like it." He looked closer at it, peering at it in the firelight.

"Apparently, it can only be smithed by an Earthmover."

Caleb grunted and tossed it back to her. "I know what you're think-ing, and that's not me. I can't smith anything. I can't move earth. I'm not an Earthmover. Not one you need."

Rose hummed and pocketed the lump. "Maybe. I used to think I wasn't more than a thief and a… well… a thief with a useful trick." She shrugged. "And now look at me."

Caleb grunted and pulled a book back into his lap. She sighed and let him. She couldn't push him, not any more than she liked to be pushed. They fell into an easy silence, the fire cracking and popping. The wind was howling through the trees outside, making them creak and sway against the small cottage. Even though it was barely past noon, the temperature had plummeted this morning, and it hadn't risen much with the sun.

A nagging sensation started on the edge of her awareness, and she cocked her head. It was like a pushing or a prodding feeling that made the back of her neck itch. She followed the feeling, sending her mind out through the few shadows of the forest. At the edge of town, where the wolves kept the barrier against strangers, she felt the pressure.

Someone was trying to get past the barrier. She sat up, bitterness filling her mouth and her heart racing. She took a deep breath and tried to settle herself. She hoped it was Ty returning with soldiers.

She focused on the wolves at the barrier, the soldiers pacing back and forth along the thick fog that made up the border. She felt the pressure again, like a squeeze at the back of her skull, and pushed further into the darkness of the mist. Dread filled her as she saw Goron pacing along the mist, fists clenched at his side.

"Coward!" he shouted, and the wolves growled.

Get ready, she told them and pulled back.

When she opened her eyes, Caleb was watching her with a frown and pressed lips.

"It's time, isn't it?"

"Yes," she said, her voice a soft whisper. "Get the others."

CHAPTER 46

They were all gathered in the meeting room again. Caleb hung nervously behind her, his hands clutching the Orthalen in his pocket. Liddia, face paler than usual, stood at the far wall with her arms crossed. Agatha was pacing in a nervous circle. Rose leaned against the wall, her own arms crossed as she watched the people of the room. Her dirks hung at her sides, and occasionally, the elders would cast nervous glances at them.

"You're sure he's here?" Mark asked again.

She nodded. "Yes. From what I'm able to gleam from the shadows, there are others with him. That might've been what took him so long to get here."

"Others, like an army?"

"Soldiers, at least, yes." She turned to Liddia and shrugged. "There is too much sunlight for me to see more details. We've assumed Gerik had returned to the Southern Territories after his escape and has partnered with the natives. He might've sent those warriors with Goron."

Collin nodded, his white beard braided today. "Gerik had friends there. It makes sense he would return."

Iris leaned on the back of a chair. "And the king's soldiers?"

Rose shrugged with a guff of air. "Assuming Ty reached the castle? Several more days."

"Do we wait him out?" Iris asked.

She shrugged again. "I don't see – "

A sharp, burning pain slashing through her mind stole her words and breath. She dropped her head into her hand with a sharp gasp. The wolves – the shadows – in the room, growled and howled. Some took form and jumped, and others howled from the darkness. The room darkened as the shadows grew.

A hand gripped her arm and held her steady as the pain eased.

"Rose? Rose, what's happening?"

She ignored the speaker as she turned her sight outward with the shadows.

"He breaks our barrier!" The shadows growled, anger and fear deepening their voices. She'd never heard fear come from them before, and that terrified her. They were always so sure, so confident. It nearly paralyzed Rose for the shadows to have fear.

"He's cutting through the barrier," Rose rasped as she turned toward the door. "Gather whatever fighters you have and move south. He's coming in."

Samson rushed past her, shouting orders to his men as they went. As Rose ran outside, people were rushing, yelling as they ran. Those that could fight were running south. Those that couldn't were running into the hills and toward the cemetery to the tomb.

Gather, Rose ordered the shadows as she ran toward the breach. Gather at the breach. A horn bellowed behind her. A warning call. Soon other young men, and even a few women, were moving behind her with swords, hoes, and knives. It was better than nothing. The searing pain cut through her again, but this time she recognized it and could brace for it. She wasn't blinded by the shock and pain and was able to think. It was the same burning pain she felt last summer when she'd tried to use her magic when the Cirkus cuffs had been on her wrists.

Her lips pulled back in a snarl as she slowed near the trees at the edge of the village. The fog swirled, thick and dark, in front of her. She could sense people moving through the fog just as Goron appeared through the mist. Behind him, more bodies emerged from the fog, bronze-skinned, dark-haired men emerged. They wore bright red skirts that fell to their knees, covered with intricate looped chains. The metal, a soft golden bronze color, must've come from the mines throughout the southern region. Their chests were bare, save for more chainmail of the bronzed metal. Dark headpieces adorned with sparkling beads cover most of their heads. The blades strapped to their hips were wicked, curved things. Matching red war paint covered their arms and faces. The combined gleam of metal and bright glare of the blood red paint was more than enough to make Rose's blood run cold.

More than a dozen of them stood behind Goron, still and silent. She didn't know what she'd expected from the warrior, but silence was not it. It somehow made them more intimidating, like a tightly pulled bowstring on the verge of snapping.

At her back, Rose sensed the crowd of people pausing, assessing, panicking. She settled into a fighting stance, her feet spaced wide and knees bent. She spun one blade in her hand and held the other low. In Goron's hand, shimmering in the sun, was a long knife, similar to her dirks, made of Cirkus Steel. The magic of the metal repelled magic; all magic. That shiny blade allowed him to literally cut through the shadow's boundary. Her eyes were drawn to it, and a hiss sounded from the shadows at the base of the trees.

"Do you like my new knife?" Goron asked as he twirled it, mirroring her. "Took me a bit to find enough to smith into this blade." He tilted it, caused the sun to gleam off its surface, and it shimmered like a pearl. "It reflects the sun beautifully, don't you think?"

"He thinks you cannot call us to you in the sun," the shadows hissed to her. She could feel them pacing at the edge of her mind. Their anger was making her skin hot and too tight. "He does not know you. He does not know the true potential."

A tight smile pulled at her lips, barely more than a grimace. No. He doesn't. She was the bridge between this land and the land of darkness. She could pull people into the shadows... she could pull the shadows to her. She was finally starting to understand what J'Teal meant when she said Rose was of the shadows.

"Bring me the Orthalen, and my warriors won't destroy the village," Goron said. "Don't make me work for it."

She slowly opened her mind to the shadows and let them in. They filled the holes and gaps and settled gently into place.

"You ruin the Balance of Nature."

Her voice was not her own, filled instead with the power of the Judges. She started to call the shadows to her, gathering them, building them up. Protecting the Orthalen was secondary to her actual goal, the Shadowstalker's goal. She needed to right this wrong. Goron needed to be erased.

Despite the sun, the brightness glaring off the patches of snow, a fog built. Dark and rolling. The mist rolled in from the trees and the depth of the forest. It came from the boundary at Goron's back and grew in substance. His eyes darted around, and his hand clenched around the hilt of his blade. The warriors he brought shifted on their feet.

"*Goron Velra.*" Her voice boomed and echoed through the fog filling the clearing. "*Your life has been sentenced by the Judges.*"

She let more shadows in. Pulled them in. She kept a death grip on her chain to Micah but let the shadows all the way in. She needed to be quick. This couldn't be sustained long without losing herself or the magic draining her entirely. She let them take her strength and pulled them into her world. Shapes formed in the thick mist, and wolves started appearing.

She moved toward Goron, her blades at her sides. Goron's face pinched in a grimace, and he shouted a loud, harsh word in a language Rose hadn't heard before and all the warriors were running. She heard the villagers and soldiers running to meet them, but she sent her wolves to attack the advancing army first.

A giant wolf, midnight black with fur-tipped in silver leapt at a charging warrior, but these fighters were swift and agile. And they knew what to expect. They didn't panic and scream like the soldiers had in the throne room. He ducked and rolled, dodging the wolf's leap, and swiped up with his long, curved blade. With a howl, the wolf split in two and disappeared in a puff of mist and fog.

Rose's back arched, the burning pain searing through her as if she'd been the one struck. Panic made her heart race faster than it already was and her blood ran cold. The shadows around them howled, the mist quivered. Goron was on her, his hand gripping her coat and hoisting her upright.

"You didn't think I came unprepared, did you?" He spun her, held her back against his chest as she watched the warriors cut through her wolves. His barrel of an arm locked around her torso, pinning her arms and dirks to her sides. The wolves howled and screamed, the sound was ear-shattering. She could feel them reforming in the Shadow World. The swords didn't kill them, she still doubted they could be killed, but it neutralized them.

"I didn't have enough for more swords, but I had just enough to melt down and coat their swords."

The wolves were regrouping in the Shadow World. Rethinking. Like a pack, she told them. They'd told her that once. She could feel in their memories mixed with hers that it had been centuries since they'd felt pain, that they'd been surprised. Hunt smarter, not quicker.

The warriors were pushing through, moving toward the villagers, but the shadows were reappearing and reattacking. This time, they hunted like a pack of wolves and not the magical beasts there were. They darted in at ankles, moved in groups to herd the warriors. They chased.

"That was a good surprise." Rose bit out past clenched teeth. "We'll adapt."

"Give me the Orthalen, and this will end."

Rose pushed into the Undertunnels, pushed herself into the Shadow Lands, and stepped out of the mist behind Goron. He spun his glimmering blade around in front of him. She twirled her own blades around her and then attacked. The Cirkus steel clanged and sung, an off-pitch sound, with each strike against her blades. Each time a wolf caught the blade of the warriors, she felt it, felt the magic drain from her bit by bit. She was running out of time. Sweat already soaked her shirt and coat. Her limbs were already starting to shake. She had to act soon, or she wouldn't have the strength to.

Goron's sword crashed into hers, and a quick spin had it flying from her fingers. Another fast parry and swipe, and her second dirk was lost.

She searched down into herself for that panicked rage she'd felt last time. The rage that fueled her. She found it in the shadows. Their rage at being challenged, at the Balance being mocked so openly. Their fury at Goron and everything he was, his warriors striking against them. That fury fueled her, steadied her shaking limbs. Their fury became hers.

To me! she bellowed at them and opened up her mind.

CHAPTER 47

They rushed her. Into her. Around her. She felt the magic of the shadows filling every last crevice. The world fell into blue and gray hues; the sun touched areas a blinding white. She pulled more mist in, more fog, and blocked more of the sun. The bright afternoon sun was blocked out like storm clouds filled the sky, but it was her shadows. Her darkness. Rose felt the strength of beings she didn't fully understand fill her limbs. And she laughed.

They would claw his throat out and make him bleed.

When she lifted her hands, black claws formed. She licked her lips and found two sharp-pointed canines, not much longer than her own teeth. She pulled her lips back in a feral grin, showing off her sharp new teeth.

The color drained from Goron's face, and she settled into a fighting stance.

"What–"

"*I am the Shadowstalker. I am the Shadows. I am the Judges.*"

Her voice rumbled with dozens of voices as they all spoke through her. She lunged at him but was met with a wall of mud and rocks. She fell through the layers of the world and stepped out, once again, in the mist. Without giving him a chance to spot her, she lunged, swiping wide with her claw. Goron spun at the last moment, and her wickedly sharp claws caught only his leather coat. She growled and lunged again, catching her claws on his chest, next to four other healing slashes.

She chuckled low in her throat at the marks on his skin.

With a grunt and a curse, Goron raised up the earth and threw her back. She hit the ground hard on her shoulder and rolled with the wave of earth and felled trees. She swiftly came to her feet and turned her eyes back to him. She closed the distance and brought herself close to him. He swiped at her with his blade, and she jumped back. A wolf snapped at his ankle, and Goron jumped, spun forward to avoid him, right into Rose's swing. He howled, now, as her claws dragged across his back. She reached forward, fingers curved like daggers, toward his neck, ready to end it, when he gripped her hard on the wrist, ducked, turned, and flung her over his shoulder.

Rose hit the ground hard on her back. Air rushed from her lungs as they seized against the impact. Her back arched, trying and failing to force air back into her lungs as she clumsily rolled onto her side. Growling and barking drew her attention as two giant wolves darted in and around him, trying to distract Goron while she lay there whimpering.

Another wave of earth threw her into the air and she fell hard onto her side, rolling and bouncing as she came to a stop.

"Shit," she wheezed, but at least now her lungs were working again.

A blade slashed in front of her face and she had only seconds to roll away. She came shakily to her feet as the blade flew in front of her more and more. She wasn't so much backing up as she was running backwards to avoid it. Goron parried, slashed, and feinted in such quick succession she could barely spot the attacks coming. She dipped and ducked and fell backwards; stumbling over her feet as she backed up.

He pulled back for a large slash, and the blade swung across her chest. She pulled herself back, arching her back, and swung her own claw at his exposed chest. She had an opening. Finally!

Rose missed the blade stabbing toward her middle until it was too late. She spun, but not quickly enough. She screamed as the blade slid through her middle, her mind going white with pain. She fell to the ground writhing, shrieking, barely able to breathe as the metal stole all magic from her. The wolves vanished. The fog thinned and disappeared. Her vision returned to normal, the light burning her sensitive eyes. Even the comforting presence of the Anchor bond disappeared, and the loss pulled a new found whimper from Rose.

She reached a shaking hand to her middle, the knife protruding from her side, and gingerly felt around. She felt no wetness, and when she looked at her hand, there was no blood. Cauterized, she thought hazily through the burning pain that stole her breath and halted all thought.

Goron looked down at her, wheezing and gasping. His body was marred with gashes and bite marks. With an angry jerk, he ripped his fist through the air, his eyes never leaving hers. The ground shook until suddenly, the earth spat out Caleb. He rolled through the mud, coughing and gagging. His body was curled around itself, clutching tightly at something he held to his chest.

"You're strong, boy. You have Earthmover blood in you," Goron grumbled at him. "Give me the Orthalen, and I won't kill you."

Caleb looked up from his hunch and then slowly moved his eyes past Goron to Rose, gasping on the ground. She saw his eyes go wide, his already pale face, go whiter, but he shook his head.

"You killed all my friends," he bit out. "You destroyed everything I knew."

"Fine," Goron sighed and jerked his fist again.

The bundle against Caleb's chest moved, pulled by Goron's magic, but Caleb held on. He clenched his jaw, his eyes squeezed shut as he held the Orthalen back against Goron's pull. Goron, his stance widening and settling, seemed to put more effort into it. Rose saw the tendons in his neck stretch against the effort. The necklace ripped from Caleb's grip but hung suspended in the air between them.

Both men had their hands outstretched, calling the metal to them. Rose smiled weakly, her limbs shaking and mind foggy with pain.

Caleb was exactly the Earthmover she needed him to be.

Goron grunted, mostly silent in his strain, but a shout started in Caleb. A shout that turned into a scream, filled with anger and loss and pain. Tears streaked his dirty, muddy face as he curled his fingers in. The An'thila warriors turned, the soldiers paused, even the towns-people turned toward the battle in the center of the destroyed clearing. Some warriors rushed toward Caleb, their shimmering swords held high, ready to end the threat.

Cracks appeared in the spikes of the Orthalen. Small at first, but they quickly grew in number and size. A dark, purple light started leaking through the cracks and Rose remembered the color from the magic D'ray had thrown at her and burned her skin, poisoned her blood. The wrongness of that magic. It had looked like this.

"Shit," Rose gasped just as the Orthalen shattered.

She rolled into a ball, the pain of the knife nothing compared to the strange, searing pain of the Orthalen's magic washing over her. It moved with the force of a summer storm. She heard bodies hit the ground around her, and the trees whipped on their trunks. Screaming filled her ears. Her own voice added to the cacophony.

Suddenly, the glen was quiet again. The screams stopped, the wind disappeared just as quickly as it had appeared. Wincing, whimpering in pain, Rose uncurled and looked for Caleb and Goron. Caleb laid in a heap, his chest barely moving. Goron knelt, his skin red from burns. His eyes were wide and unseeing as he stared at his burned hands.

Quickly, she glanced around the clearing and noticed everyone was down. Most were starting to move. They whimpered and groaned as they found their feet again. This was her only chance. Her last chance.

Grinding her teeth, Rose pulled the knife from her middle. She screamed as the blade ripped burnt flesh, blood poured down her side. Tears streamed down her face, and spots appeared at the corners of her vision.

"Don't pass out," she whimpered, gasping for breath and holding a trembling hand to her middle. "Don't pass out."

The second the metal cleared her body, the wolves returned to her. She dropped the blade in the dirt. The shadows buoyed her as best they could. Gave her what little strength they had left. She shakily eased herself to her feet, nearly falling twice. She took uneasy steps toward Goron, who was slowly lifting his head and looking around. She reached him just as he turned his head, his eyes meeting hers. With the last of her strength, she pulled the shadows to her and tipped her fingers in wolf's claws. She swiped, hard and fast and deep, across his stretched throat. His eyes went wide, his mouth a silent 'o' as blood poured out of his ruined neck.

"The Judges have spoken. The Balance has been restored."

She watched as he sank to the ground, gurgling and coughing. She pushed the shadows away and gripped the chain tight enough it hurt. The shadows went, tired and a little defeated, quietly from her, leaving her limbs shaking. They had been surprised in this fight, and Rose suspected she wasn't the only one leaving with broken pride and injuries.

"I am the Shadowstalker. And you are nothing," she bit out as his eyes dimmed, "but the shadow's past."

The world felt right again. The Balance was restored between life and death, and the shadows heaved a collective sigh of relief. She turned and surveyed the rest of the fighters. The villagers had taken advantage of the blast, and many now held the warriors at knife-point. Or... pitch-fork and hoe blade, in the case of many.

As she surveyed the survivors, she only counted three of the king's soldiers still standing. The villagers were few in number, many bleeding and burned. A great number of villagers lay strewn around the trees unmoving. Not as many as she had feared, but more than she'd hoped. The whimpers and cries of the injured and dying started to fill the quiet.

The warriors had taken a greater hit of the blast than the others. Many of them lay unmoving, most covered in burns. Vaguely, Rose remembered them running to Goron's aid right before it exploded. Iris stood some ways back, a knife in her hand and blood splattered across her coat. Her eyes caught Rose's, and they were wide and filled with fear. Rose doubted it was fear from the battle and was mostly fear of her. She grunted, unable to care, and turned once more to Caleb.

The resilient man was sitting up, a burn covering half his face. She stumbled over to him, only to collapse right as she made it.

"Told you," she whimpered, as she tried to hold back a whine of pain.

"Told me what?" he asked with tired, slurred speech.

"You are the Earthmover I need." She smiled. Or at least she tried. The adrenaline was wearing off, and the burning, throbbing pain in her middle was making her shake. Her limbs felt cold, and her lips numb. She tapped her face with fingers sticky with blood.

"Shit," she whimpered.

At the back of her mind, the constant pressure of Micah and the chain kept her centered. Kept the Speakers at bay. She knew where she was. Who she was. She tugged the chain tiredly, and in response, was a steady stream of worry and relief and... the calming presence that was Micah. He was going to yell at her when she got home. The thought made her smile again.

Out of the corner of her eye, Rose saw the flat blade of a hoe raised up in the air.

"Stop!" she shouted just as the man was about to bring the hoe down on the neck of one of the captured warriors. "They are prisoners until the king's men arrive to take custody of them. No harm," she paused to stress her order and met the eyes of everyone close enough, "will come to these men."

The hoe was slowly lowered, and heads nodded. She nodded too and sighed. Her limbs shook. Her middle burned and ached. There wasn't a part of her that didn't hurt.

"You were stabbed," Caleb squinted at her middle, her coat and trousers turning a deep red.

"Yeah," she breathed, tears threatening. "I was."

Suddenly, as if a spell was broken over the clearing, people were shouting, and orders were barked. Samson must've survived then.

Those who could move, did, those that couldn't, were loaded onto stretchers or lifted between shoulders. Someone came and scooped Rose up, her eyes trying to fall shut. She heard Caleb's angry shout before the blood loss, the pain, her injuries, and her exhaustion won, and she let her eyes shut.

EPILOGUE

ing Micah's soldiers arrived a day later. The medical supplies they brought were much more appreciated than the swords. The handful of An'thila warriors were given to the king's men, no doubt to be interrogated later. For their sake, she hoped they talked. Rose had been moved back into the small cabin she and Caleb had shared. The healer sent with the soldiers, an apprentice of Rita's she hadn't met before, was optimistic she would heal fine. The blade had cauterized the wound and stopped much of the bleeding. The healer, who adamantly informed Rose her name was Liz, not Lizzy or Elizabeth, had dryly told her that Rose did more damage pulling it out than when Goron had shoved it in, and next time to just leave it there.

"I'd rather just not be stabbed again," Rose had grumbled to the girl's back.

Caleb's dormant magical ability seemed to have been awakened with his confrontation with Goron. He was tentatively experimenting with moving the earth; he was starting with lifting pebbles. So far, the results were unpredictable.

Liz had worked on the burn on his face, and while she stated it would heal just fine, there would be quite the scar. Caleb was quiet

310

about that, and Rose watched him carefully. He'd seen too much change in the past few weeks.

She needed to make sure he ended up alright. Happy. So much of this was her fault. He'd lost his home because of her, and now she'd dragged him further into this mess. Her mess. She owed it to him.

She wanted to go home, but in the message she'd sent back with Ty for the king, she'd said she was staying. For now, at least. She needed to learn more about her clan, her magic. She also doubted she'd make the journey back to the castle just yet. Most days, she could barely stay awake for more than a few hours at a time. The strain on her from the magic, the shadows taking over so thoroughly, left her weak, and her eyes were sensitive. Even small amounts of light burned, and most days, her vision was fuzzy and gritty. Iris kept saying it would recover in time and with Subpulent berries, but a nagging feeling in the back of her mind told Rose it wouldn't. Something had shifted during the battle; something had broken. She wondered how badly she'd sped up her vision loss.

She still hadn't told the king. She didn't know why; didn't know what kept her from revealing this thing. He knew everything else. Why was this so hard for her to say out loud to him? When she returned home, she'd have to. Eventually. Rose kept telling herself she was fine. That her vision wasn't that bad, and most of it probably would return. But when she woke in the dark room, and she didn't know if it was dark because it was night or because she'd gone blind, the panic that stole her breath told her she wasn't alright.

Her days were constantly accompanied by the soft hum from the chain. Micah's calming presence helped to keep her sanity. Liz promised she would be able to travel soon. Rose hoped she was right. The tugs and pulls and sensations from the chain helped, but Rose found she was missing Micah's presence more. She wanted to sit with him in the warm solarium. Watch him draw. She wanted to see him in worker's clothes, sitting at a crowded table in a noisy bar laughing. But she suspected that was less likely.

A light knocking on her cabin door broke into her thoughts. Rose squeezed her eyes shut and covered them with her hands.

"Come," she called.

The door clicked open, and the bitterly cold wind rushed in and around her legs as the council hastily moved into the space. Caleb had graciously agreed to vacate their small cabin while the council met with her. Her eyes were far too sensitive to make the walk through town. Even now, blankets covered the windows, and the lamps burned low. She'd found, over the past few days, that her eyes could tolerate the warm golden glow of flames better than sunlight. But only barely.

The door clicked shut, and Rose looked around the bleary shapes of the council settling themselves around the room.

"Now that the pressing emergency is over," Liddia said into the silence, "we've some things we need to address."

Rose nodded and sipped the bitter berry tea. She was getting seriously tired of drinking this stuff.

"First, we need to know what your intentions are," Liddia continued.

She set her tea aside. "I sent Officer Reeson back to the king with a letter explaining that I would be remaining here for the time being. I hope you don't object," she added with a tight smile toward Liddia. She knew the woman would object.

The woman's features were too blurry for Rose to tell, but she suspected she bristled.

"You have much you need to learn," Iris said to her right. "Both of your magic and your responsibilities. We had hoped you would stay."

This time Rose definitely saw Liddia shift with a jerky twist. She bit back a smile at the old woman's discomfort.

"Only long enough for me to learn what I need," Rose said. "Then I'll be going back to the castle. Goron is dead, and the Orthalen is destroyed, but whatever Gerik is planning isn't finished."

"You are the Shadowstalker. The leader of our clan. You can't simply abandon your responsibilities."

Rose snorted at Iris' words and the irony in them. That woman knew nothing of responsibilities. After all this searching, all this silent hoping and unacknowledged wishing, she'd found her mother and realized... Rose didn't need her. Not like she thought she did. No. Rose would learn from her. And then she'd go home. To the family she'd found, the one she'd made for herself.

"I have no desire to run this clan. Liddia's been doing it all this time. I see no reason to change now."

"You don't understand," Liddia cut in, her voice sharp and loud. "The Shadowstalker isn't only the leader of the Shademaker Clan. With the help of the council, the Shadowstalker was the ruling monarch of all other magical clans."

Rose's heart stopped in her chest, and her blood seemed to turn to ice in her veins.

"You see, girl," Liddia spoke low, "you're not only our clan chief. You're also our queen."

The shadows roiled in their dark corners, and Rose could feel them pacing at the edge of her mind.

There must be a Balance!

She gapped at them and smoothed her shaking hands along her legs.

You are the Balance.

Rose pushed them out of her mind with a sharp shake of her head and held her cold hands to her cheeks.

"You have much to learn, girl."

THE END